Th

The magician sat up there on the stage, by a group of about ten children who formed a semi-circle around him. They sat motionless, curiously listless, like marionettes left unattended by an absent puppeteer.

His voice was liquid, comforting, like the gratifying waters of a relaxing stream:

"You have stepped into a world of pure magic. You are no longer bound by everyday rules. Everything is possible. Everything is permitted. All illusions are real. And everything real is illusion . . ."

Campbell Black was born in Glasgow in 1944. He was chief editor at a major London publishing house in the late sixties before moving to America where he taught Creative Writing in universities (State University of New York). His first novel appeared over twenty years ago. Now, nineteen novels later, his books are read all around the world. Under the name Campbell Armstrong his 1978 novel *JIG* was a runaway bestseller. Campbell Black lives in the sun-baked state of Arizona but has recently taken a home near Dundee where he can enjoy a frequently wet Scottish summer.

By the same author
available from Mandarin Paperbacks

The Wanting

CAMPBELL BLACK

THE
PipeR

Mandarin

A Mandarin Paperback
THE PIPER

First published in the USA 1986
by Pocket Books
First published in Great Britain 1992
by Mandarin Paperbacks
Michelin House, 81 Fulham Road, London SW3 6RB

Mandarin is an imprint of the Octopus Publishing Group,
a division of Reed International Books Limited

A CIP catalogue record for this title
is available from the British Library
ISBN 0 7493 0899 0

Printed and bound in Great Britain
by Cox & Wyman Ltd, Reading, Berks

Prologue

———•———•———•———•———•———•———•———

IN ONE UNSTEADY HAND THE MAN HELD A PEN. HE'D ALREADY written several sentences and phrases on the paper in front of him. Some of these he'd crossed out, drawing thick lines through the words because words alone couldn't convey anything he intended, couldn't describe the nature of what haunted him.

Words were as empty, as meaningless, as echoes. They were ghosts moving beyond his range of vision, leaving rooms just as he entered them.

What good was language to him now?

He put his pen down and gazed out of the window. He saw a quiet tree-lined street, the windows of houses that faced his own, a certain suburban banality. Nothing lurked out there. Everything was still. It was a shadowless place where decent people lived out decent lives.

Decent people.

But not him.

He ran one hand across his dry lips.

Closing his eyes, he was surprised to feel moisture seep through the lashes. This wouldn't do. This wasn't the way to finish the thing.

1

He picked up the pen again. His hand shook so badly he imagined his writing would be unintelligible to anyone who read his note. *My wife*, he thought. My wife will read this.

He tapped the end of the pen against his teeth. To any casual observer he might have suggested a poet pausing in composition, a man hunting a rhyme, tracking down a meter. But he was alone in this big room and there were no observers and his solitude was an unbearable thing.

He stared at the sheet of the paper.

He read through what he'd written.

It was a message of some kind, he supposed. But how in the name of God could these scribbled words even *begin* to suggest what he felt, how could they *remotely* indicate the pain that lay inside him?

He tilted his chair back.

He looked up at the ceiling.

There were sounds coming from downstairs, from the recesses of the house.

His house.

His home.

The place he was leaving. The place he had loved.

I find it hard to live with the idea that this child is dead . . .

The pen rolled out of his fingers and he watched it move across the surface of his desk. This ordinary occurrence, this simple motion of a pen, shocked him somehow. Even at the heart of the ordinary, there was a sharpness now, an angle of perception he'd never experienced before. The things that lay all around him in this familiar room seemed luminous to him, lit by an invisible light.

A pen slips. It rolls. A man writes words on plain paper. A man dies.

I have no excuses, only remorse inexpressible remorse, killing me . . .

A sadness went through him. And yet it was more than that—it was a guilt without limits, a pit into which he had

2

fallen and there was no way of climbing out of it again. Not if he lived a thousand years.

He shut his eyes once more. He touched the pen the way a blind man might, tracing its surface with the tips of his fingers. He didn't have anything left to say. Everything was inadequate, skeletal: everything was buried in a field, the field of his dreams, that place of flat land and long grass and high trees—that was where his horror lay.

The weapon was surprisingly light when he picked it up. He could feel every detail of the gun, every mark and metallic whorl.

He leaned back in his chair.

The gun, held loosely in one hand, lay in his lap.

He parted his lips. Angling the barrel, feeling it against the roof of his mouth, he thrust the gun upward and the metal touched his teeth, causing a small electric shock against his fillings.

There was a sound on the landing outside his room. A footstep. The creak of old wood.

He paid it no attention.

He paid no attention either when the door of his room opened a little way and a shadow fell into the threshold.

All sounds stopped.

All movement was still.

Death was deafness. Blindness.

He didn't hear the violent roar of the gun, didn't feel the bullet pierce the roof of his mouth or go on rising up through bone, didn't witness the way his skull cracked open and his brain—that place of both wisdom and bestiality, that arena of brute contrasts and conflicts—flew out from his scalp against the wall of his room.

The shadow in the doorway saw all this.

The shadow in the doorway—small, scared, horrified—missed nothing.

The shadow in the doorway screamed once.

Then was silent.

And the echo of the gunshot rolled through the rooms of the big house, like the fading footsteps of some monster hurrying outside into the quiet street of dense trees and solid frame houses.

3

ONE

•••••••••••••••••••••••••••••••

TOMMY SEARS, THIRTEEN YEARS OF AGE AND FILLED WITH ALL
the anxious longings of his first love, thought he had everything figured out by the time he reached Granby Street.

Three more weeks at fifteen bucks a week and he'd have
enough money saved from his newspaper route to buy the
ten-speed Schwinn he'd seen in the window of Rawley's
Sports Store out at Delta Plaza. He already had a hundred
and fifty dollars stashed inside a Folger's Coffee can he kept in
his bedroom closet, money he had sweated for through a
series of odd jobs—lawn work and housepainting and car-
washing and tree-trimming. Dog's work.

Three more weeks.

It suddenly seemed to Tommy Sears that three weeks was a
very long time when you were thirteen and impatient to
pursue your heart's first adventure and you didn't have the
wheels to take you out to the neighborhood where the
adorable Victoria Estaban lived.

He tossed a copy of *The Hamland Progressive* on to the
porch of number 24 Granby Street. It landed perfectly, flush
against the front door. Good one, Tommy. Right on the nose.
He listened to the satisfying *thump* the paper made and then

he moved on to the corner house, number 28, where old Mrs Adamsky lived.

Mrs Adamsky didn't want *her* newspaper thrown, thank you very much. It had to be folded neatly and *placed* in the middle of the porch. For a moment Tommy considered rolling the paper up and sending it through the air like a missile anyhow but he had the unsettling feeling that Mrs Adamsky was watching him from behind lace curtains. She had a face which reminded Tommy of a battered old apricot.

He walked up the pathway, laid the paper on the porch, then headed for New Castle Street. He sat down beneath an ancient elm tree where he normally rested for a couple of minutes on the last lap of his route. He had six more papers to deliver along New Castle before he was through. Six more papers and plenty of time. With his back to the elm, he took a deck of playing cards from his jeans and shuffled them carefully the way Zanzibar had shown him yesterday.

Stroke them, Tommy. Stroke them. They feel like silk in your hands. Don't work against them. And never let them work against you . . .

The cards slipped out of Tommy's hands. He remembered now how Zanzibar had taken him aside, his thin face filled with a kind of quiet strength, the odd throaty voice saying *Think of the cards as feathers. Light. Easy. Don't be scared of them . . .*

Frustrated, Tommy gathered the cards up. He shuffled the deck a couple of times, then returned it to his pocket. He'd never be any good, he didn't have the hands for it—his fingers were large and ungainly—and he certainly didn't have the kind of *nerve* it took to perform conjuring tricks. To stand up in front of people and *perform!* Holy shit!

What the hell. He was only going to Mr Zanzibar's magic class because Vickie Estaban went there and he could sit directly behind her and dream his dreams of the ten-speed Schwinn, all silver and red, that would carry him out through the streets of Hamland to Vickie's house, where she'd be waiting—slim and lovely and angelic with that wonderful mouth just asking to be kissed—on the porch. She'd come down the steps toward him, holding her hands out, and the smile on her face would be like the sunrise . . . And he'd come right out and tell her he wanted to go steady with her and she'd smile, boy would she ever smile, and just accept right off the bat!

And they would KISS!

Tommy Sears trembled, just thinking about this. Of course, he'd have to make sure he was chewing spearmint gum or had sprayed his mouth with that aerosol stuff you could buy. Not Listerine, though, never Listerine. Then Vickie would think she was kissing her dentist.

He walked along New Castle Street. He had thought recently about sitting down and writing a poem but what the hell rhymed with Victoria?

Pretoria? Astoria? He couldn't fit words like that into a poem for Vickie Estaban. Shit, he didn't even know where Pretoria was.

It crossed his mind that this business of love was more of a pain than it should have been. For one thing, Vickie Estaban had never so much as looked at him. For another, he hadn't ever worked up the courage to even *talk* to the girl. He had accidentally brushed against her one time on the way to Zanzibar's class but she hadn't even *looked* at him.

She doesn't know I'm alive!

Tommy Sears paused, adjusting the baseball cap he wore. The bike would change everything. He was confident of that. With that Schwinn beneath him, he'd be free as the goddam wind and all of Hamland would be his oyster then. (Oyster. Tommy always thought this was one weird kind of phrase, especially if you didn't like oysters and he for one *surely* didn't because it was like swallowing a great gob of salty mucus on the one occasion he'd actually tried it.)

He looked the length of New Castle Street, which was quiet and still at this hour of the morning. Dawn sunlight fell against the thick branches of the trees, barely penetrating to the houses beyond.

Tommy scratched his head. This morning, when he'd tumbled out of bed, he had had the strange sensation that he was *supposed* to do something today, something important, something he'd totally forgotten. It came back now, teasing him.

6

It was like the feeling you got when you had a word on the tip of your tongue only you couldn't for the life of you remember it.

Something important.

He tossed newspapers on to the porches of 12 and 16 New Castle Street. The feeling wouldn't go away. It puzzled and irked him, as if he had a fly trapped inside his head. *Buzzzzz buzzzz* . . . What the hell was it he'd forgotten? Something to do with his route? An instruction he couldn't remember? Had somebody cancelled a delivery?

He shook his head from side to side.

A dream maybe. A leftover feeling from a dream . . .

No, not a dream exactly. Something else.

Halfway along New Castle Street Tommy Sears paused. He rolled up one of his papers and aimed it at the porch of number 19. It struck the screen door and slithered beneath an old deck chair. Bad throw.

21 was next.

Tommy shut his eyes a moment.

21, he thought. Gotta deliver to 21.

He looked at the house. He didn't move. Shadows fell across the lawn ahead and a light breeze stirred all the trees around him. Gotta move, he told himself.

Only three papers left.

Only three more weeks for the Schwinn . . .

Three more weeks before Victoria Estaban is mine . . .

Tommy took a couple of steps toward 21 and then he stopped.

Something about that number.

But what?

He felt suddenly very strange, as if all the strength had ebbed out of his limbs. A great weight descended upon him from a place above and the breeze that soughed through the trees was whispering his name.

Tommy . . . tommy . . . tommeee . . .

He took another hesitant step toward the house ahead and the whispers flew after him like small stealthy birds on a furtive flight.

tommmeeeee . . .

7

He gazed across the lawn. A wooden disc with the number 21 on it dangled from the porch. He couldn't take his eyes away from it. The numerals shimmered like things suspended in water. He was electrified by a sense of déjà vu. He'd stood here on the same spot in exactly the same way only it was in another lifetime.

Something was happening to him. Something *weird* . . .

I'm sick, he thought.

Maybe a virus.

He placed a hand against his forehead, which was clammy. Jesus, he was shivering now, a whole series of little shivers running all through his body. What was going on? what was happening inside him? It seemed to him right then that he could hear voices inside his head and yet they weren't really voices, they were more like sing-song nonsense sounds and they echoed through him and all he could think of was how he'd read about the Sirens recently in old Fogarty's mythology class and the way those sweet singers lured unsuspecting sailors on to rocky shores, a story Tommy Sears thought pretty damn stupid because if you were any kind of sailor at all you'd sure as hell *notice* a big bunch of rocks and you'd get your ass right outta there—

And then—

And then suddenly he changed direction and turned away from the house and walked back the way he had come, going along Granby Street and crossing the old railroad tracks and passing the abandoned station-house with the broken windows.

Suddenly. Without warning.

He tossed his newspaper satchel and the three undelivered papers into a clump of dense weed, then headed toward the grassy slope that led to the freeway.

Why? why am I doing this? what is making me do this utterly goddam ridiculous thing which isn't anything like what I usually do, sweet Christ . . .

He walked purposefully, like somebody with an urgent destination in mind, a place where he was determined to be. He hesitated only once when he reached the edge of the freeway and then he turned east, walking quickly with his head down, as if he knew the way to his own ultimate destination so well he didn't even have to look.

And he walked—as certain people might think later—off the face of the earth.

On the day Tommy Sears disappeared, the five-and-dime store on Center Avenue closed after thirty-eight years in business. It couldn't compete with the new establishments in Delta Plaza out on the edge of Highway 50. Some of the local merchants came out to watch the store shut its doors for the last time, an occasion that produced some sadness, a little nostalgia, and a touch of bitterness about how the big circular plaza, balanced like a freshly minted coin at the edge of the freeway, was tearing the heart out of downtown shopping in Hamland.

Men and women stood around in defensive little groups as Charlie Woodbine and his wife Martha locked the front doors. There was a large FOR SALE sign in the window, with the name of a realtor over in Denver, and a telephone number you could call if you happened to be interested in this downtown location. Nobody was.

A damp wind blew down Center, bringing a sniff of rain from points west, from the White River National Forest and Grand Mesa and Gunnison. The downtown merchants stood around the five-and-dime, sympathizing with the Woodbines. Soon they would all go over to Scatini's Tavern and become rowdy in the big back booth, but for the moment they were loitering on the sidewalk and wondering who would be the next to close his doors.

Somebody could run a book on the deterioration of Hamland's business district, George Cheney thought. He stood across the street, his arms folded, his body resting against his car, a navy-blue Chrysler with the insignia of the Hamland Police Department on its door panels.

He gazed at the front of the five-and-dime and what he remembered was how he'd used this store as a kid, how he'd roamed its narrow aisles and looked upon its astounding assortment of goodies, his chin barely level with the edge of each counter.

You could find paper lanterns from Shantou nestled along-side plastic trombones out of a factory in Duluth, Callard & Bowser toffees from England competing with chocolates from Hershey, Pa. One time, Cheney remembered, he had come across a set of mysterious South African roadmaps, as if somewhere along the way a wrong delivery had been made to the store.

He realized now that the Woodbines hadn't been business-men at all. They'd been indiscriminate buyers, children almost, who took as much innocent pleasure in their stock as any of the kids who stepped inside to look and feel and wonder.

And now the five-and-dime, as well as the wonder, was gone.

Cheney stared the entire length of Center Avenue.

He could see Naughton's Hill and the new houses that had been constructed up there on the edge of town. At the foot of the hill lay a network of narrow, older streets, frame houses that had about them a certain dignity, like that of old men who are damned if senility is going to overtake them.

Across the street, some of the merchants were beginning to drift in the direction of Scatini's Tavern to hold their wake. The demise of one store, Cheney thought, diminishes them all. He got inside his car and drove past the five-and-dime, conscious of an aspect of his own history receding as the automobile slid down Center.

And for a second his boyhood was framed in the rearview mirror.

Then he took a left and the view changed entirely.

Courtney Sears stood in the downstairs living-room of her home on Dolores Street and looked out across the front lawn. She was a small-boned woman with a colorless face. Even her hands were white as fine china and gave the impression of fragility.

A noise from the kitchen caused her to turn from the window. Her husband, Thomas Senior, was rummaging in the refrigerator, searching for the last beer he knew he'd stuck in there somewhere.

Courtney listened to the sounds of bottles and jars rattling together and then there was the swift and purposeful pop of a beercan being opened. After a moment, Thomas Senior stepped into the living-room. They made an unlikely couple, she knew.

Thomas had swelled over the years from a trim one hundred and fifty pounds to something whalelike, something blubberous, so that on those rare occasions when he needed what he perceived as conjugal admission to her body, she felt she was accommodating a huge marine animal.

Courtney turned her face back to the window. Dolores was a leafy street and at certain times of day, especially in the late afternoons, the slant of sun through the mass of leaves created enchanting, latticed patterns. Courtney glanced at her wristwatch.

Five forty-five.

She experienced a slight anxiety, a faint shiver that passed through her quickly. She heard Thomas sit down in an armchair and the sound of air being forced out of a cushion beneath him. He was, she thought, a decent man and a good provider and if he had a problem—one she might at least single out—it was his incessant beer-drinking.

"Tommy's late," she said. Giving voice to her concern like this made her feel even more uneasy than she had been.

"He dawdles," Thomas Senior said. "You know how he dawdles. Anyhow, he's always over at Parks and Rec."

Courtney nodded. She folded her arms. Tommy was her only child and perhaps she'd always been more than a little protective of him. He was thirteen years old, tall for his age, he could look after himself.

Not that Hamland was a place of hidden menace, she thought. It was a good place to bring up a kid.

She shut her eyes a second, listening to Thomas slurp his Old Milwaukee. When she looked out at the street again, she saw two kids go past on roller skates, but neither of them was Tommy Junior.

Five forty-nine.

Parks and Rec, she thought.

Kids had a way of losing track of time. They didn't live in a

world of clocks and timetables the way adults did, especially
during the long summer vacation. She turned away from the
window and sat down in an armchair facing her husband.

"I haven't seen him since this morning," Courtney Sears
said.

Her husband crushed the beercan in his fist. She knew he
was going to get up and stroll along to Stander's Market for
another couple of sixpacks at any moment now.

"It's summer," her husband said. "Kids play. They're free.
No school. Hell," and Thomas Sears shrugged his shoulders.
"He's over at that park, I bet."

He struggled out of the armchair and, standing massively,
looked down at her. "Think I'll take a walk. Maybe I'll run
into him."

Courtney nodded absently. She said, "He left at six AM to
deliver his papers."

She was silent. A wind blew the length of Dolores, shuffling
the leaves with the noise of a cardsharp rearranging a deck.

"I wonder what he ate for lunch," she said.

She watched her husband amble toward the door, then she
heard the screendoor rattle and the sound of his heavy feet on
the porch. Alone, she realized she felt oddly insecure in her
own home, almost as if some quite unrecognizable animal
were slavering to get in at the back door.

For no apparent reason, unless it was on account of his
nostalgia attack, George Cheney drove up Naughton's Hill,
passing the smart new homes and their redwood sun decks,
and continued to drive until he was well beyond the Hill
Estates. The road yielded to a dirt path and trees pressed
close together on either side of his car. When he reached the
spot he understood he had been destined for all along, he
stepped out of the car and walked through the trees to a
clearing.

Then he paused.

It was the view that had brought him up here.

He stood perfectly still, feeding on the sight spread beneath
him.

There was an undeniable magic in this view—the way

Hamland lay below him, the reach of the mountain range beyond, the isolated canyons, dark green and mysterious, that pocked the landscape between town and mountains and vanished in the foothills where the trees were thick and profoundly silent.

Hamland below—that's what he concentrated on.

The narrow ribbon that was Center Avenue ran through the town like a thin, wasting artery. A network of streets flowed out from Center like tiny tributaries. He could see the steeples of both St Mary's and Hamland Lutheran and the green rectangle of the municipal park that lay between these churches. Beyond the park—only if he looked hard—he could make out the shingled roof of his own house which, from this perspective, seemed to lack a dimension, as if it were a child's drawing on a slat of cardboard.

A mile away, on a street of rotted houses that dated from the early 1900s, monstrous dwellings with ornate cupolas and misty turrets, his own father still lived in the home where Cheney had been raised. *Why did these houses suggest hunched dragons to him now? Or were they old crones doomed to whisper the same gossip until eternity?*

Over there, east, were the railroad tracks along which these days only the occasional freight train hauling eerie boxcars ever traveled. Flattened against the skyline beyond the tracks was the squat, chimneyed structure of Rosita's Mexican Food Company, from whose depths issued the constant aroma of refried beans and hot sauces so that on especially windy days a stroll through Hamland was like a walk around the largest Mexican kitchen in the western world.

Cheney thought how Hamland appeared to slumber way beneath him, a place of sleepy storefronts and dormant leafy streets, where even the church steeples seemed dreamy and their bells, whenever they sounded, resembled the snoring of asthmatic men.

Beyond the tall trees and the patch of brilliant green that was Sutter's Meadow lay the great wide slash of the freeway which, like a stream of adrenaline bypassing the hypnotized condition of Hamland, ferried rigs west toward Utah and east in the direction of Denver. He could see the collected signs of service stations, clusters of neon stalks—Exxon, Mobil, Texaco—reaching upward and seeming to quiver like the antennae of predatory insects.

Slowly, distant sounds filtered up toward him. The wind-whipped cries of tiny figures playing soccer in the park. The rumble of the freeway. The buzz of a power-saw someone was using in the Hill Estates. A hammer going into wood somewhere, rap rap rap, a heavyhanded stuttering.

George Cheney had been born in Hamland and only once in his thirty-seven years had he left the place for any length of time and that was when he'd spent two years at college in Los Angeles where he'd studied English Literature—and when he thought of these two years now they didn't seem quite real to him, as though they were slightly skewed, tilted pictures hanging aslant on the walls of his memory.

What he considered real was the view that lay below him from the highest point on Naughton's Hill. What he considered real were those streets and storefronts and the shingle roof of his own house he could barely even see from this distance. As real as the prints on the tips of his own fingers.

He flipped his cigarette away and went back to his car, thinking that the closure of the five-and-dime had robbed him of some essential part of himself.

This much was certain. Tommy Sears had picked up his copies of *The Hamland Progressive* at six-fifteen and had delivered all but three of them to the homes that lay along his route, which covered Granby, Craig and New Castle Streets. Three subscribers, all of them living on New Castle, had not received their morning editions. Two of them had called Eddie Delmarco, the circulation manager of *The Progressive*, to complain, which explained Eddie's presence in the Searses' home shortly after suppertime.

Eddie Delmarco was a former sergeant in the Marine Corps and liked to run his little squad of delivery persons—three boys, two girls—along military lines, which involved punctuality and considerable discipline.

"It doesn't make any sense," Courtney was saying. "Why wouldn't he deliver those three newspapers . . ."

"Last three on his route," Eddie said. "Last three houses

on New Castle Street." Here Eddie shrugged, glancing around the room and observing various framed pictures of Tommy Sears, all of which seemed highly colored with the kinds of tints you never saw in real life. He was a kid with an almond-shaped face and ears just a half-inch too large for his skull. A nice kid, well-mannered—Eddie had always had a good rapport with him.

"He hasn't been home and I haven't heard a word from him," Courtney Sears said, more fiercely wringing her hands. There was a noise from the porch and she turned her face expectantly but it was only her husband coming in with his brown-bagged beer, clutching it to his chest.

Thomas Senior disappeared inside the kitchen.

"Have you looked for him?" Eddie asked.

Courtney shook her head. "I didn't want to admit I was that worried, I guess."

Thomas Senior came inside the living-room with an open beercan. He nodded at Eddie Delmarco, whom he knew vaguely. Thomas sat down. A white slick of beer slipped across his chin. "What's up?" he asked.

Courtney told him.

He said, "Maybe the kid didn't feel up to delivering the last three papers. You know kids. Always goofing off. Or maybe he was three papers short, huh."

"That wouldn't be possible," Eddie said. "The papers are always correct."

The three people in the trim living-room were quiet for a time. Outside, the wind along Dolores scattered itself like buckshot through the dense trees. Eddie Delmarco took a Kleenex from his somber plaid jacket and ran it between the palms of his hands. One of his squad had gone *AWOL*, for Christ's sake.

"The park," Thomas Sears said. "He's always at that goddam park."

This remark, like a wounded bird, fluttered around the room for a time. But Courtney Sears noticed, for the first time, a tone in her husband's voice that was a half-note below conviction. And this worried her because Thomas Senior wasn't the kind of man who yielded to anxiety easily when it came to his son. Courtney stood up and went to the window and studied the tree-lined street. There was a mystery suddenly in the familiar things that faced her, a distinct sense—not yet shrill—that the view from her window had altered in some odd manner.

She wiped her hands against her dark green slacks and wondered where Tommy was right at this minute in time. And what went through her mind was a picture of three undelivered newspapers and she saw them, as if through psychic means, lying in a damp gutter with the damp wind making their pages flutter.

Eddie Delmarco was rising now. "Maybe you should take a run over to the park, I guess," directing this suggestion to Thomas, who had his can to his mouth. "I got to get home before my old lady sends out a search-party for *me*." He wandered toward the door and Courtney turned to look at him.

"Call me when he gets in," Eddie said.

"We will," Courtney answered. "And thanks for stopping by."

She watched Eddie Delmarco go across the lawn to his car, a small pea-green Pinto, and after he'd driven away she realized she felt more lonely than she'd ever felt in her life, that even the presence of her husband could neither touch nor change the heart of her solitude.

She fingered the edge of the curtain and she thought. *Tommy*.

Apart from a slight knowledge of the English Romantic poets, the only thing of real value George Cheney had brought back from Los Angeles was his wife, Anne. Cheney, who had never been given to public displays of affection in his life before he'd met her, found it hard at times to stop himself from touching her, impulsive caresses, abrupt moments of reaching for her—passing her in the kitchen, on the stairs, sitting down with her at breakfast, it didn't matter when because his hands seemed to take on a volition all their own and he'd find his fingers squeezing her shoulder or stroking her wrist or lightly touching the side of her face.

Even now, as he stepped inside the kitchen of their house

on Danforth Street, he placed his hands on her hips and pressed his mouth against the back of her neck, quite ignoring the fact she was at the crucial point of preparing a mustard cream sauce.

Cheney moved away, hung his jacket on the back of a kitchen chair. Home, he was home—not just in this house but in Hamland too, as if this house were a smaller cocoon wrapped inside a larger one; and he felt the extraordinary ease of a man who is completely attuned to his environment.

Anne sat beside him at the table. "No reprieve, huh? No last-minute proclamation from the Governor?"

Cheney shook his head. "None."

"Poor George," and she touched the back of his hand with fingertips that were slightly sticky. "So they really did shut the doors on part of your childhood today?"

"They really did." He smiled at her across the table. "Half the Downtown Merchants Association will probably be drunk at Scatini's by this time. I can't say I blame them."

"Change, my dear. Change," and Anne rose to return to her sauce, which she stirred a couple of times. Cheney watched her.

Her body hadn't altered much in the eleven years of their marriage; whenever he sat back to look at her he had the feeling of a time-warp in which he was caught. Even the birth of their son hadn't wrenched her out of shape the way birth did to some women. But then, he reminded himself, he was in love and love was as blind as justice and he supposed he wouldn't notice such things as a thickening of waist or small lines running around the edges of the mouth. Her reddish hair was worn long, perhaps unfashionably long these days, in the style that once was affected by hippies—center-parted and hanging on her shoulders.

She looks, he thought, the way she did when he'd first met her in the cafeteria at UCLA, when she'd sat down alongside him, bundles of books spilling from her arms, toppling all across the table in front of him. She had been a third-year drama student then, a lovely, captivating creature who had absconded with his heart. They had married, their interest in their studies had subsided, and they'd come to Hamland to live—George with the kind of relish that attended a home-coming, Anne with the curiosity of a missionary setting out for some savage, unmapped place she was determined to like.

And she'd come to like it too, not just because it was her husband's hometown but because there was a tranquility here that had taken her quite by surprise. Even when, now and then, she saw the face of a former classmate appearing on a soap opera, she felt absolutely no longing for what she might have given up by marrying George Cheney.

"Change," she was saying again, turning to look at him from the stove. "Even Hamland has to change, George."

He shrugged and got up from the kitchen table. From the window, he looked out into the backyard. The sky was overcast, turning green things gray, somber.

"You're a romantic, a sentimentalist," Anne said. "And like all romantics, you're a conservative at heart. Don't bother to deny it either."

He shoved his hands inside his pockets. He studied the shrubbery for a time. A conservative, he thought, and the word had a dismal ring to it inside his head, as if it implied a lack of adventure, an absence of impulse.

"Food," Anne said.

Cheney sat down at the table and looked at the plate Anne placed in front of him. Small pieces of meat and vegetables floated in the sauce. He ate in silence a while, then put his fork down and looked at his wife across the table.

"Something wrong?" she asked, because she knew his vibrations. She knew his moods and silences better than he did himself.

"The food's great," Cheney answered.

Anne put her elbows on the table and placed the palms of her hands against the sides of her face. "It's only another three days, George."

"Yeah, I know."

"And he's having a terrific time. You know he is."

George Cheney nodded. The absence of their son, Danny, at Cub Scout camp, created strange little pockets of silence throughout the house. For the first few days he'd enjoyed the kid's absence. He had even felt like a man who has been given the gift of a second honeymoon, because there was nobody to trespass on the intimacies he shared with his wife. But now it was different. He missed the boy, and he had a sense of incompleteness.

"We could drive over and pick him up this weekend," Anne said. "It's only forty miles."

But Cheney shook his head. "The last thing he needs is his parents," he said. "We showed up, it would embarrass him."

"So don't think about him," Anne suggested. She pushed her chair away from the table, wiping a napkin to her lips.

Cheney smiled. He finished eating and then he wandered out into the back yard. He noticed a catcher's mitt and a Wilson Little League bat lying in the grass by the corner of the fence.

He walked to the fence, picked up the mitt and the bat, weighed them in his hands a moment as he stared up at the back of the house. An old house, built around 1920, and not altogether practical with its high ceilings and big drafty rooms and heating bills that were almost criminal at times. But it was real, it was solid, and it had been constructed by men who understood wood and how to use it. And right then it seemed to him a curiously silent house, like a large dog that misses its youthful owner. A big, huffy house.

He sat down in an old cane chair on the patio and after a moment Anne came out and joined him.

"So tell me," she said. "What's it really like being the Sheriff of Hamland?"

And she stuck a mug of coffee beneath his face as though it were a microphone and she some local newscaster hanging on his response with embarrassing eagerness.

In their 1978 Dodge Colt Courtney Sears and Thomas Senior toured the neighborhood. They drove to the municipal park where a baseball game was being played and knots of kids slithered around the bleachers. They went inside the Youth Center, a brick building situated in the center of the park, where some kids played pool and others sat in trance-like states over chessboards and where, in the Center's small auditorium, somebody was doing magic tricks up on the narrow stage. They peered across the rows of pale young faces for a sight of Tommy, but they didn't see him. After, the

Searses drove down Center and traveled as far as the railroad tracks.

Bobby Bones, lingering outside the Burger Palace, hadn't seen Tommy all day. Nor had Randy Claybourne, whom they encountered outside MacMullen's Drugstore. Then they drove out to Delta Plaza and hurried through the mall, looking inside Video Dreams where kids peered myopically into screens and punched buttons and the air was filled with spacey sounds.

Nobody had seen Tommy Sears.

Nobody.

At eight twenty, when they had covered all the likely places and talked to all of Tommy's friends they could find, when they were at the end of their very short rope and young Tommy Sears had been missing for a little more than fourteen hours, they went to the police.

TWO

•——————————————————————————•

THE FIRST THINGS ANYONE EVER NOTICED ABOUT MR ZANZIBAR
were the fingers. They were long and skinny, almost as if the
bones were covered only by a single layer of flesh. They had
about them a skeletal delicacy, a sensitivity you might associate with a brain surgeon or a violinist. They seemed unat-
tached to the hands and nobody ever, *ever* noticed the wrists
or the slender arms that extended upward. When you had
registered the fingers, then you might look at the face, a gaunt
young oval whose dark eyes were set deep in the skull, thin
lips, a long chin that came to a point, as if it were a form of
punctuation to mark the end of the face.

The hands slicked over playing-cards, turning them into
goose feathers. They handled coins as if currency were
weightless. They smoothed over silken scarves in a way that
suggested a defiance of physics. White, bloodless, they took
the mundane matter of everyday shapes and forms and
transmuted them, invested them with secret powers.

Mr Zanzibar didn't speak. It was as if he had absolutely no
use for words because language couldn't contribute anything
to his magic. The kids in the audience, and the few scattered
adults as well, understood this, understood that Mr Zanzi-

bar's mute performance was essential to the mystery at the heart of everything he did. And even when his female assistant stepped forward from the shadows, a pale-faced young girl in a black costume who sometimes handed Mr Zanzibar a prop or caught things he left in his quick wake, she said nothing either—in fact, this girl somehow underlined Mr Zanzibar's total silence as she removed strings of silk scarves or shifted a table for him or took something out of his way.

Balls spun through the air, playing-cards exploded, handkerchiefs caught fire, birds were created from the ether, tubes and scarves and wands turned to flowers, cubes of colored glass, glittering orbs that floated beyond the clutch of gravity —and then the lights went on in the big darkened room and the show was over and somehow Mr Zanzibar and his female assistant had vanished behind the curtains, as if their disappearance were a part of the act also.

The kids applauded, whistled, stamped their feet. They had been hauled inside a circle of mystery and now, abruptly, that circle was broken and everything was ordinary again. This fact was emphasized by the appearance of Ellis Diamond, the young woman who ran the Hamland Parks Recreation Program, on the platform that Mr Zanzibar had just abdicated.

Some of the kids were already shuffling toward the door, eager to go watch the baseball game or play pool or just generally act chaotic in the municipal park. A few of them were pretending to be magicians, Ellis Diamond noticed, faking coins pulled from their friends' ears or shuffling imaginary decks of cards and laughing.

"Kids," Ellis Diamond said, but she wasn't really drawing attention. Who could follow Mr Zanzibar anyhow? She knew she was an anticlimax. "I know we all enjoyed Mr Zanzibar's wonderful show. I know we're very, very fortunate to have his presence here in Hamland this summer. And, as some of you already know, Mr Zanzibar is giving lessons in magic Tuesdays and Thursdays, so for those of you interested in conjuring . . ."

She paused, watching the general shuffle toward the door. "This is a terrific privilege you might want to take advantage of, but remember, there are limits to the number of kids in these groups, so . . ."

She let her voice fade out. She watched the last of the kids wander away and then she stepped behind the curtain and went down a short flight of steps, finding herself in a narrow corridor filled with all the abandoned props of last week's play, The Three Musketeers—plywood swords and plumed hats and capes. She made her way toward a tiny changing-room located at the end of the passageway. There, she paused outside the closed door a moment, turning Zanzibar's perfor-mance over in her mind.

It had been far more professional than she'd ever antici-pated. In her time as director of Parks and Recreation, she had seen more than a few performers—some amateur, some quasi-professional—come and go, but she'd never encoun-tered one as competent, as smooth, as the man who liked to be known only as Mr Zanzibar. (How had he managed to do that bit with the big playing card rising through a handker-chief when there wasn't a hole or a slash anywhere in the fabric of the thing?)

She raised her hand and knocked lightly on the door. From within the room she heard a certain rustling, a shuffling of papers, and then the door was opened and Ellis Diamond was looking into the face of the female assistant, Zena. Ellis cleared her throat and looked beyond the girl's rather large, spaced-out eyes toward Mr Zanzibar, who was hunched over a big hardwood trunk, his white cuffs extending from the sleeves of his black jacket.

"I just wanted to say, Mr Zanzibar, the show was terrific and the kids loved it. I've never really seen them this enthralled."

Ellis was aware of the enthusiasm in her own voice, the breathless quality that made her feel like some kind of groupie. She watched Mr Zanzibar straighten his body up from the trunk. He was tall and lean and he gave the impression of concavity.

"We're really fortunate to have you here this summer. Really," and this time she tried to harness her eagerness. "I've heard great things about your instruction. How patient you are with the kids."

Zanzibar said nothing. His silence might have been an extension of his stage persona. Looking at him, Ellis Diamond had the impression of great height—but surely this was an illusion created by his gauntness and the unyielding blackness of his suit. He was—what?—five eleven, six feet maybe? She turned her face away, conscious of the girl Zena staring at her, and she glanced round the small room which was strewn with props.

"Well." Ellis shrugged, smiled thinly. "I just thought you should know . . . the response you struck in the kids . . ." She stalled, searching for words. "I don't know if this is the right time, but I have to mention that bureaucratic stuff again. Your Social Security numbers, papers you have to sign . . ."

She waited for a response, which she knew wasn't going to come except in some unfathomable, quirky manner.

Mr Zanzibar stepped forward suddenly and looked at Ellis Diamond's hair with great intensity and then his hand snaked forward faster than her eye could follow and she looked up, seeing him draw a length of golden string from the strands of her hair, a string that went on and on for what seemed like twenty-five yards.

Then he crumpled the yarn in the palm of his hand and opened his fingers as if to throw the string back at Ellis, but his hand was empty and the string gone.

Surprised, she heard herself laughing. But it was a nervous sound and she was glad when the trick was finished. She had a strange sense of having been trespassed upon.

She moved toward the door. She thought about raising the subject of the paperwork again. She couldn't keep on letting it slip like this. Sooner or later, she was going to have to confront Zanzibar as *forcibly* as she could about those forms.

She had stepped along the corridor, passed the discarded Musketeer artifacts, climbed the short flight of steps and crossed the upraised platform before she realized that Mr Zanzibar hadn't said a word to her in the dressing-room. Hadn't spoken, hadn't smiled, hadn't graciously accepted her compliments, her gratitude—indeed, he'd behaved toward her as if she were nothing more, nothing less, than another prop in his magic act, a skull out of which he might draw an astonishing length of golden twine.

Now she had passed into the activities room of the Center, heading for her office, which was nothing more than a cubicle tucked out of sight beyond the restrooms and the water-cooler and the soda machines. She paused a second, looked around the room, observed a couple of kids playing pool, and then she closed her office door and sat down behind her desk.

Mr Zanzibar, she thought—and she realized, with something of a start, that the little scene in the dressing-room, which one could hardly call a scene at all, had left her slightly *unnerved* in a way she couldn't altogether define. True, Mr Zanzibar hadn't spoken. True, he had pulled a little stunt on her. True, too, that the female assistant had done nothing but stare at her—but what did all that add up to?

The door of her office opened and the custodian, Max Crouch, stood there in his blue coveralls, his hands stuffed inside his pockets. He was a thin, haggard man who seemed in need of a good meal or a vitamin infusion.

"Puts on quite a show, don't he?" Max asked.

"Quite," Ellis answered.

"Makes you wonder." Max, who was fond of cryptic sentences and unfinished remarks and mumbled phrases that he never repeated on request, ran one hand over his unshaven jaw.

Max Crouch stared at the window of the cubicle, as if he disapproved of something he saw outside in the failing light. Ellis followed the line of his vision but she saw nothing save for the sight of Mr Zanzibar, followed by Zena, getting into their big old-fashioned black Packard and the dense pall of exhaust that always came in the wake of the engine turning over. It passed through her mind, quickly, that she didn't know where the magician lived or whether the girl lived with him—an ignorance she assumed Zanzibar liked to cultivate and encourage, almost as if there were no line of demarcation between his stage and his personal life.

He arrived, he did what he had to do, he departed into the night.

"Makes you wonder what he's doing here," Max Crouch said.

Ellis looked up at him, curious.

"Guy like that," and Max opened the door, turning his face toward the cooler and the soda machines, mumbling away from her.

"A guy like that could do what, Max?"

Max was drawing the door closed as he backed out of the room. "Anywhere," was what he said. "Play anywhere he damn well liked."

Then the door was closed.

Ellis Diamond, thirty-three years of age with a degree in social psychology from the State University of New York at Buffalo, got up from her desk and wandered to the window and saw the disintegrating fumes left in the air by Zanzibar's car, of which there was now absolutely no trace—as if the Packard, like everything else about the magician, were an illusion designed only for mystification.

The broom and the dustpan and the big plastic trash container on wheels. The snotty tissues and the discarded candy wrappers and the damp waxy cups.

Sometimes, for Max Crouch, it was a little too much. He swept and picked up and stuffed the black-green trashbag with the droppings of brats and when he had worked his way to the front of the room, he paused a moment, took a cigarette from his coveralls, lit it and leaned with his elbows against the stage. During the regular school-year he was the janitor at Hamland Junior High, a place he secretly called Craig Street Zoo because kids weren't kids these days, not any more—they'd become little animals, all paws and snuffling snouts and screeches.

What the authorities should do is come in and put some drops of Thorazine in the school water-supply. Then you'd be guaranteed peace and quiet. Turn all those little assholes into guppies!

He drew on his unfiltered Camel and gazed across the large room at the door. A kid's face appeared there briefly, two bright eyes rolled, a middle finger went erect, then the kid vanished and Max Crouch could hear a shrill voice singing

Crouch the Grouch!
Crouch the Grouch!

A little echo, then the voice faded, and the big room was silent again. Max Crouch stubbed his cigarette between thumb and index finger and dropped the butt in the trashbag and some part of his mind entertained the notion that maybe—just maybe—the butt would smolder and catch flame and this whole so-called Youth Center would go up in a bonfire and with it all the bright ideas of Miss Ellis Diamond and her Parks and Recreation Program.

A Youth Center. Where kids could safely go. That was a laugh.

It was supposed to keep kids off the streets during the long summer vacations. Supposed to keep them from hanging out in billiard parlors or sneaking beer and smokes out beyond the railroad tracks. Supposed to make them nice little goodie-goodies. But he knew better than that, he knew they got up to all kinds of rotten mischief because if there was one thing in the world you couldn't trust it was a goddam kid.

They'd break your heart every time.

Max Crouch tightened his grip on the handle of his broom.

Too many kids in Hamland, he thought.

Too many in the whole goddam world!

He wheeled his trash-trolley toward the door. What he'd do, he told himself, was wait until Miss Ellis Diamond had gone home to her second-floor apartment in one of those Victorian houses over on Gunnison Avenue then he'd split and walk the streets until he was sure his wife Hildy might be asleep.

Or maybe he'd follow Ellis Diamond as she walked along Gunnison, keeping his distance from her, tracking her the way he sometimes did, admiring her legs, which were long and slender even if she hid them under calf-length skirts or shapeless polyester pants. A good-looking woman without style might as well shut up shop.

He peered inside the trashbag. My whole life, he thought. *Trash.*

What was the fucking point going home to a wife who sat up most of the night with a box of fucking Kleenex in her lap and her eyes filling up with moisture and her voice breaking whenever she talked and her head made crazy with that sherry she drank? He'd walk the streets, looking—as he

27

always did—into dark doorways and shadowy windows, like a man searching for something or somebody he couldn't name.

But this has a name, Max. Only you don't like to remember it, do you?

Max Crouch rolled the container out of the room, glanced once at the stage, then turned out the overhead light before he drew the door shut. In the dead center of his chest he experienced a certain tightness, a tension that passed almost as quickly as it had come. His eyes had become moist, his vision blurred.

It was the same old pain as always.

And he'd ease it the way he always did, with a few quick nips from the bottle of rum he kept stashed behind the steampipes in the basement of the Youth Center.

At nine thirty George Cheney sat behind his desk and drew one hand across his face, conscious through half-shut eyes of the sign that hung outside the Matterhorn Motor Lodge across the street. Small neon peaks had been made out of the Ms and the roughcut timber of the place suggested it might be a choice location for those anxious to ski—but it was at least forty miles to the nearest slopes. Nobody came to Hamland if they wanted winter sports.

He leaned forward and looked at the faces of the two people who sat opposite him. The small woman with the pitiful expression on her tiny, bony face and the large man whose thick fingers lay curled on his thighs and whose stomach hung so far over his belt you couldn't see the fly of his pants.

He'd known Thomas Sears Senior for some time—Cheney had been a freshman at Hamland High when Thomas was a senior—but it always surprised him to see what the man had turned into. He sat in his chair like a pink dirigible suddenly grounded and yet you had the feeling that gasses were being slowly pumped into him and pretty soon he'd take off again.

Cheney examined the notes he'd made on a pad in front of him.

T Sears. 13. Last seen by mother 6 AM.

13. That made young Tommy three years older than Danny.

"He made, let's see, three deliveries along New Castle Street," Cheney said, squinting at his own writing. "Then for some reason he didn't deliver his last three newspapers."

For some reason, he thought. Why wouldn't the kid finish his paper route? If he'd had plans to run away from home, surely he wouldn't have gone to the trouble of delivering any papers at all?

Courtney Sears studied the plaid sports shirt George Cheney wore and the frayed jeans and the old sneakers and she thought how different he appeared from the uniformed man she sometimes saw driving through Hamland. What she remembered right then was how some of the wives of the town found George Cheney cute. They'd wave to him from their porches and front yards if they happened to see him driving past.

"Is there a girl-friend, Courtney?"

Courtney Sears smiled. "He never mentioned anybody, did he?" And here she looked toward her husband, who stirred his big body around.

"He liked girls," Thomas said. "He was getting to that age when you first start to take notice. He used to go over to the Parks and Rec a lot of his time, so maybe there was somebody he liked down there."

"But he never mentioned anybody special?" George Cheney said.

Both parents frowned, tried to think, shook their heads.

Cheney got up from his desk. His legs were stiff and he wanted to circulate his blood. He stared from the window. Down the street, Center Avenue opened out into Civic Square, where the town hall was situated, a nondescript building erected in the twilight years of the Eisenhower administration.

He turned from the window back to the Searses, both of whom were regarding him with the kind of expressions people might assume in the presence of a guru. Tell us the truth, these expressions said. Tell us everything is fine. Tell us where the boy is, George Cheney.

The sheriff went back to his desk but he didn't sit down. He said, "Kids don't just vanish. Not here in Hamland anyhow. We'll find him." And he thought of the darkness out there in the town, the darkness that stretched itself across Hamland like a temporary skin punctured here and there by a neon sign, a porch-light, a traffic signal. Somewhere, under this sheet of night, was young Tommy Sears.

"We'll need a list of his best friends," he said.

A pause, a hesitation, and then a sequence of names poured out of Courtney Sears. Cheney wrote them all down. Some were names he knew, old Hamland names. Others were strange to him. He had six in all by the time Courtney Sears stopped reciting.

Charles Bannion, Cheney's deputy, appeared in the doorway. He was a stiffly pleasant young man who fancied himself something of an actor. Only last spring he'd appeared in the Hamland Players' production of *Henry IV,* in which he'd been cast as the King. The flattened midwestern accent, almost a drone, had made Charlie Bannion a strange kind of Henry, as if he were the Republican Party Chairman in some dismal district of Nebraska rather than a king in an English court.

Cheney looked at the officer. As did the Searses, twisting hopefully around in their seats, almost as though they expected to see their son accompany the young policeman.

Bannion said, "I have a list here of the three people who didn't get their papers this morning." He handed Cheney a sheet of paper with the names of the unhappy subscribers on it. Cheney glanced at it, then folded it and tucked it in the breast pocket of his shirt.

Cheney sat down now. Tommy Sears, he thought—where are you? And in the wake of this question came images of his own son, the small body huddled in a sleeping-bag under canvas down at the Manti La Sal National Forest, the dark trees stirring around him, maybe a campfire throwing up a few last failing sparks at the moon. Danny, the Cub Scout. Kids grew up and in the process grew sideways and away from you, their lives running at sometimes awkward tangents to your own. A momentary sadness coursed through him, a feeling of inevitability.

He slapped the palm of his hand on the desk. "Check the names on this paper, Charlie. They're all Tommy's friends."

And he tore a sheet from his desk-pad and watched the young officer seize it eagerly.

Courtney Sears said, "We talked to all those kids already, didn't we?" And she looked once at her husband, for his imprimatur, his affirmation.

"Cops talk differently," Cheney said, smiling.

Charlie Bannion, AKA King Henry, exited, and Cheney could hear him go crisply along the corridor and then there was the squeak of the front doors swinging on their hinges.

"I suggest you both go home," Cheney said.

The Searses didn't move. They stared at him, expecting more somehow, and it showed on their faces. Didn't he have a computer or something, a machine he could go press a few buttons on and out would pop the whereabouts of young Tommy?

"Go home. When I find Tommy, I'll deliver him in person," he said. "Okay?"

The couple rose and went toward the door. There, Thomas Sears paused and looked back and his mouth opened as though he were about to say something, but then he changed his mind and shrugged, following his wife out into the corridor.

Cheney, alone, leaned against the edge of his desk.

What was it Thomas Sears had been about to say?

There had been a moment just then when something glassy had gone across his eyes, something a little secretive, and his lips had been alerted for speech—but nothing had emerged.

Cheney stared at the Matterhorn Motor Lodge.

A curtain was drawn across a window and a shadow passed and a lamp was turned off in one of the rooms.

Cheney just knew that something furtive was going on inside that room, an illicit coupling, a betrayal of some sort. Somewhere in Hamland there was a lonely wife and a lonely husband, both wondering where their spouses might be, both pacing floors or staring at TVs to stall their fears and suspicions.

Goddam.

It's some imagination you have there, he told himself. And

31

he turned off the lamp inside his own mind to save electricity for the task of running down young Tommy Sears.

A cold aluminum cylinder of beer in his big hand, Thomas Sears sat down at the kitchen table. From the bedroom he could hear his wife sniffle. It didn't matter how hard he tried, he couldn't bring her any comfort—perhaps because he couldn't find any himself. You couldn't escape the iron fact that the boy was out there somewhere, that it was now ten thirty and he'd been gone more than sixteen hours.

Thomas sipped some beer but he was beginning to find it tasteless. Besides, it wasn't doing anything for him, it wasn't fuzzing the edges the way it usually did. He clasped his hands together on the table and he stared at them, surprised by their plumpness. In a moment he'd get up and go back inside the bedroom and put his arms around his wife and maybe she'd find some consolation in his embrace—but for now he couldn't move.

Something was churning at the back of his mind, something old that smelled of decay and darkness, something damp that seemed to cling to the recesses of his brain, like pictures from a moldy old family album which has lain too long in a mildewed attic.

Close it, Thomas.

It has nothing to do with the present.

Put it away, set it aside . . .

Slowly, he got up from the table and moved back to the bedroom, where he sat on the edge of the mattress and reached for his wife's small cold hand.

Thomas Sears whispered. "Listen, he's gonna come through that front door any minute now. He's gonna have some cock and bull story ready about why he's late and where he's been. You know the kid. You'll see."

His wife didn't respond.

Her hand lay motionless in his own like some tiny bird a long time dead.

Victoria Estaban saw the big black Packard draw up alongside her. Beneath the glow of the streetlamp it looked sleek and mysterious, like a vehicle from some other dimension. The girl, who was at an age when it was easier to love mysteries than dispute them, held her breath as Zena rolled down the passenger window.

Zanzibar, Vickie thought. *Zanzibar's wonderful car. And it's stopping for me . . .*

"Need a ride?" Zena asked.

Vickie Estaban hesitated only a moment. She glanced beyond the magician's assistant to Zanzibar himself, who was staring straight ahead, his face expressionless. In the pale light he looked almost unbelievably handsome. Vickie Estaban felt a small tremor go through her body. For some time now she had been conscious of the way Zanzibar seemed to pay more attention to her than he did to any other student. A flame flickered back and forth between herself and the magician, she was sure of that. She thought it was the spark of some secret unspeakable longing, of something very special between them. Didn't he always take time to explain the mechanics of magic to her? Didn't he lean very close to her when he talked? And hadn't there been at least one memorable moment when he'd clasped his hands around hers to show her how to handle a deck of cards?

At the age of fourteen, Vickie knew she was ready for a Prime Time affair, a serious passion of the heart. And Zanzibar, so unlike anyone else in Hamland—(especially that Lonnie Garrison who thought he was God's gift to girls and that Sears kid who gaped at her all the time)—Zanzibar, so *vibrant* with his own powers, so *intense,* was the only candidate she had really considered.

Sometimes, before she fell asleep at night, she imagined Zanzibar stepping inside her bedroom, his black cloak falling away, and it was the most overwhelmingly erotic thing she could think of. Lying alone in her darkened bedroom, she would gasp as the magician slid toward her across the mattress . . . Zanzibar was a lover of inexhaustible resources, inventive, a sorcerer of flesh.

And now here she was, sitting in the back seat of the magician's car for God's sake, sitting only ten or twelve inches *away* from him and all she could do was *babble* about

33

how much she'd liked his show and how hard she was practicing the card-palming he'd demonstrated and how interesting the whole conjuring bit was.

Aware of the noise she was making, she forced herself to stop. She sat back in her seat and sighed. It was unsophisticated to babble like that, especially when you were the only person talking. She glanced at the rear-view mirror and thought she saw Zanzibar staring back at her. She wanted to ask him so many things—did he believe in UFOs? life after death? had he ever seen a ghost?—but she kept very quiet as the car slid down through the dark streets. She folded her hands in her lap, wanted to tell Zanzibar how many books on the occult she'd read, wanted to talk about the biography of Houdini she'd recently finished and ask if he thought Houdini the greatest magician who'd ever lived, but if she opened her mouth she knew she would gush again and that would be an embarrassment.

Vickie stared at Zena now.

That gaunt face and those hard dark eyes and the hair so black it had to be dyed—what could Zanzibar *possibly* see in the woman? Vickie crossed her legs and wondered if Zanzibar and Zena were lovers.

Vickie stared out of the window a moment. She saw Center Avenue flit past, darkened storefronts, shadowy awnings, a blue beer light burning in the window of Scatini's Tavern.

"I live on Carberry. You know it?" Vickie directed this question at Zanzibar but it was Zena who answered.

"Just point the way, kid," the woman said. Vickie saw Zena's hand go down to Zanzibar's knee a moment. It was such a personal gesture, a lover's move, that Vickie felt a quick stab of envy. She had to look away. Center Avenue had disappeared and Zanzibar was driving now toward the freeway.

Vickie said, "This is the wrong way, Mr Zanzibar. You need to go back two blocks and take a left at the stoplight."

Zanzibar braked and the big car began to slow down. Vickie, who for a moment had imagined some unlikely abduction—a prospect that didn't fill her entirely with fear—laughed lightly. "I guess you don't know your way around Hamland yet, huh?"

Zanzibar parked the car and sat behind the wheel in silence. Zena tilted her head back and made a soft sighing sound. Vickie looked out at a field surrounded by thick trees. It was isolated from the rest of Hamland, set apart from the well-lit streets and the houses. It was known as Sutter's Meadow.

"You can turn around here," Vickie said.

Zanzibar didn't move. Zena shut her eyes.

Vickie shifted around in her seat. She looked at the rear-view mirror. Zanzibar, his eyes shadowy, was staring at her reflection. There was no expression on his face. Nothing. A little unnerved by the stare, by the depth of silence in the car, by the dark trees on the dark street, Vickie rubbed the palms of her hands together.

"If you go back to the stoplight . . ." she said. She felt that her words somehow sunk into the silence of the car, like small pebbles in water.

Zanzibar opened his door and stepped out. He reached for the rear door and Vickie watched it swing out and then she realized Zanzibar wanted her to join him but for a second she didn't move, she simply glanced at Zena who seemed to be asleep, head tipped back, lips slightly parted.

Vickie looked at the magician. He was holding one hand toward her, waiting for her. His black clothing melted into the black backdrop of trees. Only the pale sphere of his face was visible. As she stepped warily out of the back seat, Vickie felt a curious weakness in her legs. *Did Zanzibar intend to take her down into Sutter's Meadow and make love to her there in the tall grass?*

Vickie hesitated now. In her fantasies of Zanzibar there had always been an element of safety because he'd never *really* been in her bedroom, he'd never *actually* crept into bed beside her—but this was something else and she wasn't sure what she wanted, wasn't sure she was ready to go down into the meadow with him. In her dreams, she always had control. But not here. Not now. Maybe she just wasn't ready for this adventure.

He took her hand. His skin was remarkably cold.

He walked with her to the edge of the trees. She was trembling. Through the dark she could see the island of blackness that was Sutter's Meadow. She couldn't stop shaking now.

Between the trees Zanzibar paused.

He dropped her hand from his own and turned to look at her and she wished she could see the expression on his face but there were too many shadows falling from the overhanging branches. A slight breeze shivered across the tall grass, making it rustle. She felt the passage of air press against her jeans and touch the flimsy blouse she wore.

He handed something to her, something he whipped out of the folds of his cloak. It was a deck of cards. A gift from the sorcerer.

She was touched, didn't know what to say. She blurted out, "Thanks," and then she was silent. *A gift from Zanzibar! Oh God!*

A night moth buzzed at her face. She swept it away.

Zanzibar lifted an arm. His hand, the palm open, fell against her cheek and remained there. She trembled more. A sequence of tiny uncontrollable explosions went through her whole body.

She felt the coldness of his palm on her face. And then she was being drawn toward him and she wondered if she would let him kiss her, if it really came right down to the bottom line she wondered how far she'd actually go with him—

But there was no kiss.

There was only the touch of Zanzibar's mouth against her ear.

Only his warm breath. The light touch of his lips.

This was the most strangely intimate moment of Victoria Estaban's young life.

Now she really *shared* something with the magician, even if a little later, when she was lying down in the security of her own bedroom, she couldn't say exactly what. And even when she took out the deck of cards Zanzibar had given her and began to shuffle through them, she still couldn't penetrate to the heart of the mystery.

THREE

●━━━━━━━━━━━━━━━━━━━━━━━●

IN THE ROOM WHERE ELMER HUBBARD HAD BLOWN HIS OWN brains out years before, his widow Lily stood at the windows with one hand on the edge of a curtain. She looked down into Gunnison Avenue and remembered a time when a house on Gunnison meant something very special in Hamland—a certain standing in the community, a certain level of achievement. These were not mean houses even now, not by a long way, but many of them—her own included—had been turned into apartments and although Gunnison was still a good address to have it wasn't quite the same as it had been when Elmer was alive. Lily Hubbard thought of her own tenants. Miss Diamond and Mr Rigley might pay rent and possess keys and come and go as they wanted, but they would always remain strangers in her house.

She turned from the window and crossed the room, where she stood behind the door and listened to the sound of footsteps on the stairs. This was Ellis Diamond returning from the park where she worked. Her footsteps, Lily Hubbard thought, were timid sounds, like those made by scampering mice. She put one hand on the doorknob and waited until she was sure Ellis Diamond was on the landing and then she drew the door open and gazed at the young woman.

"Windy tonight," Lily Hubbard said and pulled her fringed shawl over her shoulders. She smiled and her white makeup cracked in little lines.

Ellis Diamond nodded and said politely, "Yes."

Ellis had one hand on the bannister rail. Her face was turned toward the flight of dark stairs that led to the next floor and her own apartment. A moment of fatigue went through her but she made no move toward the stairs. It had become a fact of her life—Lily Hubbard detained her like this at every opportunity. It was almost as if the older woman depended on her to bring news in from the outside world, as if she, Ellis, were a war correspondent returning daily from some brutal front that Lily Hubbard was interested in but had no desire to visit.

"I have this feeling there's a storm coming," Lily said. She put her fingers up to her frizzy, dyed hair. "The park . . . how are things at the park with the children, Miss Diamond?"

Ellis watched as the landlady's nails curled round her wrist. She pretended not to flinch.

"Oh, the kids are fine, just fine," was what she said.

Lily Hubbard, leaning forward a little, seemed to be waiting for more information. Her red mouth was parted and her eyes, bright and focussed, made Ellis think of a coroner surveying the corpse he is about to dissect.

"We had a magician tonight. A magic show," Ellis remarked. "It went off well. Really well. The kids liked it . . ." She paused. "The man was very good. We're fortunate to have him this summer . . ."

Lily Hubbard smiled again. Her painted claw fell away from Ellis's wrist.

Ellis moved toward the staircase. From the upper part of the house she heard the squeak of a door. It would have been Mr Rigley who lived at the very top of the house, perhaps opening his door, listening a moment, then shutting it. She had only seen the other tenant once and that was on the day, three weeks ago, when the man had first moved in. What did he do up there anyhow? Sometimes, around midnight, she would hear him drift down the stairs quietly and then the front door would be opened and he'd be gone.

Lily Hubbard was backing inside her own room now, as if some invisible hand were tugging persistently at her fringed shawl. "You look tired, dear. You do look tired."

Ellis said that she was and yawned to prove it. She edged closer to the stairs.

"A night's sleep wouldn't harm you at all," Lily Hubbard said. "Goodnight, dear," and she drew the door closed. She could hear the tenant go on up the stairs. Such a timid little thing, she thought. Afraid of her own shadow.

Lily moved toward an armchair and sat down, facing a second chair exactly like her own except that it was empty, quite empty.

That had always been Elmer's chair. Wingbacked, upholstered in dark green leather, it still seemed to contain a shadow of the dead man.

Lily shut her eyes and considered the dark, silent reaches of this big house. And then she thought of her two tenants, whose apartments she sometimes visited when she was sure the occupants were gone. Ellis Diamond was not extremely tidy. She often left clothes on the bathroom floor and sometimes undergarments dripped from the curtain-rail in the shower. Mr Rigley, on the other hand, was fastidious. Mr Rigley, indeed, was the perfect tenant.

Perfect.

Lily Hubbard opened her eyes.

A magic show, she thought.

What this town needed was a magic show.

New Castle Street, short and blunt and like all the streets of Hamland tree-lined so that houses were hidden from casual view, backed on to the municipal park. When George Cheney got out of his car he stared across the darkened park toward a scattering of tall white lamps that hung around the baseball lot. They were lit still—presumably because somebody had forgotten to turn them off—but the diamond and the bleachers were deserted, and the lights created harsh, eerie shadows everywhere.

Roots, George Cheney thought.

He had played ball here as a kid but that was before the Youth Center had been built. Back then, the baseball team had been coached by an Irishman called Malley, a locomotive engineer who manipulated rosary beads between his fingers during games, as if victory were dependent upon saying the right things at the right time to God.

Cheney looked away from the bright lights and moved toward the sidewalk, feeling a moist wind come down through the night against his face. There were perfumes in the dark—cut grass, old barbecue scents, a whiff of refried beans drifting out lazily from the direction of Rosita's Mexican Food Factory. He stood under a streetlamp and looked at the notepaper in his hand.

According to this information, Tommy Sears had made his last delivery of *The Progressive* at number 19. The next delivery, which he had not made, would have been at 21. Somewhere between 19 and 21 the kid had decided to take a hike. Or else somebody had made that decision for him. Cheney shook his head. Kids lived in a secret world and sometimes you couldn't get access to it, not because you didn't know the password, not because you didn't understand the jargon they used these days, but simply on account of your own age, your history, the fact that you were ancient.

Where had young Tommy gone? What furtive plans had that kid hatched?

Cheney moved toward number 19, a green frame house with a yellow porch-light. Through a window he could see inside, a living-room, a TV picture flickering, papers on a coffee table. He knocked very lightly on the door and a tall teenage boy emerged from the gloom, half-hidden from Cheney by an old screen door. The people who occupied this house were called Scully. Cheney didn't know them well. They'd never been in trouble with the law.

"Hi," Cheney said.

The kid opened the screendoor. "Sheriff Cheney?"

Cheney nodded. "Your father home?"

The boy twisted his head, called out down the hallway, and after a moment Archie Scully appeared. Scully, who was a short man with a bald, dome-shaped head, glanced at his son for a second. Cheney could hear an unspoken question in that look. *What the hell have you been up to, kid, that brings the goddam sheriff to our house?*

A light went on in the hallway. Cheney blinked against it. Archie Scully was wearing an old-fashioned V-neck sweater, sleeveless, shapeless.

"What can I do for you, Sheriff?" Scully asked.

"Your delivery boy has disappeared," Cheney said. "The kid who brings you the morning paper."

"Disappeared?" Scully said. He looked puzzled, a man dealing with a concept foreign to him. He turned to stare at his son, as if he suspected that Scully Junior had had something to do with this business.

"After he delivered your paper, he didn't make it to 21," Cheney said.

Scully looked from his porch and out across his front yard in the direction of 21, a frame house not unlike his own, and he frowned. "Would be damn hard for a kid to disappear between here and there, wouldn't it?" he said.

Cheney folded his arms. "Damn hard," he agreed.

The teenage boy said, "Maybe he got zapped by aliens."

Scully gave his son a hard look. "Tony, if you don't have anything real sensible to say, don't go opening your mouth."

"Listen, I've read about guys just vanishing inside space-craft."

"Yeah, yeah, but not around here," Archie Scully said with disdain. It was clear he dismissed the possibility of alien life having any desire to come to Hamland, of all places.

"Did you see the boy this morning, Mr Scully?" he asked.

"Nope," and Scully shook his head. "But the newspaper was on the porch like it always is. You see him, Tony?"

Tony Scully said, "He's always been and gone by the time I get up."

"Even if you was up," his father said, "you wouldn't notice anything anyhow."

"Did either of you see anything unfamiliar this morning? Like a strange car? Anything like that?" Cheney asked these questions in the manner of a man who knows the answers in advance. The only evidence that Tommy Sears had ever passed this way was the newspaper on the front porch,

41

nothing else. No sign of the kid, no strange cars, just a rolled-up newspaper.

Neither Scully spoke. Cheney shrugged, moved toward the porch steps. He crossed the spongelike grass to the shrubbery that surrounded 21, conscious of the fact the Scullys were still watching him. He parted the bushes and approached a cracked concrete path and as he did so a porch-light went on up ahead and a figure appeared on the porch.

"George Cheney," the man said. "Something must be going on."

Cheney reached the steps and looked up at Henry Hodges, who stood with his feet wide apart and his hands tucked inside his belt. Hodges was a tall man who wore a black turtleneck sweater and white slacks. He had gone to Hamland High with Cheney, where he had distinguished himself with the best academic record of any student ever at the school. Henry Hodges, everybody just knew, was going to go out and shake the world like an apple tree.

Instead, he was the local agent for a life insurance company with headquarters in Des Moines. His ambition had died, his brightness had dimmed—nobody knew for certain. He would live and die in Hamland.

On the porch, Cheney shook Hodges's hand.

"This is too late to be a social call, George," Hodges said.

Cheney nodded. "I'm looking for a lost kid. Your newspaper boy."

"Tommy? I wondered about the paper this morning. Kid's usually regular as a clock."

"He's missing."

Hodges was silent a second, studying the darkness around him. "Want to come inside, George? I just opened a nice Cabernet."

Henry Hodges, Cheney remembered, was very proud of his wine collection. It was a little touch of sophistication in a small town that didn't have much of it.

"I don't have the time," Cheney said.

Hodges leaned against the porch railing, his hands spread. "You think he's a runaway?"

"Could be."

"Seems like a good kid. I can't imagine him running away.

But I suppose even good kids run away these days." Henry Hodges paused and turned his face to Cheney. It was a dark-eyed face, mournful in a way. "Used to come around Sundays to be paid. Once or twice I had him mow the lawn. A good kid. Open, if you know what I mean." Hodges shook his head from side to side.

Cheney listened a moment to the wind moving down New Castle, then blowing out across the municipal park.

"Did you see him this morning, Henry?"

"No."

"He delivered at the Scullys."

"Strange he didn't make it here," Hodges said, as if to himself. He moved toward a wicker chair and he sat down, clasping his hands together. "I hope nothing's happened to the boy."

"Did you see anybody hanging around this morning? A stranger? Anything out of the ordinary?"

Henry shook his head. "I wish I could help you, George."

Both men were quiet for a moment.

"What did the Scullys tell you?" Hodges asked.

"About as much as you, Henry."

Cheney shrugged and turned toward the steps. The darkness around him, as the wind died, seemed empty and taunting.

"George?"

At the foot of the steps Cheney looked up. Henry Hodges stared at him from the shadows at the back of the porch.

"You ever wish you'd stayed away?"

"From Hamland?"

Henry nodded. "You ever wish you'd been a high school teacher out in California?"

"I don't think so," Cheney said.

"Or a farmer in Iowa?"

Cheney laughed. "I don't have a way with plants or animals."

"Or maybe a college professor in New Hampshire?"

Cheney moved toward the sidewalk. "You ask too many questions, Henry."

Cheney reached his car and stood very still. A farmer in Iowa. A teacher in California. He was a man who believed

43

more than a little in destiny and it had been his personal fate to become the sheriff of this small town, not a college professor in New Hampshire, not an insurance agent for a company with its headquarters in Des Moines. Not anything else but what he was.

He watched the lights go out around the baseball field and the darkness was suddenly staggering, as if he'd been stripped of a sense all at once. And, like a blind man, he could feel Hamland press in on him, he could smell the place on the tail of the wind and hear it whispering in his ears—but nothing he sensed, nothing he heard, could tell him anything he needed to know about Tommy Sears.

The girl didn't like Zanzibar's moods of silence because he sealed himself away when he was like this, locked himself inside a little box in his mind and he wouldn't be coaxed back out until he was good and ready. In many respects, there was something childlike about Zanzibar.

Dressed in a dark-green kimono, the girl stepped out on the porch and lit a cigarette with cold hands.

Wind blew in little spasms down the night-black canyon and there were misshapen clouds across a half-assed moon. She shivered. To the east, miles beyond the canyon walls, she could see a pale yellowy glow in the sky that was a reflection of Hamland. She thought that living in an obscure canyon was bad enough, but if they'd rented a place in a dump like Hamland it would have been even worse. Small towns like that gave her the willies. They were always so . . . wrapped up in themselves. Small towns and Zanzibar had that much in common, at least.

She stared at the moon a while.

From inside the large house behind her there was the sound of a door slamming. Zanzibar on the move, she thought.

But after that there was a silence broken only by the hawking of some weird night-bird out there in the canyon. It crossed her mind in a lazy way that maybe it wasn't any bird out there, maybe it was Zanzibar himself, masked by darkness and doing one of his bird noises. She had started to think like this since she'd been in Zanzibar's company. Boxes within boxes within boxes. And after you'd undone all the damn wrapping-paper you still didn't find anything. Life with Zanzibar was like a really weird Christmas when all you got was tinsel and polyurethane packing chips.

She stepped into the house, pausing in the hallway, looking in the direction of the stairs ahead. Zanzibar was standing motionless at the top, his hands pressed against his thighs.

She gazed up at the illusionist, finding her way into his eyes, but there was no expression there because when Zanzibar wanted to deny you access to himself he could do it as easily as he could work a deck of cards.

She smiled up at him. He looked at her as if she did not exist.

Her kimono hanging open, she started to climb the stairs. Halfway up she paused.

She had a sense of hidden springs coiled within the man, compressed energies, fuses smoldering in deep, dark places.

Say something to me, she thought. Say something nice the way you did before when we were in bed. Or lay me out some nice lines of dope like you did when we first met in Laughlin. Or tell me again about how we're going to Vegas after this gig closes down, I need to hear nice, nice things. *I need to hear about love and kindness and the sweet places of the human heart . . . I need to be more than your assistant in some stage act. I need to be special to you. And you can be soooo nice to me when you want to be . . .*

He moved. He moved down two, three steps, then stopped. He turned his face toward her and the corner of his mouth twisted slightly and this faint movement had the effect of making his face seem suddenly very large to her, filling her entire visual field as though the head were a balloon that had been blown up.

Zanzibar moved past her and she swung around, watching him descend. After a second, she followed him.

He smiled.

He turned his face toward the door. A clock in one of the downstairs rooms began to chime the hour.

* * *

George Cheney tried not to disturb Anne, who was asleep on the living-room sofa, but she stirred anyhow as soon as he'd turned off the TV. Rubbing her arms, she sat upright and smiled at him, watching him slump in an armchair with a strange little look of defeat on his face. It was a good, firm face, the kind most people felt comfortable with immediately —lived-in, she thought, like a room you loved—and it was odd to see his downbeat expression right then. It was like coming home to find a stranger had rearranged all your furniture.

"You didn't find the boy," she said.

Cheney shook his head. "Nobody saw him. Nobody on the street where he delivers saw him. None of his friends."

"What do you imagine happened to him?" Anne asked.

Cheney said, "A runaway. Who knows?" There was concern in his voice, there was nothing casual in the way he asked the question. There were certain areas of his life where, Anne understood, George was inflexible—and one of these was in the way he performed his job. It had to be done well and if perfection was forever just out of reach then he could at least say he had tried his best. No, he could never be casual about his job, any more than he could be careless with his family's love. Solid qualities—very far removed from the kind of life Anne had once considered, that flaky theatrical world with its upturned cheeks waiting to be kissed, its slackly insincere handshakes and loose embraces.

She rose from the sofa and stood by the fireplace, hands clasped behind her back. "If he's a runaway, George, where do you start?"

Cheney sighed. "That's just it. If he's a runaway, we note the information and it goes out over the wires and if the kid happens to get picked up by cops in Snake Pit, Alabama, or some godforsaken place like that because he's been jaywalking then maybe his name's going to pop out of the computer and he'll be sent back home. A stroke of luck. Ordinary runaways don't rate much police time."

"What if he's not a runaway, George?"

Cheney raised his face and looked at her in silence for a while. Then, "You mean—some kind of prank? Something like that?"

"That's not what I mean," Anne said. And you know it, George Cheney. *You know it.*

Cheney stood up, slouching a little. "I can't allow myself to think like that, Anne. Not yet. Not yet anyhow."

Anne closed her eyes a moment. The trouble was that George liked to think of Hamland as a fixed entity, unchangeable, a place untouched by the temper of the times as though it were a flawless moth preserved in amber. He liked to imagine Hamland as he'd seen it once through childhood's eyes. It was a town of clean streets and open spaces and fresh air. And as long as he imagined it like this, it was controllable, he could manage the place. But didn't he see how other forces could intervene? how dark things could manifest themselves even in Hamland? Acts of vandalism, random violence, senseless crimes thrown up from undercurrents of jealousy, hatred, madness?

She sometimes thought her husband had wanted to be sheriff of this small town because that way he might have a hand in preserving the place he remembered. That way he could reinforce the laws that had worked—or so he thought—when he'd been a boy growing up here. Change, sweet Christ, didn't he just hate change?

She wanted to say these things to him but she didn't. Instead, she moved silently behind him and began to rub his tense shoulders. She loved this man and she loved his town, as if one were a mirror reflecting the other, but there were times when she despaired over his refusal to see things for what they were.

"There are some people in this world, George, who are one brick shy of a full load. Who aren't operating on all pistons. I don't know if this fact has escaped your attention—"

"Anne—"

"Crazies, George. Everywhere you look, crazies." She ploughed her fingertips deep into the fibers of his muscles and she heard him sigh. "And it's not just some weirdos walking through New York or L.A. muttering into their beards either. It's everywhere." She paused. "Even in Hamland, George. Even here."

* * *

Max Crouch stood under a dark tree and stared up at the lit window of Ellis Diamond's apartment. Now and then a shadow crossed in front of the blinds. Maybe she was undressing up there. He shut his eyes, swayed, felt cold. He could see her stripping down to nothing, maybe leaving her flimsy panties to the very last, or stepping out of her pantyhose. Maybe she was lying naked on her bed at this very moment and what he imagined was Ellis Diamond *playing* with herself, stroking her clitoris with the tip of a moist finger, and beginning to moan quietly as she reached up into the Christmas tree lights of self-inflicted passion.

Max Crouch opened his eyes. He wandered out from beneath the tree and began to move down Gunnison. Christ, he didn't want to go home. He didn't want to go there at all, back to that hive of pain where Hildy was sitting up, plump as a goddam queen bee. He moved absently down through the town, barely feeling the cold edge the wind had as it pushed against him. Then he was way out in the boonies, where Hamland petered out.

He paused on Carberry Street. The people who lived here had made their little bundles and had built themselves custom homes, tailored to their individual needs. What did he have? What did Maxwell Crouch, janitor, *really* have? A dreary little walkup apartment and a weeping wife and a raging emptiness in his shriveled heart, that's what Max Crouch had, goddamit!

He stood outside the Estaban house a moment. There was a kid lived in there, Victoria, he'd seen her, he knew that type, all ass and little tits jiggling under tight T-shirts, he'd seen her all right, the flowering of her sex, he'd seen her and he knew she was one of the little brats that tease the guys, a flash of teeth and a downward flutter of the eyes and little nipples visible through her shirts and her crotch tight in her jeans, she'd come to nothing in the end because that was the way girls like Victoria Estaban turned out.

Slut! Cockteaser!

Max Crouch stood very still and looked up into a sky that

was dark and furtive. He stood in the manner of a man searching for a God that has chosen to deny him just about everything.

Everything that really mattered anyhow.

Tears welled up in his eyes suddenly and he felt abandoned under the vast and terrible empty sky.

FOUR

• •

IN THE COFFEE SHOP OF THE ROYAL HOTEL (WHERE JOHN L.
Sullivan was said to have stayed in 1893, the year after he lost
his heavyweight title to Gentleman Jim Corbett) Thomas
Sears Senior flipped pancakes and supervised bacon strips
on the big griddle and pushed sausages around with a
spatula.

He sometimes paused to wipe his palms on his greasy white
uniform or back-hand sweat from his forehead. He was
distracted, distanced from himself. He thought that maybe he
shouldn't have come to work today at all, he should have
stayed home with Courtney and waited for news of the kid.
But he felt he had to do something, go someplace, to take his
mind off Tommy.

Wanda Hartmeyer came inside the kitchen. She was a
plump girl who looked like a stuffed tomato inside the
tight-fitting red uniform the Royal made the waitresses wear.

"I just heard about your boy," she said. She slid the open
palm of one hand down Thomas's arm in a gesture of
comfort.

"What did you hear?" Sears stared at her.

"Only that he's missing," the waitress said.

"Where'd you hear that?"

"This is a small town," she said. She let her hand fall from his arm. "Listen, Tommy, he'll turn up. Kids do the strangest things. I know I can't keep up with mine, I'll tell you." She paused and gazed at the writhing bacon on the griddle. "You spank him when he does show up."

"Yeah," Thomas said. And he scooped up piles of scrambled eggs, dumping them on plates carelessly. He watched Wanda balance them in her expert way, then she was gone through the swinging doors.

He peered out through the serving-hatch again. In the dining area he saw a half dozen or so workers from Rosita's, two guys from Slattery's Meat Packing Plant in their blood-smudged white coveralls, three mailmen and a couple of well-dressed strangers who were obviously guests of the hotel because they were taking the trouble to read the menu, something none of the regulars ever did.

And then, tucked away in the far corner of the dining-room, he noticed Lily Hubbard and for a moment he felt something cold around his heart, a sensation of packed ice pressed against his ribcage. She wasn't looking at him, she was studying the menu, her long painted fingernails gripping the laminated paper like talons. Her face was an eccentric rainbow of makeup, reds and blacks and pinks against a sky of immaculate white. She set the menu down finally and her eyes roamed the dining-room a second before they found the hatch.

Her lips moved, forming the words *Good morning, Thomas.*

A silent greeting from across the room.

Thomas Sears smiled back at her and then looked away quickly.

Lily Hubbard never came to the Royal for breakfast.

So why today?

As he moved toward the griddle, he could feel an intense rush of blood through his head.

He stared down at the strips of twisted bacon and the bubbling eggs, unable to see them, his vision flooded with the sight of Lily Hubbard's face.

* * *

"And you've no leads, right?"

Cheney, seated behind the desk in his office, nodded. The man who asked the question was Ronald Kelly, a *Progressive* reporter who'd been with the paper for twenty-three years. He had a narrow, pinched face which reminded Cheney of a bruised pear.

Cheney stood up and walked to a wall-map of Hamland and the surrounding county. The gridlike pattern of the city streets suggested a maze to him all at once, a labyrinth at whose heart was one missing boy.

"Any ideas, George? Any theories?"

Cheney shrugged. He went back to his desk and sat down, still looking at the big wall-map. One little mystery, he thought. One simple occurrence and it makes the map look different in some small way. "I don't have any theories, Ron. Christ, I don't even know if there's any story in all this. It's only been twenty-four hours."

What was he supposed to do? Speculate that the kid might have been kidnapped? Brutally murdered and slung in some narrow irrigation ditch where his young body might fester for months and be turned up one day, by a farmworker or somebody passing by?

Kelly said, "Give or take a couple, there's about fifteen thousand people in this town. Which doesn't exactly make it the Naked City, but somebody out there has to know something." And the reporter wandered across to the wall-map, gazing up at it, his expression like that of a melancholy Bosc. "Somebody has to know something."

Kelly came back to the desk. "Do you have any reason to suspect foul play, George?"

"Foul play? Ron, look, the kid's only been *missing* for about twenty-four hours, I don't have a lead, I already told you that—so how could I suspect *anything?*"

Kelly smiled. A crease in the center of the fruity face. "It isn't much fun, George, when you have to churn out copy in a town where not a whole lot really happens. Sometimes, to amuse myself, I look to see if maybe a story has more stamina than it seems to have on the surface. To see if it *really* has legs. Mostly, this doesn't happen. The story is exactly what it appears to be, which in the case of Hamland is usually something pretty trifling, like the closure of the five-and-dime. You know what I'm saying, George? Pardon me if I'm hungry for a little drama."

A little drama, Cheney thought. He could see black headlines unfurling, gruesome smudges of printer's ink. "Sometimes, Ron, a kid stays out too late and he's afraid to go home because he's in deep trouble with his parents, so he stays away and it only gets deeper. Kids don't look at clocks, Ron. You know that."

Ronald Kelly was moving toward the door.

"Tommy Sears could come home at any moment," Cheney said. "I wouldn't like to see you waste your time just yet."

Kelly shrugged vaguely. "I'll give it another twenty-four hours, George. Then I'll see what shape it's in."

Cheney watched the journalist go out. Then he sat very still for a while with his eyes shut.

Tommy Sears, he thought.

Come home.

Come home—if only because I don't want a little drama of the kind Ronald Kelly needs. I don't want to see morbid headlines of the sort that would drive up the circulation of The Progressive *beyond its wildest speculations—*

What I want to see, Tommy, is a happy ending.

His telephone rang and he picked it up. He heard a girl's voice on the line, reticent, slightly breathless.

"Sheriff Cheney?" the girl asked.

"Speaking."

A pause. A beat.

"I saw Tommy Sears yesterday."

When Marge Dove came inside the kitchen Anne looked up from her copy of that morning's *Progressive* and smiled. "There's coffee," Anne said. "You know where everything is."

Marge Dove helped herself to a cup of coffee which she drowned in milk. Then she sat at the kitchen table and tilted her chair back at the wall, sipping. "What would we do without Parks and Rec?" she asked in the fashion of Karl

Malden in an American Express commercial. *"What would we do?"*

Anne filled her own coffee cup and looked at her next-door neighbor who, despite her thirty-three years of life and two kids, came off like some hapless overgrown girl, large-boned and awkward. You could sometimes imagine a satchel over her shoulder and inkstains on her fingertips and school papers tucked willy-nilly in the pockets of her jacket.

Marge said, "I just packed my two off to the care of Ellis Diamond. That woman is a treasure, I swear. I'd be crazy without her."

"What do they do over there anyhow?" Anne asked. Because Danny was away at camp, she hadn't paid much attention to Ellis Diamond's summer programs.

"It's so well-organized. Games. Handicrafts. You name it, Ellis Diamond probably has it on her agenda." Marge put her coffee cup down. "Jenny's rehearsing a play. She has the role of a dwarf in *Snow White*. God knows, she's small enough. Dozey, I think. Maybe it's Grumpy. Anyhow, it keeps her busy and out from under my feet. And Rick's into a couple of things. He keeps telling me what they are and I keep forgetting. Chess, I think. Except today it was magic. Somebody was going to teach him some card tricks. Apparently, they've got a wizard over there."

Anne smiled. "Maybe when Danny gets back I can enroll him in one of the groups."

"You should, Anne. You really should." Marge Dove paused. "How is he? Have you heard?"

"We got a phone call last Sunday. He sounded great. I thought maybe he'd be homesick and I was crushed to find out he wasn't."

Marge ran a blunt fingertip round the rim of her cup. She'd been born in Denver but had married into old Hamland blood. Fred Dove, a man whom Anne found vaguely aloof, elusive, and in some way even officious, came from a family that had been in this area when Hamland had been nothing more than a Post Office and a railroad. Fred did something at City Hall that Anne couldn't quite define; the intricacies of local politics were beyond her grasp. She realized right then that she couldn't even remember what Fred Dove looked like, as if his photograph were missing from her private mental album. A name, but no face.

Something else occurred to her, something that went in and out of her mind like a whisper, a casual item of uninteresting gossip. It was the fact that while she and Marge met a couple of times a week like this for coffee, George and Fred never socialized. They had lived next door to each other for four years and they'd never met for a drink except when it was in the company of the two women. Fred, she finally assumed, wasn't happy with social situations. It was simple as that.

Marge said, "Anyhow, you should put Danny in one of those programs as soon as he gets back. He'd have a ball."

"I don't believe I've met this Ellis Diamond," Anne said.

"You haven't? I'll take you over to the park one day and introduce you. She's sweet. Pretty," and Marge shrugged. "Well, in a frumpy kind of way. I always want to take a brush and rearrange her hair so she doesn't keep reminding me of a spinster. Is that terrible of me? And she dresses in clothes that don't exactly flatter her, if you see what I mean. She has a good face, though."

Spinster, Anne thought. What a quaint word these days.

"But she's a gem, she really is," Marge went on. "She's devoted to those kids. I mean, what more could you ask? I get the feeling she's lonely, you know? Somehow, though, I keep forgetting to ask her to come to supper some night."

Anne poured more coffee and stood at the kitchen window a second, gazing out into the back yard. In the gray morning, the beech trees that grew against the brick wall looked faintly melancholic, almost as if light and life had been sucked out of them. She was thinking of Danny's return now, trying to imagine him swinging his baseball bat out there in the yard or attempting to make a basket through the hoop George had fixed to the side of the house.

Marge was placing her empty cup in the sink. "Well, thanks for the caffeine rush," she said. "I guess I better be running along." She moved in the direction of the kitchen door. There, she hesitated a moment, gazing at Anne. "Yeah, I think I'll call Ellis Diamond soon, invite her over before I forget it entirely. She rents an apartment in Lily Hubbard's house on Gunnison Avenue, which can't exactly be a barrel of laughs. Poor woman."

"Which poor woman? Ellis or Lily Hubbard?"

"Both, I guess." Marge raised one hand to her face, pushed aside a strand of her black hair. "You don't know Lily?"

Anne said she wasn't sure she did. But the name rang some kind of faint bell way at the back of her head.

"You're talking one crazy lady," Marge said. "You must have seen her. About fifty, going along Center in an ancient fur stole and a veil. Face like a broken jigsaw puzzle. How could you have missed her?"

"I guess I shop on different days," Anne remarked.

"Her husband shot himself back in . . . I don't remember when. But he took a pistol and killed himself. It was quite a scandal. I guess I must have been about fifteen at the time." Marge shrugged. "Ancient history."

"Why did he kill himself?" Anne asked.

"Who knows why anybody kills themselves?" Marge opened the door. There was a slat of gray sky beyond her head. "It made old Lily a little dippy, I can tell you that. Anyhow, I'll catch you later," and she was gone, closing the door behind her.

Alone, Anne glanced out into the back yard. There was a large black bird—a raven, a crow, she wasn't sure which—perched among the beech trees. Its coatbutton eyes looked wintry and haunted and its hunched presence seemed to emphasize the sudden emptiness of the house. She pushed the back door open and the bird rose clumsily upward like a black umbrella slowly filling with air.

When he had been growing up on Montrose Drive, Cheney had always thought of the houses as rather dignified old men, stately and set in their ways. But now, as he drove slowly along the street, he felt the homes were more like ancient women blindly, secretively, facing the side of Naughton's Hill.

He braked in front of his father's house and glanced up the driveway at the blinds drawn down on the windows. It was a gothic house, angular and furtive. At the turn of the century it must have accommodated some entrepreneur and his colossal entourage of wife and kids and servants—but now only his father lived there, alone with God only knew what memories. For a second, Cheney thought of paying a quick visit but he pushed the idea aside for a later time. He was in no mood for the old man's elliptical manner and he didn't feel up to tracking his father as he bumbled around from one room to the next like somebody who has mislaid something and can't quite remember what.

Senility, Cheney thought. The saddest condition.

He continued along Montrose until he came to 33. A slender girl of maybe thirteen, fourteen, was standing at the edge of the sidewalk with her back pressed against an ancient oak tree. Cheney stopped the car, got out, greeted the girl, a pretty young thing.

"Amanda?"

"Yeah." The girl put her hands in the pockets of her jeans and turned round to look up at the front of number 33 Montrose. "I was going to come down to your office but I'm the official babysitter for my two young brothers, which is a drag." She shrugged her shoulders loosely and smiled and it was the kind of razzle-dazzle smile Cheney could imagine breaking young boys' hearts.

Cheney glanced at the house. Unlike his father's, in fact unlike most of the homes along Montrose, this one had been kept in good condition. It had recently been painted a pale autumnal yellow and it stood out on this street like a gold nugget among dross.

"See, some kids told me this morning Tommy hadn't come home last night," Amanda Thurston said. "They said you were looking for him."

Cheney nodded. The Hamland grapevine, he thought. He imagined it was more effective, in its own mysterious way, than smoke signals had ever been.

"You said you saw him," Cheney remarked.

"Yeah, I did. I saw him yesterday."

"Tell me about it."

The sound of a child came floating out of number 33 and

the girl turned to face the house, but the sound died and she made no move to go indoors. "Those kids just want attention," she said. "All the time. Jesus!"

"What about Tommy Sears, Amanda? Where did you see him?"

"I was going out to Delta Plaza with my mother and he was walking along the side of the freeway."

"When?"

"It was like late morning. I don't know. Before noon, I guess."

"He was just walking, that's all?"

The girl nodded. A frown passed across her face. "Just walking, Sheriff. Walking east."

"Was he trying to hitch?"

"Uh-uh. Not that I noticed. He was looking down at the ground and . . . well, just walking," and she gave a short embarrassed laugh, as if she were sorry she couldn't add much more.

"Alone?"

"Yeah."

"Was he carrying anything? A bag? A suitcase? Anything?"

"Nope. He wasn't carrying a thing."

"Did he see you?"

She shook her head. "No way."

Cheney leaned against his car and studied the big oak a moment. If he'd allowed himself, his mind would have been flooded with memories, because this tree had always caught the moon in a special way when he'd been a boy and he'd watched it on a hundred nights from the window of his own bedroom, seeing silvery phantoms in leaf patterns. This was a tree he sometimes still saw in his dreams.

"Can you tell me anything else? Like what he was wearing?"

"Tommy always wore blue jeans."

What else? Cheney asked himself.

"He had on a brown shirt. One of those thick kind. Flannel, I guess." She smiled. "Yeah, the cap, he always wore the same stupid cap. It was kinda yellow and there was a badge on it—"

"What did the badge say?"

"Tigers. What else would it say?"

Right, Cheney thought. You weren't a real kid in this town, you didn't have any clout, unless you supported the Hamland High Tigers. Crystal fall afternoons, wooden bleachers, the lazy drift of faraway barbecues—and the High School cheerleaders in their green sweaters and short yellow skirts.

"Was he still on the freeway when you came back from the Plaza?" he asked.

"If he was, I didn't see him. Anyhow, when you see a kid walking along it's no big deal, is it?"

"I guess not," Cheney said.

There was the scream of a kid from the house again. The girl looked flustered and angry. She said, "Those brats. I swear, I understand why child abuse happens. I only turn my back for a second and they feel neglected."

"It's good training," Cheney said.

"For what?"

"Motherhood."

The girl squinted at him. "You're joking."

"Right, I'm joking."

He watched the girl turn and go up the driveway to the house just as the front door swung open and two sticky-faced kids—twins—came toppling out, one clinging to the other's shoulders. Amanda hurried toward them, swept them inside, and disappeared herself behind the closed door.

Cheney heard a single, sharp shout.

And then there was silence.

From the window of his bedroom, Edward Cheney had seen his son's ridiculous car go along Montrose Drive, and for a moment he had halfway expected the boy to stop and visit—but then the car with its self-important insignia and its roof-lights had continued right past, which was when Edward Cheney let the edge of the blind slip from his fingers.

He went downstairs into the big kitchen and he made himself a cup of the herbal tea he customarily drank. He carried it out into the back yard and surveyed the dense shrubbery and unkempt trees that seemed to leap at him as soon as he opened the door. There was an old canvas-backed chair, dating from the time of his marriage, which he sat down in—and there he remained, motionless, his head shaded from the sunless sky by the brim of the broken straw hat he wore. From afar, he might have looked like a figure in an impressionist painting, because he was frail and his appearance suggested that if you were to go very close to him you might think he was composed of tightly-packed dots, atoms held together by invisible adhesive.

He sipped his tea with a trembling, white-haired hand.

When he'd awakened that morning, he had been thinking for some reason about Elmer Hubbard. He hadn't considered poor dead Elmer in a long time and what he remembered now were those sad furtive trips he and Elmer had taken up to Denver now and then on the pretext of this business or that and how Elmer had always insisted they visit two whores he knew called Satin and Brandy (such curious *noms d'amour*) who lived in an apartment near the State Capitol . . . Edward Cheney understood now that he had always looked forward to these visits, these defiances of marital fidelity, that he couldn't blame Elmer for his own sexual appetites, even though he had tried in the past.

He pictured Satin's round, eager face and the soft swell of her belly and the light glistening on her white thighs and there was an echo of an old electric excitement. He wondered if his wife had ever known the real nature of those trips to Denver. Perhaps not. And even if she had, she had the class not to say so.

Edward Cheney, he thought. Betrayer. Wrecker of things. A man of weaknesses. A man who spent hours in the company of a whore even when his own wife lay dying her quiet lonely death. Why couldn't he see Liza's face before him now? Why was it the improbably-named Satin that floated in front of him?

There had been depravities, curious foursomes involving himself and Elmer and the two whores, jumbled experiments of the flesh that had excited him because he'd always felt he was pushing his boundaries and limitations back, extending himself far beyond his veneer of respectability. He had been a small town appraiser, a man who estimated the values of properties for banks and realtors, a confining job he'd grown over the years to loathe. And the more he hated his work, the more frequently he'd gone up to Denver, as if there he might somehow balance the scales of his life with the excitement Satin gave him, the sheer satisfaction she always provided. And afterward he'd lie with his head on her breasts and she'd always say *You're learning, Eddie. I got to think up more tricks* . . . and he'd become aroused again, anxious to explore his appetites.

During these encounters he had imposed a convenient amnesia on himself. There was no wife, no Liza, she didn't exist *ergo* she couldn't possibly be sick.

Ancient history now. But why was it with him so strongly today?

He raised his face to look at the trees and what he saw there were patterns of all sorts because as he had grown older so had he come to recognize what he thought of as God's design in everything—even in the random motions of trees there was nothing whimsical, nothing left to chance.

These patterns extended beyond coincidence. It was no mere coincidence, for example, that his own son had become the sheriff of this town. External forces of a cosmic kind had made that inevitable, as inevitable as retribution.

He set his teacup down in the thick grass.

He tilted his face upward and his lips moved silently. In recent years, he had come to feel that a certain doom had begun to stalk him. It took the form of nightmares he experienced three or four times a week, those wracking, awful dreams that forced him to wakefulness when he'd lie in the dark, gasping, choking, his frail fingers clutching the sheets, when he'd feel the presence of an avenger in the big, black bedroom, a cloaked figure who stood just beyond his range of vision.

There were patterns, yes, and they were not just blind things spun out of some universal anarchy.

And the fact that his own son, his own blood and flesh, had become the Sheriff of Hamland, confirmed what the old man had known all along—that one's own history, no matter how casual certain acts might have seemed at the time, no matter how insignificant, or how important, came back with the certainty of sunrise to expose and undo you.

He rose and wandered back inside the house.

George, he thought.

George was the hooded figure.

His own son.

FIVE

"I SEEM TO GET STUCK WITH ROYALTY," CHARLES BANNION WAS
saying. "You think I look like a king, George? Is there
something regal about me? I don't want to start getting
typecast, you know?"

Cheney looked at the young officer. They were in the car
going east out of Hamland toward Delta Plaza and Bannion
was driving. Charles was concerned about having recently
been cast as the King of Siam in the Hamland Players'
production of *The King and I*.

"Yul Brynner's a tough act to follow, Charlie," Cheney
said. He glanced from the window and studied the grassy
embankment at the edge of the freeway, as if he might see an
after-image of Tommy Sears strolling along. On the other side
of the slopes, hidden from his sight, there lay fields and
isolated canyons and dense wooded areas, and the kid could
have wandered off in any direction if he'd happened to leave
the freeway.

Suddenly Cheney's mind was filled with the possibility of a
full-scale search. Helicopters borrowed from the State Police,
a volunteer posse on horseback beating the shrubs and the
shadows out there in the quest for Tommy Sears, everybody

and his cousin mounted on everything from thoroughbreds to old nags and mules, and geezers sipping on hipflasks of cheap brandy as if a search were a kind of picnic with a purpose.

Charles Bannion nodded. "Yeah, Yul had a lock on the part, I guess. I'll have to figure out some new approach. And I'm worried about my singing voice, George. I don't know if I can carry a tune."

"You'll be all right on the night," Cheney said.

Up ahead, a mile or so, the Greek letter Delta hung in the gray sky, an ornamental triangle dreamed up by the San Francisco architects who had created the new plaza and mall. It was out of place, Cheney thought—the alphabetical symbol, the big circular mall, the landscaped parking-lots. Damage had been done here, and not just to the landscape, but to an entire way of life.

What was Anne always telling him—that he lived in the past? That he hoarded his memories like a miser? He smiled to himself.

Bannion said, "You think this kid met somebody at the mall and they went off together? Maybe a friend?"

"I don't know what to think, Charlie." And that, Cheney reflected, was true enough. He didn't know—and it was a condition of mind he didn't like.

Bannion was turning the car off the freeway now, heading up the ramp that led to the vast parking-lot. Cheney looked at the store signs, the great runic mysteries of American commerce. J.C. Penney. Radio Shack. The Xerox Store.

Bannion parked the car. From the breast pocket of his uniform he took out two small colored pictures of Tommy Sears that Courtney Sears had parted with. He handed one to Cheney. "School photographs," he said. "Taken last May, Mrs Sears told me, so they're recent at least."

Cheney took one, gazed at the face. It could have been the face of any boy anywhere. A knifelike shaft of anxiety went through him quickly. Blue eyes, freckles, a small nose, lips stretched in a smile that reminded him of the tension in a drawn bow. Why was it that pictures of missing kids, those sad photographs posted in supermarkets or published inside newspapers, always suggested unspeakable terror to Cheney?

He and Bannion were inside the mall now. There were

fountains dripping on beds of ceramic tile and a plexiglass elevator carrying the infirm, the lazy and the obese upward to the second level. Muzak, too, issuing with an irksome innocence through concealed speakers. *Getting to Know You.*

"They're playing your song, Charlie," Cheney said.

The young officer smiled. He had, Cheney noticed, perfect white teeth.

"You're younger than me," Cheney said. "You take the upper level. I'll check the stores down here."

Charles Bannion moved off in the direction of an escalator. Cheney watched him vanish somewhere above and then gazed at the storefronts stretching along a delicate curve in front of him. Boutiques. Thousands of pairs of jeans at cut price. Millions of sunglasses at reduced rates. Twenty percent off the current best-sellers. A video arcade where kids blew up whole galaxies for a quarter. This entire mall struck Cheney like a huge exclamation mark.

How could Center Avenue hope to compete with this? Cheney knew the answer as well as he understood that the shortest distance between two points was a straight line. You couldn't only read the writing on the wall, you could feel it like braille could be felt—and he had a vision of Center as a collection of empty stores and broken windows and fallen canopies, *For Sale* signs wilting in rain, bleached by sun, a weathered hopelessness spread over everything.

He mourned, briefly, the passing of the soda fountains of his boyhood; then he looked at the photograph of Tommy Sears.

Let's find out if anybody saw you yesterday, Tommy.

Let's knock on a few doors.

He held the small photograph out in front of himself, the way a man might hold a key.

Lily Hubbard always referred to her late husband as The Judge, because Elmer had been about to take his seat on the judicial bench at the time of his tragic death. Even if he had never actually worn the black robe, and hadn't ever been in any position to pass sentence on anyone—save, perhaps, himself—she called him The Judge anyhow because it was a small verbal monument to his memory. She raised a mug of hot chocolate to her lips and peered over the rim at the face of Mr Rigley, her top floor tenant.

Mr Rigley, who wore a light-colored raincoat with epaulettes and a plaid scarf knotted at his throat, suggested to Lily the kind of man who bought his outfits at thrift stores, one of those lonely figures you sometimes saw working the racks and sifting outmoded clothing, looking more for fit than fashion. He had a gentle, rounded face and a slack mouth.

"The Judge liked hot chocolate," Lily said. "Some men prefer coffee first thing, but The Judge always made this. Before he left each morning for his law practice, he brought me a mug of hot chocolate in bed. He was that kind of man. We loved each other dearly, Mr Rigley."

Mr Rigley nodded his head slowly.

"Will you take a cup?" Lily asked.

Mr Rigley shook his head. He didn't speak. He appeared astonished to be inside the landlady's apartment, and the fact had rendered him quite speechless. His face, eyeglasses glinting like two transparent pennies, turned upward to study the ornamental frieze of Lily Hubbard's living-room.

Lily set her hot chocolate down. She had her feet wrapped inside a traveling-rug and her shawl pulled down over her shoulders. She observed her tenant for a while as he looked at the ceiling. There was a vacancy in his eyes and the loose flap of his weak mouth indicated a certain dim-witted quality.

"How is your apartment, Mr Rigley?"

"I like it," he said slowly.

"I'm happy to hear that. It's nice to have a place where one is comfortable."

Mr Rigley took a crumpled handkerchief from his coat and wadded it, applying it lightly to a speck of saliva at the corner of his mouth. "I'm very comfortable," he said. "The place where I lived before had rats."

"Rats?"

"Used to lie awake nights and listen to them."

Lily Hubbard shuddered.

"Behind the walls," Mr Rigley said. "Could hear them scratching right behind the walls. Scratch. Scratch. All the time."

"You won't have the same experience in this house," Lily said. She looked at her tenant. His eyes were blank, as if they were waiting for somebody to come along and stamp experience into them.

She placed a hand upon the sleeve of his coat. "This will be your home, Mr Rigley. You don't need to worry about rats or anything else so long as you live in this house."

Mr Rigley smiled.

After a time, he went toward the door.

"If you need anything, don't hesitate to let me know. You hear me?" Lily asked. "Anything. A man's got to be comfortable, after all."

Mr Rigley opened the door and moved out on to the landing where he stood in shadow. He appeared to stare into the palms of his hands—but what he found to interest him there defeated Lily.

"You've been very kind to me," he said. "I . . ." And his voice trailed off here into a choked silence. He put a hand to his face and inserted fingers beneath the lenses of his glasses. His shoulders heaved up and down for a time.

"I'm sorry," he said. "I was just thinking, you know, about the cat?"

"The cat?"

"How kind you are to let me have the cat—"

Lily waved a hand. "Hasn't anybody ever been kind to you before, Mr Rigley?"

"At the other place they said I couldn't have pets—"

She moved toward him. She touched the side of his big round face, which was the color of semolina. "This is your home, Mr Rigley. Your home! You don't need to worry about anything here."

The face smiled, the glasses glowed. "Thanks, thanks."

"And there's no need to keep saying thanks all the time."

Mr Rigley nodded. Lily watched him lumber toward the stairs. For a big man he made barely any sound as he climbed. When she knew he'd reached the landing, she closed the door of her own apartment. She made her way back to her chair, placing the rug around her feet. She finished her hot chocolate, pushing aside with a painted fingernail the skin of milk that had formed like a brown web across the liquid. Only this morning, she had tried to order hot chocolate in the Royal Hotel, but when she'd found out all they had was Swiss Maid she'd changed her mind. The Royal Hotel, like everything else in Hamland, had gone markedly downhill in recent years.

Playing with the fringe of her shawl, she thought about Thomas Sears. And she could feel something way down in the depths of herself, as if in the pit of her stomach a thread were on fire, a slow flame eating along a line of thin cotton and twisting it as it burned, and this same misshapen, smoldering thread appeared to rise up through her body to the back of her throat . . .

She turned her head around, as if she had just heard a movement behind her, a footfall, a man sighing.

"Mr Rigley is just fine," she said.

At the window, the curtains were perfectly still.

Light the color of an eggshell fell against the glass.

Lily Hubbard raised one hand. "Isn't he just fine? Isn't he, Judge?"

If there was an answer to her question it came from the silent drapes and the eggshell light and the sound, from the highest part of the house, of Mr Rigley closing his apartment door.

Cheney climbed the embankment at the side of the freeway. When he reached the top he turned to see Charles Bannion getting out of the police car.

Both men surveyed the landscape in silence. It seemed to Cheney that he stood on a thin demarcation line up here on the slope, with the freeway and the plaza at his back, the wilderness in front of him.

Charles Bannion shook his head. "I guess young Tommy never made it as far as the Plaza. Which means that somewhere between town and mall, he either hitched a ride or decided to take the plunge out there somewhere," and Charlie gestured toward the trees and the wooded canyons.

Cheney said nothing. Delta Plaza had been a blank, a waste of time. Nobody had seen the kid in the photograph. Somehow he had imagined they would get lucky out there in the mall and now he felt a weary kind of disappointment. And the landscape stretching away from the freeway yielded up nothing to his eyes. "Why the hell would Tommy Sears go out there, Charlie? For what? It doesn't make sense. A kid on his own like that. I could see him with some friends, if they all decided to take a hike together. But I just don't see him out there on his own."

Bannion agreed. "He didn't have a fight with his parents. He didn't seem to have a girl-friend he could fall out with. So what was he angry about?"

"Maybe he wasn't angry, Charlie."

"Then what kind of mood was he in to wander away like this?"

Cheney had a theory that the moods of children were as mysterious as lunar forces. That the instruments required to measure and understand those moods hadn't yet been invented.

"I don't know about Tommy's mood," he said. "I'll tell you this, though. I don't like the prospect of searching out there. I don't like that at all." He could hear the whirring blades of a chopper, the sound of hoofbeats, the whisper of feet through undergrowth, the barking of eager dogs—and these were all ominous sounds in his mind. The landscape, merely grim and gray before, seemed to suggest death to him now.

He clapped Bannion lightly on the shoulder and said, "Maybe it won't come to a search, Charlie. Maybe when we get back into Hamland we'll find Tommy Sears safe at home, sitting in the kitchen and sucking on a Coke and telling some story about how he managed to get delayed. Maybe."

And maybe donkeys could fly.

"Maybe" was a world all to itself.

Ellis Diamond considered it strange how Mr Zanzibar seemed to fill her office with his body, creating the effect of darkness around himself. It was as if he drew light toward his body, sucked it of substance, discarded it when he was through. His black suit, she thought. Nothing more than the dark of his clothing. But his presence—she was nervous in his company.

Especially now, when she had to trouble him with bureaucratic nonsense. She glanced down at the various forms that
lay across her desk. There was really no way round it, these
forms had to be completed by anyone who worked in the
Parks and Recreation Program, part-time employees included. It was a state law.

There was a Personnel Information Sheet, a tax-
withholding form, and several other papers he would have to
sit down and complete. She had already been lax enough
about these papers. She simply *had* to get Zanzibar to attend
to them.

She raised her face, looked at him. She said, "I hope you
don't mind, but I eavesdropped on your little class just then."

Zanzibar stood with his back to the window, his arms
folded on his chest. He said nothing.

Ellis Diamond looked down at her desk again. "I enjoyed
it . . . You really do have a way with the kids . . . And . . ."
Here she paused, swallowed, listened to the ticking of her
pulses. "That coin trick you demonstrated surprised me. I
didn't think you could pass the coin from one hand to the
other quite that fast. It's very good of you to share your
professional secrets with our kids. Really. It's different from
the kind of thing they expect at Parks and Rec."

Mr Zanzibar nodded. An oily dark curl slipped on to his
forehead. He made no attempt to push it away. Ellis looked
at her calendar. It was one of those in which the days of the
month each occupy a little square; in various squares Ellis had
written down the times and names of different programs.

BASKETWEAVING 11:30
BASEBALL PRACT. 2:00
CHESS INSTRUCTION 10:00
DRAMA CLUB 1:30

As she studied the squares, she had a sense of organization,
an awareness of how the parts of her program added up to a
whole she was proud of—indeed, the entire town was proud
of having the best-run Parks and Recreation program in all
the state. She had testimonials from contented parents, a

diploma from Richard P. Bacon, the mayor of Hamland (a conjunction of names that always amused her), a certificate from the Chamber of Commerce and several inquiries from other communities that looked to Hamland as a model. Why, then, did she feel in the presence of Zanzibar a consciousness of how fragile her organization was in reality? His very presence seemed to remind her of the flimsy line that divided organization from chaos, as if she walked constantly on thin ice. The fact he wouldn't complete the paperwork, for example, menaced everything she'd worked to build right here in Hamland.

But all this, she decided, was illusion.

Her real problem was not so much with the magician as it was with herself. All her life she had allowed other people to inordinately affect and influence her—as if her own personality were nothing more than a small voice crying in a locked room. And naturally when she encountered someone such as Zanzibar, a man of silences prepared to let others do the talking while he seemed simply to look on in cool, analytical detachment, she felt insecure and vaguely threatened.

Zanzibar took an old-fashioned timepiece from his vest pocket and flipped the lid open. He looked at the time, clicked the watch shut again. His face was expressionless. He stepped away from the window and stood against her desk, his shadow falling across the papers lying there.

Ellis cleared her throat. One of her hands fluttered nervously in the air. "These forms," she said. "I mentioned them to you when you first came here. I hate to trouble you, but they do have to be completed. Officialdom, you know? Everybody who works here in any capacity has to fill them out."

As she slipped the forms toward him, a strange thing happened.

A deep voice emerging from a place behind her said, *"Zanzibar does not fill out forms,"* and she swung her chair around in surprise but there was nobody standing at her back, nobody at all—and when she turned back to look at Zanzibar she understood. The magician had performed a simple act of ventriloquism, which had disoriented and flustered her.

All she could think to say was, "You fooled me," although she knew she shouldn't have fallen for such a childish trick. She felt herself blush. He throws his voice, he makes objects disappear and reappear in impossible places, his is a world of fantasy and tricks, of dislocations and disturbances.

He had picked the forms up and was looking them over and Ellis half-expected them to turn to fire between his fingers or become birds that would flap nervously around her office. Nothing like that happened—instead, Zanzibar took the forms, folded them over and with fingers that moved too quickly for Ellis to follow began to pick and tear at the folded sheets, manipulating them this way and that, filling the room with confetti that fluttered through the air and when he was through he straightened the paper out to reveal a row of linked girls, can-can dancers whose paper legs angled upward.

He let the dancers slip from his hands and they floated gently down to the desk.

How do you follow an act like this? she wondered.

What do you say to a man like this?

Zanzibar went through the motions of disdainfully wiping worthless crumbs from the palms of his white hands—and then he was gone in one fluid gesture and she listened to the click of his heels as he walked away.

She got up and moved to the window in time to see him striding across the grass toward his black Packard. He got inside his car and Ellis turned back to the paper scraps across her desk.

Mr Zanzibar had just told her, in his own inscrutable manner, that he was beyond forms.

Beyond *any* forms, paper or otherwise.

It was Edward Cheney's custom to leave his house every day at one PM and drive his maroon 1955 Studebaker to Center and Third Street where he would have a drink in the bar of the Crawford Steak & Chop House before seating himself at his usual table in the dining-room. He had followed this routine regularly since the death of his wife many years before; there were people in Hamland who swore they could set their watches by the eccentric sight of the straw-hatted man in the old car. Others claimed they could tell the date of the month from the length of Cheney's white hair, which he had cut on the second Wednesday of every month and which he allowed to grow out between visits to his barber.

Now, as he stepped inside the darkened bar of the Crawford—looking in his beige suit and straw hat like a tobacco-plantation owner of the 1930s—he saw that the barman was already shaking the dry martini he always had before lunch. Cheney stepped up to the bar and placed his hands flat on the counter, nodding to Norman Sachs, the barman.

"What's the special today, Norm?" Cheney asked. It was the question he asked every day.

Norm Sachs, a balding man with a slight lisp, placed the dry martini on a paper coaster and answered, "Rocky Mountain trout in lemon garlic sauce. We also got some oysters fresh."

Cheney propped himself against a stool. He sipped his drink, turning his face toward the doorway that led to the dining-room. From out of the gloom a large figure emerged, blocking the doorway a moment, then shambling in Edward Cheney's direction.

When he recognized the man, Cheney turned aside quickly. A cold feeling, like that of snow pressed to flesh, touched the sides of his face and he found himself gazing down into his drink, stirring it nervously with the tip of his index finger. A gust of beer breath blew at him.

There was no way out of this, he thought.

There was no exit from the inevitable. There never was.

Thomas Sears hauled himself up on to a stool and let one of his large hands drop heavily on Cheney's shoulder. Cheney looked at Sears and managed a smile, a little frozen effort— but it was apparent that Sears was drunk and in no state of mind to notice such things as deceptive expressions. In one bear-like hand he clutched a mug of beer. There was a grease stain on the front of his white shirt—presumably, Cheney thought, a consequence of Sears's employment as a short-order cook at the Royal Hotel.

"How are you, Thomas?"

73

The big man was silent and in his silence Cheney could hear the beating of his own dilapidated heart and the screaming of his pulses.

"My boy's gone," Sears said.

"Gone? How do you mean?" For a second, Edward Cheney was confused. What boy? But then he remembered there was a son, Thomas Junior.

"Gone. Vanished." Sears looked into his beer. "Since yesterday, Ed. Since early morning. Gone."

"I'm sure he'll turn up," Cheney replied.

Sears raised his face as if with monstrous effort. There was moisture in his eyes and Cheney feared that the big man was going to break down right there in the bar of the Crawford. Reluctantly, Cheney put one hand on Sears's arm, as if to console him.

"Thomas," he said. "I am sure there's a perfectly reasonable explanation for the boy's absence."

"Yeah yeah yeah."

"And I'm sure he'll turn up."

Suddenly, Thomas Sears's face fell apart. It broke into little lines like a shattered windshield and tears slid over the grooves of his cheeks and from the back of his throat there emerged a dreadful, choking sound.

"Thomas, please. Pull yourself together. Now." And Cheney patted the man's arm, glancing at Norm Sachs, a discreet soul who went about his business as if he noticed nothing unusual in the sight of a fat man sobbing in his bar.

"He's gone, Ed. Gone." The face went down on the bar now and the plump hands hung loose and useless. "I think . . ."

"What do you think?"

Sears raised himself upward, twisting his neck to look at Edward Cheney. "I think things keep coming back, Ed, that's what I think, I think you get what you deserve, but I don't want to settle old accounts if the price is my own kid."

"You're being unrealistic." Cheney tried to steer the man to a far-off table, but he failed. "Nothing has happened to your boy. Absolutely nothing."

Sears seemed suddenly to find a moment of calm at the

heart of his personal storm and looked at Cheney in a lucid way. "I was remembering—"

"You do not remember, Thomas."

"Sure I do—"

"There is nothing to remember—"

"Ed—"

"Let me take you home. You need to lie down. Come on, Thomas."

Sears stumbled down from the stool and looked at Edward Cheney, as if he were trying to decide whether this was a man to whom he could entrust his welfare. Then he leaned against Cheney and went with him to the door of the restaurant. Cheney put one arm around the big man's waist, assisting him out into the street.

They moved like mismatched partners in an unlikely waltz toward the place where the Studebaker had been parked. Somehow, Cheney managed to get Thomas Sears into the passenger seat.

Sears said, "And Lily Hubbard was in the restaurant today. What was she doing there? She never comes there. Never. So why was she there the day after Tommy vanishes?"

Lily Hubbard, Cheney thought. He felt a door closing in his mind but he could sense the dark, stifling room beyond it. "Presumably the lady wanted breakfast, Thomas. That's all."

Breathless, wheezing from the effort of supporting Sears, Edward Cheney leaned against the side of his wine-colored car a moment. He had the feeling that much more than just his daily routine had been upset. Much more.

He glanced in through the window at Sears, who had his head tilted back. Again, tears were streaming down the fat man's face and his mouth hung open. Cheney clenched his hands and jammed them in the side pockets of his linen jacket. His whole physical being seemed to him just then like a complicated knot in the center of a tense rope, something you could not undo no matter how hard you tried.

"Nothing ever goes away, does it, Ed?" Thomas Sears asked. "I mean, nothing ever fucking goes away."

"It does, Thomas. It does if you let it." Cheney slipped in behind the wheel. It was a lie, he thought, a terrible lie. In his rambling, drunken way, Thomas Sears was absolutely right.

Some things would not go away.

"I'll drive you home, Thomas," Edward Cheney said. "Perhaps your son will be there by this time."

"Yeah," the fat man said hopelessly.

When George Cheney returned to his office from the fruitless thirty-mile round trip out to Delta Plaza, there were two telephone messages waiting for him. The first was from Anne, an inquiry about when she might expect him for dinner. The second was from a certain Mrs Liz Estaban—no message, but Cheney was asked to return the call because the matter, according to the note, was urgent. Liz Estaban was a schoolteacher at Hamland Primary and married to an accountant named Hugh, an old friend of Cheney's father.

Cheney went into the corridor and moved toward the front desk. Officer Arlene Flagg, a young woman of pert efficiency who wore her uniform as if it had been tailored for her personally by a seamstress who watched nothing but Hollywood cop shows on TV, turned her bright little face upward and smiled.

"Arlene, did Liz Estaban say what she wanted?"

"Only that it was urgent, Sheriff."

"That's all?"

"End of message," Arlene said.

Cheney wandered back inside his office and dialled the number left by Liz Estaban. It was answered immediately by a woman whose voice was filled with distress—and Cheney instinctively knew that whatever he was going to be told here would throw him further into that black place in his mind presently occupied by Tommy Sears. He picked up a pencil and drummed the eraser end against his desk.

"Liz, this is George Cheney returning your call."

"I'm so glad you called, George."

A pause.

"What's the problem?" Cheney asked.

"I need to report something . . ." Her voice faded away into a sniffling sound and there was a soft papery whisper, like that of Kleenex pressed to her face.

"Liz," Cheney said. "What is it? What's the matter?"

"It's my daughter Victoria—"

"What about her?" Cheney heard a chill in his own voice.

"I think I need to report her as a missing person."

The pencil in Cheney's fist snapped abruptly in two and a yellow splinter pierced his finger, bringing a faint thread of blood up to the surface of his skin.

SIX

·•·•·•·•·•·•·•·•·•·•·•·•·•·•·•·•·•·•·

LIZ AND HUGH ESTABAN LIVED ON THE OUTSKIRTS OF HAMLAND
at a place where the town had simply stopped growing.
Beyond their house, a large red brick ranch-style affair,
scruffy meadows yielded to trees and then to open countryside. Liz Estaban, a tall woman who wore black tailored
slacks and a matching blouse, paced up and down the
living-room. She had short hair and a large face that was
attractive in an equine kind of way. She had always reminded
Cheney of women he'd seen in *Town and Country* magazine.

Hugh Estaban, the accountant, sat on a sofa and nervously
watched his wife. He was as crumpled as Liz Estaban was
immaculate. What you could imagine Hugh doing best was
cooking corporate books, laundering money for wealthy
clients through Switzerland and the Bahamas. *Slightly seedy*
was the phrase that came into George Cheney's mind.

Liz Estaban stood at the picture window of the living-room
and looked in the direction of the wild meadows. She twisted
the ends of her beige chiffon scarf together. "She said
goodnight last night, the way she always does, George. She
went to her bedroom. It was about eleven."

"You didn't happen to check on her later?" Cheney asked.

Liz smiled. "She's fourteen years old, George. I haven't tucked her up in bed since she was eight. Anyhow, when I went to wake her around noon . . . " The woman paused, frowned.

Cheney wrote in his little book, using his own curious shorthand. *G1 L8 slpr*. He gazed a moment at Hugh, who was wearing a dark suit, the texture of which was creased and cracked, as if the man had slept in his clothes. The odd couple, he thought. Elegant and inelegant.

"The bed hadn't been slept in," Liz Estaban said. "The window was wide open and the bed hadn't been slept in."

The woman moved toward the sofa, sitting down beside her husband. She crossed her legs in a tidy fashion, hitching her slacks up from the knees.

"I called her friends," Liz said. "Nobody had seen her. She hadn't spent the night with any of them."

Cheney said, "Does she have a boyfriend?"

"Vickie's a pretty girl. She attracts boys," Liz answered.

"Would she spend the night with one?"

It was, Cheney thought, an awkward question. It hung in the air unanswered. He knew it had to be asked; he wished he'd formulated it in some other fashion, except he couldn't think how.

Hugh Estaban coughed into his hand, breaking the silence. "It's hardly likely, George. She's only fourteen."

Cheney closed his notebook a moment. Fatherly illusions, he thought. For a second he was about to say something about how quickly kids grew up these days and how even some ten-year-old girls were on the pill, but he decided against it.

"Did she have a special boyfriend?" he asked.

Liz Estaban answered, "If she did, she never mentioned anything to us. I'm not saying Vickie is Little Miss Innocent, George, so don't get me wrong, but I don't think she spent the night with a boy unless it was against her will."

Cheney nodded. He imagined darkness. He imagined Victoria Estaban closing her bedroom door at eleven o'clock, waiting perhaps until the house was silent, and then slipping out through the open window into the night.

"What kind of mood was she in at bedtime?" he asked.

Liz Estaban shrugged. "She'd been out. She'd been over at

Parks and Rec. When she came in she just said she was tired and was going to bed. That's it. I didn't notice anything else."

"Has she ever stayed away before?"

Liz Estaban shook her head. "Actually, she's pretty good about phoning when she's going to be late, or when something's happened to delay her."

"Can I see her room?" he asked.

He was led out into the hallway. Hugh Estaban opened the door of Vickie's bedroom. The single bed was made. Smooth sheets, uncrumpled pillow, a patchwork quilt that was obviously an antique. On the walls there hung pictures of rock stars, strange creatures who stared toward the Sheriff as if they resented him.

Something about this room didn't seem right to Cheney. Maybe it was all too neat, too tidy—where were the discarded clothes that kids tossed on floors and hung over chairs, where were the books and playthings they never remembered to put away?

It's the damn bed, he thought.

That's what it comes down to.

If Vickie Estaban had waited until her parents had gone to sleep, if she'd planned on taking a nocturnal hike, wouldn't she have slipped under the covers and *pretended* to be asleep at the very least? Wouldn't she have done that much just in case her parents happened to look in on her? But this kid must have said goodnight, closed her door, and sneaked immediately out through the window. Slick movements in the silent dark. Maybe she just sat in her darkened bedroom and waited until she was sure her parents were asleep.

Or else—

Or else the kid was in a real hurry to split. But why? why the urgency?

"Anything missing? Clothes? Anything like that?" he heard himself ask. His throat was dry.

"I already checked," Liz Estaban said. "Nothing I can see, George."

"What was she wearing when she went to her bedroom?"

"A yellow cotton blouse. One of those Madras types that always shrink and wrinkle. Blue jeans. And red Nikes."

Cheney wrote this down. Yellow and blue and red. He

moved to the window of the bedroom, conscious of the parents staring at him. Like Courtney and Thomas Sears the day before, they had expectations. Below the window some shrubs grew; then there was a stretch of lawn that reached to the sidewalk. He turned back to face the room.

On the bedside table, under a lampshade covered with decals that said *Van Halen* and *Kiss,* there was a short tidy stack of books. *Flying Saucers Have Landed, The Sleeping Prophet,* and *An Introduction to Card Magic.* Occult books and conjuring tricks.

Liz Estaban said, "She's into psychic phenomena, George. It's something of a phase. You know how young kids can be."

Cheney picked up the book on card magic, flipped the pages, looked at the illustrations of disembodied hands holding cards.

Hugh Estaban said, "She's interested in card tricks."

"Intriguing hobby," Cheney said.

"It's something they have over at Parks and Rec," Estaban said, shrugging. "She spends a lot of time there."

Cheney moved toward the door. Parks and Rec, he thought. When he'd been a kid growing up in Hamland, Parks and Rec, a loosely run organization in those days, was decidedly uncool. You wouldn't be caught dead going there because the socially acceptable behavior back then was to hang out in Buzz's Soda Parlor or Caporelli's Ice Cream joint, both establishments long gone. It was different now: these days Parks and Rec was run by an efficient young woman they'd imported and she'd gone at it with a missionary's zeal. Her name, he recalled, was Diamond.

He followed the Estabans back inside the living-room. He remembered that years ago Hugh Estaban had done Edward Cheney's tax returns but for some reason there had been a falling out between the two men, a parting of the ways whose cause he'd never known.

"What I'll need is a list of her friends. Names, addresses. Everybody you can think of." Cheney paused a moment. "Also some indication of her haunts. Places she habitually went to. And a recent photograph."

When he made this last request he thought he could feel the temperature in the room fall. *A photograph,* the Estabans were thinking. *Why would George Cheney want a picture?* A photograph was serious, something you flashed under the faces of people when you asked the question: Have you seen this girl? A photograph was a public admission of something neither Estaban wanted to admit—that their daughter had really gone.

Liz Estaban said she thought she could provide these things. "You'll find her, won't you?" she asked suddenly. There was in her voice a crack of desperation, an anxiety she had hoped to conceal beneath her smooth appearance. "I mean, this is such a small town, George. She couldn't have gone very far away, could she?"

"I'm sure she'll turn up," Cheney replied, which was not entirely an answer to the question he'd been asked. "Why don't you get together all the information I need and call me when you have it? By that time, I guess she'll have come home anyhow . . ."

He walked toward the door. The Estabans followed him.

Gray light flooded the hallway as he opened the front door and looked in the direction of his car. "One other thing," he said. "Does she know a boy by the name of Tommy Sears?"

"Sears," Hugh Estaban said, and looked at his wife, as if he were incapable of answering the simple question himself.

"The name doesn't ring a bell," Liz Estaban said. "Is it supposed to?"

Cheney said, "I'm not sure. Except Tommy Sears is missing from home as well, which may or may not be coincidence."

He paused a moment, looking at the Estabans.

He walked toward his car and sat behind the wheel. He flicked the pages of his notebook, although he wasn't really reading the shorthand messages scrawled on the sheets.

Something, he thought.

An edge of some kind.

Hardly that. Hardly as sharp as an edge.

But when he'd mentioned the name of Tommy Sears a certain expression had gone across Hugh Estaban's face that reminded Cheney of faint tracks left by the claws of a light bird on a surface of snow. Just that: an almost imperceptible disturbance. And then it was gone.

He turned the key in the ignition.

He had a headache and he was weary and he was filled with the odd sensation that Hamland, the town of his heart, was as unfamiliar to him as the far side of the moon.

Arthur Rigley, his cat tucked against his chest, listened to the sound of Ellis Diamond climbing the stairs. He stroked the cat's head, listened to the way it purred a moment, then he opened his door and stepped on to the landing, seeing Ellis Diamond come up below. She moved wearily, he thought. A tired woman.

He leaned over the bannister. "Miss Diamond?"

She looked up at him, surprised.

"I am Arthur Rigley," he said. "I thought it time we got acquainted."

"Why, yes," she said.

Arthur Rigley raised the cat in the air. "This is Mumps. Say hello to Miss Diamond, Mumps. Say hello! Come on, Mumps." He waggled one of the creature's paws in the air. Then he began to descend as Mumps scurried up his arm to perch precariously on his shoulder. When he reached the landing where Miss Diamond stood, the cat dropped away from him and bolted upstairs into the shadows.

"Nice cat," Ellis Diamond said.

"We're very close." Arthur Rigley took his glasses off and wiped the lenses on the cuffs of his navy-blue cardigan.

The woman was fumbling in her purse for the key to her apartment. She had a pleasing face except for small lines of fatigue that ran from the corners of her eyes. She'd found the key now and was reaching toward the lock.

"You work at the park, don't you?" he asked.

"That's right."

"With all those kids."

She nodded, smiled uncertainly, inserted her key.

"You always come home for lunch, though. I hear you."

"I usually find I need a break in the middle of the day. It recharges my battery."

"I know what you mean," he said. He put his glasses back on. He remembered that for some days he had been planning this encounter but all at once he realized he couldn't quite recall why, as if a void had opened up in his mind. It was something that happened to him frequently, this weird lapse in memory. All through his life, in fact, he had run into spaces in his recollections that were like small dark rooms through which he had to stumble blindly because he wasn't sure what he was doing in them.

Dr Frye had told him the medical name for this but he'd forgotten that as well. What he remembered for certain, though, was the fact that it was connected to the accident he'd had when he was twelve years old. Until that time, his brain had functioned normally, he'd been a kid like any other—

He watched Ellis Diamond turn her key, saw the door open. He had a glimpse of her apartment beyond. On a small round table by the window he noticed a cup and saucer, a half-eaten donut on a plate, and a pair of pantyhose lying on the floor beside an upturned shoe. Despite his flaws of memory, he understood he had a gift for absorbing details. He noticed things.

"Dr Frye said I could have been a painter," he remarked.

"I'm sorry?" She was stepping inside the room.

"A painter. An artist. I have an eye for detail."

"That's . . . nice, Mr Rigley."

Arthur Rigley heard Mumps patter around somewhere overhead. He observed the woman's face as she backed toward her apartment.

"Do you enjoy living alone?" he asked.

"I'm used to it . . ." She glanced at her wristwatch. "I really must eat lunch, Mr Rigley. I have to get back to the park."

Rigley said, "You must like children a great deal, Miss Diamond. I mean, you must really enjoy them to spend all the time you do with them. It has to take *great* patience. Personally, I adore children, I like to watch them play. I sometimes go past your park just to look at them. I think I envy their energy, you know?"

"I'm really *very* pushed for time, Mr Rigley."

Arthur Rigley heard the echoes of his own words reverberate around inside his head. It was strange, but there were times when he found words flowed out of him quickly and easily, times when he didn't stutter, didn't stumble over what he needed to say, and then it was as if he could hear his words

84

rolling round and round inside his brain like tiny pebbles rattling together. Sometimes he thought it was because of the medication Dr Frye told him to take.

He said, "I should flush those pills. Sometimes that's all I think about. You know, flushing them away."

Ellis Diamond smiled. "Well, if you feel that way," she said, and she shut her door, a haunted little smile on her face.

He knew that smile. He knew that *kind* of smile very well. It was the one most people used when they talked with him.

Arthur Rigley lingered a second, conscious of the fact that he felt suddenly very small in this vast dark house. And then he turned and began to climb the stairs, calling the cat's name as he moved. *Mumps. Mumps.* He reached the landing outside his own apartment just as the cat leaped out of shadows and bounced against his chest and he caught it, kissing the top of its soft furry head.

He shut the door of his room.

He carried the cat to a chair by the window and he sat down. Then he raised one hand and gently searched through the thinning hair on the left side of his scalp, touching the ridge of scar tissue there. He understood it would always be there, that for the remainder of his life he'd always have the same ridge of scar tissue on his skull at the place where the big metal bolt had punctured his head.

He sat very, very still.

Tea, he thought.

That was it.

He'd meant to invite Ellis Diamond to have tea with him! But his clumsy mind, his careless memory, had betrayed him again. Moisture filled up his eyes. He squeezed them tightly shut. He *hated* himself for his own failings.

He moved his fingers slowly upward to the neck of the cat, feeling cartilage and bone under layers of fur. He let the hatred course through him savagely until the insides of his eyelids were a blood-red color and his brain was on fire and his hands had created a tight manacle around the cat's neck and then he had no control over himself at all—

The cat howled, squirming to get away from him.

One fast open claw tore the flesh on his wrist and he suddenly dropped the creature to the floor.

Arthur Rigley opened his eyes. Its back arched, the animal was standing by the wall, staring at him.

"Oh God, oh God," he said. He went down on his knees. "I'm sorry. I'm so sorry, Mumps. Please forgive me. Please . . ."

The cat regarded him warily now.

"Please . . ."

He put one hand out tentatively in front of himself and the cat, relaxing, its spine straightening, moved slowly toward him. Arthur Rigley touched the animal's head gently. The creature looked at him with feline pity. *You poor human.*

The cat purred faintly under the man's open palm. Arthur Rigley picked it up, snuggled it against his chest, then wandered to the window of his room in time to see Ellis Diamond go down the driveway toward the street. She was hurrying back to the park.

To her kids.

He would ask her to tea some other time.

If he didn't forget.

Charles Bannion said, "Maybe they eloped, George. Maybe they ran away together. Maybe Tommy Sears and Vickie Estaban had a great passion going."

"You're serious?" Cheney asked.

"Hey, it's a possibility. Why not?"

Cheney looked from the window of the car as Bannion drove down Center Avenue in the direction of the municipal park, where it was Cheney's intention to see if he could turn up anything at the Youth Center in connection with the missing kids.

Bannion turned the car past the Royal Hotel where two bloodstained men were stepping out from the coffee shop. They were butchers from Slattery's Meat Packing Plant and they regarded the passing cop car with a kind of muted interest.

Cheney tilted his head back in the passenger seat and closed his eyes. As a kid, he'd thought the meat-packing plant the most sinister building that could conceivably exist in the entire world. Great trucks loaded with doomed animals would drive up to the unloading yard and then the beasts would be herded down a passageway to their execution. There had been a rumor back then that the butchers drank cups of freshly-spilled blood in some weird ritual test of their manhood. Even now, when he passed Slattery's plant, or when he saw workers in the streets, he'd remember that old legend of the secret society of blood drinkers.

Opening his eyes, he sat forward in his seat. Something in the idea of elopement appealed to him. It wasn't the youthful romance of it all either. It was the fact that it would explain the disappearance of two kids in terms that weren't altogether unacceptable when you considered other, darker possibilities. He wished he could buy the idea.

He said, "Tommy Sears disappears very early in the morning. Vickie Estaban waits until after dark. It's a strange kind of schedule for an elopement, Charlie."

"Okay. Suppose they have a secret rendezvous. Suppose they don't want to raise suspicion by taking a hike at the same time as each other. Wouldn't that make sense?"

"I don't buy it, Charlie," he said. "I'd love to buy it, but I don't. At least not until we establish some kind of romantic connection between these two kids and so far as I can tell nobody's mentioned any such thing."

"Kids keep secrets," Bannion said.

"Secrets aren't airtight, Charlie. None of Tommy Sears's friends said anything to you about Vickie Estaban, did they? None of them even hinted at her, did they?"

"True. In fact, I got nothing out of Tommy's friends. Nothing at all. If he'd been planning to leave home, he sure as hell didn't tell anybody about it."

Cheney sat back. He crossed his legs awkwardly under the dash and tried to relax. "So we put elopement on the back burner until something comes up to make it feasible. In the meantime, Charlie, all we've really got in common between these two kids is a high school and a Parks and Recreation program, which is what a thousand kids in this town have in common. It's not exactly a stunning revelation."

Bannion was turning the car in the direction of the municipal park. Cheney could see the Youth Center and the flag that flew all summer long from the roof of the building. Crumpled stars and limp stripes hung in the still afternoon air. Streams of kids swarmed around the building.

Bannion parked the car alongside a black Packard. Both he and Cheney got out and strolled round the Packard, which had formerly been a hearse. Cheney realized he'd seen this automobile cruising down Center one afternoon, perhaps a couple of weeks ago, and he recalled noticing it in an absent-minded way.

Bannion, who was something of an auto enthusiast, touched the Packard with a gesture of awe. "Mint. Absolutely mint," he said. "Must be 1947. Maybe '48. You don't see these things any more, George."

Drapes, neatly held back by satin sashes, hung against the rear and side windows. It was such a somber vehicle that it was easy for Cheney to imagine it transporting the dead from funeral parlors to cemeteries.

Bannion said, "This belongs to the guy who does the magic shows here. Mr Zanzibar."

"Zanzibar?" Cheney asked.

Bannion shrugged. "Some kind of stage name, I figure. I hear he's pretty good. Slick."

Cheney looked at Bannion across the hood of the big black car. There were moments when Bannion's knowledge of what was happening in Hamland surprised him, moments when Charlie Bannion would come out with a snippet of information that he could only have culled from a network of gossips. But then Cheney remembered that Bannion spent most of his off-duty hours with the Hamland Players, which was a hotbed of gossip and trivia.

Just the same, Cheney had the faint sensation that he wasn't listening closely enough himself to the pulse of Hamland, that things were slipping past him now and again—an insight he didn't like because maybe, just maybe, it implied that he was taking Hamland for granted.

"What else do you know about Mr Zanzibar?" he asked.

"That's about it." Bannion shrugged. "I hear he lives with a girl in a house out in Gowrie Canyon."

"There's only one house out there," Cheney said. "That's

the old Burford place. Been empty for ten, twelve years." He put his hands in his pockets, understanding that what he had just done was to try and impress Bannion, as if he were saying to the young officer: *You might know who owns the Packard, Charlie boy, but I know the family that used to own the house in Gowrie Canyon—bet you didn't know that one, huh?* He felt a vague sense of foolishness suddenly.

Tense, Cheney thought.

There are two kids missing and I am tense as hell and it made me petty just then.

He walked with Bannion toward the Youth Center. He said, "This Zanzibar must really enjoy isolation if he lives way out there."

Charlie Bannion nodded. "I guess he does."

"You artistic types," Cheney added. "You're in another world."

The young officer smiled because he enjoyed this description of himself. Both men paused at the entrance to the Center where kids milled around, jostling past them and paying them absolutely no attention. They moved inside.

There was a pool table in the center of the room and various partitioned spaces along the sides, creating smaller rooms within the bigger one. In each space there was some kind of activity taking place. Cheney had a quick jumbled impression of things—the click of a chesspiece on a board, a girl's nimble fingers working a strand of raffia, a plump woman he recognized as Jane Howitzer, the retired principal of Hamland Primary, saying *The important thing, girls, is to remember that the soil must be kept damp but not ever waterlogged,* a small boy with an outsized pool cue taking aim at a ball with all the concentration of a physician about to perform neurosurgery. It was a large space filled up with inexhaustible sources of energy in the form of both movement and sound. If you could somehow harness this energy, he thought, you could keep the whole town of Hamland warm through one entire, cruel winter.

Followed by Bannion, he crossed the floor to the back of the Center, where there was a small sign with the word OFFICE written on it. Some cute kid had filled the O with a crayoned Groucho moustache and glasses. He passed beyond the sign to a narrow hallway where a door lay half-open and a young woman sat behind a desk looking at him in surprise.

"Miss Diamond?" Cheney said. "I'm George Cheney. This is Officer Bannion."

Ellis Diamond stood up very quickly. Her fingers moved toward a desk calendar, which she touched lightly as if it brought her reassurance. "Is something wrong? Some trouble with one of my kids?"

Cheney smiled. "We thought you might be able to help us."

Ellis Diamond stepped forward. "How? How can I help you?"

"We're making inquiries about two kids who are members of your program—"

"Inquiries? I don't understand what you mean—" She gave the word *inquiries* a breathless quality.

George Cheney wanted to reach out and lay his hands on the woman's shoulders and perhaps knead some of the obvious tension out of her body. He glanced at Charles Bannion, who was gazing out of the window toward the baseball field.

"I don't think there's any real cause for alarm, Miss Diamond," Cheney said. "Two of your kids are missing from home."

Ellis Diamond walked around her desk. "Two of the kids?" she said. "Two of *my* kids?"

Cheney nodded. "Tommy Sears. And Vickie Estaban."

She leaned against her desk now. She had, Cheney noticed, a good body which for some reason she contrived to conceal under very loose clothing—a wide skirt, a blouse two sizes too big for her.

"How long have they been missing?"

"Tommy was last seen yesterday around noon. And Vickie Estaban about eleven last night." Cheney paused. He was conscious of movement behind him and he turned his head to see the custodian of the place, Max Crouch, go along the hallway with a bucket in one hand. Crouch was a known factor. Cheney had arrested him twice for being drunk and disorderly. He had a sinister, angular face with eyes that seemed to be forever looking into some private distance. It was a face made for hatching plots. If you could have arrested a man for his expression, Max Crouch would be doing ten to twenty. Cheney turned back to Ellis Diamond.

"We wondered if you knew of any relationship between the two of them, Miss Diamond. Anything at all that might help explain the fact that they're simultaneously missing . . ."

Ellis Diamond was trembling very slightly. "You imagine they ran away together? Something like that?"

"It's just one angle to explore," Cheney said, conscious of hollows in his own voice. Just one angle, and not a very good one either.

"Well, as far as I ever knew, they were never especially close to one another. Acquaintances, nothing more. They were both involved in various activities together here, that's all."

"What activities?" Cheney asked.

"Vickie and Tommy both take Mr Zanzibar's magic lessons. And they both play on softball teams. Beyond that, I'm not aware of any special friendship. In fact . . ." And here she smiled slightly, an expression that changed the shape of her face entirely, softening her features and making her look pretty, as if her smile were a light she kept concealed in dark places . . . "I understand that Vickie Estaban was seeing a boy called Lonnie Garrison."

"Is Lonnie a member of your program?"

"He comes and goes. He blows hot and cold. He's something of an outsider, Sheriff. He's maybe fifteen, sixteen. I hear he dropped out of high school."

"You have an address for him?"

Ellis Diamond shook her head. "All I know about Lonnie Garrison is that he lives over on Mulberry somewhere. Exactly where I'm not sure. I suppose he wouldn't be hard to find."

Cheney was silent a moment. Mulberry was a street of broken down houses between the railroad tracks and the edge of the freeway. If Hamland had a ghetto of any kind, it was the area of narrow streets around Mulberry.

"They're both nice kids," Ellis Diamond said. "Tommy and Vickie. I mean, they were never any trouble around here.

91

Never any kind of disciplinary problems or anything like that. I can't imagine them running away from home. I'm sure they'll turn up pretty soon . . ."

"Let's hope so," Cheney said. He edged toward the door. Charlie Bannion followed him.

Bannion said, "It looks like you're doing a real fine job here, Miss Diamond."

"I like to think we've got a good program for the kids," she answered. She blushes, Cheney thought, in an age when the blush was supposed to be an extinct reaction like the swoon and the fainting spell. "If you have time, why don't you look around? Maybe if you asked some questions among the kids, you might get some answers . . . I do hope the children show up. Their parents must be going crazy."

Cheney stepped out of the office.

At the far end of the hallway a door was halfway open. It led into the auditorium. A couple of years ago, when the Center had first been built, he'd come to the dedication ceremony, a hot dog and kegged beer affair where city councilmen had demonstrated their aptitude for getting drunk at the city's expense. Cheney moved toward the door, remembering now that the auditorium had been the damp, inebriated heart, so to speak, of the whole ceremony.

He peered through the space in the direction of the lit stage. Fourteen or fifteen kids sat up there in a circle at the center of which stood a tall skinny young man in a black suit who held his arms out in front of him, his sleeves rolled back a little way. Out of nowhere—or so it seemed to Cheney—playing-cards appeared in the young man's long fingers.

"That's Zanzibar," Charlie Bannion said from behind Cheney's shoulder.

Cheney watched as the kids stretched out their arms the way they'd seen the magician do. And then they made passes with their hands and the air was filled with flocks of falling cards and a lot of awkward laughter. Apprentices of the sorcerer, Cheney thought. Tommy Sears and Vickie Estaban should have been sitting up there alongside the others, trying to mimic Zanzibar's magic. But they weren't.

Now the magician was showing them again how to do the trick. He spoke rarely and when he did his voice was an inaudible whisper Cheney couldn't catch at the very back of the auditorium. But the kids were all hushed and attentive, leaning forward to listen to the magician's instructions.

Now the young magician had singled one of his students out for a private conversation. Cheney saw Zanzibar's arm go round the shoulder of a small fairhaired boy, saw Zanzibar lead the kid to the edge of the stage where he talked to him with his head bent low to the boy's face. Cheney suddenly realized the kid was Rick Dove, Marge and Fred's son, Danny's friend. Rick, a well-mannered if somewhat grace-less child whom Cheney couldn't imagine doing subtle con-juring tricks, was nodding his head up and down slowly as Zanzibar whispered to him. And then Rick was released and went back across the stage to his chair, where he sat down fanning a deck of cards in his hands, a small smile on his lips.

Zanzibar moved to the center of the stage and gazed slowly around the circle of children and again the kids tried to do the trick he'd been teaching them. For a second time there was a brief flurry of dropped cards.

Cheney observed a moment longer before he turned away.

"What now, *Kemo Sabay?*" Charlie Bannion asked.

A slight wind blew down the bleak canyon. It flapped around the porch of the old house and shook the loose shutters. Zena moved the length of the porch until she reached the rocking-chair, where she sat down and let the breeze flap at the hem of her cherry-colored kimono.

She shut her eyes, tilted her head back, tried to imagine she was elsewhere. A big city, say. A place where there was action and high rollers and some *glitter*. Anywhere but this nowhere dump.

She stood up and went back inside the house. Whenever Zanzibar took the car and drove off to his little seminars of magic—as he was inclined to call them—she was totally stranded. The house had begun to touch her with dread and the sight of the barren canyon filled her with an awful kind of loneliness. She wandered inside the kitchen, scratching the backs of her arms casually. She picked up a bottle of Chianti, read the label, set it down again.

Zanzibar had promised he'd supply her with dope but so far he hadn't produced a goddam thing.

Typical Zanzi.

A man of few words and most of them fucking lies.

She went into the living-room. Where would he score anyhow in a place like Hamland? Maybe he didn't have to. Maybe he already had a supply stashed somewhere.

Like upstairs.

She sat slouched in an armchair, spreading her legs. She could see part of the stairway through the open door. Up and up and up, like levels of a nightmare. What I ought to do, she thought, is get out of this place before . . .

Before what?

She stared at the telephone, which lay concealed behind some of Zanzibar's magic equipment. She turned over in her mind the idea of calling her mother in Davenport, Iowa, but it had been two years since she'd done that and even then it had only been because of the trouble she'd gotten into in San Diego and needed the old lady to bail her out.

Hi, Ma, she'd say, *Guess who? Your daughter Martha, now known as the amazing Zena . . . Yeah, right, the very same Martha Jane, formerly Miss Davenport Dairy Industries, 1978.*

That would be a laugh. Probably the old lady would hang up right away.

She got up and walked into the hallway, where she stood looking up the stairs to the dim landing above. Stairs, goddam stairs, why were they always so creepy?

Because of landings. Because of other rooms up there. Because because because.

She went back inside the living-room.

She wandered toward the telephone and let her fingers slide over the smooth plastic surface of the instrument.

Hi, Ma, this is your errant daughter, and I think I got more trouble than I know how to use . . . I can't exactly explain it, Ma . . .

She shut her eyes, bit her lower lip.

She tried to remind herself that she was Martha Jane Beecher from Davenport, Iowa, just a kid who grew up a spit from the shore of the Mississippi, that she wasn't this other person, this Zena that Zanzibar had christened her when he'd picked her up in Laughlin, Nevada, where she'd been doing her cocktail waitress routine in a crummy gambling joint and staying up nights strung out on cocaine. She was Martha Jane Beecher and she was a lost soul and she had a sorry history of placing her vulnerable heart in all the wrong hands.

Losers and bruisers and two-timers and flakes. She'd never picked a winner yet. Zanzibar had rescued her from the clutches of a practicing alcoholic called Maxie in Laughlin, he'd taken her away from the cheap apartment and Maxie's violent attentions and for a moment, for one wonderful moment in time, she'd let herself imagine that maybe, just maybe, her relationship with Zanzibar wasn't going to turn into the usual bloody masochistic enterprise that all her relationships had become.

A knight in a black suit.

Somebody to love. Somebody to reach for in the desperate hours. Somebody who'd give her that vision of love she hungered after.

He changed the way they all changed. He became indifferent to her. And yet she still hungered. She still longed for that tenderness he had shown her at first when he'd been kind and filled with promises of the future—until they'd come here *to this place.*

Call me a cockeyed optimist.

She reached out, picked up the telephone, tried to remember the number of Elizabeth Conway Beecher of 4090 Oskaloosa Road, Davenport.

Area code 319.

319. Then 555-2443.

That was it.

She punched out the numbers, the receiver tucked between her cheek and shoulder, her face turned toward the open door and the sight of the staircase.

She waited for the sound of her mother's telephone ringing all the way up there in Iowa.

Click. Whir.

Clickwhirclick—but no ringing tone.

The bastard had it rigged! He had the goddam telephone rigged so that whenever she wanted to make a phone call all she could get was the pre-recorded message she heard now uttered in Zanzibar's curiously low, metallic tone of voice!

This line is dangerous to the user's health.

This line is dangerous to the user's health.

Over and over, recorded somewhere on some looped tape he had concealed in this crazy godawful house.

This line is dangerous to the user's health . . .

Martha Jane Beecher slammed the receiver back in place and walked back out into the hallway of the big drafty house and stood at the bottom of the stairs, looking up.

I don't want to know, I don't need to know.

She put her hands against her ears and swept out on to the porch.

The canyon was large and silent and lifeless.

Even birds didn't like it here.

Max Crouch watched the cop car move out of the parking-lot. He spat one time into the bucket he was holding. When the car was gone, he relaxed. George Cheney gave him the willies. The way the guy had looked at him before had upset Crouch, who thought the sheriff was just looking for a goddam reason to run him straight into jail.

Crouch turned back into the Youth Center, where the screams of kids assaulted him. Their voices might have been razor blades snipping away at the soft center of his brain. Why couldn't they just shut the fuck up? Why did they go on and on, whining the way they did? It was all kids really knew, how to make noise, how to upset you.

He tried to shut the sounds out of his head as he passed the open door of Ellis Diamond's office. Miss Goody Two-Shoes was standing beside her desk, a worried look on her face. Crouch paused, the bucket dangling in his hand. Whatever George Cheney had said to Ellis Diamond had obviously troubled the woman.

Crouch licked his lips. "Trouble in Paradise?"

Ellis Diamond gazed at him. "I didn't hear you," she said.

"Too bad," said Crouch and continued along the corridor. He opened the basement door and went down a flight of steps into darkness. The basement was his place. He was a creature of the depths. He paused beside the boiler. A spider's web brushed against his forehead and he wiped it aside. Even down here, through layers of floorboards and insulation, he could still hear the voices above.

Those little angels.

Those whining bastards, why couldn't they ever be silent?

Crouch shut his eyes and swayed slightly in the dark of the basement. A single sound went through his mind like the muffled beat of a drum. *Mona* . . .

Startled, Crouch opened his eyes.

He didn't want to think. He didn't need to think.

But the sound came back to him again, like some abandoned item ferried toward him by a tide.

Mona . . .

And he drew from the pocket of his coveralls a ribbon, a pink ribbon that a girl might have worn in her hair, letting it slide between his fingers before he crumpled it tightly in the center of his skinny fist like a useless old relic.

SEVEN

⦁————————————————————————⦁

BY FOUR O'CLOCK IN THE AFTERNOON THIN RAINCLOUDS HAD
rolled in around Hamland, creating a mist that hung against
Naughton's Hill like a pale gray aura materialized at a séance.
Edward Cheney, who enjoyed this kind of weather, sat in his
living-room and gazed through the window along Montrose
Drive.

He saw the Thurston children playing under the big oak
tree some houses down the block. Amanda Thurston had a
bright pink umbrella opened over her head. Cheney watched
a while, remembering when his own son had climbed that
very same tree.

Back then, Liza had been alive.

Back then, years back, he had seen Montrose Drive and the
town of Hamland through other eyes. Back then he had a son
who would climb to the uppermost branches of that oak and
then cry because he couldn't find a way down again and
Edward would have to fetch a stepladder and go to the boy's
rescue. Time after time, George had stubbornly climbed that
oak as if he were driven, and each time he'd have to be
rescued—until one glorious revelatory morning when he'd
found his own way down.

That was George, Cheney thought: somebody who persisted. Somebody who stayed with a thing until it was over and done with.

Back then, too, he had a wife whose life and vitality overflowed into the high-ceilinged rooms of this lonely house. It was a time, he thought, of music and tears and laughter.

And love . . .

Edward Cheney considered love: if he had felt so much of it for Liza, then why had he ever gone on his grubby little sorties to Denver with Elmer Hubbard? Why had he spent so many philandering hours away from this house, when he could so easily have passed that time with his wife? He remembered Liza now, brought her back physically in his mind: a small woman with quick dainty movements and an easy humor, a woman who drew around herself firm boundaries—home and husband and son, and that was all she had ever seemed to want. There had been, alas, an absence of what Edward Cheney thought of as passion.

Did you find at the heart of your love for this woman a certain tedium? Cheney asked himself. A certain weariness at the progression of your marriage and the downhill slide to the gray years? He thought of the girl called Satin in the small apartment near the State Capitol in Denver and he knew what she had offered him that Liza didn't.

A chance to be base. A chance to explore the abysses of yourself. To go down into the damp secretive recesses of yourself, a deranged pilot of inner spaces.

He got out of his chair and moved toward the kitchen. He filled a kettle with water and set it on the stove. When the water was ready he made himself a cup of herbal tea and carried it back inside the living-room, thinking now of Thomas Sears and the big man's drunken behavior at lunchtime. Edward Cheney had always disapproved of public spectacles, emotional scenes played out for general audiences. Thomas Sears, he thought, had been very foolish—and not for the first time in his life.

A missing child.

It was probably only some mischief. Nothing more. Why did Thomas Sears have to think it was anything else?

Back at the window, Cheney sat down again and sipped the

weak tea. The Thurston children were gone now and the street was desolate for a time in the increasing rain. Then he saw, at the far end of the block, a figure moving under a black umbrella. Moving, not moving—he realized he wasn't absolutely sure. There was something faintly familiar about the shape but because the features were masked by the black hood of the umbrella he couldn't be certain.

He set his teacup down on the sill.

The figure beneath the black umbrella was passing close to the oak tree now. Something in the movement, in the stiff little steps, made Edward Cheney feel a small stifling sense of alarm. He ran the tip of one finger round the rim of his teacup and moved his face closer to the glass.

The umbrella came closer.

Cheney stood with the palms of his hands pressed to the windowpane. The umbrella was being folded now and shaken and the woman beneath it, Lily Hubbard, was gazing up at him and smiling.

Lily Hubbard, moisture making a mockery of the thick makeup she wore, moved toward the driveway. Cheney watched her. When he heard the doorbell ring the sound went through him sharply. He shivered.

Lily Hubbard. Here. Why was she here?

He went out into the hallway where he could see the woman's shadow pressed against the stained-glass panel in the middle of the door. He hesitated only a moment before he opened the door a little way and looked out at her face.

"Edward," she said. "I was in the neighborhood and I thought to myself *Why not? Why not drop in on an old friend?* And here I am . . ." She held one hand out for him to grasp. It was damp and cold and there were slicks of moisture on her purple nail varnish. Cheney took her hand and held it as long as he could before he stepped back, allowing her to come inside the house.

"Do you want tea?" he heard himself ask. It was the only question he could think to ask.

"Don't you remember, Eddie? I never drink tea. It's hot chocolate, always hot chocolate." The smile hadn't gone out of her face and Edward Cheney saw something both dreadful and elusive there in that expression.

"Of course—"

"Which you never had, did you?"

They went into the living-room. Lily Hubbard trailed a thin stream of water behind her as she moved. The little protective plastic covers she wore over her shoes squelched.

He stopped in the middle of the floor. He shook his head. "No, we never kept the stuff around." And he attempted a weak smile, making an empty gesture with his arms stretched.

"The Judge and I always kept things in the house strictly for guests, Eddie. Things we wouldn't keep in the normal run of things. Little amenities for those who might happen to drop in on us unexpectedly . . ." She turned her head and looked at the room. Whatever she saw caused an expression of distaste to cross her face. "This house," she added. "I've always felt this house had an empty heart."

An empty heart, Cheney thought. He stared at Lily Hubbard. Rain had cut deep grooves through the layers of makeup, giving her face the appearance of a wrecked birthday cake in which her dark-rimmed eyes were like two cherries. What came back to him was a quick image of the man she called The Judge, Elmer Hubbard, a slender little person with the smallest hands Cheney had ever seen on any man. Elmer Hubbard—his memory distilled in hands and the echo of a gunshot in a dark room. Cheney wondered if Lily knew about Denver and decided it didn't matter if she did. She had always had a remarkable ability to tune out the unpleasant things of life. And Elmer Hubbard had been more to her than a husband: he had been something of an idol for her to worship. Her whole life ran its orbit around The Judge.

"I haven't been in this neighborhood since Elmer passed on," Lily Hubbard said. "And you, Edward Cheney, why haven't I seen you in almost seven years? Now how is such a thing possible in so small a town? Why don't our paths cross more often? Strange." She pursed her red lips a moment. "In fact, I haven't seen you in any social sense since poor Elmer's burial, have I?"

Cheney made a sound that suggested he'd been remiss but had no excuses for his behavior. He looked down at the floor. He remembered now that Thomas Sears had babbled something about Lily Hubbard being in the restaurant of the Royal

Hotel that same morning. Was this Lily's day for going through Hamland like some godawful apparition, reminding people that she existed?

She sat down and her coat made a moist sucking sound on the sofa. "Do you ever see any of the old crowd, Eddie?"

"Hardly," he answered, his voice dry.

"The same for me," she said. "I see faces in passing, but nothing more. A month or so ago I caught a glimpse of Hugh Estaban and that fashion-plate wife of his out in the new Plaza. We didn't speak. I don't think they saw me. Do you ever see Hugh, Eddie?"

"It's been a while," Cheney said.

"They have a daughter, don't they?"

"I believe so."

Lily Hubbard poked the rug with the tip of her dripping umbrella. "Victoria, I recall."

Cheney nodded. There was, he thought, a purpose in her being here: at least, the *outline* of a purpose—but it was a map done in a projection with which he wasn't familiar. Lily Hubbard had always unnerved him, even before the Judge had died. There had always been this quality to her of cunning—he could think of no better word—as if everything she did, every tiny act she performed, was part of some larger, inscrutable mosaic.

"It's funny how people drift away from one another, even in a place like Hamland where certain bonds go very deep. Don't you think that's strange, Eddie?"

"It's natural, I suppose—"

"Natural." She made a snorting sound and the nostrils of her narrow nose flared. "We go back a long way together. How can it be *natural* to just drift apart?" She got up and wandered round the room and when she reached the old upright piano she stopped, plunking the keys with her fingertips. It took him a moment to realize she was laboriously picking out a melody.

"Remember that?"

"Yes. I remember."

"That was Liza's favorite."

Cheney nodded. Why in the name of God was she playing that particular tune? He glanced briefly at her, then looked away. He wished she'd stop striking the keys, wished she'd gather her umbrella and all her unfathomable purposes, and just leave. The tune Lily was picking out so hesitantly was *Charmaine*.

When she stopped he heard her approach him from behind. She laid the palm of one hand lightly on his shoulder.

"How is that son of yours?" she asked.

"I don't see him as often as I might," Cheney said.

"I sometimes wonder why he came back here from Los Angeles to become Sheriff of Hamland," she said. "It puzzles me."

A puzzle, Cheney thought—but only if you didn't see the patterns all around you of retribution, only if you didn't appreciate unholy irony. He moved away from the woman's touch. He said, "I think George always had something of the policeman in him. He never entirely wanted to do anything else, although he often made a decent pretense at it. When he was very young, he told me he was either going to be a detective or a poet. So, when the poet part faded away, he was left with the residue . . ." Edward Cheney shrugged slightly and tried once again to smile. But he couldn't assemble his face for that expression. He stared ahead at the rainy window.

"Our sheriff by default," she said.

"Something like that." Default, he thought. But that wasn't really it either. George's other ambitions, those brief goals he entertained from time to time, had been watery things, undertaken without sincerity of purpose. The English degree that was going to enable him to teach. The time he took a correspondence course in the then nascent science of electronics.

These had meant nothing to George, compared to being Sheriff of Hamland. Perhaps it came out of his boyhood when he'd been a dreamer of dreams, a fabulist who escaped into nightly fantasies concerning cowboys and Indians or cops and robbers. Perhaps it was an overflow of youthful fancies into adulthood.

"And your grandson? How is he?"

Cheney turned. The woman was gazing at him and those eyes which before he had fancifully likened to two cherries were something else altogether now—hard and flat and purposeful. Cheney thought that if Lily Hubbard were a book he would have returned her to the library unopened.

"Danny's fine, I guess," he said. "I don't see him as often as I might either. I understand he's at camp right now." Danny, he thought—the bloodline continues through Danny Cheney. Little Daniel, so proud in his uniform, so eager to go to camp, so anxious to prove his maturity. Cheney realized he missed the small boy in ways he couldn't quite express. There was a tiny ache in his heart at times when he considered the fact that he would be long dead before Danny had grown into manhood, that he'd never know the kind of man the small boy would grow up to be.

"I saw him, Eddie," Lily said. "I saw him in his little uniform about five weeks ago. He was in the car with George and they were both in their different uniforms and it looked so . . . well, cute. Father and son like that."

"Cute," Cheney said. He picked up his empty teacup and looked inside it.

"You know, young Danny looks so much like you, Eddie. More like you than he does his own father." Lily Hubbard had picked up her umbrella and was shaking drops from its folds into the fireplace. "The resemblance is uncanny."

"I've heard that," Cheney said.

"Family, Eddie. Family is all. In the last analysis, family is everything."

Cheney stared across the room at the woman. She was telling him something, she was saying *something* to him, but it fell outside his scope of comprehension. All this talk of children and families had direction, he was sure of that. Where, though?

"Why did you come here, Lily?" he asked.

"I told you. I was in the neighborhood, Eddie."

"Visiting somebody? Is that it?"

She didn't answer his question. She began to move toward the hallway. Cheney followed her, filled with a curious sense that was somehow both relief and anxiety. She was leaving, but behind her lay clues to her visit he couldn't understand.

"I don't entirely believe you, Lily," he said. "You walked all this way just to see me, didn't you?"

"You always flattered yourself, Eddie Cheney. You always had a streak of vanity a mile wide," and she smiled at him.

"You wanted to tell me something—"

"I don't think so," she said. "What could I possibly tell *you* that you don't already know?"

She regarded him a moment longer, then she turned her face toward the stained-glass panel in the door. She twisted the umbrella and opened it and tiny sprays of water struck Cheney's face.

"Some people say, Eddie," and she leaned toward him conspiratorially, "that it's bad luck to open an umbrella indoors. But personally I don't believe that. Do you? Do you believe that, Eddie?"

She was gone nimbly, before he had time to form a response in his mind. He watched her go down the driveway in the rain, a crazed figure whose crazed purpose had eluded him.

Bad luck, he thought. There was no such thing as luck. You created your own destiny.

Closing the door, he shut his eyes and rested his face against the stained glass.

Why had she come to his house? he wondered.

Why, after all this time, had she come to Montrose Drive?

He wondered, for the first time in many years, whether Elmer Hubbard had left a suicide note behind before he applied the handgun to his head, whether he had left his widow a legacy of information.

A note, he thought.

It was this that haunted him now.

The area of Hamland that lay squashed between the railroad tracks and the edge of the freeway was a hodgepodge of narrow streets and mixed architecture, where small frame houses stood alongside Victorian monstrosities that had been turned into apartments. Here and there, a relatively new duplex had been built, chipped cinderblock dwellings with overgrown yards. These buildings were tax write-offs for corporations in Denver or Los Angeles or Phoenix.

The entire neighborhood, dotted here and there by small bars and tiny groceries, had arrived at that stage of neglect which is apathy. If the landlords didn't care to maintain the properties, then why should the tenants worry? There were broken windows covered over by sheets of cardboard, front yards filled with rusted tools, piles of warped wood, cars that hadn't gone anywhere in years and sat now in a stupor of shattered windshields and flat tires and spiderwebs.

In the rain, the whole area had a gloomy, forsaken look, a bleak emptiness.

On Mulberry Street, the heart of the neighborhood, Charles Bannion parked the car at Cheney's request across the way from Howie's Tavern, a long narrow bar with a squat jukebox glowing at the back of the room. In the dim interior several figures could be seen on stools, their darkened faces turned toward the sight of the sheriff's car.

"Nice lady," Bannion said.

"Ellis Diamond?"

Bannion nodded. "Yeah."

Cheney gazed at the porch of a large rundown house, where a grubby kid of about three or four was staring morosely at him. "A little nervous. A little on the high-strung side," he said.

"Maybe," Bannion remarked.

"I guess anybody would get that way if they were sur-rounded by screaming kids all day long." The kid on the porch was blowing up a balloon, which grew fatter and fatter and then popped suddenly. The kid began to wail. A bright slick of broken rubber adhered to his cheek.

Cheney got out of the car. "You said Lonnie Garrison lives at 38 Waddell?"

"According to the phone book," Bannion answered.

"Let's walk, Charlie."

"In this rain?"

"Why not. It's refreshing. Blows the cobwebs away."

They reached Waddell Street, where the houses stood very close together, the spaces between them creating narrow alleys. Number 38 was a two-story frame house that had been converted into two apartments. There were two bells and nameplates at the side of the door, and one of them had the name GARRISON written on it in ballpoint that had become smeared from rain.

Cheney pressed the bell. He could hear it ring in the upper part of the house, followed by the sound of footsteps coming hurriedly down the stairs. The front door was opened and the kid who stood there was a hulking figure of about fifteen, sixteen, black T-shirt, muscular arms folded against his thick chest in a defensive posture. Cheney observed the various tattoos that covered the flesh. Snakes, birds, a stag's head—there was a whole menagerie inscribed on the boy's flesh.

"Lonnie?" he asked.

The kid nodded. He had, beneath the small blemishes of acne, a kind of sullen beauty. His thick hair, dark and glossy, grew to his shoulders.

"Lonnie, we're looking for Vickie Estaban—"

"Hey, I hardly know the chick," Lonnie Garrison said, a little too defensively. He had a spectacularly deep voice for an adolescent. It boomed out of his chest. "What she is is jail-bait."

Cheney felt rain come through the broken roof of the porch and slither down the side of his neck. "When did you last see her, Lonnie?"

The boy shrugged. He turned his head and glanced back down the hallway behind him. A broken stroller, a bowling-ball, and a pile of *National Geographic*s sat against the wall at the foot of the stairs.

"Couple days ago. I don't know. What's she done anyhow? Robbed a bank?"

"She didn't do anything, Lonnie, except vanish."

"Vanish?" The kid smiled. "She really vanished?"

Cheney nodded. "Yeah."

"How about that," Lonnie Garrison said. The notion that Victoria Estaban had disappeared seemed to bring him some pleasure.

"Did she ever talk to you about leaving home, Lonnie?"

"She didn't talk to me much about anything."

"You were friends, Lonnie, that's what we understand—"

"Friends," the kid said derisively. "If that's what you want to call it."

"What would you call it?"

"Listen, there's a word for Vickie and that word is airhead, man."

"I don't know what you mean, Lonnie."

The kid shrugged. He moved his arms and all the tattooed animals stirred. "She talked like her head was in the clouds, is what I'm trying to tell you. Like a dreamer. You understand?"

Cheney shook his head. He wanted this kid to be more specific. Lonnie Garrison looked frustrated and glanced at Charlie Bannion a second, as if to see whether Bannion understood what he was trying to tell the sheriff. The kid took a small box of dental floss from the pocket of his jeans, snapped a length off, and began to work it between his lower teeth.

"Look," Cheney said. "When you're through with the oral hygiene, maybe we could get back to Vickie Estaban?"

Garrison crumpled the floss, tossed it aside. "I don't know anything, Sheriff. I'm trying to tell you that."

"You said she was a dreamer, Lonnie. I want to know what that means."

Garrison peered across the porch into the rainy street. He twisted his lower lip downward, touched it with a fingertip. There was a core here of reluctance, Cheney knew. When you lived in this neighborhood you didn't want to talk to cops; more important, you didn't want to be *seen* talking to them.

Lonnie said, "She talked about flying saucer bullshit and reincarnation and some guy called Edgar who could cure sick people while he was asleep. Crap like that." The kid paused. "Then there was this magic shit."

"What magic shit, Lonnie?"

"She was doing these real *childish* magic tricks, you know? She was always saying 'Pick a card, Lonnie' or something like that. She was always bugging me."

"What's wrong with that?"

Garrison shook his head slowly. "It got on my goddam nerves, that's what's wrong with it. It was always Zanzibar this or Zanzibar that or Zanzibar says, like the guy was holy, you know?"

Jealousy, Cheney thought.

A bad case of old-style envy.

It made certain tiny things clear in his mind—such as the kid's reluctance to admit any relationship with Vickie

Estaban—but it didn't touch the central problem remotely: where was the goddam girl? And where the hell was Tommy Sears? Down and down and down, Cheney thought: he felt like he was tumbling through layers of slick levels, slippery rungs he couldn't grasp. A margarine world.

"I had Zanzibar up to here," Garrison said.

"You told Vickie this?"

"Damn right I told her. I told her she had the hots for the creep."

"You think she went away somewhere on account of Zanzibar?"

"Who knows? Who cares?" Lonnie Garrison looked suddenly glum. "Magic. Big deal. I mean, it's all tricks. But she thinks magic is something else, the way she talks about it. Like it really exists."

Cheney wiped rainwater from his forehead. Drops drummed on the decrepit porch roof overhead. The girl is in awe of Mr Zanzibar and Lonnie doesn't like that and maybe they argue . . . It was an old story: conflicts of the young heart. Now Cheney tried to picture the girl sitting on that stage in the half-lit auditorium, writing mental love-letters to the man known as Zanzibar.

Dreams in the secret places of the night.

The seductive motion of fantasies.

What Lonnie Garrison had called "the hots" was what George Cheney would have described more sedately as "a crush"—an occupational hazard of adolescence.

Charlie Bannion stepped away from the rail of the porch and asked, "The name Tommy Sears mean anything to you, Lonnie?"

"Father or son?" Garrison asked. "If it's the father, sure, I know him because sometimes I run into him out at Six-Mile Lanes bowling. The kid I spoke to maybe once or twice, that's all. Why you asking about Tommy Sears now? I thought you came here to talk about Vickie Estaban?"

"They've both gone, Lonnie," Bannion said.

"*Both* of them?"

"Yeah."

"Well shit." The kid scratched his head. This new item of information appeared to baffle him.

"You happen to know any reason why they might leave home together?" Cheney asked.

"What? Vickie and Tommy? You kidding?"

"I'm not kidding, Lonnie," Cheney said.

"They hardly knew each other, man. What the hell would they run away together for, huh? That don't make any sense."

Garrison hooked his thumbs in the belt-loops of his jeans and sniffed. He stared at Cheney and added: "I swear to God, man, I don't know where Vickie is. It's been a couple days since I saw her and like I said all she wanted to talk about was this real stupid magic."

Cheney moved toward the steps. He felt bleak as the street that faced him. "If you see either Vickie Estaban or Tommy Sears, call me."

"Yeah. Sure," the kid answered without conviction, as if a call to any cop would be a waste of dimes.

"I mean it, Lonnie," Cheney said.

"I hear you, Sheriff."

The door was shut slowly.

Cheney and Charlie Bannion went toward the sidewalk. They walked a little way in silence.

Then Bannion asked, "You believe him?"

"I don't know," Cheney said. "I believe it's possible Vickie Estaban had a crush on the magician."

When they reached the car, Cheney got in on the passenger side.

Charlie Bannion drummed his knuckles on the steering-wheel.

"What do you know about conjuring, Charlie?" Cheney asked.

"When I was a kid I got a magic set one Christmas, I remember that. I had a wand that broke in two as soon as I touched it and some bad card tricks and a weird box that was supposed to make a coin disappear. Only it never worked. That's what I know about conjuring."

Cheney smiled. He told Bannion to drive.

Magic and mystery, he thought.

Other dimensions.

He closed his eyes and tipped his head back against the seat and he imagined that somebody in Hamland had their own weird box which, instead of causing coins to vanish, worked another kind of disappearing magic on children.

Danny Cheney, who sat alone on the bank of the river, listened to the sounds of his Cub Scout troop float toward him from between the trees. He had become separated from the others in the course of a game which was a variation on Hide and Seek that Bubba Shankland, the Scoutmaster, had dreamed up.

Danny was The Master Spy, the man with the important microdot in his possession, and the other Cub Scouts were supposed to find him by tracking.

Bent grass and disturbed shrubbery. Footprints. All that good stuff Bubba Shankland thought Scouts ought to know.

Danny, bored at being the object of the hunt, stared down at the gray water of the sluggish river. The voices that reached him were shrill.

He musta come this way. Here's a candy wrapper!

Danny didn't have any candy, cowbrain!

Danny yawned and lay back on the slope of the bank, safe in the knowledge it would take the troop a while to find him. He stared up at the sky which was bloated with rains about to fall. He hoped somebody had repaired the leak in the tent. During the last rain his sleeping bag had turned to wet mush and everything inside the tent had floated on a half-inch of water.

The joys of Scouting.

It was okay but it wasn't really the adventure he'd expected. Bubba Shankland was a man with an overwhelming interest in string, and insisted on showing off all kinds of fancy knots. If it wasn't string it was bird-watching. Old Bubba had been really excited yesterday when he'd seen something he called a Siberian Ruby Throat. Andy Saxon said it wasn't a Ruby Throat at all but Bubba dismissed the notion. He knew his birds, he said. Been watching them all his life, he said.

At nights, round the campfire, Bubba liked nothing better than to have sing-songs, which he accompanied with his autoharp. Danny thought if he heard anything more about

The Old Gray Mare he was going to just puke. Last night, Andy Saxon—who riled Bubba something wicked—had asked the Scoutmaster if he knew any Iron Maiden tunes.

Danny pushed himself upright. He thought about his Mom and Dad a moment, understanding that he missed them more than he was prepared to admit. It was one thing to go away to camp—but who said it had to last *this* long?

He strolled to the edge of the river.

As he stood there, gazing at his own colorless reflection in dull water, he was aware of the bushes behind him being parted, and then there was the sound of someone coming down the bank toward him.

Danny turned.

It was a guy with a fishing-pole.

Danny smiled at the man, who moved down the bank with a kind of easy grace. He carried a tacklebox and the pole was propped against his shoulder, the line hooked into one of the eyes of the rod, so that the pole bent a little like a taut bow. The man stood a couple of feet away from Danny and opened his tacklebox, rummaging through it. He wore a red plaid jacket and dark glasses and a baseball cap pulled down over his forehead so that his face was shadowed.

"Many fish here?" Danny asked.

"It's a good place for trout mainly."

Danny stared inside the tacklebox. There was a pile of lures, different colors, each of them shiny, as if sunlight were trapped in that box. The man fingered through them and then removed one that was silvery. It glistened as he attached it to his line. It dangled in the air in front of Danny's eyes.

"I've had good luck with this one," the man said.

The lure caught light and glittered, swinging back and forth. It was an elongated disc, slightly hollowed in the center, and it reflected the trees like a small mirror. What it reminded Danny of was a miniature satellite dish, one that was tuned into faraway galaxies.

Danny gazed at it.

The man reached out and clasped the lure, turning it over and over in his hand as if he were trying to get something right.

"It lulls the fish," the man said.

"I guess." Danny was drawn to the core of the silvery lure and for a second saw his own reflection there, distorted and misshapen.

"Puts them to sleep, I guess. They come up, see the lure. The silver gets them. The light. Reflections. Makes them feel very peaceful."

Danny continued to watch. The guy cast his line out and the lure made a *plopping* sound as it broke the surface of water. After a moment he reeled the line back in and the lure, slick and dripping, hung in front of Danny's face.

"You ever fish?" the man asked.

"Sometimes."

"It's all a matter of patience, I figure. You got to have great patience. And a bunch of luck."

Danny turned his face away from the fisherman as he heard footsteps coming down the bank and then there were boys shouting at him.

He was caught. The Master Spy was trapped.

It was a silly game anyhow.

"Gotcha!" said Martin Axelrod, a boy with a constant globe of mucus on the tip of his nose. Snotty Martin.

"Terrific place to hide," Robbie Stokes said, with the heavy sarcasm for which he was famous. "I mean, nobody would ever find you out in the open like this. You're a clever guy, Danny. Anybody ever tell you that?"

Danny Cheney allowed himself to be captured. His hands were held behind his back and he was taken up the bank in the general direction of camp. At the top he paused a second, twisting his head round to look back down at the river.

The guy with the fishing-pole was gone and the bank was empty.

Courtney Sears sat in the darkened corner of the bedroom, her legs tucked up under her body as she watched her husband sleep off his midday drunk. Sometimes he mumbled in his dreams and moved his head restlessly from side to side. Every now and then, when she heard a sound that didn't emerge from Thomas Sears, when she heard the stirring of wet leaves or the passage of a car in the street or an unexpected creak from the roof, she would lean forward in her chair and pull the curtain back a little way from the window and look out into the street—because she knew, she *knew,* that sooner or later one of these sounds would be that of Tommy coming home.

Outside, the porch-light burned brightly. She thought she would keep it on day and night until Tommy was back, the way some people had tied yellow ribbons to tree trunks when all those embassy personnel had been held hostage in Iran.

She rose, walked to the bed, gazed down at her husband.

He was not an insensitive man, she knew that. His problem was that expressions of feeling didn't come easily to him, he managed to block them somehow—so instead he went out and got so drunk that old Ed Cheney had had to practically carry him inside the house.

She thought of Ed Cheney now. Always the perfect gentleman. Always kindly and courteous. He'd acted toward her so solicitously at lunchtime that she felt flooded with gratitude. *Young Tommy will turn up, my dear. You'll see. Everything is going to be just dandy . . .* And then he'd hugged her for comfort and she'd been surprised by the strength in that old man's arms. He'd helped Thomas to bed, then he'd gone into the kitchen and brewed some weak tea, forcing her to sit down at the table and drink it for relaxation. A kind man. A man of class and integrity.

The sudden sound of the telephone startled her as she stood beside the bed. She turned and went out of the room toward the kitchen, which was in darkness. Without taking time to flip on the light switch, she hurried toward the telephone and answered it breathlessly.

The Sheriff, she thought.

It had to be George Cheney with some news of Tommy.

"Hello," she said.

There was no response.

"Hello," she said again. Inside her all at once there was a tiny, terrible feeling she knew was going to grow: it was a tension that rose from deep in her stomach to her throat, where it would congeal and she wouldn't be able to breathe.

"Hello, hello, this is Courtney Sears speaking," and her voice came out sounding strangulated. "Is anyone there?"

The reply came from a million miles away. It came through

sudden bursts of static and interference as though it were travelling at incalculable speeds through galaxies, through the awesome expanses of deep space.

It was a single, terrifying word and it made Courtney Sears's heart stop dead.

"Mom?"

EIGHT

ANNE CHENEY SAID, "THE FIRST THING YOU DO, GEORGE, IS GET into the bathtub and *soak*. Soak until your skin feels like rice paper and you look like a totally revolting wrinkled old man. Then come back out here and I'll feed you. How does that sound?"

Cheney sat down, kicking off his shoes.

Anne, perched on the arm of the sofa, caught her husband's feet in her lap and began slowly to massage his toes. His socks were slightly damp. She knew what he was going to say to her proposal even before she'd suggested it. There were two kids inexplicably missing out there and George wouldn't rest until he knew why.

"I don't have time, Anne."

"Make some."

"Look, I'm up to my neck in worried parents. I expect Ronald Kelly to come bursting in through the door at any second hounding me for a story. How is it going to look when he finds me in the bathtub, for Christ's sake? I can *hear* the headlines he'd write. *Sheriff Soaks in Tub While Anxious Parents Wait . . .*"

Anne slowly lowered her husband's feet from her lap.

116

"Kelly's an old hack. You can handle him without any problem. At least eat, George," she said. "I bet you haven't eaten since breakfast."

"I had a hamburger somewhere along the way," he answered.

"At Greasy Freddie's Drive-In? At the Palace of Botulism?"

"Someplace like that."

"Ulcer City, George." Anne rose from the sofa and walked to the fireplace, where she folded her arms across her breasts. Normally, she could read her husband's face and the expressions there as surely as if they were bold print on white paper, but the way he looked right then eluded her. She sensed his concern, his anxiety, but there was another quality she couldn't quite grasp. There was a darkness in his eyes, as if blinds had been pulled down across them.

"Are you going back out again?" she asked.

He didn't answer her.

"What are you going to do? Drive the streets?"

"I'm not sure." He sat upright, running a hand through his hair. "Kids don't vanish without a trace. It's impossible."

Anne moved toward him. She had an urge just then to undress him, to take him upstairs to their bedroom and make love to him, as if that act might somehow compensate—or, at the very least, remove his tensions. She caught his hands in her own and kissed them softly.

"Maybe there's no connection between the two kids," she said. "Maybe that's the wrong approach. You're being swayed by coincidence. After all, they don't seem to have a great deal in common. You said so yourself. They go to the same school but they're apparently not even in the same classes together. They go to the Youth Center and participate in some of the same programs—but what does all that amount to, George?"

"I don't know," he answered, and there was something forlorn in his voice, a hollowness that came from far inside him. For a moment she listened to the rain beat against the window beyond drawn curtains and she thought of this house as an island of comfortable light at the heart of a storm.

"Let me fix you some food anyhow," she offered.

"I'm not hungry, Anne. Really. I can still feel that hamburger in my stomach." He made a noise suggestive of queasiness.

Anne said, "Poor George," and as she did so stared across the room to the bookshelves, where family photographs stood in their dark frames. The one that caught her eye just then was a picture she'd taken last summer of George and Danny when they'd all gone on a camping trip to Montana. George had one arm around the boy's shoulders and Danny was squinting because the sunlight was flowing directly into his eyes. It had been a good time, a time of freedom and carelessness, when every new day arrived filled with lazy possibilities. There hadn't been any tensions, any distress.

Now she thought of Danny, but the strange thing was she couldn't quite get an image of him fixed in her mind. What was he doing right now? What kind of Cub Scout activity was he involved in at this particular moment? Maybe he was asleep already. Maybe the day had worn him down by this time.

George got up from the sofa and went inside the kitchen. She followed him, saw him open the refrigerator and pour a glass of club soda which he drank by the sink. Under the bright kitchen light, his skin looked pale.

"If you won't eat, and you won't take a hot bath, then at least change out of those damp clothes into something else," she said.

"And what would I change into?" he asked. He made a claw of one hand and distorted his face terribly. It was his Monster Look, the one he sometimes used when he was fooling around with Danny. Only this time he did it without humor, without enthusiasm. A very feeble joke. He didn't even bother to drag one foot behind him the way he usually did.

"Change into something dry, George," she said.

The Monster vanished. The Cop came back.

"Come over here," he said.

She went across the tiled floor toward him.

He drew her body against him, holding her so hard that for a moment she had difficulty catching her breath. Then he released her, smiling as he did so.

"What was that for?" she asked.

"Gratitude," he answered.

"Sometimes you're pretty schmaltzy, George, you know that? For a cop, my love, you've got a real soft center."

"And you love it," he said.

"Yeah, I love it."

He finished his club soda, placing the empty glass inside the sink. "No regrets?" he asked. He made a loose gesture with his hand, indicating not only this family and this house, but the town that lay around them.

She shook her head. "Even if I had any, would I mention them to you? All the women in my family are the strong supportive type. They keep their disappointments to themselves."

"Do *you* have any disappointments?"

"Except for the fact that you won't hang around long enough for me to drag you off to bed—"

"Later," he said.

"Is that a promise?"

He nodded. "I swear," he said.

She slapped him lightly on the ass. "Go change those clothes."

He went to the door and there he paused, turning back to look at her. "Can I tell you something?"

She nodded.

"I'm a little bit scared," he said.

"Scared?"

"Yeah, scared I won't find those kids. Scared I don't have the competence to find them. Scared that I'm out of my goddamn depth."

She strolled across to him and held him. She had never heard George Cheney worry about his competence before now. She had never heard him admit to being afraid of anything either.

"You're not out of your depth, George. It's going to be okay. You'll find those kids. I know you will."

Cheney stepped back from her and smiled in a weary way. "Is that the kind of reassurance the strong supportive women in your family have always given their men?"

Anne put one hand out and touched the side of Cheney's

face. She said, "It's really very simple, George. I have a lot of faith in you."

Cheney smiled again. He went out of the kitchen. She could hear him climb the stairs to their bedroom. She listened carefully. There was one point when his footsteps stopped and she knew that he was looking inside Danny's empty room, as if he meant to remind himself of something. Don't be scared, George. Don't ever be scared.

The telephone rang and she went to pick it up.

It was Courtney Sears asking for George.

Max Crouch climbed the stairs to the door of the apartment he shared with his wife on Strasburg Street. He clutched the bannister rail as he moved because he was in a mild state of inebriation.

He reached the landing and fumbled in his coat for his key.

He pushed the door open. The room into which he stepped smelled of cheap sherry. A TV was playing. His wife, Hildy, stared at the picture and didn't look round when he deliberately belched. He gazed at the top of her braided hair. These braids were always a fucking bad sign for Max Crouch because they usually meant Hildy had spent a whole lot of time in front of a mirror, which in turn meant she was depressed by her wrinkles, which in turn reminded her of all the passing years.

He slung his raincoat over the back of a chair and sat down on the floor, glancing at Hildy as he did so. The TV show was some bullshit game where newlyweds were supposed to answer questions about their spouses and then they won these prizes for trips to Waikiki or someplace. It all seemed too bright for Max Crouch, too colorful, but that was the way Hildy liked the picture to be—maximum color, total sound, everything designed, like the sherry she sipped, to turn her brain to oatmeal.

"Maxwell," she said, during the commercial break. "I didn't hear you come in."

I should've farted, Max Crouch thought.

"How was your day?"

"It was a day," he answered. "Wait. I take that back. It was a little different."

Hildy inclined her big face questioningly.

"We had the cops down there today," Max said.

"Cops?" Hildy's face, you could see, was being drawn back toward the TV where a woman was busily whizzing through her kitchen with a floormop.

"Yeah, cops. The Sheriff himself, Hildy."

"Why?" she asked.

The guy on the TV grinned and asked: *Will your husband say he likes to eat in bed or prefers to do it at the table?*

Laughter. You had to be in on the sly jokes here, the sexual undertones. Max Crouch wanted to put his boot through the screen.

"They were looking for something, I guess." He wasn't going to say what exactly. Hildy lived much of her life too close to tears. She had a cistern in her brain that frequently overflowed.

"Like what?"

"Beats me."

"Is one of the kids in trouble or something?" Hildy asked.

He looked at his wife now. She had this peculiar notion about his job—she thought he was a kindly old janitor, the guy all the kids came to when they had bloody noses or had wounded themselves, the old custodian who dispensed good cheer and wise counsel. He had allowed her to retain this image intact. All the balances in Hildy's life had become so goddam *delicate* you always had to be careful to ensure her illusions.

"Nah, who knows?" He shrugged. He watched as she became engrossed in the show again. She was a big woman with enormous breasts and thick thighs.

"Well," she said. "I hope nothing's happened to any of the kids."

Max stood up.

It was always worse than ever at this time of the year. *Birthday time . . .*

Max went in the kitchen. It was clean, all surfaces spotless.

He squirted some dish-washing liquid on his hands and ran hot water over them. Then he dried himself with a paper towel. In the course of a day, he figured he washed his hands maybe twenty, twenty-five times.

He went back to the living-room.

He thought: *Two less kids to deal with at Parks and Rec. Two less to clean up after.* And he recalled the look of horror on Ellis Diamond's face after the cops had gone. *Two kids missing! Two of MY kids missing!*

He went to the sofa and sat down alongside his wife.

He put one arm around her wide shoulders.

"I hope nothing's happened to any of the kids," Hildy said again, chewing on her lower lip.

Max Crouch shut his eyes just as a pair of the newlyweds on the TV took greedy possession of their Grand Prize: new suitcases for their all-expenses-paid vacation to Waikiki. It was a big deal. "Nothing's happened," he said. "Nothing at all."

When Ellis Diamond heard the sound of somebody knocking at her door, her first thought was of Arthur Rigley from upstairs. Since she had no desire to see the man, she thought that if she didn't answer he'd think she was asleep and just go away. Arthur Rigley had unnerved her earlier—the rambling nature of his speech, the non-sequiturs, the way he'd continually put one hand to the side of his head as if he had a pain there he couldn't altogether locate . . . She wasn't sure whether she should feel sorry for him or afraid of him. And the idea he might be on the other side of her door at this very moment was not exactly reassuring.

The whole day, though, had been an unsettling one. The missing children. The visit from the police. The unsettling sense of chaos creeping round the edges of things.

Now, sitting in front of the small electric fire and trying to get her damp hair dry, she listened to the soft *rap rap rap* on her door. Whoever stood out there was extremely persistent. She tutted impatiently, tightened the belt of her dressing-gown, walked across the room.

Say nothing, she thought.

He has to go away eventually.

Rap rap rap.

God. She looked quickly round the room, picked up some discarded items of clothing, stuffed them inside a closet, then went back to the door.

"Miss Diamond?"

It wasn't Arthur Rigley's voice anyhow.

"Who is it?" she asked.

"Charlie Bannion."

"Bannion?"

"We met at the park today?"

The young policeman. She remembered him now. She opened the door a little way and looked up at him. He had one of those sharp well-defined faces she always associated with track athletes. It was lean and open, but without any gaunt quality.

"Is something wrong?" she asked. "Have you heard something about those children?"

Charlie Bannion, clothes dripping with rain, shook his head. "Sheriff Cheney wants me to ask you a couple of questions, Miss Diamond. That's all."

"Perhaps you should come in," she said.

"Thanks."

He stepped inside the room and followed her toward the sofa in front of the electric fire. He stretched his hands to the heat, rubbing them together.

Ellis Diamond experienced a moment of awkwardness. It was the first time she'd ever had a man inside this apartment and she felt suddenly clumsy, as if she'd forgotten anything she'd ever known about social graces. "Would you like some coffee? I have tea if you'd prefer that."

"Nothing, thanks," he said.

A silence.

She felt a vague sense of inner collapse all at once, almost as if all the disturbing events of the day had come together in one lump in her heart. She sat down and looked at the red glow of the fire.

"You haven't heard anything about Tommy or Vickie?" she asked.

"Not yet," Charlie Bannion answered.

She placed the palm of one hand against the side of her face. "I find it hard to believe they'd just run away, Officer."

"Charles, please. Or Charlie. I don't like Officer."

"Charlie," she said, smiling thinly. Charlie was a good

name, she thought. It had a raw, easygoing feel to it. "You don't have any information at all?"

Bannion said, "No clues."

Ellis Diamond turned her hands up in her lap and looked down into the cups of her own flesh. Her fingers had always seemed very wrong to her, square and thick and so workmanlike. She longed for delicacy. "What do you do when you don't have any clues, Charlie?"

"We keep right on digging," he answered.

"It must be very difficult for the parents. Maybe I should telephone them or visit them . . ."

"They might appreciate that," he said somewhat uncertainly.

She gazed up at his face now, sticking her hands in the pockets of her robe.

"Sheriff Cheney wants me to ask you a few questions about this Mr Zanzibar . . ."

"Go ahead. I'll try my best to answer." She had a strange, airy sensation in her chest: this was going to be awful. She wasn't going to be able to tell the young cop anything. And it was all her own idiot fault.

"First, you have to understand that this is routine. I mean, we don't suspect him of anything. It's just that Zanzibar is a common factor with the two kids. Okay? I'm saying this because I don't want you to think he has anything to do with the situation—"

"You're exploring," she suggested in a voice that was glumly quiet.

"Right. That's all we're doing."

From somewhere, Bannion had produced a small notebook. The pages were damp and curling. The pencil he used was a blunt stub. Something in this combination of things touched Ellis Diamond. She wasn't sure what. An insight into Charlie Bannion's life presented itself to her. Blunt pencil, tatty little notebook, muddy shoes—he lives alone, she thought. He doesn't have anyone to help take care of him. He has nobody to hurry home to.

"How long has he been with your program?" Charlie Bannion asked.

"Four weeks. Roughly."

"What's his real name?"

She was silent. Suddenly her sense of inadequacy struck her like a mallet. *I couldn't get him to fill out the forms,* she wanted to cry aloud. *I couldn't get him to do any of the necessary paperwork. I don't know a damned thing about the man!* It was a mistake, she shouldn't have taken him on without knowing who he was, she should never have done a thing like that. But then she'd never met anybody quite like Zanzibar anyhow, who had a certain aura of force about him, an elemental thing as basic as a flood or a thunderstorm or a fork of lightning in the sky. He had this way of just flowing over you and there was nothing you could do to stop him.

"His real name," Charlie Bannion repeated. "I mean, it can't be Zanzibar, can it?"

"I don't know," Ellis said. "He didn't tell me."

"How did you meet him?"

"He came to my office one day. He said he was interested in helping out. I asked him what he could do . . ." Ellis Diamond shut her eyes. All this was so vivid to her, and at the same time so unreal. "He didn't answer the question. At least not directly. He asked me to write my name on a slip of paper. Which I did. It was a weird request, but I did it anyhow. Then he told me to fold the paper and hold it in the palm of my hand tightly. Then he asked me to raise the hand in the air above my head. And . . ."

"Go on," Bannion said.

"And then he said I should open my hand and look at what I had written on the paper."

"What was on the paper?"

"I still have it," she said. "Would you like to see it?"

"Sure."

She went to the writing bureau, opened a drawer, found the slip of paper and handed it to Bannion, who read it. The words were in capital letters:

I AM ZANZIBAR, MASTER OF ILLUSION

"That's quite a trick," the cop said. "How did he make the switch?"

"I don't know. He must have done it at some point, but I

can't remember when. I was puzzled, you have to remember that. Probably I was a little flustered too. Perhaps it was easy for him to switch paper. I don't know."

"What happened next?"

"He said he wanted to teach magic to kids. And put on a couple of shows now and again. I was so impressed I suppose I asked him if he could start immediately—"

"Without checking his background?"

"Without checking his background," she said. She looked down at the floor. She thought of her entire program, that intricate organization of interlocking pieces, that edifice she'd constructed herself block by block, and it was as if she saw—halfway up the facade of her own skyscraper—a terrible crack in the concrete.

"I know it was wrong. But I was enthusiastic, you see. I was carried away. Even when I asked him to go to work, I knew it wasn't the proper procedure because you've always got to be really careful when kids are involved. I mean, there are guidelines, you're supposed to check references, crosscheck them so that you can keep out the crackpots and the molesters and sex offenders. There are definite guidelines and I chose to ignore them . . ."

"Hey," Charlie Bannion said. "Relax. I told you, I'm not accusing Mr Zanzibar of anything. I'm not even *hinting* at his involvement in any wrongdoing. This is routine, Ellis. That's all. And nobody's pointing a finger at you either."

"I know, I know." She wandered to the window, parted the drapes, looked out into the rain, which fell in great silvery threads through the streetlamps. "I just feel so bad, though. But the man won't fill out the forms I give him. He won't do anything like that. He just refuses. He laughs at me."

"Why does he do that? What possible objection could he have to some simple paperwork?" Charlie Bannion asked.

She said, "I don't know. Maybe it's part of the whole mystery of what he does. Part of his *style*. And that girl who works with him—God, I don't even know anything about *her* either. You must think I'm terrible. I'm inefficient."

"Did I say that?"

Ellis Diamond shook her head. He was too kind to come right out with it, that was all.

126

"Tell me about the girl," he said.

"She calls herself Zena. That's all I know."

"No last name, I guess."

Ellis shook her head again. "Maybe that's a stage name like Zanzibar."

"Zanzibar and Zena. It has a certain ring," Bannion said. "If they're on the payroll, they must have provided you with Social Security numbers, right?"

She didn't answer him. This absence of all the raw data she should have obtained as a matter of course was making her feel worse by the moment. She imagined she was naked, suddenly stripped of all her clothing in some public place. Humiliation.

"No Social Security numbers, huh?" the cop asked.

"Not yet. I'm sorry. The girl said she'd give them to me about a week ago, but so far I haven't received them . . ."

He wrote something in his notebook. "Have you any idea of the background of these people? They ever mention where they came from? Why they turned up in Hamland?"

She said, once again, that she was sorry, knowing that sorry didn't quite cut it, didn't quite cover her failures.

"I don't have any excuses, you know. I've never done this kind of hiring before, Charlie. Maybe I was just swept away by my enthusiasm for Zanzibar. He *is* quite a find for a program like ours. Also, he has a weird manner that makes it damned hard to communicate. The things that might be important to you and me, well, they don't seem to mean a damned thing to him." She paused. "And that's no excuse either. You must think I'm dumb."

Charlie Bannion closed his notebook. "Not dumb. A little on the eager side, I guess, but not dumb. Anyhow, like I said, all this is just routine." He paused, looking round the apartment. "It sounds to me like Zanzibar's just protecting his image of mystery. When you're in his racket, you need all the gimmicks you can lay your hands on. You really need an *image*—"

"Sometimes I think he's all image. Sometimes I think he's going to vanish inside that black coat he wears and there'll be nothing left behind."

Charlie Bannion sighed. He started to move toward the door, where he paused. His smile was firm and honest. It wasn't the kind of face that could hide anything easily.

"Maybe when these kids are found and safely home tucked up in bed, you and I can go out some night to dinner. They do a good trout dish over at the Crawford. You ever been there?"

"I'd like that," she said. "I've never been to the Crawford." Or anywhere else, she thought. Her life had become as self-contained as an unpeeled grapefruit: work and apartment, nothing between.

"I'll keep in touch," the cop said.

"Please." She saw him to the door. "And please keep me posted about those two kids."

"Don't worry."

Charlie Bannion stepped out on to the landing.

He watched her close the door with a tiny gesture of an upraised hand. He stood motionless for a time at the top of the stairs. A small smile went across his lips and he felt . . . *sly*.

Actually, George Cheney hadn't sent him to see Ellis Diamond at all. It was what was known as *initiative*. And a little more. Call it curiosity. Call it a quietly brooding lust that had been nagging at him ever since he'd gone to the Youth Center.

What the hell, he had picked up some information that might be useful somewhere along the way because George Cheney would get round to this Zanzibar character sooner or later.

Probably sooner, if he knew the Sheriff at all. George Cheney was not fond of mysteries, especially those that affected the tranquil operations of his domain.

He patted the pocket containing his notebook. He felt more than slightly pleased with himself. *Two birds, one stone. Way to go.*

A click from the dark spaces overhead made him look up. Somebody moved there briefly.

A cat issued a quick horrible scream. There was a scuffling sound and a door was closed very quietly.

THE PIPER

Inquisitive neighbors, Charlie Bannion thought.
Hamland was full of them.

She was sitting on the porch and listening to the rain fall out there in the black canyon when she saw the lights of Zanzibar's Packard coming along the dirt road.

She rose and went inside the house. Earlier, she had tried to light a fire, but the kindling was damp and wouldn't catch and now only a dense smoke rose from the grate into the chimney. Look, Zanzibar, it's been fine, but the time has come to take a hike . . . No hard feelings? She shivered. Could she really tell Zanzibar that this dump gave her the creeps? that she wanted to go without complications? that she no longer liked living here with him?

It occurred to her suddenly that he wouldn't be nice about it. He wouldn't want her to go.

Not now.

She heard Zanzibar in the hallway.

What you do, Zena, is be nice to the man. You smile at him. You sleep with him. You go on as if nothing was wrong. Then, next time he's in town, you get your shit together and you walk until you hit a highway and you hitch the first goddam ride you can get.

She saw him in the doorway. A lock of black hair hung down on his high forehead. His long coat almost brushed the floor. Blackness, everything was blackness with Zanzibar, everything was an absence of light.

When she greeted him, her voice was thin. "Hi."

Zanzibar stepped inside the room. He had his black leather bag in one hand and suddenly he reminded her of a young mortician come to do an embalming. She thought of her blood being drained away and of formaldehyde filling the empty veins.

He stepped toward her, looking this way and that around the room as he moved.

He went to the telephone, making an abrupt change of direction. Does he know? she wondered. How could he possibly know that she'd tried to use the instrument before?

She had the impression of omniscience about him. He knew things and you couldn't understand how he managed to

know, but then she remembered the way he had with
gadgetry, the way he could build things and connect tangles
of wires with those long amazing fingers of his—and all at
once she was assailed by the idea that whenever she was here
alone she was being photographed by hidden cameras, her
voice and movements captured on concealed tapes.

He looked at the telephone, then smiled, turning his face to
her. For a long time he didn't move. He simply stood there,
watching her. She saw it in his eyes: *he knew she'd tried to use
the telephone.* Probably he even knew the number she'd tried
to call. Even that.

She said, "I wanted to talk to my mother . . ."

Zanzibar dropped his bag on the floor, left the room, stood
a moment in the hallway looking up the stairway, and then
came back. He snapped his leather bag open and dipped one
hand inside among the playing-cards and the silks and the
coins he used to teach kids magic tricks. He took out a small
plastic envelope that contained a white powder, and he held
this up where she could see it.

"For me?" she asked. "A present for me?"

She watched the little envelope as he shifted it from one
hand to the other. Don't spill it, she thought. Dear Christ,
don't spill it. Back again, left hand to right, right to left.

"Quit teasing me," she said. "I hate being teased when it's
something as serious as dope."

She moved toward him, watching the envelope go from one
hand to the other, quick, then quicker still.

Why doesn't he just give me the goddam stuff? Why play
these asshole games?

She put her hand out to catch the envelope but Zanzibar
was too quick for her, stretching his arm away, folding his
fingers around the drugs. His free hand went between the
folds of her kimono and she felt his icy palm close around her
left breast.

She held her breath. Then she said, "Either you give me
the shit or you don't, I don't care one way or another, it's
nothing to me. I'm over that particular nasty little habit."

She stared into his eyes. There was flint in there, a pitiless
knowing quality because he could see straight into the heart
of her. She shut her eyes and tried to withdraw, tried to find

some private head-room where she could float away from the drug, from Zanzibar, from this mad house and everything in it.

Zanzibar was never going to be the same guy who had rescued her from mad Maxie back in Laughlin. You might as well face it. He was never going to go back to being kind and considerate and sweet. Maybe he'd never been like that anyway. How could she be sure? She'd been pretty fucked-up in her head back in Laughlin.

Write this one off, Zena. Write Zanzi off like all the other clowns you imagined you loved. Then try to grow up a little. Why had Zanzibar dragged you here in the first place anyhow? Because he wanted a cheap assistant, somebody he wouldn't have to pay? Because he needed a piece of ass on the side?

She bit hard on her lower lip. She could feel his fingertips on her nipple. She tried to ascend, reaching up inside her own mind, into high, dark realms where she wouldn't have to deal with any of this. Make a plan, she thought. Make a plan to get away from this dump, to just get the hell out of here before you're too involved in whatever it is Zanzibar is doing in the upper rooms of this house—plan, plan, plan, anything.

His hand fell away from her breast now, the palm flat against her stomach. She didn't open her eyes. She felt his fingers move down to her inner thigh, soft stroking.

She looked at him and said, "The dope, Zanzi. What about the dope?"

He took a step back from her. The appealing little envelope lay in the palm of his left hand.

Don't, she thought.

Please don't fuck around with it.

But you're going to, aren't you, Zanzi? You're going to screw around with it anyhow and it doesn't matter a damn what I say.

She watched, her eyes wide, as he switched the envelope from one hand to the other.

Or so it seemed.

So it only seemed.

Because somewhere in midair it disappeared entirely, vanishing inside Zanzibar's world where everything was drawn down and down into that place where no light fell and no air entered, where there was only emptiness and secrets you couldn't fathom and things that never returned once they had been made to go away.

He turned away from her now.

She watched him go to the telephone and pick it up. He held the receiver in the air for a second.

Make that vanish too, Zanzibar.

Make everything disappear.

Make me disappear too.

He let the receiver fall and it clattered back in place.

Then he turned and strode out of the room and after a moment, she could hear him go up the stairs.

She understood now. It had been a punishment for trying to make a phone call. The little envelope of dope, the hand on the body, the fingers between the legs, the vanishing act—all this had been a punishment.

She went to the foot of the stairs.

From above came the sound of a high-speed electric drill, a harsh grinding noise that made her want to scream. Start. Stop. Start again. She imagined the drill bit piercing wood and fine sawdusty fibers filling the air around Zanzibar's hands.

He was constructing something.

Something he'd told her once would be part of his greatest illusion of all.

After a while the strong scent of melted wax floated out of the upper part of the house, sickening her. Air, she thought. She needed air more than anything else.

Whenever he encountered a blank in his memory, Arthur Rigley was inclined to panic. Although he was accustomed to them, just the same he never felt entirely at ease with the inconveniences of these lapses and he supposed he never would. In one way, he was like the drunk who suffers blackouts and who can't remember his behavior from the night before or how he managed to drive his car home.

He held the cat—which he had punished severely a moment ago by squeezing one of its paws because the animal had taken the liberty of scratching his arm—and carried it to the armchair in front of the electric-fire.

He tried to relax. He breathed very deeply and noisily.

The cat squirmed in his grip and he rapped his knuckles on its skull. Ungrateful creature, he thought.

The thing that was troubling him surfaced again. He couldn't begin to relax. He rose, still carrying the struggling cat—which was gasping now—and went inside the bathroom.

There he swallowed one of his pills. He looked at himself in the mirror. There was a flaw in the glass and his face appeared slightly distorted.

He walked back into his living-room.

He could not for the life of him recall how he had come in possession of the object he had discovered hanging on the small hook on the back of his door. For one thing, it didn't fit him. For another, there was no reason on the entire face of the planet why he should purchase such a thing.

Perhaps he found it.

Perhaps that was it.

Stumbled across it somewhere.

He went to the door now and gazed at the object.

Reaching out, he took it down. He turned it round and round in one hand.

I just don't remember, he thought.

He hung it back on the hook and walked across the room and turned to regard the object another time.

It was a child's yellow baseball cap.

It had the words HAMLAND TIGERS written across it in maroon letters.

NINE

⦁————————————————————⦁

As HE DROVE THE DARK WET STREETS OF HAMLAND, A TOWN
boxed in by walls of rain like some fortress withstanding an
assault, George Cheney wondered why he was satisfied with
this place.

The answer to his question lay, he assumed, in his emotional makeup. It was as if somebody had given him a kit at birth
and said to him *Here, George Cheney, these are your attri-
butes. Loyalty. Honesty. A certain intelligence. A dash of
persistence. Some stamina. This kit, however, contains no
ambition at all . . .*

It was more than that, though.

It was as if he were paralyzed by a sense of place, as if this
small town and his own personality had somehow become
welded together so seamlessly he couldn't imagine one without the other. Some men dreamed ambitious dreams. George
Cheney dreamed less aggressive things, smaller things. He
dreamed his boyhood and his adolescence and these memories were so connected to Hamland and the countryside
around it that sometimes it seemed to him his life couldn't
ever be lived elsewhere.

Now, as he stepped out of the car and looked toward the

Searses' home where Courtney Sears stood under the porch-light, he felt a sense of fragmentation, an uncomfortable fracture: his dreams had taken on an edge of nightmare, and his peace had been eroded, and something in Hamland had changed around him without his noticing it.

He moved up on to the porch. Courtney Sears, who seemed diminished, shrunken in some way, looked at him sadly. She wore a heavy plaid jacket a size too large for her and she had her hands way down deep in the pockets. George Cheney wanted to hug this little woman and tell her how everything was going to be just fine. Even more, he wanted to surprise her, he wanted to bring her Tommy gift-wrapped. He wanted to say *Here he is, here's the wandering boy, now go on with your lives . . .*

"Tell me about the call," he said. "You're absolutely sure it was Tommy's voice?"

The woman nodded. It was a small gesture of certainty: a mother couldn't ever mistake her own son's voice.

"And all he said was Mom?"

"That's all, Sheriff. One word."

She broke down and wept into her hands a moment, then she raised her face and sniffed. "I'm sorry, Sheriff. I just don't understand. I don't understand why he'd call and say only one word and hang up. He could have told me where he was or that he was fine. But just one word . . . It was cruel, and Tommy's not a cruel boy."

Cheney put one hand on Courtney Sears's shoulder and she lifted up her face, smiling sadly at him. She asked, "I don't suppose there's anything new? There can't be, otherwise you'd have told me . . ."

There's nothing new, Cheney thought, and peered into the dark rain. There were times in Hamland when it would rain for days on end. "Do you know a girl called Vickie Estaban?" he asked.

"I don't think so. Why?"

Cheney told her.

She said, "And you think there could be a connection?"

"It's possible. I don't like coincidences, Courtney. They always have this strange smell to them."

Courtney Sears thought a moment. She was running names

through her mind, scanning them, looking for associations, half-remembered links, anything that would bring light to her dark little corner. "Tommy never mentioned the girl to me. At least I don't think he did."

The door swung open and Thomas Sears half-stumbled out under the light. He rubbed his eyes with the big paws of his hands. Then he looked at Cheney and said, "You think he's been kidnapped, Sheriff? You think the next time that phone rings there's gonna be a ransom demand, something like that?"

Cheney shook his head. "Nobody's said anything about kidnapping, Tom. Who'd want to kidnap Tommy?"

"Listen, I got seven hundred and eighty bucks in Hamland Savings and Loan. There's another five hundred in bonds someplace. That's a grand total of twelve hundred and eighty. If somebody took Tommy for ransom, they're not exactly going to stumble into a fucking bonanza."

The man was trying, Cheney knew, to make light of it. But his voice was thick. Cheney said nothing for a time.

A phone call. One small word. Nothing else. Why would young Tommy Sears do a thing like that? Unless it hadn't been *Tommy* at all, but somebody else—another kid playing a particularly malicious joke on the Searses, calling up and pretending to be Tommy, which was something Courtney Sears, in her present frame of mind, might fall for all the way. She desperately wanted it to be her son's voice: so it was. He didn't have the heart to say any of this aloud to the Searses.

Courtney Sears looked at her husband. "The Sheriff says there's another kid missing. A girl called Vickie Estaban."

Thomas Sears said, "Estaban?"

His wife nodded. "That name mean anything to you, Tom?"

Sears reached for the porch-rail. As his face passed directly under the light, Cheney could see the papery paleness of the man's skin and the way a small pulse ticked beneath his right eye.

"Vickie Estaban," the fat man said. He ran the cuff of his sleeve across his lips. He stared off into the rain and said nothing for a time. Then, "Hugh Estaban's daughter?"

136

"Right," Cheney said. "You know the girl?"

Sears moved one hand dismissively. "No," he answered.

"But you know Hugh?"

Sears didn't look at the Sheriff now. "I haven't seen Hugh in a while. Christ, it must be a couple of years. Used to do taxes, didn't he?"

Cheney said he thought he still did.

Thomas Sears moved back from the porch-rail and lowered himself into a chair where he sat silent for a time, his eyes fixed to the floor.

"Were you and he friends, Tom?"

"Nothing like that," Sears said, raising his face now. "Passing acquaintances, I guess. You know how it is."

George Cheney said, "Yeah," but there was something else here, a center to all this he couldn't quite locate, just something that bleeped on the edge of his own radar and then passed out of the screen again. It was inscribed in Thomas Sears's manner, the tone of his voice, the small light that went in and out of his eyes, as if he were tracking a memory but letting it go because he didn't want it.

Hugh Estaban, Cheney thought, had flickered in a way similar to this when he'd heard the name of Tommy Sears. What went across Cheney's mind now was the notion that somewhere in the past Hugh Estaban and Thomas Sears Senior had had some kind of disagreement, something that lay tainted between them.

"Tell me about this passing acquaintance, Tom," he said.

"What's to tell, Sheriff? I knew the guy vaguely because one time I was thinking of getting him to do my tax returns, but after I spoke with him I changed my mind."

"Why?"

"He didn't seem interested in bush-league clients. Guys like me. That's all. That's it. He was interested in bigger fish."

Cheney looked a moment at Courtney Sears.

She said, "You never mentioned this man to me, Tom."

"Was it important?" Sears stared at his wife.

"I guess not," the woman said. "I guess it wasn't important."

"Anyhow, it's got nothing to do with Tommy," Sears said. He got up out of the chair, shaking his head from side to side, inflating his fat cheeks and expelling air through a funnel he made of his lips.

Cheney had the distinct impression of invisible pressures bearing down on the man. Somewhere in the past Hugh Estaban had rubbed Thomas Sears the wrong way—was that all there was to it? Hamland, he thought: it was a town of half-forgotten grudges, old sorrows, buried resentments, and in that sense it was like any small town anywhere. Perhaps Sears had never forgotten the way he'd been brushed off by Estaban. Perhaps Sears, taking all his tax papers to Hugh Estaban, had seen something in the accountant he didn't want to see—the successful CPA disdainfully leafing through the short-order cook's piddling receipts and turning them aside with a smile of barely concealed contempt. And maybe Thomas Sears, who was nothing more significant than the guy turning strips of bacon and scrambling eggs in the Royal Hotel, had seen his own lowly station reflected in Hugh Estaban's face.

When you were a failure in a small town, you always failed in a big way.

Cheney moved to the edge of the porch. The wet night pressed against him. Out there in the darkness this rain would be filling the washes and causing streams to overflow their banks and turning the earth into a quagmire. He wondered briefly if it was raining in the place where Danny was camped. A sound, a sensation, out of his own childhood: the beauty of rainwater dripping on canvas and the feeling you got that you were safe and warm as long as your tent held.

He turned to look at the Searses.

"If he calls again, I want to know about it immediately. It doesn't matter what time it is. Day or night, you know where you can reach me."

The couple nodded their heads. They reminded him of two birds incongruously locked together in a cage that was too large for one, too small for the other.

"I'll be in touch."

He went in the direction of his car. He felt curiously tiny all at once, engulfed by the vast noisy secrecy of the night around him.

Victoria Estaban had cried almost ceaselessly on the day she was born and through many long, long nights after that. Hugh Estaban had walked up and down the floors of his house with the small screaming bundle wrapped in his arms, trying to restrain his temper, trying to resist the nervous urge he had to stifle his offspring with a cushion.

Now, as he sat on the edge of his daughter's narrow bed, Estaban blinked at the dark window and remembered how Victoria had stopped crying around the age of two because she had come to recognize that small battles could be won by stubborn silences, that you didn't have to waste energy screaming your lungs out. And so she had gone through childhood, exercising her will fiercely by withdrawing—when it was necessary—into the sullen depths of herself. There she would remain until Hugh had yielded whatever point she was trying to win.

He rose, touched the books that lay on the bedside table, moved to the window.

He put one hand up to the glass. It was cold.

Beneath Vickie's pretty surface, there was a steely core. Even the way she went in pursuit of each new interest was one of relentless determination: she had devoured almost every book Hamland Public Library owned on the subject of psychic phenomena. When her latest interest—conjuring— had come along, she'd shut herself inside her room practicing card tricks hour after hour: she'd die before she admitted failure. Hugh felt sorry for any man she might set her sights on. He was going to get his balls busted.

He went out of the bedroom and down the three short steps into the conversation pit. Liz looked at him, her large dark eyes moist.

"I keep seeing pictures of her out there in this weather. I keep seeing her with the rain in her face and her clothes soaked through and then I hear her coughing and the sound of her sniffing, and she's shivering, Hugh, she's shivering and miserable and hopeless . . ." Liz Estaban paused. She did something unexpected then. She removed Hugh's cigarette from between his fingers and took a quick brutal puff from it before replacing it.

"First time in almost ten years," she said.

Hugh nodded. Once, she'd had a two packs a day habit, which she'd kicked finally through five awful days of withdrawal symptoms, but she'd been determined, taking to bed and chewing gum and pulling the blankets up over her head.

Liz stood up now. "I don't feel like sitting. I feel I should be doing something . . . only I can't think what. I can't think what I should do. Then I have these other feelings. Like the telephone is going to ring and it's going to be news I can't stand to hear, Hugh."

He reached forward and caught her by the wrists. "You can't do anything but wait."

"I hate waiting. I was never good at waiting. You know that." Liz stepped away from her husband, roaming the conversation pit. "How come you're so calm, Hugh? How do you manage that?"

"Calm?" He smiled at his wife. "I only look that way. Cut me open and I'd bleed Jello. I'm not calm, Liz. It's my front." He rose now and went to his wife and put his arms around her and said, "Vickie's strong, Liz. You raised a tiger there. I know . . . I *know* there's got to be some really logical reason for all this."

Liz didn't speak. She was breathing heavily, her face pressed against her husband's chest. What Hugh Estaban suddenly thought about as he held his wife close to him was something that hadn't occurred to him in years, something that caused him a flicker of pain, something that lay buried in their marriage like the corpse of a relative whose name was too shameful ever to mention: it was the recollection of the time, two years before Victoria's birth in the first year of their marriage when Estaban—in a crazed drunken mood, when an animal had been set loose in his brain—had systematically tried to tear this house apart: he remembered very little of it now, a confusion of destructive rage, a chaos of broken objects flying through space, shattered dishes, glasses, bottles, overturned tables and chairs, a sofa to which he had taken a carving knife, a whole room filled with razored pieces of foam, shards of glass from broken windows. He remembered Liz running after him through the rooms of his house as if she might stem this unexpected spate of destructiveness. He recalled her white face and the horror in her eyes and something else came back to him now: *it was the terrifying idea he'd had at the time of killing his own wife in the midst of all the other destruction.* It was something she must have read in his face because she'd locked herself in the bathroom, sitting with her back to the door and sobbing hour after hour. Perfect madness released: insanity unfettered.

Hugh Estaban, holding his wife, shut his eyes. When he brought this distressing incident back to mind, he tried to think of it in terms of a newspaper headline describing the behavior of another person. *Young Accountant Goes Berserk. No Reason Given.* But when he brought the memory up close, when he examined it carefully, what scared him was the idea that something dark and uncontrollable existed inside, an entity he didn't know, didn't recognize, a monster liberated by alcohol. It was as if his personality were a large house where, in one locked attic room, a violent creature separate from himself paced back and forth restlessly. An amorphous thing, a gargoyle imprisoned in his own brain.

If alcohol undid the traps and chains, the easy answer was never to drink again. And for a year after the bewildering incident that's what he'd done. One sober year.

And then, on a fine summer night twelve months after he'd tried to demolish his own home, he'd gotten drunk again . . .

Hugh Estaban opened his eyes. *It was dead. It was all a long time dead. He hadn't touched alcohol in fifteen years. He'd killed the monster.*

Liz freed herself from his arms and went to the telephone. "I had an idea," she said. "I should call this woman—"

"Which woman?"

"Mrs Sears—"

"Mrs Sears. Whatever for?"

"You know, mutual support."

Hugh shook his head. He could feel a faint film of perspiration begin in his armpits. "Mutual support," he said. "I don't think so, Liz."

"Why not? We're in the same boat. We've both got kids missing, haven't we? Maybe we can help each other—"

Hugh shook his head even more aggressively. "All you'd do is multiply the misery by calling her. That's all you'd achieve, Liz."

He reached out and took the receiver from her hand and set it back in place. He went down on his knees beside her and held both her hands between his own.

"I thought it was a good idea," she said. "You know, somebody to talk to, somebody who understands, I thought maybe we could give each other some courage, Hugh."

She stared at him.

Her hands went up to her face. It was only an enormous effort of will that prevented her from breaking down and crying. She made a tiny choking noise at the back of her throat.

He went back to the long white sofa and sat down, lighting another cigarette. He gazed a moment at the telephone.

Courtney Sears, he thought.

Mrs Thomas Sears.

He backed away from the thought of the name like a frightened horse balking at a hurdle. He imagined he heard hoofbeats pound in the distance. And then he felt pain in the center of his chest, a closed fist between his ribs.

Liz said, "Don't cry, Hugh. I couldn't take it if *you* cried."

"Was I crying?" He looked at her, aware of how blurry the room had become. "I wasn't conscious of it."

"Two small tears," she said.

And now it was her turn to hold him as fiercely as he'd held her a moment before. He wasn't sure if he was crying because of the monster that inhabited him or whether his tears were for his lost daughter.

In his office, George Cheney gazed out of the window at the Matterhorn Motor Lodge across the way. A red neon VACANCY sign hung in the rain, the letters flickering. He watched them a moment, then turned to Charlie Bannion, who was standing by the doorway. Little pools of liquid had gathered around Bannion and these shone in the stark fluorescent light of the room.

"She's probably broken a couple of state laws," Cheney said. "And she's probably flouted some kind of federal guidelines. I'd say she acted out of enthusiasm more than any urge to falsify."

"Ellis Diamond's not the type to falsify," Bannion said, a little too defensively. Then, "At least, she gives me the impression of honesty, George. If she employed Zanzibar and this girl of his without sufficient documentation, she was being over-zealous, nothing more."

Cheney sat up on the edge of his desk. Staring up at him from a transparent plastic envelope was the face of Victoria Estaban. It was a school photograph, similar to the one of Tommy Sears. Cheney picked it up. The girl had a good face, a cheerleader's face, and what he remembered as he looked at it was the way he'd lusted after the cheerleaders of Hamland High when he'd been a student there. He put the photograph down alongside a list of names the Estabans had compiled. These were Victoria's friends. It was a long list and Cheney felt exhausted just gazing at it.

He set it down on top of the picture and said, "It doesn't matter how honest she is, Charlie. The point is, she's employed somebody she doesn't know anything about. And she's set this person loose among kids. It would bother me at the best of times and these, Charlie, are not the best of times."

"Well," Bannion said. "She knows she's blundered."

Cheney looked at the young cop. It surprised him a little to think of Charlie Bannion going to Ellis Diamond's apartment. What had been the real motivation for that? Was Charlie harboring notions of a horny nature?

"Blundered is right," he said. "It leaves us with the mystery of Mr Zanzibar and his female companion. Who are they? Where did they come from? What the hell brought them to Hamland of all places? Too many questions, Charlie. I get a headache."

Bannion shifted around uneasily. He squinted at his wrist-watch a second and a slick of rainwater slithered from his wrist to the floor.

Cheney was on the edge of saying something about taking a drive up to Gowrie Canyon where Zanzibar lived in the old

Burford house, when he heard a sound from the corridor and saw a shadow fall across the doorway.

The man who stepped inside the room was Richard P. Bacon, the Mayor of Hamland. He had a heavy black coat slung over his shoulders and the sleeves flapped loosely at his sides. His hair, which was dark and greasy, lay covered with little globules of rain that couldn't penetrate the oil he used. He was about five foot two inches tall and somewhat overweight and he waddled when he moved. He always gave Cheney the impression of a tub of margarine that had somehow acquired locomotion.

Richard P. Bacon took a newspaper from his pocket and thrust it into Cheney's hand.

"Tomorrow's paper, George," he said in his strange throaty voice, which suggested very old Parmesan cheese being rubbed against a grater. "Tomorrow's *Progressive*, George. Read it. Interesting. Engrossing."

Cheney looked at the Mayor a second. He remembered how Bacon's political opponents had made jokes out of Bacon's last name and its similarity to the name of the town itself. Since all politics seemed a huge joke to Cheney, he considered it only appropriate that Hamland had found itself a Mayor with a porcine name.

"Read, George," Bacon said. "Front page."

Cheney opened the newspaper, smoothing it out.

The headline came off the page at him.

HAVE YOU SEEN THESE CHILDREN?

Beneath the headline were photographs of Tommy Sears and Victoria Estaban. The story was attributed to Ronald Kelly. Cheney saw the print squirm away from him as he stared at it. Bacon was looking at him grimly, his pugnacious little jaw set forward.

"This hits the streets in the morning, George," Bacon said. "Nice stuff for people at breakfast. The kind of thing that makes folks feel safe about raising their kids in this town. So what's the story, George? These kids been abducted or what? Runaways?"

Cheney gazed at the faces of the two kids. "Ron Kelly has been doing his homework," he said, his voice dry. The faces that looked out at him from the newspaper had innocently smiling expressions. He wondered how Kelly had managed to get a hold of the photographs. Inscrutable journalistic sources, he thought.

He scanned the article, which was an accurate documentation of the times the kids had disappeared. In both cases, Kelly had written brief descriptions of what the kids had last been seen wearing. There was no mention of the reporter having talked to either set of parents, so presumably he hadn't done so. But in a town the size of Hamland he wouldn't have to—information eddied from mouth to mouth, house to house, store to store, ruthless and reliable and efficient, right down to such small details as Vickie Estaban's yellow shirt and Tommy Sears's brown flannel one.

"Well, George? I'm waiting." Richard P. Bacon, empty coat sleeves flapping, strode up and down the office. "How the hell can two kids disappear in a town like Hamland?"

"We're working on that, Richard," Cheney answered.

"A word like *working* doesn't tell me anything, George. A word like *working* is about as useful as a hog at a vegetarian cook-out."

Cheney spread his hands and glanced at Charlie Bannion. "We don't have any leads."

Richard P. Bacon stepped to the window and blinked in the direction of the Matterhorn Motor Lodge. He flattened the palm of a hand against the glass. He suddenly reminded Cheney of some small-town Napoleon, scrutinizing the horizon for new victories. "You can't give me anything. Is that what I'm hearing, George? When my phone rings off the wall I'm supposed to tell people I don't know anything about these kids, right?"

Cheney nodded. "You'll be the first to know when a break comes, Rich. I promise you that."

"Yeah," Richard P. Bacon said. "Meantime, I stonewall."

"Right."

The Mayor sighed and said, "I don't like this situation, George. One thing I promised when I won the election was that I'd bring new industry to this town, I went out on a limb saying that. As it happens, I got the interest of a couple of companies, nothing's signed—but these guys are looking for cheap space, some tax breaks, and available housing for their personnel in a pleasant small-town atmosphere. You get my drift? Jesus Christ, these companies want their employees to bring their kids to a place that hasn't heard of urban blight and mugging and armed robbery."

The Mayor had the newspaper in his hand now and was waving it in the air. Cheney studied the guy a moment. There was a demented edge to Bacon, a slight flush of hysteria. Cheney had seen it during last year's mayoral campaign, when all Bacon's speeches were infused with lethal injections of effervescence and bombast.

"I hope you can clear this up, George. I really hope you can get some kind of handle on this before it becomes more than a little damaging," the Mayor said. He thwacked the rolled-up paper against his thigh like a riding crop.

Damaging, Cheney thought. The kind of damage Richard P. Bacon was thinking about was to his own reputation, to the promises he might have made in the heat of a political campaign. He wasn't thinking about two missing kids because that wasn't the way his mind worked. He was defined by one notion only: the chances of re-election. Cheney, who rated all politicians in a category just above that of those criminals who steal purses from blind old ladies, turned away from Bacon and picked up the list of Vickie Estaban's friends. Maybe, if he simply pretended that Bacon wasn't in the office, the guy would go away.

The Mayor moved to the doorway, where he took an aluminum cigar-tube from his coat pocket. He removed the cigar, tossed the band aside, stuck the thing in his mouth and lit it. For a moment his yellow face vanished in blue smoke. He said, "I mean, this town is a place where people feel safe. Christ, they've always felt safe here, you know that. You grew up here, George, so you should know that better than anybody."

Cheney nodded, but said nothing. He had a tight feeling in his stomach, a sharp little knot. *You grew up here, George*

. . . *so you should know*. The trouble is, Mr Mayor, I don't know. I don't know where the hell those kids are. I don't know how to find them. I don't know how to track them down. And maybe this place *is* changing and I'm too goddam blind or too goddam nostalgic to see it.

Bacon moved out into the hallway. He was still rapping the rolled-up *Progressive* against his leg.

"Find them, George. Find those kids."

"I will," Cheney answered.

"I'm counting on you. Don't forget that." Bacon went down the hallway a little way. He stopped, turned around, called back aloud: "I want people to know they can feel safe in Hamland. I want them to know they can raise their kids here with peace of mind. I want them to feel they're a part of the growth and prosperity of this town."

Rah-rah-rah, Cheney thought.

Bacon waved the newspaper, then he was gone, his footsteps quick and nervy as he vanished along the corridor. Cheney listened to the outer doors swing shut, then he stared at Charlie Bannion.

"Don't look at me, George. I didn't vote for the guy," Bannion remarked. "Did you?"

"What do you think?" Cheney asked.

"I didn't vote for the other guy either," Bannion added. "It was asshole against asshole and too much of a predicament for me. So I didn't vote at all."

Cheney stifled a yawn. "I want you to check this list out for me, Charlie. These are Victoria Estaban's friends."

Bannion looked at the list, then at his watch. "It's ten o'clock, George. You want me to get to this right now?"

"Listen, don't you want to help make Hamland a safe place, Charlie? Don't you want to play a part in Richard P. Bacon's dreams of glory? Don't you want to share in all this growth and prosperity?"

"Sure, sure," Bannion answered, tucking the paper in his pocket. "I want to be in on all that good stuff."

Cheney picked up his car keys from the desk. He rattled them a moment in the palm of one hand before he said, "I'm going out to Gowrie Canyon."

Bannion stepped into the hallway. He peered down the dark length of it toward the front door. "The roads out that way are going to be pretty damn bad in this rain. You sure you want to do it tonight?"

"Yeah, I'm sure," Cheney answered.

When he was sure that Liz was fast asleep, when he was absolutely certain the ten milligrams of Valium he had insisted she take had edged her over into a comfortable darkness, Hugh Estaban went into the living-room and picked up the telephone, holding the receiver uncertainly in his hand. He sat motionless, his appearance that of a man who has wrestled a long time with a problem and who is still perplexed.

He set the receiver down. He got up, wandered around the room, drew the curtain back from the window, gazed out at the black rain. He lit a cigarette, placed it in an ashtray, forgot all about it and promptly lit a fresh one.

Then he walked back to the phone.

Once again, he picked up the receiver and held it to his ear, but when he heard the dial tone he replaced the thing.

You can't do this, he thought.

He smoked for a while, listened to the rain, wondered about the night, tried to picture his daughter out there in that awesome darkness—but no images came to him.

He picked up the receiver again and—with a long sigh—checked the Hamland directory before punching out the number he wanted.

The voice that answered was abrupt and hoarse. "Yeah?"

Hugh Estaban hesitated. It was a moment of choice, only he couldn't choose because his mind emptied like water rushing into a drain. He couldn't think what to say.

"Who is this?" the voice demanded.

Estaban crushed out his cigarette and whispered, "Tom?"

"Yeah, this is Tom Sears. Who am I talking to?"

"Hugh."

A pause. A silence.

"Estaban?" Sears asked.

"I heard about your son," Estaban said.

Another pause. A darkness in Estaban's brain.

Thomas Sears said, "Your daughter's gone too."

"Late last night," Estaban said.

"It's got to be a coincidence, Hugh. What the hell else can it be?"

"That's what I keep asking myself. And that's what I keep failing to answer."

"It couldn't be anything else. How could it?"

Hugh Estaban looked across the room. A vague noise had captured his attention, something that wasn't the rain beating against shrubbery or the wind harping through trees. It came from just outside the house: it was a solid noise, like something brushing against the outer wall.

A cat, he thought. A stray dog.

"Listen. Listen, Hugh. If you start thinking there's a connection here, if you start thinking along those lines, then you're out of your mind! And don't call me again, okay?"

Thomas Sears hung up abruptly. Estaban held the receiver for a while before he set it back in place. He rose, walked to the window, flipped the curtain back.

Nothing. There was nothing out there.

He pressed his face to the glass.

He heard his daughter's voice.

It floated down the hallway from the open door of her bedroom. He listened a moment then turned, hurrying in the direction of the sound.

Vickie, he thought. *Vickie* . . .

Outside the door of her room he paused.

For a second he didn't want to go inside, didn't want this sudden sense of gladness to evaporate, didn't want his expectations destroyed.

But it was *her* voice.

It was *unmistakably* his daughter's voice.

Vickie. Vickie . . .

He stepped into the room.

The curtains, blown by wind and rain, flapped back and forth at the open window, great pink sheets of light that seemed to explode in front of Estaban's eyes even as he looked.

THE PIPER

He looked round the room, shivering in the chill damp blast coming in out of the darkness.

He heard Vickie's voice again.

She was saying, *Over here, Daddy. I'm over here* . . .

Hugh Estaban turned round.

TEN

RICK DOVE BROKE THINGS. YESTERDAY IT HAD BEEN A SMALL porcelain doll belonging to his sister Jenny which caused no end of grief. Two days ago he'd accidentally dropped a plate containing mashed potatoes and Salisbury steak on the kitchen floor, a royal mess. Last week, when his father had told him to wash the car—in that really cold voice his Dad often used—he'd somehow managed to scrape paint from a door panel, which meant his allowance had gone down the toilet for the next month.

Sometimes, his own clumsiness filled him with despair. He saw his life stretching in front of him as one long sequence of broken objects. He imagined his future wife forever bitching at him, *Can't you get anything right without breaking things all the time?* Some kids had a kind of natural grace. His friend, Danny Cheney, for example, hardly ever broke things. And his little sister, Miss Goody-Goody, never had accidents. Rick imagined there was a spiteful God in the sky frowning down on him and saying *Hey, what can we get this kid to break next? Let's really DUMP on the little chump.*

Rick tossed playing-cards into an old hat of his Dad's,

which he had upturned on the floor of his bedroom. He had a vague idea that if he could learn to control cards, then it might somehow help cure his clumsiness in general. He watched a Jack of Spades hit the brim of the hat and then slither into the crown where it lay among the other cards he'd managed to get inside. He figured he scored one out of three hits, which wasn't exactly terrific, but it was some kind of start along the road to grace.

The door of his room opened and his father looked inside. Rick glanced at the man and then went back to tossing cards. He always felt nervous under his father's stare.

"Bedtime," his father said.

"Yeah."

"Lights out."

Rick lay back across the bed, drawing a blanket over himself. One day his Dad would actually give him a goodnight kiss and hell would freeze over, Rick thought. Some fathers were pretty physical—Danny Cheney's Dad was always hugging him, for example—but Fred Dove had a whole different attitude. No kisses, no hugs, just this general aloofness. Rick shut his eyes, knowing his Mother would come up later to kiss him and make a fuss of tucking him up for the night.

"Goodnight, Rick."

"Night, Dad."

The light went out. Rick stared at the dark curtains. Then he shut his eyes. Later, if he didn't fall asleep first, he'd get out of bed quietly and go on tossing cards into the hat. One day he'd score a perfect fifty-two and that was something he could tell Zanzibar, who had recommended the pitching exercise in the first place as a way of getting *the feel* of the cards.

Zanzibar was nicer to him than his own father. An awful thing to think, maybe, but true.

Zanzibar took time with him. Zanzibar was committed to teaching him something. Zanzibar had promised him he'd overcome his clumsiness if that's what he really wanted to do. That first time, when the magician had come up to him in the bleachers and talked him into joining the magic class, Rick had been reluctant—Christ, if he couldn't carry a dinner plate without breaking it, how could he ever do a simple card trick?

I'll teach you, Zanzibar had said. I'll show you how you can have confidence in yourself. Trust me.

It was the *trust me* that had convinced Rick.

Okay, Rick said. I'll join. Besides, he was secretly flattered he'd been singled out like that.

He sat up in bed, turned on his bedside lamp, picked up a fresh deck. From the edge of his mattress he started to toss cards at the hat.

He hit eight out of the first dozen, his best yet.

He scored seven out of the next twelve.

His total for the whole pack was thirty-six. Nothing to write home about but not bad anyhow. He went across the floor, gathered up all the discarded cards, then turned off the bedside lamp because he was suddenly very sleepy.

He hoped he dreamed.

He never broke anything in his dreams.

It was ten o'clock when Anne Cheney heard the sound of a car turn into the driveway, and her first thought was that George had come home. She went to the window, looked out. She saw Edward Cheney's Studebaker parked there in the rain. The old man stepped out and hurried up the driveway, his head bent against the weather. Anne went to the front door and opened it, and her father-in-law smiled at her as he moved inside the hallway.

She pressed a small kiss to the side of his damp cheek.

"What are you doing out in this weather?" she asked.

She led him into the living-room and made him sit down by the fire, where he spread his hands toward the logs.

"It's crazy driving around in all this," Anne said. She looked fondly at the old man.

Edward Cheney rubbed his hands together. "Are you scolding me?"

"You deserve to be scolded," she said.

"At my age, I don't sleep a whole lot," Edward Cheney said. "And tonight I fancied taking the car for a spin around our fair town . . . Then, when I found myself in this neighborhood, I knew my daughter-in-law would take pity on an old waif like me and force something liquid and warm down my throat."

"What would you like, Dad? Tea? Coffee? Something stronger?"

"Something much stronger, Anne."

She poured him a glass of scotch.

"George out?" he asked.

Anne nodded. "He's looking for those two kids."

"Which two kids?"

"You haven't heard? Tommy Sears. Vickie Estaban."

"Estaban . . .?" Edward Cheney rose from his chair and drained his scotch in one extravagant gesture. "I'd heard about the Sears child. But not the other one . . ."

Anne took the empty glass, refilled it. "This is all you get, Dad. So make it last."

"First you scold me, then you put a limit on my drinking. What's an old man to do?"

His hand trembled as he reached for the fresh drink. Anne thought about him sitting in the coldness of his big empty house over on Montrose and the picture touched her sadly. Once or twice when she'd gone over there to visit, usually in the company of Danny, she'd found Edward Cheney sitting in total darkness, simply staring off into space the way a blind man might. (*Is something wrong with Gramps?* Danny had asked once. *What does he see sitting there in the dark? What is he looking at?*)

George, she knew, didn't go there very often, at least not as often as he might. The only reason he gave was that the house depressed him since his mother had died and he didn't have the heart for it.

Edward Cheney sipped his whisky. "You did say Estaban, didn't you?"

"A girl called Vickie," Anne answered.

"I don't think I know her," the old man said. He moved back to his armchair and gazed quietly into the fire a moment.

"You must have been walking as well as driving," Anne said. "Your shoes are soaked."

"I parked the car. I walked a ways. I confess."

"Why don't you take the shoes off and dry your feet?"

He sighed, bent over, undid the laces.

He slipped his bare feet out of the black shoes.

"Dad, have you ever heard of socks?"

"The term isn't unfamiliar to me—"

"Then why aren't you wearing any?"

"It's called living dangerously."

"I'll lend you a pair of George's before you go." She watched him wiggle his toes before the flames. He had white feet networked with dark blue veins. "It might be thrilling to live on the edge the way you do, Dad, but I'm not sending you home until you put some socks on."

She sat down on the arm of the old man's chair and leaned her head a moment against his shoulder. She had always liked Edward Cheney, right from the very start when she'd first come to Hamland. There was a musty attractiveness about him, a certain whiff of a time that no longer existed.

"Heard from Danny?" he asked.

"He called."

"And?"

"He's having a great time. Sounded kind of grown-up. Mature. He said he'd call again before the camp folded."

"Give him my love," the old man said.

"I always do."

"I mean it. I don't mean empty words. Empty phrases. I'm talking about something else."

Anne moved her face away from her father-in-law's shoulder, a little surprised by the firmness of his tone. "I know what you mean, Dad."

"Danny's important."

"Of course he is."

Edward Cheney pulled his feet back from the flames and sat with his eyes closed for a time. Anne watched his face. There were tiny nerves working just under the surface of the old man's flesh. She wondered what was going through that head right then. Why the sudden insistence in the voice when he spoke about his feelings for Danny?

He opened his eyes, smiled, finished his drink. "When he gets back from this camp, bring him over to see me."

"Sure."

"I've missed him," he said.

"We've all missed him, Dad," and she patted the back of his hand. "I'll get you some socks."

She went upstairs to the bedroom and came back with a

pair of George's socks. Edward Cheney was looking at a framed photograph of his grandson. He stood in the center of the room, the picture tilted toward the lamp on the coffee table. He appeared to be studying it, like someone trying to memorize material for an examination. There was longing on Edward Cheney's face, longing and sadness and concern. Anne felt as if she were intruding here on a special private moment, a communion.

He set the photograph down. "They grow up so fast, Anne."

"Yeah. I've noticed."

"They start to grow outward," he said. "One day, you turn around and they're no longer there, they've gone. It's a final thing. They go. They never come back."

Puzzled, Anne went toward her father-in-law. What was he talking about? What was this maudlin strain in his words?

He went on, "Oh, they come back bodily. They come back and they create some kind of presence. But that's not the same. That's not the same thing at all. Because when they go, they go for good."

Anne touched the old man lightly on the arm. She handed the socks to him. "Good ones," she said. "George is a man of quality and so he insists that his socks be of the best wool. No synthetics in there. No polywhatever. Pure wool." She listened to her own voice, realizing that she was babbling about socks because she wanted to steer Edward Cheney back into a world of tangible items, mundane things, away from the mood the photograph had seemingly imposed on him.

"I'm telling you to enjoy the boy while you can," he said.

"Dad . . . I *understand* that."

Cheney stared at the navy blue socks. He went back to his chair and pulled them over his feet. When he'd finished, he didn't raise his face, he simply went on staring at his feet.

"Is something wrong?" Anne asked. "Has something happened to upset you?"

"This weather oppresses me," he answered.

He drank what remained of his whisky, then rose, setting the empty glass down on the mantelpiece. He looked frail and infirm. She had the impression that only paper stretched across his bones.

"Are you going to be all right?" she asked. "You could stay over tonight if you wanted. You could sleep in Danny's room . . ."

"I'm fine, Anne," he answered.

"You're a poor liar, Dad."

He smiled at her. "On the contrary, I'm a wonderful liar. I've learned the whole craft of lying, my dear. To be a truly good liar, to be a *great* liar, you need more than an inventive mind. You need only one wonderful lie, one amazing lie, and it has to be powerful. Then you create a total fiction to accommodate this single overwhelming fabrication. And you need to believe in this world you've created yourself without ever having a single doubt. It takes single-mindedness. Stamina. Obstinacy. It takes everything you can give it, Anne. Even then, it demands more and more. You've mortgaged yourself to a lie."

She went toward him and touched the back of his hand. He was suddenly lost to her, adrift in his own strange realms. "Stay, Dad. I don't want to think of you driving in all this crap."

"I'll be fine," he answered. He tied his shoelaces. "Bring Danny. You won't forget that."

She shook her head. What was all that stuff about lies? she wondered. What was that all about anyhow? Confused, concerned, she followed him toward the hallway.

"You worry me," she said. "I wish you'd stay."

"Goodnight." He turned, embraced her briefly, kissed her forehead with cold lips. Then he went out to his car, bending his face away from the rain. She watched him get in, saw the car back out of the driveway. She shut the door.

For several moments, she could still hear the sound of the Studebaker's engine turning over. She wondered if perhaps he wasn't going to drive away, if he was sitting out there right at this moment pondering her invitation to stay. The engine had a slight metallic undersound to it, as if something were loose beneath the hood.

She waited.

The Studebaker continued to stutter.

Did the old man have a sudden car problem? Was it something like that which prevented him from driving away?

She opened the door and looked out.

Engulfed by its own exhaust fumes, the old car was parked outside the house next door where Fred and Marge Dove lived. Anne watched for a time, wondering why Edward Cheney had stopped his car right there. She saw the fumes rise into the dark rain where the wind shredded them. Suddenly she had the weird impression of a ghost car with nobody behind the wheel. A vehicle that drove itself—like old tales of horse-drawn coaches thundering through the night with no driver.

The Studebaker didn't move.

What was Edward Cheney doing in there?

She saw him open the door and start to get out of the car, moving in the direction of the Dove house, moving with all the purpose of a hungry man who has been invited to a late-night meal. But then he stopped, turned around as if he'd suddenly changed his mind, and climbed back into the Studebaker.

This time he drove.

This time she saw the old car vanish in smoke and red lights down the street.

She closed the door. Odd behavior.

But then all Edward Cheney's behavior tonight had been odd.

She went toward the kitchen, her hands in the pockets of her jeans for warmth. Senility, she thought. The tragic drift of old age, the blunting of memory, the tiny errors and small confusions. Perhaps Edward was on his way down that terrible road.

The telephone rang. Shrill, echoing.

The washes were running through the canyons. In the far sky a fork of lightning burst through the mass of cloud cover and thunder bickered distantly. George Cheney, driving across the frail bridge that hung over Gilchrist Gulley, blinked as the lightning startled him.

The wind swept at the car. In the full beams of the lights, Cheney could see the track curve and twist ahead of him. He was cold and tired and hungry and now he was questioning the wisdom of this trip to Gowrie Canyon. A little daylight would have helped. He should have waited. *You couldn't wait, though. That touch of fear you felt before, that's what drove you out here. That chill feeling inside you.*

Thunder rolled again, setting up a little chain reaction of echoes that carried down Gilchrist Gulley. Once, freeing itself from clouds, the moon appeared: it was a forlorn old thing up there in the bleak sky, like a smallpoxed face peering down at you. Then it was gone and the clouds darkened everything.

The old Burford house was located halfway up Gowrie Canyon, an isolated stretch of land hemmed in by low hills. Until the early 1970s, the house had been lived in by Walter Burford and his wife Laverne, two Mormons with an enormous number of kids. Then, around 1972, the whole brood had upped and moved themselves to Salt Lake City, and the house had lain empty ever since. Cheney couldn't remember ever hearing of the place being sold or of new tenants moving in—so far as he'd always known the gloomy house sat up here neglected in Gowrie Canyon, still owned by the Burfords. Had Zanzibar rented it? Or had it been purchased from the Burfords?

In front of him the treacherous road twisted sharply. The vehicle bumped and shuddered and then the road became steep, sloping sharply under him in the direction of Gowrie Canyon.

He maneuvered his car carefully now because he could feel the wheels sliding on the slick watery mud. Through the dark, deep in the fold of the land, he saw a pale light from the house. He steered downhill toward it and suddenly the road was submerged in five or six inches of rain, which rose over his tires and slapped at the panels of the car.

He pressed the gas-pedal gently. The big car rolled through the water until it had reached a stretch of track less deeply immersed. When he was ten yards or so from the house, Cheney parked, got out, and walked around Zanzibar's black Packard toward the porch.

He climbed the steps quickly: the rainy wind that blew down the canyon seemed to catch in his throat, making it hard to breathe. When he was under the cover of the roof he realized somebody was watching him from the dark shadows at the far end of the porch. A girl, her face invisible to him, stepped forward a couple of feet.

"Saw your car coming," she said. "Shitty weather."

Cheney looked at her as she moved in front of the light falling from a window. She was in her middle twenties, though it was hard to be sure. She had long black hair and a pale oval of a face and her eyes were little caves created out of eye-shadow. When he saw the face for the first time in the full light, Cheney had the strange fleeting impression of unhappiness—something to do with those eyes, the downward set of lips, the weary way the girl moved.

He introduced himself. The girl took his hand limply in her own for a second.

"I'm Zena," she said. "You like that name?"

She drifted past him to the door. He mumbled something about how it was a pleasant, unusual name, but she seemed not to hear. She was gazing through the screen door into the house, pulling on her lower lip with the tip of one finger. She seemed to be turning something over in her mind, deciding something. For a second she looked reluctant to enter the place.

"What brings you out here?" she asked.

"I wanted to ask a couple of questions."

"They must be very important questions to bring you all the way out here on a night like this," she said.

"They could be," he answered. He moved after her as she pushed the screen door open and stepped into the house. A long hallway led to a flight of stairs. To his right there was a large room, which was where she led him.

"I don't know if I like questions, especially when they come from the law," she said, and she glanced past him toward the stairs, almost as if she were afraid of something now. "You want to ask me or you want to ask Zanzibar?"

"Both."

"I don't know. Sometimes he doesn't speak for days at a time. Sometimes he goes into this silence and he won't come out of it . . ."

Cheney looked round the room. It was filled with all kinds of weird apparatus. He saw a small guillotine. A lacquered

Chinese trunk. Various sets of chains and handcuffs. There were empty birdcages. Bizarrely shaped bottles. Whole sets of brightly-colored canisters. Decks of oversized cards. Oriental screens. A ventriloquist's doll, dressed in tux and striped pants, hung over one of the screens like a limp midget. Cheney felt he had stepped inside a sorcerer's showroom. A room of secrets, illusions, a place where things were not quite as they seemed.

The girl said, "Strange stuff, huh?"

Cheney nodded. "Real strange," he agreed.

He looked at her. In the lamplight she seemed younger than she'd appeared on the porch. She had a very narrow mouth and her lips barely moved when she spoke. There were tense cords in her neck and a suggestion of redness in her eyes. She *is* afraid, he thought. Was it because *he* had shown up? Was she afraid of Cheney asking questions she didn't like to answer?

He wandered among the equipment.

"He doesn't like people to touch anything," she said. "He doesn't even like it when *I* touch something and I'm part of his act." She swung her face in the direction of the hallway, where suddenly Zanzibar had appeared.

Dressed in a black kimono, the magician came into the room. He had a strange smile on his long face: it was slightly off-center, crooked, like a picture hanging at a bad angle. The impenetrable blackness of his garment, which hung as far as his ankles, emphasized the curious whiteness of his face.

"This is Sheriff Cheney," the girl said. She moved slightly to one side and her body brushed against Cheney, who felt a vague pressure from her. Was it deliberate? he wondered. Had she meant to touch him? He watched her pass across the room to a sofa, where she sat down, unmindful of the way her robe slinked open and her pale thighs appeared. She sat motionless, staring at him in a manner he found unsettling.

Zanzibar had one hand stretched forward. Cheney took it. The magician's grip was like concrete: when Cheney removed his fingers from the young man's grasp, his hand ached. Nevertheless, Cheney smiled, gazing into Zanzibar's face. The young man's eyes were almost as dark as the garment he wore. For an odd moment, Cheney experienced a passing dizziness, a light-headed sensation that made the face before him swim and the room tilt. You haven't eaten, he thought. No food and too much bad coffee along the way: it was a sure prescription for weakness.

The girl said, "What are these questions you wanted to ask, Sheriff?"

Cheney felt his eyes being drawn to the sight of her pale thighs. He said, "I'm making inquiries about two kids. Tommy Sears and Victoria Estaban. They're both members of Mr Zanzibar's magic group—"

"Has something happened to them?" the girl asked.

"They've disappeared." There was a strain in Cheney's voice, a dry quality. He looked back at Zanzibar, who appeared quite content to let the girl do the talking for him. There was a secretive expression on his face, something almost mischievous. Cheney had the feeling he was going to come quickly across the room and produce a plum from the air or pull silks out of the pockets of the sheriff's uniform.

"Disappeared?" the girl asked.

Cheney nodded.

"What makes you think we'd know anything?"

Cheney went to a chair and sat down. "This is routine," he said. "I'm not saying that I expect you to know anything. My problem is simple. The kids vanished. Maybe they vanished together. Maybe it was planned between them. Maybe not. I have to explore whatever connections I can . . . Believe me, I don't have much to go on."

The girl was quiet a moment. She looked in Zanzibar's direction. The magician moved to the center of the room, stretching his arms so that the wide sleeves of his kimono gave him the appearance of a black kite in a wind. Again, Cheney half-expected something—a trick, an illusion, a sudden transformation. But Zanzibar slowly lowered his arms and smiled at him.

"I know those kids," Zanzibar said.

Cheney had to strain to hear the young man's words. They were spoken in a muted voice, low and deep and slow, as if the pronunciation of each word gave Zanzibar some difficulty.

"They're very pleasant kids," Zanzibar said. "I can't imagine them leaving home without some kind of message."

The conjurer sat down in a chair that faced Cheney. He seemed to sink a moment inside his black kimono, as if he were on the point of disappearing himself. It was disconcerting, Cheney thought, to be here: to be in this room and to keep feeling this peculiar sense of expectation—that a trick was about to be performed, that something was going to materialize in mid-air, that birds were suddenly to be set free from invisible hiding places. It gave his private reality a soft core: it skewed his senses.

"There must be some good reason," Zanzibar said.

"I haven't found one yet," Cheney said.

Zanzibar made a little steeple of his long fingers, placing them beneath his chin. "Do you believe in magic, Sheriff?"

Cheney glanced across the room at the girl. She hadn't moved in a while: her hands still lay on her thighs. "Magic?" he asked. "I guess I believe in illusions, sure."

"Not illusions," Zanzibar said. "I don't mean illusions. I mean magic."

Cheney shook his head. "I don't think so, not in the sense I take you to mean."

Zanzibar smiled lopsidedly. His hand dipped a second into the folds of his garment and Cheney, impaled on his own sense of expectation, waited for a trick. But nothing happened. The hand reappeared, empty. It's a game, Cheney realized. It's a very strange game here. Zanzibar *knows* I expect an illusion of some kind and he's playing around with me. Cheney sat back in his chair. A strange game—for what purpose, though? To confuse and bewilder?

Zanzibar said, "If I could materialize those two children for you, right here in this room, what would you say then?"

Cheney, unable to measure or control his reactions to the man, moved his hands in a nervous, aimless gesture.

"I'd still say it was a clever illusion," he remarked eventually. Across the room, the girl stretched her legs and her robe slipped completely from one leg and her thigh rose up into shadows. She hadn't taken her eyes off Cheney, and the stare was disconcerting.

"No matter how magical it might seem, you would still argue that all I had done was to create an illusion?"

"Right." Cheney nodded.

There was a long silence. A small determined look crossed Zanzibar's face.

Cheney saw a thought flash through his own brain as if it were words on a tickertape: *He's going to do it, he's about to do it, he's going to make those two kids appear right in front of my eyes* . . . He got up out of his chair and wondered what the hell he was thinking. He was tired and beat and Zanzibar was *playing* with him. That's what it came down to. He should have waited until morning before coming out here.

"But since you *can't* make the children appear," Cheney said, "I'd like to ask you some more questions."

Zanzibar smiled again. He inclined his head, waited.

"Did either of those kids ever talk to you about any plans they might have had? Did they ever mention anything to you about going away?"

Zanzibar simply shook his head.

The girl stared, didn't move.

Cheney was quiet for a second.

He saw Zanzibar stretch his hands out in front of his body and produce a large crystal attached to a thin silver chain. He did this without any flamboyance; he might have been a man checking the time on his wristwatch. It might have been a perfectly ordinary occurrence: maybe, in this house, it was.

"I had the feeling something was going to happen," Cheney said. "That was good. Swift."

Zanzibar absorbed the compliment. The crystal swung from his fingertips. Cheney followed the orb of light with his eyes.

"Mere trickery," Zanzibar said. "Mere technique. Nothing to do with magic. Anyone can do what I just did."

Cheney watched the moving crystal a moment. Zanzibar swung the chain in the air and then it was gone as suddenly as it had come, in a sleight-of-hand so smoothly undetectable that Cheney was impressed.

"You must have played some good places," he said.

The magician didn't answer. He rose from his chair and

wandered around the magical equipment, touching this, fingering that.

"With your skills, I guess you're pretty much in demand," Cheney offered. He was searching for an opening and failing to find one.

Zanzibar looked down a moment at a small glossy black box. He pressed something, some concealed lever, and doors sprung open, revealing the stark emptiness of the container. "You could come to the point, Sheriff," he said. "You could simply ask us about our backgrounds. You don't have to beat around bushes. You could ask us where we came from, why we're here, what our intentions are."

Surprised by Zanzibar's insight, Cheney said nothing for a while. "I guess I could," was all he thought to say eventually.

"After all, isn't that the real reason you're here? You began with the mystery of two missing children and then you stumbled into another—namely, myself and Zena. And you wonder if these two mysteries are somehow related, don't you?"

Cheney nodded his head. He had the same unsettling feeling as before, that a game was being played at his expense. Only this time it was at some other level, down in a place he couldn't reach. He watched as Zanzibar tapped the top of the black box and the doors swung sharply shut beneath his fingertips. And Cheney waited, waited for those doors to burst open, revealing a bird, a rabbit, something— but nothing happened. Zanzibar simply walked away from the box and approached Cheney and stood there, looking down at him, scanning him.

"You have expectations," Zanzibar said. "You expect answers. You expect your small mysteries to reveal themselves."

"At the very least, I expect you to provide me with some background," Cheney said. "Two kids are missing, and what they have in common is you and your magic, and when I find out that nobody knows anything about you, then sure, sure I have expectations—"

Zanzibar interrupted. "My profession is mystery, Sheriff. To a certain extent, so is yours. The difference is that you try to solve them. I encourage them. I enlarge them. I need them." The young man hesitated, lowering his hand. "In my profession, which is the better name? Mr Zanzibar? Or the fact that I'm really Stanley Oakes, a former shoe-store clerk, from Potsdam, New York, whose Social Security Number is zero seven four, zero five, zero five six five? If you were a magician, Sheriff, which would you prefer?"

"I take your point," Cheney said. "But you have to understand my situation. When I'm faced with the mystery of two missing kids, I don't give a damn about your profession or your stage name or your image, all I'm interested in is some hard data—"

"And I've just given you some, Sheriff," Zanzibar said. "Do what you like with it. Check it out if you need to."

"What about the girl?" Cheney asked. He'd taken his notebook out and had started to scribble down the information Zanzibar had just offered him before he had time to forget it. Nor did he want to give Zanzibar the satisfaction of repeating himself. It was, Cheney thought as he scribbled, a tiny, petty victory. But over what? Over the way Zanzibar seemed always to be at an advantage? Over that knowing expression and those penetrating eyes?

"Why don't you ask her," Zanzibar said.

The girl leaned forward, adjusting her robe. She looked at Zanzibar as if for assistance. Then she said to Cheney, "What do you need to know, Sheriff?"

"Your real name. Your Social Security number."

The girl moved her lips, said nothing.

Zanzibar came to her assistance. "Her real name is Mary Beth Orlando. From Minneapolis. Her Social Security number is five eight three, four zero, six seven three four."

Cheney looked at the girl. She was nodding her head emphatically. Why hadn't she told him herself? Why had she relied on Zanzibar?

"Does that satisfy you, Sheriff?" Zanzibar asked.

"It helps," Cheney said. He got up from his chair. His limbs felt locked, his muscles tight. He added, "It doesn't explain why you came to Hamland. You must have had your pick of places—so why here?"

Zanzibar smiled. "I like working with kids. Kids are so

open, Sheriff. They still have the capacity to believe in magic. Their minds are uncluttered."

It wasn't an answer, Cheney thought. It was a signpost *pointing* to an answer. It fell short. "But why Hamland?"

"Because it was on the way to somewhere else," Zanzibar said.

Cheney closed his notebook. He saw the girl get up from the sofa. She turned her face in the direction of the door, the hallway beyond—and there was something in this gesture, something he couldn't quite read, almost as if she were trying to convey a message to him with the movement of her head. Puzzled, he followed the line of her eyes out into the hallway, but by then the girl had turned back to look at him and the moment was gone, the impression had passed.

Zanzibar stepped between Cheney and the girl suddenly. In his strange whispering voice he asked, "Do you truly think we have anything to do with the missing children?"

Cheney said, "No," but as he spoke the word he realized he wasn't sure. He wasn't sure of anything. All he had accomplished by coming out to Gowrie Canyon was a deepening of his uncertainty.

"If you think of anything else," he said. "Remember to get in touch with me."

He moved toward the door.

As he did so, a faint cry made him stop.

He turned around, looking first at Zanzibar, then at the girl. "What was that?"

"I didn't hear anything," Zanzibar said, his face sly now, his mouth set in a half-smile of mischief.

Cheney looked toward the small black box Zanzibar had been toying with before. The little doors swung open abruptly. A large white rodent sat there in the space, rearing up on its hindlegs, pawing the air blindly around its head, squeaking.

Cheney forced a small tired smile. "How did you do that?" he asked.

"Do what?" Zanzibar said.

"It doesn't matter." Cheney went toward the front door. Zanzibar and the girl followed him slowly, like good hosts ushering their guest out after a party.

Cheney opened the front door, stepped out on the porch. Rain, black and windblown, swept down through the canyon.

"Thanks for your time," Cheney said.

"You must come again," the girl said. She offered her hand and Cheney took it. She dug her fingernails into his palm, hurting him a second. *What the hell is it? What is she trying to say?*

Zanzibar said nothing. He merely moved one limp hand in a slack gesture of farewell. Cheney went down the steps toward his car.

When he'd driven a little way, he glanced back once.

But the lights in the house had gone out and he had the uneasy feeling that it had ceased to exist—nothing more than some rainy illusion which Zanzibar, with one pass of a hand, had conjured out of existence.

Max Crouch stood at the open bedroom window, letting the damp night air blow against his face. Hildy snored. Open-mouthed, her sinuses blocked, she made porcine sounds that night after night kept him awake. Tonight, the idea of going out into the rain magnetized him. There was a certain sense of freedom in the roar of the dark wind and the way the trees trembled. He rubbed his cold hands together, then he put an old raincoat on over his striped pajamas and he left the small apartment softly, like a man who had come to steal, only to leave empty-handed.

Outside, he paused on the empty street. He experienced a sense of freedom that was weird in its unexpectedness, as if some part of himself, shackled for so long, had been suddenly liberated. Unconscious of any particular direction, he walked. He let the rain slide over his face as he strolled past darkened storefronts and then he found himself turning away from Center Avenue, entering a street of dark suburban houses, big old houses with overgrown front yards and ornate porches. Lovingly restored by their inhabitants, he thought, right down to the stained-glass panes in doorways.

He moved quietly under dripping trees. People slept in these houses. People slept their safe little sleeps. Dreamless and still as the air on a warm summery night. They drifted down into the comfortable depths of themselves, like animals burrowing into the security of their warrens.

Max Crouch paused now. At the end of the street, at the place where the houses stopped, there was the darkened parking-lot of the Crawford Steak & Chop House. A faint beer neon hung in the front window even though he knew the joint was shut for the night. He hesitated a moment before he continued toward the restaurant, then he stopped before the window and the blue neon that said *Coors*. He felt like a moth drawn upward into the neon, a place where he might batter his wings time and again uselessly. He shut his eyes, moved away, crossed the deserted parking-lot: whatever brief liberation he'd felt before was gone now and he was suddenly impaled upon the night, trapped in the rainy dark, a prisoner of more than the elements.

He touched the tip of his nose, wiping away a drip of rainwater. Then, motionless, he gazed across the lot. His raincoat was soaked through and his pajamas adhered to his pale skin.

This was the last place he wanted to be, he thought.

The last place he needed to visit. There was pain here and he didn't have an anodyne against it. The weather seemed to clutch at his heart.

He moved slowly to the far side of the lot, conscious of another presence passing nearby. Max Crouch stepped beneath a tree and watched as a tall figure passed in front of him, a big man in a bulky raincoat who carried a cat pressed against his chest. Max Crouch held his breath, didn't move. The man with the cat stopped in the center of the parking-lot, raised the creature up to his face, then pressed his mouth against the animal's snout.

A kiss. A weird goddam kiss, like a touch shared by lovers for Chrissakes! It was the dark that brought them out of the fucking woodwork, Crouch thought. It brought them scuttling out from under stones.

When the stranger had passed out of sight, Crouch moved from under the tree. He was conscious all over again of his own dreary solitude in this place—and yet he knew, if he listened closely, he would catch the distant whimper of a ghost because here, if you discounted a solitary passing loony with a damp cat, a ghost was his only real companion and it whispered in his ear in a voice filled with a very old anguish.

He began to walk, pausing only once, his blood chill, when he heard the terrible scream of some animal in the dark.

Marge Dove woke suddenly, her body cold. Somewhere in her sleep she'd kicked aside the blanket and now it lay in a heap on Fred's side of the bed. She reached for the hem of the blanket to draw it back over her body but then she realized that the cold she felt was drifting in through the open bedroom door. She turned on the lamp, stepped quietly into her slippers—strange childish furry things—and, careful not to disturb Fred, made her way out on to the landing. Both doors leading to the kids' rooms were closed. Beneath the slit of Jenny's door there was a bar of electricity falling from the girl's night-light.

Marge Dove shivered. She pulled the collar of her night-dress up to her throat and stood at the top of the stairs, looking down into the lower part of the house.

That cold had to be coming from somewhere, forcing its way inside the house. She shrugged and began to go down the stairs slowly. Fred, who smoked a pipe, sometimes left a window open when he came to bed, so that the smoke would be released before morning. Fred disliked the smell of trapped tobacco fumes. Maybe he'd done that tonight. Maybe he'd forgotten to close the window.

She reached the hallway. The grandfather clock ticked loudly, its mechanism wheezing. It was colder down here than upstairs. She fumbled for the lightswitch, turned it on and saw to her surprise that the front door had been left wide open. Hurriedly, she moved toward it, closing it shut and making sure it was properly locked.

How could that have happened?

The wind, she thought.

The wind must have blown it open that way.

Shivering, rubbing her arms for warmth, she headed back toward the stairs, pausing to check the downstairs rooms as she did so. They were empty, tidy. Nobody had come in, nothing had been disturbed.

THE PIPER

The significance of the open front door wouldn't occur to her until morning. She would go back to sleep, slide into a vague dream about a large ramshackle house she sometimes visited in her sleep—a big warm place, always friendly, always welcoming—and then she'd waken in the morning and remember and the recollection would fill her with horror.

ELEVEN

"OVER HERE, DADDY . . . I'M OVER HERE . . ."

George Cheney pressed the stop button of the small cassette player, then rewound the tape to the beginning. He pushed PLAY.

"Over here, Daddy . . ."

STOP.

He placed the cassette player on the kitchen counter and looked across the room at Hugh Estaban, who stood with his back to the refrigerator. Anne, her elbows propped on the counter, ran one hand through her hair. The recorded voice of the girl seemed to linger in the room, a fragile little echo. Cheney stared at the cassette now, even as he listened to the noise of his own heart like a man trying to interpret the messages of a tribal drum.

"I didn't see anybody," Estaban said. His voice was small. It might have come from another room. "When I found the recorder I went outside immediately. I searched all over the garden, the street. I didn't see a soul . . . Then I came running over here . . ." He paused, raised a hand to the side of his nose: an expression went across his face that reminded Cheney of a man struck swiftly in the midriff with a two-by-

172

four. "I thought Vickie had come back. I thought she was in her bedroom . . ."

Cheney looked back at the cassette player and suddenly the whole day filled all the passages of his brain, the whole weary rainy day reared up and fragments of himself lay out there in the wet streets of this town, bones scattered in isolated canyons, nerve-endings burned in pursuit of two ghostly kids.

The Humpty-Dumpty Sheriff.

He picked up the cassette player again. It was a tiny black Sony. He turned it over in his hand, looked at the serial number and saw that the small digits had been scratched beyond recognition.

He put the player down on the counter.

Anne opened a pack of Benson and Hedges and lit one. Then she poured three cups of coffee. "It doesn't make sense," she said. "Before you arrived, George, I was telling Hugh about the phone call Courtney Sears received. I get the awful impression that somebody's playing some kind of horrible game in this town. I just don't understand it. It's sick."

Hugh Estaban said, "I can't figure it out either. I can't understand what it means. Why would somebody go to the trouble of breaking into Vickie's bedroom and leaving a recording of her voice? It would make *more* sense if it was a different kind of message. If it was something to do with . . . something to do with having been kidnapped. If she'd said something like *I'm okay, Dad, and you'll hear from my kidnappers shortly* . . . then I might have understood it." He sipped his coffee and slumped against the door of the refrigerator. "That message just doesn't add up to *anything*."

George Cheney thought of Tommy Sears and the single word *Mom* spoken into a telephone. Nothing added up. There was no sum he could arrive at, no equation he could understand. He was sinking down into some murky place where the algebra of missing children was beyond formulas.

Hugh Estaban said, "Another thing I don't understand is why she'd *make* a recording like that. Why she'd speak those particular words—"

"Maybe she had no choice," Cheney said.

Estaban nodded. "I considered that. I thought about

somebody forcing her to say what she did. The trouble with that is, I don't detect any stress in her voice. She sounds normal. She doesn't sound like a girl with a gun at her head, George."

Cheney regarded Hugh Estaban a moment. The man looked crumpled, his dark suit hanging on him in ridges and folds. Cheney said, "When you think about it, it's a godawful risk to take breaking into the kid's room and leaving a recorder. If you've snatched a kid, the last thing you want to do is risk exposing your identity the way this character did. *If* there's a kidnapper, he's not exactly your run of the mill."

"*If* there's a kidnapper?" Estaban asked. "What other explanation could there possibly be?"

Cheney felt a small hopelessness clutch his heart. Everybody wanted explanations. Everybody wanted solutions. And he had nothing to give them so far beyond half-assed speculations that led down the road to nowhere. He said, "All I'm saying is that if we're dealing with a kidnapping here, the perpetrator is going about his business in an unorthodox manner. No ransom demands. No instructions about any pay-off. No direct communication from the kidnapper. Nothing." He paused. A dark wave of fatigue crossed his brain, leaving shadows. "Courtney Sears gets a cryptic phone call. You get a message on a cassette. What if the abductor isn't interested in holding kids for ransom? What if there's some other reason that's got nothing to do with money?"

"Like what?" Estaban asked.

Like what? What exactly?

Cheney looked at his wife a moment and Anne gazed back at him with sympathy. She could feel her husband's frustration. She could see it in the way he stood against the kitchen counter, his body angled awkwardly. She reached across the counter and caressed the back of his hand. Poor George, she thought, cast abruptly adrift in a world that he couldn't control, couldn't harness under the banner of good old reliable common sense.

Cheney strolled around the kitchen. He opened the door leading to the back yard. It was no longer raining but the night was damp, the air filled with the smells of wet trees. He stared out across the black grass. Then he turned to face Hugh Estaban.

"Do you have anyone you'd say was an enemy?" he asked.

Estaban reacted to the question as if it were the silliest thing in the world. "An enemy, George?" He laughed. "I don't think I have the kind of enemies who'd go to the trouble of stealing my daughter, if that's what you're thinking."

"Maybe enemies is too strong a word," Cheney said. "Is there anybody you might have slighted? Anybody who would be crazy enough to take Vickie away?"

"I don't think so," Estaban answered. "There are some people I might have rubbed the wrong way over the years, but I can't imagine any one of them doing something like this, George."

Cheney saw that Anne was shivering a little, so he nudged the kitchen door shut with his knee. Even if Hugh Estaban *had* rubbed somebody in such a wrong way that the injured party had indeed seized his daughter, how would that explain the disappearance of Tommy Sears? He was back in the land of lost connections again, looking for links, interlocking parts, anything that might weld Tommy Sears to Vickie Estaban.

"Did Vickie ever talk to you about Mr Zanzibar?" he asked.

"Once or twice," Estaban said.

"Did you ever meet the guy?"

Estaban shook his head.

Cheney propped himself up at the counter again. "Did you get the feeling she might have had something of a crush on Zanzibar?"

"A crush?" Estaban shook his head.

Anne poured more coffee, lit another cigarette. Estaban picked up his fresh cup. "Why are you asking me about Zanzibar anyhow?"

Cheney said, "Because Zanzibar is about the only damn thing your daughter and Tommy Sears had in common." *Had,* he thought. The unfortunate use of the past tense, as if Vickie and Tommy were already history, already dead and buried, cold names in a cold obituary.

"You think he had something to do with the kids?"

"I don't suspect the guy of anything," Cheney answered. "Not right now anyhow." He gazed up at the ceiling, thinking of the house out in Gowrie Canyon, turning Zanzibar and the girl over in his mind. They were a curious pair living in a curious house—but that didn't make them guilty, for God's sake! He stared into the palm of his hand, remembering how Zena had pressed her fingernails into his skin in a way that was almost urgent. Had she been coming on to him? he wondered. Or was it something else altogether, something he couldn't quite comprehend? He couldn't think any more: all the avenues of understanding were dead-end streets.

"Where do we go from here?" Estaban asked. "What happens now?"

"What happens now is that you go home, Hugh. Go home, stay with your wife. If anything happens, you'll be the first to know."

He heard Anne show Hugh Estaban out, the sound of the front door closing quietly. When Anne returned she put her arms around her husband.

"You need to rest, George."

"Yeah."

Anne stepped away from him. "I feel so sorry for Hugh Estaban," she said. "I feel sorry for all the parents."

Cheney nodded. Anne picked up the small Sony and held it away from her body as if it might be contaminated somehow. Then she set the machine down on the counter without taking her eyes away from it. Small and black and ugly, she thought, and terrifying in its complete banality of design and function.

Anne reached out and put the palm of her hand against Cheney's face. "You're cold, George."

"Cold and tired," Cheney said.

"Come to bed."

She led him out of the kitchen. Upstairs in the bedroom she helped him undress. When he lay down he closed his eyes. She stepped out of her blue jeans, slipped off her blouse, and got under the covers beside him. She placed her hand over his. Bone-cold, she thought. She rubbed the backs of his hands to bring him warmth. Then she propped herself up on an elbow and gazed at his face. She examined the closed eyelids, the tense mouth, the small lines that cut into the forehead. For a moment he wasn't George, didn't look like George: she might have had a stranger in her bed.

"Your father was here," she said.

Cheney opened his eyes. "What did he want?"

Anne shrugged. "I don't really know if he wanted anything. It was just a visit." She paused, ran a fingertip down the side of Cheney's face. "You ought to see more of him, George. He's your father, after all. And he loves to see Danny. You know that."

Cheney closed his eyes again. "I've been meaning to go see him. I just haven't got around to it yet," he said. Which was true enough in its own way. It was just that the idea of crossing the threshold of the house and following the old man on one of his rambling walks from empty room to empty room depressed him. "Maybe I'll drop in on him tomorrow . . ."

"I wish you would, George. I have the feeling he'd like to see you."

Why not? he wondered.

There was always the chance—which had the likelihood of an icicle in hell—that Edward Cheney, who in his long career as an appraiser of residential and industrial properties had come to know everyone and everything in Hamland, who knew its public faces as well as its innermost workings, could offer an educated speculation about the missing kids. Besides, the old man had been pretty well acquainted once with Hugh Estaban and maybe there were tired old skeletons waiting to be sprung from closets. Maybe there were shards of dead gossip.

A wild goose chase, Cheney thought.

He knew what would happen. He'd go see his father and the visit would fade out in silences, things unsaid. Or worse, the old man might set off in pursuit of fragmented recollections, sniffing after memories as he shuffled through the rooms.

Anne placed her face down on the pillow. "Why don't you like that house, George?"

"I used to love it," Cheney answered. "When Mother was alive, it was a warm place. Now it's gloomy. He should sell it, buy himself a small apartment. What's the point in living all alone in that vast hulk of a house?"

Anne said, "Maybe he doesn't want to live elsewhere, George." She moved nearer to him, pressing her body against his.

Cheney moved his lips slightly but said nothing. He was drifting now, his mind roaming, his limbs floating, he was drifting out through dark spheres toward the enclosures of sleep. He barely felt it when Anne's arm dropped across his chest. And when she kissed his shoulder, the touch came from a million miles away.

He dreamed he found the two missing kids inside the house on Montrose Drive. But the house had turned into a great sailing ship that was sinking into an ocean and the two missing kids had somehow multiplied themselves into four and green sea-water was rising against the windows—

He forced himself awake, his mind filled with the sense of drowning. He rose, went briefly inside Danny's room—which in the boy's absence was uncharacteristically neat, books in tidy piles, boxes of games stacked, the bed with the crazy red and yellow patchwork quilt made-up—and then descended into the living-room where he sat on the sofa and stared at the last feeble glow from the fire.

How could he sleep?

It was after one AM when Lily Hubbard heard Arthur Rigley's door close. She opened the door of her own apartment and watched Mr Rigley through a narrow slit. He passed without noticing her, his bulky shape filling the landing. He paused for some reason halfway down the stairs, like a man who suspects he might have forgotten something. Then, shrugging, he continued his descent. After a moment there was the sound of the front door opening, closing quietly.

Lily Hubbard climbed upward. She stopped briefly outside Ellis Diamond's apartment, listening. All quiet, nothing to hear.

Grasping the rail, Lily continued up the next flight of stairs. Before Elmer had died, the rooms that were to become Mr Rigley's apartment had been The Judge's study—two small rooms located at the top of the house, a private place where Elmer Hubbard had spent hours with his old lawbooks and the various legal periodicals to which he subscribed. The Judge liked it up here. Sometimes he'd say *Well, Lilygal, I'm off to my eyrie,* and she'd listen to the sound of him going up the stairs. She often took him up a cup of hot chocolate, carrying it as if it were an offering to a minor god. He'd be seated behind his big desk, shirtsleeved, vest hanging open, pipe in his mouth, and when she stepped into the room he'd raise his sharp little face and grin at her and say *Lilygal, what in hell would I ever do without you?*

She stood now outside the door of Mr Rigley's apartment. She took a key from the pocket of her lilac robe, slipped it in the lock, entered the room.

It was extraordinarily tidy. Even the small kitchen, where you might have expected a mess, was a place of gleaming surfaces and saucepans hanging from little hooks. On the circular table there was a half-loaf of whole-wheat bread wrapped neatly in cellophane, a jar of peanut butter, and a dish containing dark jelly the color of old blood.

Mr Rigley was nothing if not fastidious.

She moved back into the other room, sat down on the arm of the sofa a moment, remembering how The Judge would walk back and forth across the floor of this room as he harried some elusive thought or other, some legal complexity. *Pardon me, Lilygal,* he'd say, *if I spend too much time up here and not enough with my wife and son, but I got to put on my serious thinking-cap a while . . .*

His thinking-cap. He was always thinking.

She rose from the sofa.

She walked to the window and looked down into Gunnison Avenue, seeing wet sidewalks shine beneath streetlamps and great trees assume phantasmagorical shapes as the wind stirred them. Elmer had looked out of this window a lot—especially toward the end of his life when The Silence had come over him.

The Silence. That's what Lily had called it. That condition of retreat, when he'd say nothing for days on end, when he'd sit up here with the curtains drawn and a bottle of Jack Daniels on his desk and his papers strewn all across the floor, when his face was glazed and tortured and secretive and he'd fail to notice his wife and son as if half of his brain had been amputated and his storehouse of recognition ransacked by private vandals . . .

Leave me be, Lily. Leave me alone. I need the darkness now. More than ever, I need the darkness.

She twisted her hands together. She moved toward Mr Rigley's narrow bed. It had been made as if by a nurse in an institution, the sheets tightly tucked in and folded back on the diagonal. On the bedside table there was a paperback edition of Ripley's *Believe It Or Not!*

Lily Hubbard flipped it open and read

Jas P Yarrow, of Ruckport, Ohio, has a collection of false teeth dating back to Roman times. He has more than 2,000 sets altogether. He calls his hobby DENTIQUITY.

She shut the book, replaced it.

Then she leaned forward and touched the pillow lightly.

She tried to imagine Mr Rigley sitting up in his bed, his head filled with useless reams of knowledge, tiny oddities mined from the pages of paperbacks. She sat down on the edge of the bed now, hands in the pockets of her robe.

She gazed toward the corner of the room, to the place where The Judge had kept his desk. A sideboard occupied the space now. The desk, a handsome mahogany thing created by a Mexican craftsman, lay gathering dust in the cellar. It was at that desk where Elmer Hubbard had written the last words of his life.

His suicide note.

His letter of farewell.

His testament . . .

She stood up, took her hands from her robe, walked toward the door.

She paused there, looking up at the baseball cap that hung on a metal hook. She reached out, took it down, turned it round in her hands.

Then she let herself out of the apartment, pausing halfway down the stairs to listen to the dark sounds of the house all around her—rainwater slithering down drainpipes, wind sloughing across slates, and the quietly satisfied murmur of Elmer Hubbard's approval.

When the hawks of darkness had dispersed in daylight, Edward Cheney left his house and walked slowly, as was his custom, in the direction of Pascoe's Market, a small convenience store located on Hinsdale Drive. There, six days out of seven, he purchased a copy of *The Progressive* and took it home to read over his first cup of herbal tea. On this morning he walked more slowly than he usually did. He passed in front of the big houses on Montrose Drive and when he reached the corner of Hinsdale, he stopped. His whole body ached: his muscles felt like lead.

The hawks of darkness, he thought.

Somewhere in the night the sound of a bird had wakened him. The rattle of wings, the swift passage of air, a cry. He had opened his eyes and stared into darkness, possessed by the sensation that something was climbing the stairs to his bedroom.

He had lain motionless, listening for footsteps.

Waiting for the bedroom door to spring suddenly open.

He shivered, even though the day was not cold. Brisk, yes, but not worth a shiver. Outside Pascoe's, he stopped again.

A small group of people were standing round the counter. Some drank coffee from styrofoam cups. Others smoked cigarettes. As Edward Cheney entered the store, faces rolled toward him, mouths opened and closed in greetings, and Lew Pascoe slid a copy of *The Progressive* across the counter. Lew was a small man with a misshapen face, the result of a stroke some years before. Half of his face was fine, normal, the other twisted. One had the impression of a painting done by a schizophrenic patient in an asylum.

Cheney picked up his newspaper.

Somebody said, "Seems like we got some missing kids on our hands."

Cheney glanced at the front page. "I heard about it."

Lew Pascoe said, "Your son say anything about it, Ed?"

Cheney shook his head. He looked at the headline. Tommy Sears, Victoria Estaban, photographs. He folded the newspaper over so that he didn't have to look at the front page.

"What's the inside story?" somebody asked.

"I don't know any more than it says in this newspaper," Cheney answered. He tucked his newspaper under one arm and dropped a quarter on the counter, then hurried out of the store and along Hinsdale Drive, passing under the giant oaks that still sparkled from last night's rain. When he reached Montrose and turned in the direction of his own home he had an urge just to take the newspaper and tear it in pieces and let the scraps fall to the ground where a sudden wind might blow them away forever. *HAVE YOU SEEN THESE CHILDREN?* Dear God, he didn't need to read that kind of thing. He looked up at the sky where pale clouds hung motionless. It was a sky the color of unwashed laundry.

His house came in sight.

He paused, faltered.

George Cheney's car was parked at the curb.

Edward Cheney folded his newspaper inside the pocket of his jacket, and wondered what had brought his son here at this hour of the day. Now he could see George standing with his arms folded, gazing down at the ground.

My son, Cheney thought. *My executioner.*

George Cheney smiled. "I thought I'd sample some of that herbal tea for which you're famous."

"Notorious is the word you want," Edward Cheney said. He tapped his son on the shoulder, noticing the drawn expression on the younger man's face, the purple under the eyes, colorless lips.

They went inside the house together, George Cheney following his father. Edward closed the door and beckoned his son toward the kitchen. The old man filled a kettle with water and set it on the stove, then turned toward George.

"What brings you here this early?" he asked.

"It's been a while since I stopped by," George Cheney said. "Anne said you came over last night when I was out."

The old man nodded, then tossed his newspaper down on the table. "You've got problems, I see."

George Cheney sat down at the table, glanced at the newspaper, sighed. When the kettle came to a boil, Edward made two cups of tea from one tea-bag.

"Drink, George. They claim this stuff gives you strength and vitality. You look as if you need everything you can get."

George Cheney sipped some tea, then set the cup down. "Unusual," he said.

"Dandelion and burdock. Rose hips. Lemon peel. Quite possibly spleen of toad and meadowlark bile. Who knows?"

George edged his cup aside. "I dreamed about this house last night," he said.

"Was it bad?"

"It felt like a nightmare," the Sheriff said, smiling.

Edward Cheney watched his son a moment. There was something hidden behind the younger man's expression, but he wasn't entirely sure what. George had always had the capacity to surprise, the knack of concealing his true feelings and motives behind a mask that gave nothing away. A deadpan trait. The face of a poker player.

"You should come more often, George," the old man said. What crossed his mind briefly was the notion that George—who must have access to the gossip of Hamland, who must keep his ear close to the chatter that was interwoven into the fabric of this small town—might have heard some rumor about the trips to Denver all those years ago. Maybe it was this knowledge that kept George away. The old man dismissed the prospect as quickly as it had come: it was his own paranoia, that was all, his own hot fears. He glanced at George: the poker-face showed stresslines.

"You know how it is," George said. "I get bogged down. Time slips away from me. I never get around to doing all the things I should."

Edward Cheney tapped the surface of the table. "You didn't come here for tea, George. I can still read your face, you know. I can still see the small boy back there every now and again. He's stuck halfway up an oak tree and calling for help. I can still see the face of the young man who cried at his mother's funeral. I didn't help raise you without gaining a couple of minor insights into your heart."

Edward paused, sipped a little more tea, glanced at the newspaper on the table. Half of a headline reared up at him: *ESE CHILDREN?* A picture of the girl, bisected by the fold of the newspaper, gazed up at him with only one eye. Uneasy, he placed his cup on the paper. He said, "You didn't come here for tea and you didn't come here out of some nostalgic impulse to resurrect your boyhood. So speak."

George Cheney rose from the table. He stared out into the back yard in silence for a while. His father gazed at the pistol that hung at the son's hip. Involuntarily, he found himself thinking of Elmer Hubbard, thinking of that precise fatal moment when a bullet from just such a weapon went through Elmer's brain and out again, tearing tissue, splattering a whole man's life in the air.

George turned from the window and said, "I'm still up that oak tree, Dad. Nothing's changed. My voice has gotten deeper but I guess I'm still looking for help."

Edward opened his eyes. "What kind of help?"

"Those two kids."

"What about them?"

"Hugh Estaban is a friend of yours."

"Used to be. We don't see a lot of each other any more." *A friend of yours,* Edward Cheney thought. He saw Hugh Estaban's face drift before him: it was like some comet flashing out of the long night of the past.

The sheriff returned to the table and sat down, leaning toward his father. "What can you tell me about Estaban?"

Edward Cheney shrugged. "He's a reliable kind of man. He's ambitious. At least he used to be. Something of a snob, I'd say. Not so that he was objectionable, I'm not saying that. When he got married to Liz Yardley, he started to raise his sights. Maybe she pushed him. I don't know. Suddenly, he didn't see a big future in filling out tax returns, so he started calling himself an investment counsellor or some such thing . . . People change, George. And I haven't talked with Hugh in a long time. He used to have a problem with drink, I recall. Then I heard he took some cure over in Colorado Springs. Apparently it worked."

George Cheney was silent a moment. "What about Thomas Sears?"

"I only know Tom Sears vaguely," Edward said. Gray light flooding through the kitchen window filled his son's face,

184

stripped it of shadow. There was an odd naked intensity to the way George looked, which made the old man uncomfortable.

"What I'm looking for is some kind of connection between those two," George Cheney said.

"Connection? I don't think you'll have much luck there, George. I really can't imagine those two having anything in common." Edward got up from the table and wandered around the room, absently picking things up and setting them down. A connection, he thought. A darkness streaked through with red, with violence, filled his brain. When he reached the window he pressed his nose to the glass.

George said, "I've got nothing. I've got two missing kids and a whole lot of nothing and I'm desperate, which means I'm prepared to consider any angle, no matter how goddam pointless it might appear. And it crossed my mind that maybe somebody has some kind of grudge against Hugh and Tom. And if that sounds farfetched to you, then it's a measure of my desperation."

Edward turned round and looked at his son. "It would have to be one hell of a grudge, George. But I don't see any future in exploring a link between Hugh Estaban and Tom Sears . . . So far as I know, they don't even live in the same world." He leaned against the window-ledge, his arms folded on his chest. He could feel his tired heart pound beneath his shirt. *You expected this, Edward Cheney. You knew the road would unerringly lead to this.*

The sheriff glanced at his watch, sighed, then stood up. The old man walked with him out of the kitchen and along the hallway to the front door. George turned and looked in the direction of the stairs.

You used to charge down those stairs, George, the old man thought. *Used to come roaring down those stairs pretending you were a marine or a pirate or God knows what . . . Plastic sword in one hand and a tiny helmet on your head and laughter, always laughter . . .*

"You'll find your kids, George."

"Yeah."

Edward laid a hand on his son's shoulder. He felt very

185

small all at once, shrivelled, diminished by the deceits of his life. "You always did have a persistent streak a mile wide."

"I need something more than simple persistence right now. I need a break. I feel like somebody who's digging and digging, only he doesn't have a map to where the treasure's buried."

Edward Cheney thought, *It isn't treasure.*

George opened the door. Silence now. Awkwardness. A smell of damp greenery floated around the house.

"Will you do something for me, Dad?"

"I'll try."

"I want you to sit down and think hard and see if you can remember *anything* that might link Estaban and Sears together. Can you do that?"

Edward Cheney nodded. "I can do it, George. I don't think it's going to lead anywhere, but I can try. Will you do something for me in return?"

"Sure."

"Bring Danny."

"As soon as he comes home," George Cheney said.

"A promise?"

"For sure."

Edward Cheney watched his son go down the driveway toward his car. He saw the vehicle slide away from the curb, then he closed the door slowly. He had a feeling of barbed-wire coiled around his heart. His eyes watered. His flesh was clammy.

He moved along the hallway until he reached the bathroom. He knocked the door open, stumbled inside the small windowless space. He reached for the lightswitch, then remembered that the bulb in here had popped weeks ago and he hadn't replaced it. Blindly, he splashed cold water over his face, then raised his eyes to the dark reflection in the mirror, seeing nothing but pale glimmers of distant daylight drifting from the hallway, staining the edge of the glass.

Hugh Estaban. Thomas Sears.

Threads . . .

The old man buried his face in a towel and cried quietly into the folds of the material. He cried as if his life had become lodged in his throat. He cried until his eyes ached and his head throbbed.

When George Cheney reached his office, he found Charlie Bannion standing by the water-cooler.

The young officer said, "I figure I should have been an orthodontist, George. I could have made my fortune by this time. There are an awful lot of braces in this town. Last night, when I made the rounds of Vickie Estaban's pals, I counted maybe six sets. Are those things safe in electrical storms?"

Cheney said nothing. He sat down behind his desk. Charlie Bannion drew a conical cup of water from the cooler and sipped from it. It was clear to Bannion that the Sheriff's mood this morning was somewhat delicate and more than a little grave.

Bannion carried his water to the window and stood there with the gray light framing him. "Her friends don't know why Vickie would have disappeared. They don't know where she might be." He shrugged his shoulders loosely. It had been a long night for him: he hadn't fallen asleep until one AM and even then his sleep had been restless.

Cheney tore a sheet of paper out of a notebook and passed it to Charlie Bannion.

"I want you to run a check on these Social Security numbers," he said. "I got them from Zanzibar and his girl-friend. See what you can find out."

Bannion glanced at the paper. "Will do," he said. "What did you make of the guy?"

Before Cheney had a chance to respond, Officer Arlene Flagg stepped inside the office. She was frowning and glum. In one hand she held a slip of paper as if it had once been used to wrap a rancid fish. Cheney stared at her, noticing the unhappy appearance, the little lines of worry that wrinkled her brow.

"Don't tell me," he said. "Whatever it is, I don't think I want to know."

Arlene Flagg touched her hair nervously. "Some days don't start right," she said. "Some days stink just as soon as you open your eyes."

Cheney braced himself, expecting—what exactly? a corpse in a ditch? a body discovered in some lonely canyon? He shut his eyes and squeezed his hands together and tried to shake the gloom that had tracked him all the way across town from his father's house, but it wouldn't be shaken.

"I think we've got another one, George," Arlene Flagg said.

Max Crouch peered through the crack in the doorway, studying Ellis Diamond's face. She was busy busy busy, scribbling on pieces of paper, and her small mouth was puckered in concentration. She hadn't noticed the janitor. Max Crouch liked being able to observe people without being seen himself. It was one of the few times in his life when he felt slightly superior to anyone. He stood motionless a while, enjoying his tiny exultation, then he rattled the handle of his broom on the doorjamb and Ellis Diamond looked up.

Her face was pale, dark circles beneath the eyes.

Tragic, Crouch thought. She hasn't been sleeping and now she looks tragic.

"What can I do for you, Max?" she asked.

Max Crouch said nothing. He moved the head of his broom against the floor, a rustling sound.

"Max, I'm pretty busy."

He nodded. "I was wondering about the kids," he said.

"I don't have any fresh news," she said in a weary way.

Max Crouch leaned on his broom now. "I was thinking," he said. "I was wondering if we're going to lose any more of them."

Ellis Diamond stood up. "I don't think that's an appropriate remark to make, Max. I really don't. It's negative and it's irresponsible, in the circumstances."

Crouch picked a flake of tobacco from the corner of his mouth. "If we do, hell, it's going to make your whole program look bad."

The woman's face was red suddenly. "I'm aware of that," she said, fighting with her anger.

"They might just decide to close you down."

"I don't think I want this conversation to continue, Max."

Max Crouch appeared not to have heard her. "Like a condemned building," he went on to say.

"*Max.*"

Crouch moved away, pushing the broom before him. He was conscious of Ellis Diamond slamming her office door shut behind him. He reached the end of the hallway and placed his broom against the wall. The sounds of kids herding into the Youth Center reached him and he whistled loudly, as if to drown the din.

Like a condemned building, he thought.

He turned his face and gazed along the corridor, seeing the kids milling stupidly around, staring at him, making faces, smirking.

They had this special mean way of smirking.

Their faces were filled with contempt.

Hell. He could match them. He could cut their contempt with his own any old day of the week. He reached for his broom and turned away, sweeping and whistling, his heart filled all at once with an emotion as perfect as any he had ever felt in his whole life: *hatred.*

TWELVE

SMALL MODEL AIRPLANES HUNG FROM NYLON THREADS PINNED to the ceiling. There were Messerschmitts, a couple of Spitfires, a De Havilland Dragon Fly. The planes shivered in the air that stirred through the room from a half-open window. Cheney ducked his head to avoid colliding with the models. At the bookshelf, he picked up a replica of the Goodyear blimp, turning the plastic dirigible around in his hand.

Marge Dove stood in the doorway. Her eyes were red and frightened, her large mouth twisted by worry. Behind Marge was her husband Fred, a tall skinny man whose long nose was red around the nostrils and whose eyes watered behind thick glasses. Whenever Cheney had encountered Fred Dove in the past, the man had always seemed to be in the throes of a cold—sniffing constantly, pulling Kleenexes out of his jacket, coughing. Today wasn't any exception: he yanked fresh tissues out of his right pocket, brushed his nose with them, then placed them crumpled in his left—all in one smooth transaction.

Cheney gazed at Rick Dove's bed. A pillow with a Super-man motif. A bedspread embroidered with football helmets.

He wandered to the bookshelf and looked at the various titles. *The Random House Encyclopaedia, Mad Goes To The Movies*—there was a whole series of Mad paperbacks—*The Stories of Rudyard Kipling*. He ran a fingertip across the spines and specks of dust adhered to his skin.

Fred Dove said, "Marge woke in the middle of the night and found the front door open. She went down. Closed it. Then she came back to bed and fell asleep. She didn't think anything of it at the time, George. But now we realize Rick must have gone downstairs and left by the front door without closing it after him."

From the hall beyond the bedroom door a girl's voice could be heard. *"Has my brother run away from home?"*

Then Anne Cheney was talking to the girl in comforting tones. *"Of course he hasn't, Jenny, he'll be back, you'll see."*

Anne, who had come here out of neighborly concern and a genuine fondness for Marge Dove, seemed to have taken control of the girl Jenny. There was the sound of a door closing and then silence.

Cheney sighed quietly. He had the feeling he was pursuing rainbow bubbles across a meadow, only the wind was quicker and faster than he could ever be and all the bubbles were doomed to pop long before he could reach them.

"You didn't hear the boy leave?" he asked.

Marge Dove's big girlish face looked red and raw. She shook her head. "I didn't hear anything," she answered. "I didn't know he was gone until I went to wake him for breakfast. Even then I didn't think anything about it. I imagined maybe he'd gone to the convenience store. Maybe he'd risen before anyone else and decided to go get something —a soda, bubblegum, I don't know—and that's the only place open at that time of morning . . ." She shrugged feebly.

Fred Dove cut in. "After Marge told me about the front door being open like that, I began to worry a little, especially when I looked at the headlines in the morning paper . . ." Here, the man stared at Cheney as if he were challenging him. He blames me, Cheney thought, for the disappearance of those kids—and this perception didn't exactly surprise him. Christ, somebody had to shoulder the blame and wasn't the sheriff the logical candidate?

"I went over to the store to look for him but nobody there had seen him. I came back here, called a couple of his friends . . . but he wasn't with any of them." Fred Dove paused, glanced at his wife. "After that I took the car and drove around for a while. I checked along Center Avenue. I even went down to the park but Rick wasn't there."

The park, Cheney thought.

Always the goddam park.

It was as if that park were the secretive green heart of everything that was happening.

"Was Rick a member of Parks and Rec?" he asked. He knew the answer anyway. Now, for the first time, he noticed the battered playing-cards stacked neatly under the bedside lamp.

Marge replied, "He played baseball. He took magic lessons."

Magic lessons . . . Cheney felt suddenly lightheaded.

Coincidences took his breath away, suffocated him. There was a place where the skins of coincidence peeled away and you were left with something else: an undeniable design, a fabricated shape. If I had the eyes to see it, he thought.

He stared at the bedspread, the pillow with its shallow impression of the boy's head. He tried to imagine Rick Dove—a kid who often played around the neighborhood with Danny—rising in the dark and going downstairs and drifting away into some bizarre realm of nonexistence: conjured, so to speak, out of the world.

"What time was it when you found the front door open?" he asked.

Marge Dove looked perplexed. "I didn't look to see, George. It was dark, I know that. If I had to guess, I'd say it was maybe three AM. It could have been four."

"What time did you go to Rick's room?"

"It was just after eight. Ten past maybe."

Cheney sat down on the edge of the mattress. What he felt all at once was a sense of being trapped inside the clockwork of a machine going haywire. No matter how hard he pushed there was no exit from this crazy mechanism called Hamland that made kids disappear.

He stared at the window, a square of gray light. He stood up.

Fred Dove said, "Have you found out anything about those two kids in the newspaper?"

"Not yet."

"And now it seems my son has joined them."

Cheney moved out into the hallway and the Doves followed him downstairs. Fred Dove, he knew, was some kind of administrative officer in City Hall, a man who hovered on the edges of power in Hamland. He had never enjoyed Fred Dove much, finding the man somewhat officious and dogmatic, with a hair-trigger sense of righteousness.

Cheney gazed toward the front door. *The kid comes this way at three, maybe four in the morning, it's dark, he's going somewhere—why, for Christ's sake? and where? And weren't ten-year-old boys afraid of the dark anyway? Or had somebody come in the black hours before dawn and snatched the child?*

"Did Rick know the other kids?" he asked.

"He never mentioned them by name," Marge Dove said. She broke off abruptly and moaned. Then, as if she were embarrassed by the sound of her anxiety, she turned her face away and clutched her husband's arm. Fred Dove looked at his wife in a critical manner, like a man who doesn't care to be touched. But that was the impression Cheney always got from Dove—a guy who went through life enclosed in Saran Wrap, enveloped and always somewhat aloof.

Now Dove comforted his wife, patting her arm the way a man might console an infant. *There, there, there.* When he was through he sniffed, drew a Kleenex across his nose, and said, "What do you propose to do, George? What steps are you taking to find these kids?"

Pinned by the questions like a butterfly stapled to a cardboard sheet, Cheney made an empty little gesture with his hands. He might have said that the connection of three missing children to Mr Zanzibar was more than his outraged sense of coincidence could take, but what he imagined was Fred Dove rushing off to City Hall and squawking about Zanzibar all over the place, demanding an investigation of the guy, banging desks and throwing paper darts at anything that moved—and Cheney didn't want this to happen. If there was deeper digging to do into the life of the illusionist, it would have to be done quietly, the way he wanted it done. A berserk administrator at City Hall was the last thing he needed.

Anne, holding Jenny Dove's hand, appeared at the top of the stairs. The little girl said, "Has my brother come back?"

"Not yet," Anne whispered, looking down in her husband's direction.

Cheney read his wife's expression. *George, this is the house next door to our own, this is our neighbor's kid that has vanished, this is a little too close to our own center* . . . He looked away from Anne, thinking how the Searses had received a bizarre phone call and the Estabans a cassette message—*What were the Doves going to get?*

Fred Dove said, "I asked you a question, George. So far you haven't answered me."

"I can't give you a simple answer, Fred. An investigation like this is complex—"

"Complex," Dove snorted. Marge raised her face and stared at Cheney with an expression of embarrassment. Dove went on, "Three kids are missing, George. I want to know what you're doing about that simple fact."

"I'll tell you *exactly* what I've told the other parents," Cheney said. "This is an ongoing investigation and until I have more relevant information, there's nothing I can possibly add to what's in the newspaper." Blah blah blah.

"That's bullshit," Dove said.

"Fred, please," Marge said. "George is doing the best he can—"

"And I'm standing here trying to find out what his best is," Dove snapped. "So far, he hasn't told me a goddam thing. I always knew he was a fast man with a parking-ticket and when it came to shuffling paper he could rank with the best. Maybe he's out of his league this time."

That hurt, Cheney thought. That went right down into his soul like a spike.

"I've told you all I can," Cheney said. "When I know more, so will you, Fred."

Dove paused a moment. He had the appearance of someone gathering all his strength for a frontal assault. In a very quiet voice he said, "Richard Bacon is a friend of mine, George. A close, personal friend."

"I'm impressed," Cheney said.

"You should be. You don't want a man like Bacon to start thinking that his own *Sheriff* is an incompetent, do you?"

Cheney, backing toward the front door, struggling with the sudden unfocussed anger he felt, managed to force a quiet smile from his lips. "Dick Bacon's thought processes have never enthralled me, Fred. In fact, I'm surprised to hear you say he has any." It was a weak retort, a blunted barb, but he wasn't able to think of anything else. Now he wished he could take it back. It was beneath him. He had responded to Fred Dove's outbreak with childishness. He felt like a kid with a broken plastic sword.

He reached the door, opened it.

Fred Dove, with all the pomposity of the career civil servant, said, "I'm going to forget you said that. I'm going to put that right out of my mind . . . for now. But you better find those kids. That's all I have to say to you, Cheney. And you better do it fast."

Dove turned and moved down the hallway. Marge stood very still, searching Cheney's face with her large, suffering eyes. A door slammed in the recesses of the house and Marge said, "Fred's upset. He loses his temper quickly. I'm sorry . . ."

Cheney reached out and touched Marge's hand lightly. "There's no need to be sorry." He raised his face, looking to the top of the stairs. Anne was gazing down at him without expression.

He stepped outside, closed the door.

He stared at his own house: empty, lifeless, it appeared frozen in the gray morning light like something trapped underwater.

He reached his car, sat behind the wheel, drummed his fingers anxiously.

George is doing the best he can . . .

Sure, he thought. That's what George is doing.

His best.

He slammed the car into drive and listened to the angry sound his tires made on concrete: a small satisfaction which soon faded, leaving him with a familiar ache inside.

He drove in the general direction of Center Avenue. He realized he no longer scanned the sidewalks and the doorways of stores for kids as he drove. It was as if he had given the children up entirely and no longer expected to see them lurking anywhere in his range of vision.

Goddammit, George. You're letting it all slide.

His car radio came to life abruptly. He heard Charlie Bannion's through thickets of static, like the voice of a man on the moon. Cheney reached for the dashboard microphone.

Charlie Bannion said, "George?"

"I'm right here," Cheney replied.

"I've been talking with the Social Security people over in Denver, George."

"What did you find?" Cheney asked.

"Somebody's been feeding you bullshit," Charlie Bannion said. "A whole crock of it."

Ellis Diamond watched Mr Zanzibar walk around the edge of the baseball lot on his way to the Youth Center. Her breath fogged the window of her office, so that her perception of the magician was unclear. His cloak floated out behind him and he glided smoothly over the grass as if on skates. Ellis placed a hand against the side of her face. Her nerves were shot. Already this morning she'd had to deal with two fights, one minor accident (little Willie Pasani had fallen from a tree and was convinced the cuts on his knee would lead to something he called "jawlock" if he didn't get fast medical attention), and the seemingly endless questions of those kids who'd read the front page of *The Progressive*.

Are they dead, Miss Diamond?

Has somebody killed Vickie and Tommy?

Ellis rubbed her eyes. She couldn't avoid the idea that she was in some terrible way to blame for the missing children. And now she suspected that a third child had vanished because only an hour ago she'd been visited by Rick Dove's father, who was searching for his son.

Sweet Jesus.

Wasn't there an end to this thing?

She watched Zanzibar until he was gone out of sight. Then she turned from the window and gazed across her tiny office at the half-open door. Two squabbling kids were banging coins inside the soda machine. Why was everything so loud today? Why did their squealing little voices seem to razor their way inside her brain? She sat behind her desk, swallowed two aspirin, thought about Zanzibar. Although the young cop Charlie Bannion had told her that Zanzibar wasn't suspected of anything, nevertheless she had the feeling Bannion wasn't exactly telling her everything he knew.

Cops worked that way, didn't they? They revealed only what they had to. They left the rest to your imagination.

What if Zanzibar *did* know something about the missing children?

It would mean that she—who had been in such a screaming *hurry* to employ the man—was just as culpable as the conjurer.

She shut her eyes: a headache rolled through her brain. She picked up the newspaper that lay open on her desk and she stuffed it inside a drawer—out of sight if not out of mind. Then she stared back at the doorway, waiting for a sight of Zanzibar.

His shadow preceded him. A darkness fell over tiles.

Ellis Diamond stood up. The soda machine outside her door clanked out cans of carbonated chemicals.

"Mr Zanzibar?" she said. The sound that emerged from her mouth was a dry whisper.

The magician looked at her from the doorway. He inclined his head slightly in what may or may not have been a greeting. He set his black leather bag down on the floor between his feet and for a moment Ellis thought of him as a travelling quack with a bag full of patent medicines and miraculous tonics.

"A policeman came to see me last night," she said. "It appears that I might have broken some law by not getting your Social Security number . . ." She lifted several sheets of paper from the desk and held them out to the man. "I must insist you fill these in, Mr Zanzibar. Otherwise . . ." Here she swallowed hard and her heart raced. "You just can't go on working here. It's as simple as that."

She couldn't look at him. Turning her face, she stared through the window and out across grassy slopes, trees, the wire fence around the baseball field. Anywhere but Zanzibar's face. The hand that held the papers trembled. Take them, please, she thought. Take them, fill them out, please.

She heard the sound of the black leather bag creak and the movement of Zanzibar's feet, but still she didn't want to look at the man. She had to be firm because the situation demanded it. And if she looked into his eyes she was afraid she'd weaken under his gaze, and then the documents would never be filled out.

She tried to control her trembling hand. Why did Zanzibar cause her to feel like this? So feeble, so out of *control*? She needed resolve, determination, she needed to erase all her earlier mistakes and blunders and oversights, to redeem herself in both her own eyes and those of Charlie Bannion.

Please, Zanzibar . . .

She moved her head slowly back toward the doorway.

Zanzibar was gone.

Infuriated, Ellis stepped out of her office and moved along the hallway that led to the windowless auditorium. How could he have done that? Slipped away like that? Didn't he realize how goddam important it was to complete the paperwork? Little streaks of anger, red flecks, raced through her brain. Zanzibar had treated her as if she didn't exist!

She pushed open the auditorium door and stopped.

The magician sat up there on the stage, surrounded by a group of about twelve kids who formed a semi-circle around him. An overhead light shone down on the man's skull, making his black greasy hair seem blue. He had oversized playing-cards in his hands and he was showing them to the children, who watched with curious intensity as if they were scared of missing a beat. Ellis felt a strange pulse beat in her throat.

She started forward, determined now to interrupt the lesson in magic and thrust the papers into Zanzibar's hand like some kind of process-server; and if he wouldn't complete the necessary data then she'd have him ejected from the Youth Center, even if that meant calling the police.

Halfway down the center aisle she paused.

She listened to the low, soporific rumble of Zanzibar's voice.

"In any form of illusion, in any kind of magic, your own belief is the most important thing. If you believe, so will your audience. If you have faith in what you're doing, your audience will have that same faith, only stronger. Geometry and logic and common sense do not apply in magic. You have to believe that you are beyond those kind of restrictions."

Ellis Diamond listened, although she hadn't meant to—but there was a quality in the way Zanzibar talked, a certain firmly insidious quality that bored gentle passages into your brain—his words ceased to be sound and became liquid, and the liquid was warm, comforting, like the gratifying waters of some relaxing stream.

"Once you have gone beyond those restrictions, anything becomes possible. You are no longer bound by everyday convention. You have stepped into a world beyond technique and trickery. You have entered a world of pure magical forms . . ."

Yes, Ellis thought.

Yes. Pure magical forms.

And the serrated edge of her anger became smooth.

Zanzibar talked like a voice in a soothing travelogue, except that he took his listeners to places recorded on no maps.

Ellis blinked her eyes, felt tension go out of her shoulders, almost as if she'd been touched by a faith-healer.

"Everything is possible. Everything is permitted. Remember that. If you do, then all illusions are real. And everything real is illusion . . ."

Zanzibar rose and his cloak fell around him. He rubbed his hands together and the cards rose upward in a single column as if they were stapled together to create a kind of ladder. The spots on the cards, the diamonds and clubs and hearts and spades *glowed*, like things illuminated by a soft concealed light. Then he made the ladder collapse abruptly and the cards were gone and his hands were as empty as those of a newborn baby.

Ellis shook her head like someone awakening abruptly from a dream.

She had been drawn in just then, sucked into the center of Zanzibar's world of illusion—a dreamy moment—but now she remembered the papers she held in her hand and her irritation returned.

Zanzibar came down from the stage and approached her. She shook the papers at him. "Please," she said.

Zanzibar took the papers from her. He surveyed them slowly, then reached out and cupped Ellis's chin in the palm of one hand. For a second she wondered if he were going to make her disappear the way he had the playing-cards. His fingers were cold as he turned her face round toward him.

Her eyes met his.

She felt weak and impressionable. It was as if all the codes to her behavior were written on flimsy paper that Zanzibar could read.

Zanzibar smiled, a white smile in the center of a white face. "Leave the papers with me," he said. A whisper, a whiff of words.

She had to strain to hear him. "You promise you'll complete them? I must have your word."

The magician nodded. He folded the papers and put them inside his cloak. Ellis had a sinking feeling she'd never see them again, that anything placed in the folds of the magician's cloak never reappeared.

"I must have them soon," she said. "Today." She was conscious of how her words echoed inside the auditorium. "Today," she said again. "Please."

Zanzibar continued to smile.

She could no longer look at him. She turned and walked up the aisle toward the doors. There, even though she had no desire to look back, she paused and turned and saw that Zanzibar hadn't moved.

What struck her as strange was the semi-circle of children who sat on the stage behind him. Faceless in the overhead light, their features blank and flat, they sat motionless, curiously listless, as if they were waiting for Zanzibar to breathe life back into them.

She pushed the doors open and moved out into the hallway. A small boy was savagely kicking the soda machine. *"Sonofabitch don't work—"*

She went inside her office, closed the door, sat down behind her desk. She began to shake. She shook so badly that she had to fumble inside her purse for half of an Equanil, medication she hadn't taken in months.

Max Crouch came in the room without knocking. Normally she would have said something about good manners and the nature of privacy, but she let this minor infraction slide too.

The impossible way she'd felt about Zanzibar for that wicked flash of time—

Dear God. What had gotten into her? Something serpentine had moved through her, affecting her senses, dictating her responses.

Max Crouch slouched toward the desk. The rims of his eyes were red and moist.

"Looks like you got a visitor," he mumbled.

Ellis Diamond heard his words but didn't absorb them.

Max Crouch jerked his head toward the window. "Sheriff Cheney," he said.

"Cheney?"

"The very same. Strutting this way like his pants are on fire." Max Crouch smiled in his peculiar manner: it was like a sudden fissure in a leather glove.

Ellis Diamond rose and looked out of the window.

Below Naughton's Hill there was an ancient stream, a nameless ribbon of water that slid through Hamland on a journey to nowhere. Sometimes it vanished underground on its course; at other times it took detours through a system of man-made pipes. But here, under the shadow of Naughton's Hill, it wandered idly for a mile or so, green and sluggish and fertile with mosquitoes. Overhanging trees crowded the surface of the water, creating a shadowy bower.

The two men who stood on the bank of the stream were

hidden by the density of branches and leaves. They could not be seen from any point on Naughton's Hill, nor from the road that ran past fifty yards away.

One of the men, Hugh Estaban, dropped a stone on the surface of the water and watched the green liquid engulf it.

The other man, Fred Dove, stood at the very edge of the bank and looked down into the water a while before he cleared his throat and spat.

Dove squatted, his long arms hanging between his legs. Estaban, who hadn't wanted this encounter, moved his body uneasily, causing branches to rustle against him.

"I called Tom," Fred Dove said. "He isn't coming."

Dove the organizer, Hugh Estaban thought. When something had to be put together, Fred Dove was the one who would do it. At least, that was the way it always had been in the past. Fred was the kind of man who always ended up being the secretary of whatever club he joined. Some people had a talent for that kind of busy-work. They needed to be indispensable.

"He refuses to see this thing clearly," Dove said, sniffing as he spoke. "He won't admit certain things to himself."

"I don't blame him," Estaban said drily. "I didn't want to come here either."

Fred Dove stood up, straightening his long angular body. From somewhere above, from one of the houses that lay against the side of the hill, there came the sound of a power lawnmower. It sounded curiously sharp, unmuffled by the surrounding trees.

"I wanted to call the old man," Dove said. "I thought about it, then I changed my mind. The last time I talked with him, he was wandering a bit. Later, if I have to, I'll get in touch with him."

The old man, Estaban thought. What could the old man do? He was a machine running down, rusted, too far gone into decay. Once, years ago, he'd been strong and intelligent and alert, but he was only a shadow of that former self. Sometimes Estaban saw the old man in town, walking along the sidewalk like a man trying to pick his way between cracks.

Estaban saw a small bird pick the surface of the stream, then dart away between trees: a plump insect for lunch. He plunged his hands in the pockets of his baggy pants. "I don't see the point in any of this, Fred. I don't see why you want us to get together."

"Use your head," Dove said, doing something nervously strange with his hands—unconsciously wrapping a snapped twig inside a Kleenex as if he meant to send it on a long hazardous journey through the US Mail. "We're in this together. All of us."

Estaban figured that Dove would say something like this sooner or later. It was the kind of phrase Fred Dove would use because he was a man who still had something of the Boy Scout about him. He believed in the pooling of ideas, in people getting their heads together. He was a team player. No matter how dirty the game, he was first and always a team player.

"We're talking about our kids, Hugh," Fred Dove said.

"I don't need to be reminded of that."

"We're talking about their lives—"

Estaban looked away. For the past few hours, ever since he'd talked with George Cheney, he had been obsessed with the feeling that his daughter was no longer alive. Not dead, but *no longer alive,* as if there were some terrific difference when you used a euphemism. He had tried to sleep, clutching his wife's silent body, his mind filled with images of Vickie in the most violent of situations.

If she was dead, if Tommy Sears and Rick Dove were also dead, then what the fuck did anything matter? Why the hell had he agreed to meet Fred Dove by the banks of this rancid stream as if they were a couple of spies exchanging microdots in a cheap espionage novel?

"We've got to have a plan," Dove said.

"Plan?" Estaban looked at the other man, fascinated by the cold practicality in the guy's voice.

"We've got to decide what we're going to do, Hugh."

"What *can* we do?" Estaban was suddenly impatient. He wanted to get away from this place, he wanted to go home. He didn't want to stand here and listen to Fred Dove while his wife was sitting, rigid and afraid, by a silent telephone.

"The way I see it, Hugh, we're going to be asked to make a cash contribution before we ever see our kids again. Personally, I could raise twenty grand. Maybe twenty-five. What about you?"

Estaban felt the day tilt around him. "Who's going to ask for money, Fred?"

"The kidnapper is—"

"What makes you so sure?"

Fred Dove smiled. "It's obvious. It's no goddam coincidence that he took these three kids in particular, is it? It's not exactly something he did at random, Hugh. He waited. He waited a long time. He planned like a crazy man. And then he struck. I don't have to spell it out for you, do I?"

Estaban shook his head slowly. Fred Dove lived in a cut-and-dry world, a universe of tidy compartments. For him, it was simple: the kids had been snatched, there would follow a ransom demand, you paid up and you got your children back. The account was closed. The matter was finished.

"Fred, listen to me. There haven't been any ransom demands."

"That's because he wanted all three kids before he did anything, don't you see that? He wasn't going to ask until he'd finished what he started out to do."

Estaban looked down into the stream. For a second, he imagined his daughter floating just beneath the opaque surface, her hair spread in death, her big eyes open. Christ, Christ—he shut his eyes and although he had no sense of religion these days, he understood he was offering up some kind of prayer to whoever might be listening.

Fred Dove said, "How much can you raise, Hugh?"

Estaban opened his eyes. "What makes you think it was *him?*"

"Who else could it be? There's no other candidate."

"Fred, it was a long time ago. How the hell could he have ever found out?"

"That doesn't interest me, Hugh. You play the game the way it's set up, you don't go asking for the motivation behind the rules. And it's his game now. All we want is to get our kids back."

"What if it isn't him?" Estaban asked.

"Christ," Fred Dove said, exasperated now.

"I see him around, Fred. He doesn't look like the kind of guy who's planning much of anything. I haven't ever seen him sober. Okay, okay, suppose it is him—what's to stop us from confronting the guy?"

"As soon as you did that, you could kiss your kid goodbye. If we confronted him, you could be sure he'd never tell us where he's got the kids stashed."

"I'm still not sure you're right about him, Fred—"

Fred Dove waved Estaban's objection aside. "How much cash can you get your hands on?"

"I don't know for sure," Estaban said. "Maybe about thirty thousand. But it would take a couple of days."

"Start arranging it now, Hugh. Save some time. I'll talk with Tom. See what he can come up with. God knows, it probably won't be very much." Fred Dove paused. He tossed the twig and the Kleenex into the stream, where the tissue absorbed water and started to sink. "I don't think you should have any doubts about this. The guy wants money. He's never had any. He's had nothing but a bad taste in his mouth for years."

Estaban moved nearer to the water's edge.

All at once he wished more than anything that he could turn the clocks of his time back to a certain summer night in Hamland when the sun had just gone down and the landscape was filled with a lingering golden light and a girl's laughter hung in the warm air like the resonant sound of a sweet bird—

Turn them back—

Back and back and back—

Paying ransom money couldn't give you back your decency. It couldn't restore the still center of peacefulness to your life. Money, which Hugh Estaban had juggled and computed and hidden and laundered on behalf of his clients for years, seemed suddenly a senseless thing to him.

Fred Dove said, "Now all we can do is wait to hear from him. But at least we can be prepared."

Estaban turned away from the stream.

Out there ahead of him, like a vision seen between trees, his daughter's face appeared to float. He was filled with the urge to throw himself on the ground and beg her forgiveness even as he knew that all the begging in the world would never bring back balance to his existence.

He knew he was damned.

Charlie Bannion, standing by the reception desk at the station and sipping water from a waxy cup, saw the front door swing open and Lily Hubbard step inside. The old girl was carrying a large canvas shopping-bag and grunting as she moved. A veil hung lightly against her face but Bannion could see vivid streaks of makeup beneath the flimsy material. She wore a hat which reminded Bannion of a nightmare he'd had as a kid, when he'd been carried off into a dark sky by a creature that might have been the unnatural offspring of an albatross and a giant anteater.

Bannion, who had been pondering the fake SS numbers Zanzibar had fobbed off on George Cheney, moved toward the woman. He had some idea of perhaps assisting her with her burden, but she scowled at him as she whipped her veil away from her face. He stepped back. It was well-known around Hamland that Mrs Hubbard had become deranged in her widowhood. She was, however, said to be harmless.

"Where's George Cheney?" she asked. There was a wintry snap in her voice.

Bannion, who had a soft spot for eccentrics, smiled at the woman. "He's out right now, Mrs Hubbard."

"When's he coming back?"

"I'm not certain. Maybe I can help you?"

Lily Hubbard gazed at the young cop. She plopped her bag down on the surface of the desk. "What's your name?"

"Bannion."

"You're too young to be a cop," she said.

Charlie Bannion hitched his belt up. "I'm twenty-five, Mrs Hubbard."

Lily Hubbard appeared to take this information and analyze it. Her eyes, two dark trenches in her face, became glassy for a second. "I'd rather see George Cheney, but I guess you'll have to do, Mister."

"What's the problem anyhow?" Bannion asked.

Lily Hubbard rummaged through her bag, hauling out

things as she dug. Pantyhose. Lipsticks. A ragged hairnet. "I got it somewhere," she said, wheezing a little.

"What have you got?" Bannion asked, amused.

"Yeah. Here it is."

From the depths of her bag she produced a yellow baseball cap, which she placed on the desk with flair.

"I figure you might be looking for this," she said. "If I believe what I read in the newspapers."

Puzzled, the young cop examined the hat.

"The boy's initials are inside, if you know where to look." Charlie Bannion turned the cap over, looked inside. In pale ballpoint ink were the letters: TS.

THIRTEEN

IN THE SMALL PASSAGEWAY BEHIND THE STAGE GEORGE CHENEY was surrounded by plumed hats and wooden swords and extravagant capes, all of which had been stacked carelessly against the wall. He saw Zanzibar come toward him from the direction of the stage. The magician had his hands concealed inside his dark cloak. Cheney imagined taking that cloak and going through it stitch by stitch, fold by fold, uncovering its secret recesses and hidden mysteries.

The magician brought his long white hands out from beneath the cloak and spread them. Despite himself, despite his resolve to ignore those hands and with them any expectation of trickery, Cheney found himself watching the fingers.

"What can I do for you, Sheriff?" Zanzibar asked.

"You know I'd check out the information you gave me," Cheney said. "What I can't understand is why you lied."

Zanzibar looked surprised. "Lied? Did I do that? What makes you say that?"

"It's an age of computers," Cheney said. A tiny nerve of excitement worked in his head. When Charlie Bannion had called him to say that the Social Security numbers were false, he'd had to struggle with a sense of elation, to keep damped down the idea that Zanzibar's lie was the first apparent break in the case. After all, the magician might have reasons for lying that had nothing to do with missing kids: it wasn't good policy to jump to conclusions and make connections when all you had were the thinnest of thin threads. Just the same, the excitement died hard. Even Zanzibar's coolness, in the face of the discovery, didn't cause Cheney dismay. Not yet.

"Computers," Zanzibar said scornfully. "Computers are so unpredictable. Do you really trust them, Sheriff?"

"Up to a point," Cheney answered.

"Enough to come here and accuse me of lying to you?"

Cheney nodded. "I want to know why you gave me phony numbers and fabricated names." Cheney took out his notebook and flipped the pages. "One of the numbers belongs to somebody called Altman, who lives in Arizona. The other to a person named Schleyer in Oregon. You claimed to be Stanley Oakes from Potsdam. And the girl was supposed to be Mary Beth Orlando from Minneapolis."

Zanzibar said nothing for a while. He turned his fingers over and studied them casually. "Did I really do that, Sheriff? Oh dear, did I really mislead you?"

"Don't play games," Cheney said. "I'm not in the mood."

Zanzibar, who turned his eyes down and looked for all the world like a small boy scolded for having his hand in the cookie jar, said, "I must have given you the wrong numbers, Sheriff. After all, it's so damned hard to keep nine digits straight in your mind, isn't it?"

"Some people find it quite easy," Cheney said. "Like remembering their own birthday."

"I have no head for numbers."

"What *is* your real name, Zanzibar?" Cheney asked.

"Didn't I tell you I was Stanley Oakes from Potsdam?"

"You want to keep that one? Or do you want to change it to something else?"

"Why deny my own given name, Sheriff? Mundane as it is—"

"And the girl is still Mary Beth Orlando?"

"I can only tell you what she told me. Do you think she's a

209

liar, Sheriff? Do you think *she* misled me and in turn I sent you off in the wrong direction?"

Cheney glanced at his notebook. "Maybe you can explain why the Social Security Administration, with all its computerized link-ups, has no record of a Stanley Oakes from Potsdam. While you're at it, maybe you could also explain why there's no record of a Mary Beth Orlando in Minneapolis. I'd be fascinated to hear."

Zanzibar looked devastated. "It must be a computer foul-up. Maybe Mary Beth and I have somehow slipped between the floppy disks. Something like that can erase your entire life, Sheriff."

"I'm sure it can," Cheney said. "Let me get this straight. You're saying that although you gave me the wrong SS numbers, just the same your real name is Stanley Oakes and the girl is really Mary Beth Orlando? You're still sticking to your original choices? Does that sum it up?"

"Accurately," Zanzibar said, his tone one of slight amusement.

Cheney, who felt he was being mocked, angrily slammed his notebook shut. "Then what I'd like from you, Zanzibar, is your real SS number and that of the girl. When I have them, I can run them back through the SS computers and that way we can make absolutely sure that your alleged names match the numbers. Then we'll all be happy. Is there some possibility you can conjure these numbers back into your mind and let me have them right now?"

"Sheriff, Sheriff. Do I detect sarcasm?"

"You detect fatigue," Cheney said. "You detect weariness. I told you before, I'm in no mood for games. Give me the numbers. That's all I want. If I find they're false this time, I promise you I'll come out to your house and turn the place upside down—"

"Which would be quite an illusion—"

"It would be more than that, Zanzibar. If you're hiding something, you can bet your ass I'll get to it sooner or later. Given the mood I'm in, it's going to be sooner. If you're interested in a peaceful life, you better get your memory cells working pretty damn fast." Cheney leaned against the wall.

There was a tightness in the center of his chest. He saw Zanzibar's technique clearly—it was simple confusion, nothing more. The magician hoped to muddy the waters with numbers and names until he had Cheney going round in circles. But why? Why did the guy need to play that kind of game when he must know that Cheney, with his access to computers, would uncover any lie in the end?

"I'm waiting," Cheney said. "I've got a lot of time."

Zanzibar smiled. "You only think you do, Sheriff."

"Meaning?"

"As I understand it, your time is limited. I read the newspapers. I hear certain gossip. You're going to come under all kinds of pressure."

"Likewise," Cheney said. "If you don't start being honest with me."

Zanzibar ignored this. "Three children are missing, I believe."

"How did you know that? There were only two mentioned in the newspaper, Zanzibar."

"Is that meant to be a trap for me, George? Am I supposed to have made a blunder or something?" Zanzibar laughed, a brittle sound. "How did I know there are three missing kids as opposed to the two in the newspaper? Simple, George, simple. All I need to do is keep my ears open around this wonderful Parks and Recreation program. The scuttlebutt is like wildfire." Zanzibar laughed again and held his hands forward, his expression one of unconcealed pity for a Sheriff who had a case he couldn't solve. "Here. Handcuff me, Sheriff. I fell for your little ploy. You're so intelligent, how did I ever think I could baffle you for long? Please, take me in for questioning, I'm all yours—"

Cheney, who thought he could hear a nerve inside him snap, did something then that he immediately regretted. Stepping forward, he seized Zanzibar by the collar of his cloak and pushed him back at the wall, surprised by the weightlessness of the man and the way he didn't resist the sudden display of force. With his face only an inch or so from the magician's, Cheney understood that he wanted to inflict pain here, break a bone or two, wipe that smile off Zanzibar's face for good, destroy the smug core of the man. Rage created a white-hot hollow in the center of his brain and his breathing was labored and his blood seemed to churn through him as though it had become somehow clotted in his veins.

Christ, what was he doing? What kind of shapeless desires had caused him to attack Zanzibar? All Zanzibar had really done was point out Cheney's own inadequacies: that was it, that was enough.

"I'm impressed, George," Zanzibar said. "I'm really impressed by your strength. God, you're a tough guy."

Cheney wiped the back of one hand across his mouth. He was trembling. It was as if somebody else had taken control of his body for a split second, somebody to whom violence was as ordinary as breathing air.

Zanzibar smoothed his cloak with a flutter of his hands.

Cheney looked at the young man. A silent apology formed in his mouth but he didn't utter it. What he knew now was that he'd lost whatever slight advantage he'd had in the situation. His leverage, such as it was, had evaporated when he'd succumbed to a brute gesture of frustration. Zanzibar, smiling, knew it too.

"That wasn't very smart, George. Was it?"

Cheney said nothing.

He looked down at the notebook in his hand, then began to flip pages. It was a matter now of getting back to interrupted business, but the atmosphere was different than before. A balance had shifted. Cheney's earlier anger had gone and he felt empty, like an unrehearsed actor going through motions in which he has no belief and even less understanding.

"We were talking about numbers," he said in a quiet voice.

"Yes," Zanzibar said. "I believe we were."

"I hope you've remembered them."

"Unfortunately, no."

Cheney closed his notebook.

Zanzibar said, "May I make a suggestion?"

Cheney nodded.

"I'll telephone you. When I go home today and check the numbers, I'll call them through to you, George."

George, Cheney thought. The intimacy made him feel strange.

"I'll wait for your call, but I won't wait too long," Cheney said. Sighing, he put his notebook in the pocket of his shirt. He felt dissatisfied, vaguely foolish. You handled this like an asshole, he thought. A complete moron. Now he had to re-establish himself from the very beginning. "If you don't come through for me this time, or if you lie to me again, I'm going to come down hard on you. Is that understood?"

"Perfectly, George. It couldn't be more plain."

Cheney turned away, going toward a short flight of steps that led around the side of the stage. He was aware of Zanzibar watching him, conscious of eyes burning into the back of his neck. He knew, without looking, that the magician was smiling.

When he reached the top step, a tiny shrill voice made him turn and look around.

Zanzibar had one hand inside a glove-puppet, a white furry rabbit with exaggerated front teeth and long floppy ears. The rabbit had its head cocked in Cheney's direction. Zanzibar was making the thing talk in a high-pitched voice. His fingers worked the rabbit's small arms, causing them to gesticulate wildly.

"I don't tell lies, Mr Cheney, sir. I never tell lies. You ever hear of a poor bunny telling lies, Mr Cheney, sir? Georgie-Porgie, pudding and pie . . . Lost some kids, it made him cwy . . ."

Cheney fought to ignore this. What he was supposed to do anyhow? Run the guy in for impersonating a rabbit? stick him in the slammer for the crime of ventriloquism with malicious intent? He reached the empty stage area. The shrill voice followed after him. He paused, staring out across the darkened auditorium. Beneath his feet lay a couple of discarded playing-cards.

Playing-cards. Talking rabbits. Disappearances.

Where the hell was the real world and why had he lost his grip on it so completely? First with Fred Dove, when he'd tried to slash out at the man with a childish retort. Now with Zanzibar and the brief flurry of violence.

Dismayed, he moved to the edge of the stage.

He was annoyed with himself, the way he'd mismanaged

things, his failure to cope. He was tired of the fractures in himself.

The doors opened at the top of the center aisle.

Charlie Bannion was standing there in shadow.

"George," the young cop said. "There's a man called Arthur Rigley I think we should talk to."

Marge Dove, who started at every small sound, placed her coffee cup in the saucer without sipping from it. Anne had laced the coffee with brandy, hoping it would help settle her friend's nerves. The two women were sitting in Marge's kitchen.

In the back yard, seemingly unaware of the trauma inside the house, the girl Jenny soothingly spoke to a bevy of Care Bears and Cabbage Patch dolls. The small faces were all lined up as if in a classroom for the mentally retarded.

Anne lit a cigarette, passed it to her friend. Marge took it absently and puffed, her fingers shaking. Then she crushed it in an ashtray where it continued to burn.

"Drink," Anne said. "It'll help."

Marge blinked, as if the light were too strong for her eyes. "Where's Fred?"

"He went out," Anne answered. "He said he'd be back quickly."

Marge turned her face to the open door and gazed out across the back yard. She watched her daughter for a time. Sounds drifted into the kitchen, gentle admonitions.

"Beatrice, you haven't done your homework . . . You can take that smile off your face, Paddy O'Bear, because you haven't done yours either . . .

Marge laid her hands on the table, palms flat. "I keep wondering if there's something I overlooked," and she gave a strange giggle. "I wonder if I sent Rick to stay with his grandmother and I forgot all about it or if I asked him to run an errand for me and it slipped my mind . . . the middle of the night, though, I wouldn't send him anywhere at that time, in the dark, would I?"

These were the sounds of somebody breaking in pieces, Anne thought. These were threads snapping. She edged the coffee cup toward her friend. "Try to drink this, Marge. If

214

you like, I'll see if I can find a Valium for you. I think I have some at home . . ."

"Valium?" Marge got up from the table and wandered to the open door. She rattled her fingertips against the screen. "George will find the kid, won't he? I mean, he's going to find all of them, isn't he?"

"Yes," Anne said. She thought of the burden of other people's hopes her husband was carrying and she felt sorry for him. He'd find those kids, though. She still had that kind of faith in him even if she saw that he no longer had it in himself.

"What have I overlooked, Anne? What could I possibly have forgotten?"

Anne went to her friend, gently stroked the back of her neck. "Nothing. You overlooked nothing, Marge."

"It's a horrible feeling, Anne. Somebody must have come here and opened the door and then he went upstairs to Rick's room and just took the boy, just *took* him . . . Somebody came here while we were asleep . . . I keep thinking how strange it is we didn't hear anything . . . I mean, if somebody took Rick, why didn't the boy cry out . . ."

Anne nodded slowly. She studied Jenny for a second: one of the Care Bears had apparently smartmouthed her and was being duly spanked. *Ow ow ow ow!* "I don't know the answers to your questions, Marge, but it seems likely that the boy did call out, only you were fast asleep and didn't hear anything. Maybe something was clamped across his mouth . . ."

"I don't like to think of him . . ." Marge shut her eyes, swayed against the doorjamb. She didn't finish her sentence. Tears squeezed themselves out from under her eyelids.

Anne held the woman tightly for a time. Earlier, when Fred Dove had left, she had thought it strange any husband would disappear at a time when he was badly needed for support. But Fred, who had gone upstairs for a while and made a phone call in an inaudible voice, had departed a little furtively.

"Did Fred say where he was going?" Marge asked.

Anne shook her head.

Marge stepped into the back yard, looking lost and vulnerable beneath the gray sky. Somewhere there was a milky suggestion of sunlight, pallid and hidden by cloud cover.

Anne followed her outside. The air was heavy and clammy, like the inside of a moist glove. Marge walked across the grass toward the rear wall of the yard, where she paused to pick something up.

It was a deflated soccer ball, imploded yellow and black hexagons of leather, soft and misshapen. Marge held the ball against her chest.

Anne said, "Listen, Marge, maybe Rick hasn't disappeared like the other kids. Maybe he's got nothing to do with them. It might be something different. He could have wandered off early this morning without telling you . . . That's possible, isn't it? He might have made arrangements with a friend to go fishing and like any average kid overlooked the need to tell his parents." Babble babble, Anne thought.

Marge Dove dropped the punctured ball. "Rick wouldn't do anything like that, Anne . . . I know my own son and he's too considerate to wander away without telling me where. I know him."

Marge spoke with the all the mystical certainty of a mother's instinct. She went toward the wall and stood with her back to it, gazing across the yard at the house. A crooked cottonwood tree slanted in front of the kitchen window. At the center of the tree was a treehouse, hammered together out of hardwood boards and assorted two-by-fours. Rick Dove sometimes took Danny into that treehouse for hours at a time. Anne felt a strong sense of longing. Why the hell couldn't everything be put back the way it had been a few days before? Why was it all so fragmented? All these fault-lines, all these corrosions, which had developed in the peaceful heart of Hamland, were running through Marge Dove's heart too.

"He's been gone a long time," Marge said.

Anne, conscious of an edge of hysteria in her friend, wondered whether Marge was referring to Rick or Fred. She wasn't sure. Marge swayed a little, closing her eyes, sighing. Anne gazed at her with concern.

"Let's go back inside, Marge."

"I like it here."

"Fine. That's fine. I thought maybe you'd want to lie down." Anne listened to the cautious note in her own voice. Being around Marge in the woman's present mood was like walking across a field of buried landmines. A careless step and everything would go up.

"Uh-uh," and Marge shook her head, staring once more at the cottonwood tree and the ramparts of the treehouse. "Fred didn't say where he was going?"

"No, he didn't."

Marge turned her face upward to the sky and blinked like a blind person, feeling a source of light without seeing it. "He's been unfaithful, did you know that?"

"Marge—"

"Really. He has."

"You don't need to tell me this—"

"It's okay." Marge pressed her knuckles into the lids of her eyes, but she didn't cry. "It's not much of a home for a kid when there's that kind of tension between the parents."

Anne, listening to this as if she were seated at the sick-bed of a terminal patient, absorbing it half-heartedly so she could dispose of it easily later on, twisted her wedding-ring round and round. She wanted to interrupt her friend, to still this confession, but what she realized was that for Marge Dove right then it was easier to talk about her husband's infidelity than to go on exploring the painful mystery of the missing boy.

"Fred wanders, you see. That's how I think about his behavior. A kind of wandering. I never confronted him with it. It's all just below the surface. Maybe that's unhealthy, I don't know . . . Maybe if we'd brought it out into the open it might have been different. Fred can't help himself. He just can't help himself."

Marge paused, appearing to hold her breath for a long time. A pulse beat in her throat visibly. Anne looked away.

"Young girls," Marge said. "He likes very young girls—"

"Marge, don't put yourself through this."

"Once, I even had to deal with the complaints of two outraged parents because Fred was paying what they called unhealthy attention to their daughter. A fourteen-year-old, Anne. Fourteen years of age . . ."

Anne picked at the grass with the toe of her sneaker.

"I had to defend my husband for his behavior and then I had to go on as if nothing had happened because he told me it was a moment of weakness and it wouldn't happen again. Then it did. Another moment of weakness. You see, that's Fred's life, Anne. All these moments of weakness, one after the other, because he's sick and can't help himself—"

"You could have left him, Marge—"

"Where would I go? What would I do with the children?" Marge laid her face against Anne's shoulder. She was strangely quiet now, withdrawn—yet Anne could feel small clouds of pain building through her.

"The boy's gone," Marge said eventually and her voice was thin, obstructed by tears she didn't want to cry. "You know what I think, Anne? You know what I really think? We're being paid back for Fred's behavior. We're being paid back for all the goddam awful things Fred has done. Like we're paying off some terrible debt and the price is our own son—"

Anne, patting her friend's shoulder and shushing her, stared toward the house. Fred Dove was standing in the kitchen doorway, watching the two women.

When he started to move across the grass, he did so briskly, coughing as he walked. Marge raised her face from Anne's shoulder and looked at her husband and her slack unhappy mouth formed a misshapen oval.

"You should come indoors and lie down, dear," Fred said.

"Yes, yes, I should." She held her arm out for Fred to take.

"Maybe if you sleep for a while, things will look better later," and Fred wheeled toward the house, his wife's arm linked to his own. He turned back to look at Anne. "Thanks for staying with her. We appreciate it. We really do."

Fred Dove smiled. He vanished inside the house, his wife attached to him like an invalid unable to walk under her own power. Anne tried to imagine him attracting young teenage girls, but couldn't. How did he do it? It couldn't be charm unless there was a side to Fred Dove she'd never witnessed. It certainly wasn't his looks or any overwhelming masculinity he projected. Perhaps young girls fell for flattery and attention, with a dash of the illicit thrown in for good measure. Young girls who enjoyed the idea of a married man spending money on them . . .

Anne moved toward the back door and stood there for a long time. Jenny went on playing with her dolls, lost in a world of her own making. Once, Anne thought she heard Fred Dove's voice drift out. He was saying something about how he'd do everything in his power to bring the boy back, Marge would see, a day or so and everything would be normal again. Marge sobbed once, a drawn-out sound, before a door was loudly shut and everything closed down in total silence.

Silence and emptiness.

Feeling burdened by Marge's secrets, Anne kneeled down beside Jenny in the grass.

"This bear has been very bad," the girl said, turning one of the sickly cute animals over in her lap.

"Yeah? What did he do that was terrible?"

"He tried to run away from home," Jenny said.

She spanked the creature twice.

Ronald Kelly, who always had trouble with the new word processors installed in *The Progressive*'s offices, tapped cautiously on the keyboard in front of him. He gazed at the console as if he were staring into the face of an enemy.

STILL NO LEADS ON MISSING CHILDREN

Kelly sat back, stroking his jaw at the place where he had cut himself shaving that morning. Across the newsroom, known as the bullpen, Kelly saw young Tony Morrison tap away at his own keyboard. Morrison, keen and fresh and outrageously ambitious, understood the new machines at least as well as the technicians who had installed them. He had a grasp of such jargon as "megabytes" and "baud rate" and "sysgen" and Kelly envied him his easy familiarity with something he personally found complicated. Hell, it was a New Age and young Morrison was one of the New Men and that was all there was to it: Kelly knew he was becoming a fossil himself.

Morrison stood up and looked across the room.

Kelly went back to his keyboard, pecking at it like a man who suspects his supper is poisoned.

Morrison leaned over his shoulder and read the console.

"No leads," Morrison said.

"The kid reads," Kelly said.

"What do you think, Ron? Where do you think those kids are at?"

Kelly shrugged. He looked up at the young man, whose territory on *The Progressive* was limited to sports and minor local events—flower shows, weddings, church socials. Kelly's dominion covered the big features, such as they were, and those stories categorized as in-depth human interest articles. But Kelly, given his experience of human nature and its labyrinthine ways, knew that Morrison was angling for his job.

"I only report the shit," Kelly said. "I don't need to analyze it as well."

Morrison had beautiful white teeth and so he smiled a lot. Kelly compared those choppers with his own broken-down bunch and his receding gums and the contrast dismayed him.

Smiling, the young man said, "It's got all the texture of a terrific story, Ron."

Texture, Kelly thought. It was one of those new words. Like *scenario*. Like *theme-oriented*. Like *interface*. All this new language depressed him.

"It's not going to be so terrific, Tony, if you stand over my shoulder jawboning me while I should be writing the goddam thing."

"Excuse me," Morrison said. "Pardon me for breathing."

"You're excused." Kelly laid his hands on the keyboard. There was a bad taste in his mouth left over from a lunch of salami and cucumber salad. Plus his eyes ached from the strain of staring at the goddam little TV screen in front of him. He started to type, hitting some wrong letters because Morrison was still hovering and making him nervous.

THE PIPER

ACCORDING TO SOURCEX WITHIN THE SHERIFF'S OFFICQ

"You want to borrow my Webster's?" Morrison asked, crumpling a paperclip and tossing it toward the wastebasket. "Better still, you want me to type for you?"

"Get out of my sight," Kelly said. He pressed a couple of keys and the sentence disappeared. Drifting back to his own desk, Morrison began to sing *The Age of Aquarius*.

Kelly started to type again, but this time the sound of his telephone interrupted him.

He picked it up and heard a woman's voice.

"You're the one writing the story about the missing kids? Kelly?"

"That's me. Who am I talking with?"

"You don't need to know my name," the woman said. "But you'll be interested in what I've got to say."

Kelly said nothing. He always distrusted people who were reluctant to give out their names: it was an axiom of his that those who didn't like to see their names in print were freaks of nature with something to hide.

"Well?" the woman asked. "You interested or not?"

"Depends on what you have to say, I guess."

"Two things. First, the cops are about to take somebody into custody."

"How would you know something like that?" Kelly asked.

"Never mind," said the woman. "I know. That should be good enough for you. Second, another kid has vanished. The name of the man the cops took is Arthur Rigley. The kid who disappeared is called Rick Dove. You got that?"

"I've got it, but I'd still like to know who I'm talking to—"

"Don't push it. I'm only interested in the press having access to information the public has a right to know about. I don't want my name in your paper. But if you're interested in certainties, you can take it from me that this Arthur Rigley is the man responsible for the children. All three of them. You can bet on it."

Then the line was dead.

Kelly put the receiver down. He looked at the scratch-pad where he'd written the information the anonymous caller had given him. Arthur Rigley was unknown to him. The other name, however, was not. Rick Dove's father, Fred, was some kind of asshole at City Hall, one of those faceless bureaucrats with a spread-sheet instead of a heart, a guy who thought he had been given a mandate from God personally. A year ago, Kelly had written a series of boring interviews with local functionaries under the general rubric: The People Who Keep Hamland Ticking.

Yeah. Like a grandfather clock.

He stood up, switching his word processor off.

It would be easy to get something out of Fred Dove, because the guy had an insatiable appetite for getting himself into the paper.

Sheriff Cheney, on the other hand, wouldn't give jack shit away until he was good and ready.

Wondering about the anonymous caller, he stepped toward the door.

Morrison looked at him. "A hot one, Ron?"

"Yeah. A real live wire."

"Don't step on any manhole covers. I read your horoscope this morning and it ain't good, Ron. It ain't good at all."

When Lily Hubbard hung up the telephone, she left her apartment and went out into the back yard of her home on Gunnison Avenue.

She was carrying something in one hand.

She sat down in a deck-chair of striped canvas and looked at the sky, gray patches of which were visible through thick branches of oak and cottonwood. In the distance, she heard the sound of kids shouting. She shut her eyes: she had a sudden feeling of inner tranquility, a sense of deep peace. It seemed to her she was drifting out over the rooftops of Hamland, as if she were a bird. Below, she could see the streets the way a bird might, gray ribbons winding through greenery. She floated above Naughton's Hill, over the steeple of Hamland Lutheran, over the tiny figures playing in the municipal park, up and over Slattery's slaughterhouse and Rosita's food factory, seeing as she drifted the homes of Fred and Marge Dove, Hugh and Liz Estaban, Courtney and Thomas Sears.

Pausing a moment, she found herself looking down at the house where George and Anne Cheney lived. And then she was gone again, flying over the freeway and the land that sloped away from that artery toward the foothills and such remote locations as Gowrie Canyon . . .

When she opened her eyes the illusion of buoyancy was gone. She tilted her head to one side in the fashion of a person listening. There was a rhythmic ticking sound inside her brain and she imagined tiny wheels turning, gears rolling and slipping one against the other, a rotation of shafts in harmony.

The Judge had always said that in all creation there was no artifact more magnificent, more complex and yet more base than the human brain. *It can be made to create great poetry, Lily, or it can be used to devise the most terrible schemes . . .*

The Judge was always right. She had never questioned his opinions and comments.

Lily placed her hands in her lap.

She touched the object she had carried into the yard with her. She picked it up, turned it over. It was a child's sneaker. A Converse that had seen better days.

A kid's sneaker.

Pale blue.

Size 4½.

Zena, a city girl, with no sense of direction unless she was aided by street signs and intersections, had walked some little way from the house before she turned to look back. When she realized she hadn't come as far as she *felt* she'd travelled, and the house seemed only a hundred yards away, she understood that distances in the canyon were deceptive. The dirt road she was walking along sucked at her ankles and everywhere she looked there were the flat muddy surfaces of puddles left from last night's rain.

The low hills surrounding the canyon were deceptive also, seeming at times to be very close to her, then at other times to be inconceivable distances away; you couldn't tell where the gray hills ended and the sky began because there was a fusion of grayness out there.

It was humid too, one of those days that dragged at you, settling on your flesh with the persistence of a mosquito.

I'm doing the right thing, Ma, she thought. *I'm blowing this joint which is what I should have done days ago . . .*

She paused, turned to look at the house again. Its blank windows gazed out at the canyon like glaucomic eyes. She chewed on some spearmint gum—the only provisions she'd thought to bring—and watched the house as if at any moment she expected it to rear up and give pursuit.

You had your chance last night when that sheriff was here . . . why didn't the guy get your message?

She surveyed the canyon around her now. This mud road led, she knew, through the gray walls and out to the freedom of a narrow blacktop highway. There, with any luck, she'd hitch a ride and then she'd be gone for good to a place where Zanzibar couldn't touch her.

She was wearing a black leather jacket and bluejeans, and boots that weren't suited to this terrain. She walked furiously, her head down and her hands clenched. When she next stopped to look back, the house had dwindled at last, though not by as much as she would have liked. She felt like a mouse on a treadmill, going nowhere at a frantic rate.

Every now and again she had to stop to yank her feet free of the mud that clutched at her. Already, her boots were splattered and spotted. The gum in her mouth had lost its flavor but she kept chewing it anyhow because she was nervous, goddam nervous. But at the same time she sensed freedom, and it was the idea of the blacktop highway that kept her going—that, and the understanding she was finally getting away from Zanzibar and his house.

No more weirdness.

A few months back in Davenport and she'd be okay, touching base with normal things. Ma and the little frame house and nice smells coming from the kitchen and maybe her own bed with the floral printed sheets and matching pillows— *I'm coming home, Ma—*

Normal, she thought. No more Mr Weirdo. He could do whatever it was he had to do, but she wasn't going to be a party to it. She had a life to live and it didn't include Zanzi. It didn't include the strange house and the smells of wax and all the electronic gadgetry and phones that wouldn't work when you wanted to make simple calls.

Sweet Jesus, how she longed for *normal*.

The track led upward now. Somewhere nearby a stream made choking sounds as it drifted through the canyon. Two buzzards winged through the air ominously.

She watched their flight pattern: they hung in the air as if supported by invisible silver threads.

Keep going. Gotta get a move on. Can't loiter.

Keep cruising, babe.

The incline was steeper, the going slow. She spat her gum out and, with her face lowered, trudged her way upward through mud. How far to the blacktop? She had only travelled this way in the big car so she wasn't sure: what could it be? five miles? six? Jesus, that seemed such a long way with the mud holding her back and the clammy weather pressing against her and the sense she had of melting. She removed the leather jacket and slung it over one arm.

She reached the top of the incline now. She could see the canyon stretch away on either side of her, drab and colorless, like a big box admitting no light. The house was small now and she was glad of that, glad she couldn't make out the details of the place. It might have been something left to rot in the landscape. Along with all its contents.

She walked a little farther.

Under the rattle of the stream, there was another sound now. She stood very still. Her mouth was dry and something that might have been a moth beat at the back of her throat, only she knew she hadn't swallowed any kind of insect, she was listening to her own pulse. *Ba-rum, ba-rum, ba-rum.*

It was the sound of a big car.

Zena didn't move.

She stared the length of the mud track, aware of the bare canyon all around her, an insane landscape that offered nowhere to hide.

Ba-rum, ba-rum, ba-rum.

Over a rise in the land, at a place where the mud track climbed upward again, the vehicle appeared. Black, reflecting nothing, grinding through soft earth, it might have been empty, coming forward of its own accord, coming forward with a terrifying inevitability.

It was the big black machine of all her worst nightmares.

Her mouth hung open.

The car slid alongside her and the passenger door swung out toward her.

And Zanzibar said, *"Going my way?"*

FOURTEEN

FOR ALL THE YEARS HE HAD LIVED IN HAMLAND, GEORGE Cheney had never been inside Slattery's Meat Packing Plant —and now he understood, as he had known all along anyhow without paying any attention, that the name which hung on a gaudy sign at the front of the building was a euphemism. *Meat-packing* was the gruesome end of a deathly process in which animals were stunned, suspended, sliced, their blood spilling away into gutters that ran through the plant and their slit carcasses moving on noisy hooks.

In a yard outside the building he'd seen cows packed in freight trucks, their brown eyes seemingly stripped of casual innocence as if they could smell their own deaths on the air. They pawed, moaned, scratched at the wood surrounds fencing them in. Shortly, they were to be rendered into the dismantled parts of themselves, intestines here, livers and kidneys there, bone and gristle elsewhere, steaks and ribs cut quickly out of bodies that were still warm with life. Nothing seemed to be wasted: death had its own savage economy.

Arthur Rigley, who was the night watchman at Slattery's, sat in the manager's office, looking himself rather like an animal about to be churned into hamburger. Cheney studied the guy, encountering a vacancy in the moon-shaped face that gave him reason to pause before he asked the questions he had come to ask. He turned away from Rigley, glanced at Charlie Bannion, then wandered to the big window that overlooked the floor of the slaughterhouse. Disembowelled cattle went past on hooks: a pile of intestines steamed, oozing blood on the tiled floor.

Arthur Rigley took his glasses off and wiped the lenses on his sleeve.

"When does your shift start, Arthur?" Cheney asked.

"One AM," Rigley answered in a monotonous voice. "I finish at noon."

"A long shift," Cheney said.

Arthur Rigley nodded slowly. Cheney moved around in front of the man's chair, trying to avoid the scene beyond the window as he did so.

"It suits me," Rigley said. "I like it."

"You're here from one AM until noon every day?"

"Except Saturdays and Sundays, of course." Rigley scratched the palm of his hand. "The workers come on at four AM. When they arrive, that's when I do some chores around the place. I'm not only a night watchman."

Cheney smiled. "What sort of chores, Arthur?"

"Cleaning. Tiles to hose down. The lavatory. A lot of cleaning."

"You like it?"

"It's a wonderful job."

Cheney glanced again at Bannion. The young cop was watching Rigley as if he had some new specimen under scrutiny.

"Do you ever leave this place at any time during your shift?" Cheney asked.

"No, I don't."

"Never slip away for something? Food? Something to drink?"

"Uh-uh," Rigley said. "I wouldn't do that. Mr. Jakowski, the manager, puts a lot of faith in me, I wouldn't let him down, you know. Anyway, I bring my own food and drink with me when I come here."

Cheney, despite his attempt to talk with Rigley in a normal

voice, found himself slipping into the kind of tone you used when you were addressing a child. It was hard to avoid, because Rigley seemed like an overgrown kid. The big blank face. The old-fashioned glasses. There was a deficiency in Arthur Rigley.

"How long have you worked here?" Cheney asked.

"Two weeks." Arthur Rigley cleared his throat.

"Where were you before?"

"I wasn't working before."

"I mean before you came to Hamland."

"Oh." A pink tongue appeared, slid across lips, vanished. "I was in a place where they wouldn't let me have my cat."

"What place was that, Arthur?"

"A place with rats, rats behind the walls."

"The name of the place—"

"I don't recall."

"Try, Arthur." Cheney wandered round the office. Jakowski, the plant manager, had loaned his office for this meeting. It was filled with trophies from various meat retailers, plaques and shields attesting to the quality of Slattery's products.

"It was a hospital," Rigley said. "Dr Frye was the doctor's name. He was kind to me."

Cheney sat down in Jakowski's chair, which squeaked beneath him.

"You like it at Lily Hubbard's?"

"She's good to me," Rigley said. "She's a nice woman."

Cheney saw Charlie Bannion shift his weight, tilting his body. There was strain on the young cop's face and pale circles beneath his eyes.

Cheney said, "Lily Hubbard claims she found this in your apartment, Arthur," and he laid the yellow baseball cap, Tommy Sears's cap, on the big mahogany desk.

Arthur Rigley, as if his antennae were quivering, leaned forward and poked the cap with a finger. "It was hanging on my door," he said. "I remember it."

"Where did you get it?"

Arthur Rigley blinked. His mouth turned down. On his flat brow a single drop of sweat stood out. "I don't recall."

"Arthur, it's important," Cheney said. "Take your time."

Rigley gazed at Cheney and looked hopeless. "Honestly. I don't recall. It was hanging on my door."

"One day you just saw it there? Like that?"

"Right. Just like that."

"Out of the blue, Arthur?"

"Right."

Cheney sighed. Then he rose and took Bannion aside and together they stepped into the hall, where they whispered.

"You better check on this Dr Frye," Cheney said. "See what hospital Rigley's talking about. See what you can find out. I don't know any Dr Frye locally."

"Will do," Bannion said. He peered back inside the office. Arthur Rigley was studying the palms of his hands. "This guy isn't exactly wrapped too tightly, George. What do you think?"

"I agree with you," Cheney said. "But that doesn't make him Tommy's kidnapper, does it?"

"Lily Hubbard says he comes and goes at all kinds of weird hours. She's pretty adamant Rigley's our man, George. Claims she knew the moment she set eyes on him that he was not a man with a full deck."

"Which makes you wonder why she rented to him if she thought that," Cheney said. "Did she say what she was doing in Rigley's apartment in the first place?"

Bannion shrugged. "Nope. Cleaning, I guess."

Cheney gazed through the crack in the door at Arthur Rigley. The man was turning the baseball cap round in his hands now and his expression was one of furious concentration. Cheney, who was often moved by homeless kids and stray animals in pounds, felt a strange little stab of sadness at the sight of Rigley. The man was one of the world's meek, destined to inherit something, though not these days the earth: destined, more likely, to take a lot of shit.

He turned his mind to Lily Hubbard. Now and then he would see Lily going down Center Avenue, colorfully dressed in a style he called Provincial Tack, a lot of gaudy shades clashing about her body like silent fireworks. He had Lily Hubbard pegged as one of Hamland's "characters," a diminishing species that included, to some degree, his own father. The late Elmer Hubbard had often visited Cheney's father in the old days in the house on Montrose Drive, when George's mother would play the piano and Elmer might—depending on his state of inebriation—break out singing *The Road to Mandalay*.

It was quite a day when Lily Hubbard claimed that *somebody else* wasn't playing with a full deck, he thought.

Rigley put the baseball cap back on the desk, then examined the tips of his fingers. Observing him through the slit in the doorway, Cheney tried to see Arthur Rigley in the role of monster, the kidnapper of three children. He remembered occasional newspaper stories he'd read about mass murderers and what their neighbors had to say about them. *He was such a quiet family man. I never thought in a million years he'd do something like this. He was a Scoutmaster, Church elder, a member of the Kiwanis Club, all-round model citizen, completely nice bore.*

The quiet ones, Cheney thought. Always the quiet ones.

When Bannion had gone to find a telephone, Cheney went back inside the office and sat down facing Rigley. The baseball cap, yellow and crumpled, lay between the two men.

"Remember anything yet, Arthur?"

The man shook his head. "My memory . . . It isn't what it should be, you see. Sometimes I see things in great detail. Then there are these blanks. The cap is a blank."

"You had to get it somehow," Cheney said.

"I know that." A little flicker of irritation went across Rigley's face: it was the first real response Cheney had seen in the man. "I get annoyed when I don't remember things, Sheriff."

"Does the name Tommy Sears mean anything to you, Arthur?"

"No."

"That's Tommy's cap. Did you know that?"

"I didn't."

"Try to remember. Did you meet Tommy? Did you take him somewhere maybe?"

Rigley closed his eyes. He screwed them tightly. His mouth became a small tense circle.

"We'll come back to that, Arthur. Okay? Do the following names mean anything to you? Vickie Estaban?"

Nothing. No reaction.

"How about Rick Dove?"

"Dove?"

"Dee oh vee eee," Cheney said.

"Should I know all these names?"

"I don't know. It's why I'm asking, Arthur. To find out." Cheney clasped his hands on the desk. "Why were you in hospital?"

Rigley shrugged. "They never told me. I asked them. They didn't say. It had something to do with my childhood . . ." Rigley's face contorted with pain for a second, then the look was gone.

"How long were you there?"

"Years. Years and years."

Cheney fell silent. Rigley puffed his cheeks out for no good reason, then ran a fingertip across his lower lip. Again, Cheney was pierced by a sense of pity. What Rigley reminded him of was a large witless dog awaiting instructions from its master.

"The cap couldn't have been hanging in your room by accident, could it, Arthur?"

"No."

"It had to get there somehow."

"Maybe I found it. Brought it home."

"Where could you have found it, Arthur?"

Rigley went blank again. His whole body sagged. His rounded eyeglasses slipped on his nose and he nudged them back in place with a fingertip. "I walk a lot, Sheriff. I like to walk."

"Any special places?"

"The park mostly."

Cheney stood up. His legs were stiff, his blood sluggish. "You like the park, Arthur?"

"Sure I do. I like to watch the kids play. It's noisy. I don't know how Miss Diamond takes all the noise." Rigley smiled.

"You know Ellis Diamond?"

"We live in the same house. She has the apartment below mine."

Cheney hoisted himself up on the edge of the desk, swinging one leg back and forward. He had the frustrating feeling that even if he were to question Arthur Rigley until doomsday, he wasn't going to get anywhere. Just the same, the physical evidence of the cap was the first evidence of any kind that had come his way and he couldn't just brush it aside and set the whole thing down to Arthur Rigley's curious amnesia. Amanda Thurston, after all, had seen the cap on Tommy Sears's head the day the boy disappeared: it was Cheney's only link with the kid and Arthur Rigley must have come across it somewhere.

"Maybe you found the cap in the park, Arthur."

"Maybe so." Rigley was quiet a moment. Then: "Am I in some kind of trouble, Sheriff? Have I done something wrong?"

"We don't know that yet," Cheney answered.

"I've tried to remember. When you were out of the room, I just sat here trying as hard as I could to remember—"

"Don't force it." Cheney sat down again.

"Tommy Sears." Rigley, his eyes still shut, moved his lips slowly. "I can't say. I don't rightly know if that name's familiar to me or if it isn't . . ."

Cheney, tilting his chair back at the wall, stared at Rigley and tried to see him moving in the dark places of Hamland, stealing kids from their homes or while they delivered newspapers, tried to see this man covering a kid's face with one of his big hands, dragging Rick Dove down a flight of stairs or hauling Vickie Estaban out of her bedroom or snatching Tommy Sears on his paper route—and then? Where did he take them? Where would he go with them?

Charlie Bannion appeared in the doorway, gesturing to Cheney. The sheriff went out into the corridor.

Bannion said, "This doctor Frye runs a mental institution in Rio Blanco, about a hundred miles north of here. Arthur was in the institution for a long time, George. Seems he had an accident when he was twelve. He was playing on a construction site when he fell and a metal bolt went through his skull. The kind of thing they use to reinforce concrete. Affected his memory. His motor skills. Frye had Arthur on heavy medication for years. He got his motor skills back pretty much, but his memory's still iffy."

Bannion paused. Cheney asked, "Is that all?"

"There's a kicker, George. You'll love this. It seems that Rigley has a strange kink concerning cats."

"Cats?"

"Yeah. He tortures them . . ." Bannion hesitated a second. "Then he kills them."

"He kills cats?"

"He killed three of them at Frye's clinic. He tortures them then buries them after he's had his merriment with them. Frye said he personally found two in the rose-garden and another in the septic system. Arthur keeps them for a while as pets, then when they step out of line he doesn't take it too well."

Cats, Cheney thought. He peered through the door at Rigley's face. Goddam cats. What he wondered now was whether Rigley, capable of killing animals, could somehow have extended his talents to children. He couldn't see it: couldn't make the transition. It was a long way from killing furry creatures to abducting kids, wasn't it? It was one hell of a leap. Cheney ran a hand over his face. Arthur, you're full of surprises. Do you have any more surprises stashed away for me?

Rigley looked up, smiled at the sheriff. Cheney pulled the office door shut and turned to Bannion.

"We'll take him down to the station, Charlie."

"Then what?"

"Then you'll keep him busy while I have a look at his apartment."

"Busy? How?"

Cheney smiled. "Talk about cats."

"Is that supposed to be funny?"

Cheney didn't answer.

Anne was cutting lettuce by the sink, wondering if it were worth the trouble to prepare a meal that George presumably wouldn't come home to eat, when the telephone rang. She picked up the receiver. An operator asking her if she would accept a collect call from Danny Cheney.

Danny's voice seemed incredibly distant to her, as if it were coming from more than a mere forty miles or so.

"Mom?"

"How are you babe?" Anne asked. Through the kitchen window she saw Rick Dove's treehouse across the wall that divided her yard from the Dove property: it looked abandoned to her, a sad construction hanging up there between branches.

"Ready to come home, I guess," the boy said.

Anne wanted to say, *No, stay where you are, things are bad here.*

Danny said, "Can you pick me up at the Lutheran Church at seven? That's when the bus is *supposed* to arrive. If it doesn't break down on the way, that is."

Tonight at seven, Anne thought. Stay where you are, Danny. Can't you stay for a few more days? "I'll be there with bells on," was what she said. "Have you had a good time?"

"Yeah," the kid said. "It's been decent."

No conviction in his voice, she thought. Why did kids always sound so flat and lifeless on telephones? She glanced up at the treehouse again.

"When I get home there's something I gotta do," Danny said.

"Like what?"

"Join Parks and Rec."

Anne turned her face away from the treehouse. The sight of it filled her suddenly with a certain vague dread. "Parks and Rec," she heard herself say, a small echo. "Yeah, that sounds like it might be fun."

Fun. Fun had a dark edge these days in Hamland.

"I gotta go," Danny was saying. "I'm calling from some kind of ranger station and a guy wants to use the phone. See you at seven!"

And then the line was dead.

Anne put the receiver down.

She stared through the kitchen window at the empty back yard. What was the kid coming back to? she wondered. She picked up her cutting knife and drove the blade deep into the heart of the lettuce.

Ellis Diamond watched from the window of her office as the fat man wandered the length of the fence around the baseball field. He moved a little drunkenly, with that stiff attempt at dignity drunks so frequently assumed. He looked in the direction of the Youth Center next. Ellis turned away from the window.

She sat down behind her desk, scanning paperwork she had no intention of doing. She hoped the fat man wasn't going to come inside and bother her because she wasn't in the mood for intrusions. She sat very still with her eyes shut, listening to the sounds of the Youth Center around her.

George Cheney had come here a short time ago. He'd gone inside the auditorium to talk with Zanzibar and she'd waited tensely in her office, imagining the Sheriff was going to arrest Zanzibar—

But then Cheney had left alone. She wondered what had passed between the two men. Cheney's expression, which she'd glimpsed as he passed her office window on the way to his car, was one of rather weary unhappiness, a sad inward look of fatigue.

Ellis opened her eyes now, listening to the noises around her.

The click of billiard balls. The squawking of a small child-monster. The knock of a basketball on concrete. The laughter of a girl from inside the auditorium where Ms Alyn Wheelwright, High School English teacher, was rehearsing a stage version of *Rumpelstiltskin*.

Every sound seemed to suggest hysteria to her.

The fat man was knocking at her half-open door.

Ellis looked at him. His white shirt was stained dark in places with grease spots. He looked vaguely familiar but she wasn't sure how.

"Can I help you?" she asked stiffly.

"Crouch here?" the fat man asked.

"Max?"

"Max, yeah."

"He's busy right now. He's down in the basement. A drain is clogged and he's trying to open it up and—"

"Where's the basement?" the man asked.

Ellis stood up. "It's off-limits to anyone but staff," she said, and her voice was surprisingly firm.

"I'll find it," the drunk said, and staggered away.

Ellis went after him. She saw he was moving in the direction of the door marked BASEMENT, reaching for it and then plunging through to the dark stairs beyond.

"Look, you can't go down there," she said.

"Stop me."

Ellis followed the man to the stairs. He was stumbling ahead of her, his way lit only by a weak bulb overhead. He threw an enormous shadow. She went down behind him. It was a world of pipes and gloomy corners below.

Something brushed Ellis's face as she followed the man. Sticky and sickening, it floated a moment against her lip.

"Please," she said. "You can't come down here—"

At the bottom, the fat man stopped and peered into the darkness. Drunkenly, he turned his face toward her. "Where's Crouch?" he asked.

"I don't know what you want with Max," she said. "But it will have to wait until his free time."

The man ran a hand over his big face. A huge paw. When he made a fist Ellis felt the violence that was running through him. She flinched, half expecting him to swing at her with that mighty hand, but he wasn't interested in her. He was saving all this violence for Max Crouch. He turned, stumbling into the darker regions of the basement, banging his head against a low-hanging pipe and cursing as the pain shook him.

"Crouch! Crouch!" His voice pierced the shadows, then echoed in unlit recesses of the large room. "Crouch! I want to see you!"

Ellis approached the fat man and placed a hand on his clenched fist, but he shook it aside effortlessly.

"I'll call the police if you don't leave," she said.

The man laughed at her.

"You've been drinking, you should go home, sleep this off," she tried.

"Eat shit, lady."

Ellis watched as the man—his head bent at an angle—charged into the darkness. She could hear him clattering around, colliding with things, spilling old boxes of nails in his clumsiness. She stood at the edge of the dark, straining to see him. He appeared around the side of the boiler, watching her.

"Crouch isn't here," he said. "You told me he'd be here."

"I thought he was."

"I can't find the fucker."

"Please," Ellis said again. "Go home. Sleep it off. There are kids in this building and I don't want them frightened—"

"I only want Crouch," the man said. He had that astonishingly incontrovertible stubbornness of the drunk. The world had to be the way he wanted it: nothing could be permitted to interfere with his scheme of things. He stumbled around again, searching the black corners of the basement.

"Why do you want Max?" she asked.

"Personal," he answered. "A personal matter."

"It could wait—"

The drunk laughed. "It's waited too long already, lady."

Ellis, hearing the door at the top of the stairs open, held her breath. Max Crouch, unaware of the intruder, was coming down into the basement, whistling as he moved. The drunk said "Ah," and went toward the foot of the stairs. Ellis turned to look. Halfway down, sensing trouble, Max Crouch stopped dead in his tracks. Whistling died on his lips. The fat man, swifter than Ellis could ever have imagined, reached the stairs and started to climb, stunning Max Crouch with a two-handed blow to the side of the head. Crouch buckled and slipped, sliding down the stairs on his spine. When he reached the bottom, Max Crouch sat upright, his face dazed. Blood was coming from his hairline.

"Max." Ellis went to the man and bent down beside him. "Are you all right?"

Crouch shook his head. He looked toward the stairs. "What the hell was that about," he mumbled.

The fat man, descending quickly, reached between Ellis and Max Crouch and dragged the custodian to his feet, slamming him hard against the wall. Crouch closed his eyes and braced himself to be hit again. He covered his face with his hands but this time the fat man brought up a knee into the custodian's groin, causing Crouch to moan and double over and slither in a broken fashion to the floor.

The drunk stood over him. Sweat made streaks out of the dust on his face and his huge belly wobbled from the sheer physical effort of assaulting Crouch.

"Where is he?" the fat man asked.

Crouch answered with a moan. Ellis stepped between the fallen janitor and the drunk, and spread her arms like a policeman holding a crowd at bay.

"Leave him alone," she said. "You've hurt him—"

The fat man pawed Ellis aside, placing one foot on Max Crouch's chest.

"Where is he, Crouch? You gonna tell me or do I have to beat the hell out of you?"

Max Crouch raised his head slowly, blinking up at the drunk. "I don't know what you're talking about—"

"The kid," said the fat man. "I'm talking about my kid! Goddam you!"

"What kid?" Crouch asked, shaking and wheezing where he lay.

The fat man drew his belly in, swung one leg, launched a kick at Crouch's head. Max Crouch lifted an arm, which absorbed the blow. But something snapped. Ellis could hear it—a bone in his arm breaking like dry kindling. The sound sickened her. She caught the drunk by the sleeve of his shirt and tried to haul him aside. Useless: she was only swatted away again, a fact that made her realize her own frailty.

"Crouch," he said. "What'd you do with him?"

Tears ran down Max Crouch's face and his eyes were glazed with pain. His mouth opened and closed silently. He clutched his wrecked arm with a hand, rocking his body in time to the spasms of pain that went through him.

Ellis Diamond said, "What kid are you talking about?"

"My son. Tommy Sears."

Sears, she thought. Suddenly she remembered the fat man from before, weeks ago when he'd come to pick up his son one night after a baseball game at the park. "What makes you think Max has anything to do with your son?"

Thomas Sears Senior glared at Max Crouch. "He *knows*."

"I'm sure he doesn't know anything," Ellis said. "Can't you see that? Or are you just too drunk?"

The fat man ran a hand over his mouth. "He knows," he said again.

Max Crouch rolled on to one side, holding his broken arm

239

against his hip. He made it to an upright position. "I don't know anything, I don't know what this maniac's talking about. He's *busted my fucking arm.*"

Thomas Sears, breathing heavily, sweating, stepped back from the custodian, staring now at Ellis. She experienced a strange wave of nausea, a churning inside her stomach. In her life she had never been exposed before to violence and now it was beginning to affect her, the swift brutality of it, the insane way certain human beings succumbed so easily to it as though it were some kind of substitute for reason. She clutched her stomach.

Behind her, Max Crouch moaned.

"He took my son," Thomas Sears said.

"Why? Why would he do a thing like that?"

Thomas Sears swayed. In the last few seconds all the violence appeared to have gone out of him: he seemed to deflate in front of Ellis's eyes and, smaller now, was far less awesome. He had spent all his drunken rage and, like someone finding the well of his emotions suddenly dry, appeared baffled as much as anything else.

Sears said, "Nobody else . . . Nobody else would do it."

"Why? What possible reason do you have to think Max Crouch would take your boy, Mr Sears?"

Thomas Sears, dwindling, seemingly flustered now by the act of violence he'd done, stepped away, still running the back of a hand across his lips.

Crouch, standing now, half-leaning against the wall, had the useless arm against his side.

"Max, do you know this man?" Ellis asked.

"I've seen him in bars a couple times," Crouch said, his teeth clenched.

"And that's all?"

"That's all."

Ellis stared at Thomas Sears. "You come in here drunk, you attack this man for no good reason—"

"I'm sorry," Sears said. "Look . . ."

"Sorry won't repair this man's arm," Ellis said.

"What the hell do you expect me to say?"

Ellis pressed the palms of her hands flat against her stomach. A column of hot air was rising into her throat. "I understand how you must feel about your boy, Mr Sears. But it doesn't give you license to come in here and act violently against one of my employees."

"Yeah," Sears remarked. He was looking down at the floor now. Every now and again something tense crossed his face and Ellis understood that, if she didn't handle this with care, Sears might fall back into violence. It would have to be reported to the police, she was certain of that much, but she wasn't about to tell this to Thomas Sears. If she could just get him out of the building and off the premises, she'd feel safe.

"Why don't you go home, Mr Sears," she said. She managed to smile. "You're going to have one hell of a hangover, you know that. I'm sure we can forget this little incident. What do you think, Max?"

Crouch mumbled. "This fucker busted my arm."

"We'll get you fixed up, Max. Don't worry."

"Don't worry, she says." Max Crouch moaned again.

"Listen," Sears said, raising a limp hand in the air. He didn't finish whatever he'd started to say. He turned away and, like a great bear that has raided a food-dump without satisfying his hunger, moved toward the stairs.

Max Crouch started to say something, but Ellis Diamond cut him off quickly: "Let him go, Max. Just let him go."

She watched Thomas Sears Senior stop at the top of the stairs, turn his face, look down at them, and then leave slowly, letting the basement door swing shut behind him.

"Crazy sonofabitch," Crouch said. "What in hell was all that about? I hardly know the guy. I don't know the first goddam thing about his son. Why would he come here and beat up on me like that?"

"I don't know," Ellis said.

She helped Crouch up the stairs. By the time they had ascended, there was no sign of Thomas Sears. They went inside Ellis's office, where Max Crouch slumped in a chair and lit a cigarette one-handed. He trembled.

Ellis stood at the window. Thomas Sears was gone.

She smiled because she thought she had handled the whole awful scene with a certain courageous diplomacy. If she hadn't been there, it might have been worse. Max Crouch might have had more than his arm broken.

"Puzzling," she said.

"Yeah. Real puzzling."

"Why would he think you had anything to do with his son, Max?"

"Search me."

Ellis stared out at the baseball field. In the gray sky, parting the cloud cover like a wand, a stick of white sunlight poked through.

Clawing at George Cheney's arm, Lily Hubbard pursued the sheriff up the stairs toward Arthur Rigley's apartment. She was telling Cheney how she had known there was something not quite right about Rigley from the very start.

Call it a feeling. Call it an intuition. Call it an old woman's experience. Anything you like, Lily Hubbard said, she had known Arthur Rigley wasn't altogether right in the head. Cheney, who tried not to listen to this tirade, smiled politely. The stairs were dark, darker still as they rose upward, as if all light were being systematically drained away. A gloomy house.

He paused on a landing. He faced a door. "Who lives here?"

"Miss Diamond," Lily Hubbard said.

Cheney nodded, climbed again. Lily Hubbard, rattling a chain of keys in one hand, came scampering after him.

"He goes in and out at strange hours," she said.

Up and up into the shadows. What this house needed, Cheney thought, was an infusion of light. What Lily Hubbard needed was a muzzle. She had this case solved and shut already.

Arthur Rigley had stolen the kids. End of the matter.

Outside the door of Rigley's apartment, Lily Hubbard inserted a key and allowed Cheney to enter the room beyond.

"He's tidy, I'll say that for him," Lily remarked, looking around the place. "You ask me, he took those kids to a place that's really out of the way—like Sutter's Meadow or somewhere—and he buried them. That's what he did. Strangled them, buried them."

Cheney, astounded by the woman's persistence, looked at her. "Lily, I hate to let you down. But I don't even suspect

242

Rigley of anything. This is just routine, you know. There's Tommy's baseball cap, I know—"

"I don't suppose that's any big deal, is it?" Trying sarcasm now, Lily Hubbard made a sweeping gesture with one hand. "I suppose if you came across the boy's severed head, you'd want to find the rest of the body before you officially declared him dead, George Cheney."

Cheney maintained his silence.

Lily rattled her key-chain again. "I knew you as a boy, George. Don't forget that. I knew you when you were this high. You always were a cautious individual."

Cautious, Cheney thought. He couldn't remember ever having been that. He wasn't, he knew, a reckless person: but he hadn't ever perceived himself as cautious. He ignored Lily Hubbard and began to move around Rigley's room. The woman went on bickering and making suggestions but in the absence of response she tired quickly. Finally she left him alone and wandered back down the stairs to her own apartment.

Cheney looked inside the kitchen.

He went to the refrigerator, opened it, looked inside.

Rigley had covered a number of dishes with plastic wrap. They contained portions of peas, oatmeal, a half-eaten apple. There was none of the usual gunk in the refrigerator, none of the strange blue molds you sometimes found stuck far in the back. Everything here was tidy, the shelves sparkling and clean.

He went back into the other room. The bed was neatly made up. A paperback book lay on the bedside table. A pair of slippers sat together on the rug. Folded on the sofa was a copy of yesterday's *Progressive*. Inside the narrow bathroom he looked at the medicine cabinet. There was a prescription drug called Nardil, a bottle of Visine, Scope, a tube of McLeans toothpaste, a brush, hair cream, a comb, Bayer aspirins.

He returned to the room that was a combination bed and living-room. There, he sat down on the sofa and gazed at the window. Arthur Rigley's private little world, fastidious and clean, and not altogether real. You could tell nothing about Arthur Rigley's life from this apartment: it was a blank page.

Cheney rose.

He moved toward a chest of drawers in the corner. The first drawer contained shirts, each folded and freshly laundered. Rigley's taste in shirts ran a gamut from white to off-white. Exciting. The second drawer had underwear and a couple of handkerchiefs and—perhaps Arthur Rigley's only item of flamboyance—a checkered silk scarf. In the third and final drawer there were four pairs of inexpensive corduroy jeans and a solitary sneaker.

One blue sneaker. A child's. A Converse.

Cheney took it out and held it in his hand.

Why this? Why this item of footwear so casually placed on a pile of cord pants?

There had been no attempt to hide it.

No effort to conceal the damned thing.

Just as Arthur Rigley had made no effort to hide the baseball cap.

Holding the sneaker, Cheney sat down at the end of Arthur Rigley's bed. The sneaker was scuffed and worn. The laces were knotted in the wrong places. (A boy's sneaker, obviously. Girls were better with laces.) The Converse brand-name could barely be read. He balanced the shoe in the palm of his hand. What he felt suddenly was a strong despair, as if intuitively he knew that the child who had worn this sneaker was dead. The sensation that passed through him caused him to feel like one of those psychics cops sometimes called in to help solve difficult crimes.

He turned his face to the window. A baseball cap. A sneaker. He stood up and continued to search the room. It was a task he carried out quickly, moving with frantic gestures—opening drawers, slamming them shut, searching a closet and spilling jackets and coats in his haste.

A baseball cap. A sneaker.

He didn't know what he was going to find next: he only knew to whom the article would belong.

It was stuck inside a roll of toilet paper beneath the bathroom sink, a slender silver bracelet with a disc hanging from it.

In the center of the disc was the initial V.

George Cheney closed his fingers around the bracelet.

It was the neatness of everything that took his breath away. It was the orderly manner of the arrangement that made him pause.

Tommy Sears's cap.

Vickie Estaban's bracelet.

And a sneaker that in all likelihood belonged to Rick Dove.

An unholy trinity. A perfect triangle.

Real life was never so neat. So tidy.

Real life was always frayed at the edges. The clues that existence threw up in your face were always dishevelled and inscrutable and imperfect.

He stood at the window for a while, looking down into Gunnison Avenue, seeing a quick sharp gust of wind stir trees.

Bracelet, sneaker, cap.

He took the sneaker, placed the bracelet in his breast pocket, and he left the apartment. Lily Hubbard was standing on the landing below, staring up at him. Cheney hesitated a second before descending. *She's waiting because she expects something,* Cheney thought. *She's waiting because she knows what I have found.*

Why, though?

Why in God's name would Lily Hubbard plant these items in Rigley's room? If she had done so, it opened up locked doors into other dimensions where the questions were harder and more mysterious: *How had she managed to get hold of these things?*

No, Cheney thought.

It doesn't add up.

The woman was leaning forward, peering at the soft blue shoe.

Cheney stared at her face. Beneath the painted surface he could find nothing to confirm the suspicion that had flared inside him. This harmless old woman, this *character,* what possible motive could she have for implicating Arthur Rigley in a crime? Now Cheney thought of the tenant, that large guileless face, the emptiness in the eyes. Was Rigley capable of stealing three kids? Was he?

"Where did you find the shoe?" Lily Hubbard asked.

"Rigley's apartment."

"Ah."

"Can I use your telephone?" Cheney asked.

"Sure thing."

He followed Lily Hubbard inside her apartment, which was large and filled with old furniture and smelled of mustiness, dead air, stale things.

"Small sneaker," Lily said.

Cheney nodded, still watching the woman.

"A kid's?" she asked.

"Looks that way," Cheney said. "Of course, it could be Rigley's. He might have small feet." It was a mild misplaced attempt at humor: he put no effort into it.

"Real small," the woman remarked. "Phone's over there," and she pointed to a little table by the window.

The telephone sat surrounded by framed photographs.

Cheney, absently looking at the pictures, dialled the number of the station. When he was put through to Charlie Bannion he told Bannion to check with the Doves about the kind of sneaker Rick might have been wearing. He knew the answer in advance: this was a formality, and pointless.

Cheney hung up. He stood motionless, gazing at the photographs. Mainly they were old, Lily and the late Elmer snapped in this or that vacation setting, standing alongside an ancient convertible or making faces under an umbrella or lying on sand. There was one that was slightly different: it was more formal, a studio shot, showing Lily and Elmer and a small boy in a dark suit seated between them.

Cheney stared at it.

A small boy with a long sallow face, a sullen little mouth, black hair, eyes bored with the whole photographic procedure.

Cheney picked it up and studied it.

Lily Hubbard reached out and removed it from his hand, setting it back down on the table as if it were precious.

A small boy, Cheney thought.

There was something now at the back of his mind, a pale movement. But recognition eluded him. Who was the kid that sat between Lily and Elmer?

"The boy," he said. "He looks sort of familiar . . ."

Lily clasped her hands in front of her face. "Why would he

be familiar to you, George Cheney? You hardly ever saw him."

Cheney was puzzled. Again, there was a sense of muted recollection, but nothing emerged from his memory. He looked back down at the picture.

"Maybe you saw him one time when Elmer and I took him over to your father's house. That would be two, three years after your mother passed away. He was only four at the time. Then you went running off to Los Angeles to become a teacher or some such thing."

"Your son," Cheney said. "I'd forgotten all about him."

Lily Hubbard was silent. A darkness crossed her face.

"It was while you were away that the boy took sick," she said, and her voice was soft, filled with a hint of old pain.

Cheney was silent. Somewhere in the catalogues of his memory there was one half-legible entry about Elmer and Lily Hubbard's boy. It contained a suggestion of a name. Mark, Michael, he wasn't sure. Beyond that, the index card was blank.

"He was five when he died," Lily said.

"I'm sorry . . ."

"What have *you* got to be sorry about? You never knew Michael."

Cheney shook his head.

"He was a good boy," Lily Hubbard said. "A smart boy. Always quick to learn."

She gazed at the photograph.

"Five when he died," she said. "Five when he was taken away from me. I miss him."

Cheney looked at the photograph again. His recollection of the boy was scant, almost nonexistent.

"I know how those parents are feeling, George Cheney. I know how they're suffering, wondering about their kids."

Cheney moved toward the door.

Lily Hubbard followed after him. "People don't appreciate their kids the way they ought to," she said. "It's only after they're gone that you realize you could have done more with them while you still had them and then it's too late . . . First my husband. Then my son. I could have done more, George."

Cheney stood on the landing, turning once to look back at the woman. She reminded him of a bag of colored rags and ribbons, badly stuffed, things spilling.

"Arthur Rigley," she called after him.

Halfway down the stairs, Cheney looked back up.

"He deserves whatever he's got coming to him."

Cheney continued to the bottom.

Outside, standing in the dull light of Hamland, aware of Lily Hubbard watching him from a window above, he wondered.

Was Lily Hubbard so far gone in mad grief that she had done something to those kids?

Was it some twisted sorrow that devoured her inside? Was she trying to blame Rigley for something she'd done?

Again, Cheney answered his questions in the negative.

An old woman, sure. A little crazy, sure. But capable of stealing children? You had to draw a line somewhere. And he drew one in his mind right then.

Stepping toward his car, carrying the pale blue sneaker in one hand as though it were a trophy that reminded him of his failures, Cheney dismissed Lily Hubbard and the deaths surrounding her.

What he hoped now was that Arthur Rigley's memory, by some miracle, would open doors into brightly-lit rooms.

Rooms containing three kids.

He drove through a Hamland which seemed squat and shadowy in the bad light, like a face with a terrible complexion.

FIFTEEN

SUTTER'S MEADOW, A FIELD OF TALL GRASS AND WILDFLOWERS, lay boxed in by thick oaks and cottonwoods at the edge of Hamland. Once or twice over the years this parcel of land had been placed in escrow by corporations intending to develop the property, but nothing had ever happened, and in the general economic decay of the town nothing was ever *likely* to. The meadow, which had been named after a long-forgotten settler, was as pastoral as it had ever been, a swath of green hidden from the highway running a hundred yards beyond it. The people who came here were either lovers destined for a nocturnal tryst or kids chasing butterflies out of blades of grass—or solitary strollers such as Edward Cheney, who paused on the edge of the meadow and stared across the long glistening grass toward the trees.

Two crows, disturbed by his presence, cawed and rose loudly through branches. The old man moved across the field, his straw hat angled forward a little on his head. Insects buzzed in the thickets and bees circled wildflowers for pollen.

Edward Cheney stood in the center now. The crows, as if they had judged him safe, came flapping back down into high branches.

THE PIPER

He looked up at the glossy birds.

They were creatures of death. It was written in their malignant eyes. They sat stiff and aloof in their vigilance, giving Cheney the impression of two dark warriors who had taken part in unspeakable slaughters.

The grass grew as high as his knees, pressing wetly against the material of his pants as he moved. When he reached the trees at the far side of the meadow he stepped under the branches of an oak and stood there in shadow, gazing back the way he had come.

He inclined his face against the rough bark of the oak, which was still moist from yesterday's rains. It had been a long time since he had come to Sutter's Meadow and he wasn't sure what had brought him here today. Some morbid desire to grasp the past? Some sick senile urge to confront dead things? A communion with ghosts? Sutter's Meadow, despite its placid appearance, was not a restful place.

Cheney moved out from under the tree.

Someone was watching him from the other side of the meadow.

The sight of a stranger so startled him that his first reaction was to withdraw under the cover of the tree again. But the man coming across the grass now—which parted before him like stale green water—was vaguely familiar.

Cheney stood perfectly still.

Hugh Estaban.

A sliver of perspiration ran down the old man's nose and gathered in the indentation above his upper lip.

Estaban. Had the same insane impulse which had brought Edward Cheney to this place driven Hugh Estaban too?

"Edward," Estaban said, when he had crossed the grass. "I didn't expect to find you here."

Cheney nodded his head slightly. Between himself and the other man there lay something that had always been unutterable: were they supposed to address themselves to this now? Cheney didn't have the heart for such an excursion. He felt weak, distanced from himself, as if this old man in a white suit and straw hat were something that followed his real self around.

Cheney cleared his throat. "I always thought they'd build

here. I always told myself that one day they'd come in with bulldozers and tear this field apart. Put up apartments or a grocery store. They never did."

"I can't imagine this place done over with concrete," Estaban remarked.

This was how it was supposed to be then, Cheney thought. Two old associates meeting by chance and passing the time of day. An innocent surface, beneath which there was a malignancy, a black flower growing. Cheney touched the corners of his mouth with a crumpled handkerchief.

Estaban smiled sadly. "I didn't think I'd ever come here again—" He cut his sentence short, killed his explanation.

There are no explanations, Cheney thought. There's no more left to say. Cheney saw the pair of crows take off from the branches and slap their wings through the air like paint-brushes dripping black.

The meadow was empty, still.

As is my heart, the old man thought.

Hugh Estaban looked down at his shoes, which were wet, streaked green by grass. "I had a meeting with Fred Dove, Edward."

"Dove?" Cheney raised a hand and made an old man's indeterminate gesture: he might have been trying to hold water in his palm.

"His son's gone."

"His son?" Cheney said. "I thought that's what would happen. I thought that boy would be next. I *knew* it."

Despite the foreknowledge, the old man felt as if he'd been kicked in the chest. He couldn't breathe for a moment. Something buzzed inside his brain. He loosened the collar of his shirt. In his mind he was looking along a dark road and every so often there were sinister intersections, tributary roads called Sears and Estaban and Dove.

Ahead, there was still another junction to come—

But he didn't want to reach it, didn't want to see the name on the sign even though he knew it anyhow. His hands trembled. Hadn't he thought, only last night, of warning Fred Dove? And then blindly ignored his own intentions? You didn't want to believe, did you? Even after those first two kids went missing, *you still couldn't bring yourself to believe.*

"Dove is raising money," Estaban said.

"Is he?"

"There's going to be a ransom demand, he says." Estaban kicked at loose soil.

"Is that what *you* expect, Hugh?"

"I don't know. I don't know if I have any expectations, Edward. Especially where Vickie is concerned . . ."

The wind blew again, flapping around the edge of Cheney's jacket. He wished Hugh Estaban would go away.

"Fred Dove says he knows who took the kids," Estaban said.

Edward Cheney shivered. He watched the meadow: *I knew this place would draw me back again.*

"I don't necessarily think he's correct," Estaban said. "Sure, there's only one logical candidate, we all *know* that, but you have to presuppose so many things for that person to be responsible for the missing kids. For one thing, he had to have knowledge—how did he get it? How did he find out? For another, you have to assume he's been planning this thing for years and years and that seems a hell of a long time to me. All that scheming. The effort. The concentration . . . It would drive a person mad. It would eat them away inside."

Cheney, barely listening to his companion, felt the meadow draw him out from beneath the trees. He might have been standing at the edge of a cliff, hypnotized by the abyss below him. He clenched his hands together, closing his eyes.

"Sometimes I don't believe any of it ever happened," Hugh Estaban said. "Even now, there are moments when I imagine I'm going to wake up."

It happened, the old man thought.

And it still happens.

Night after chill night.

He said, "Fred Dove was always a man who jumped to hasty conclusions, Hugh. The quicker he arrived at a decision, the more convinced he was of being right. Never once in all the time I knew Fred did I ever hear him say he was wrong about anything. What an awful burden to go through your whole life thinking you're right about everything all the damned time. Perhaps he's wrong about the kidnapper. Wrong about the expected ransom."

Cheney turned to his companion. Hugh Estaban's face, drawn and colorless beneath this flat light, was filled with a weary expectation. He was hanging on Cheney's words, the old man knew. But for what? Was he waiting for reassurance? Absolution? Cheney had nothing to give him.

"Perhaps," Estaban said quietly. He was quiet now for a long time. Then he looked at Cheney and his eyes were moist. He lifted a hand, placing it on the back of the old man's arm. "Are we abnormal? Is there something in you and I and the others that's bad? Something that's evil?"

Abnormal. Evil. Cheney shook his head. "I don't think we're any different from anyone else, Hugh. Maybe you find that answer more depressing than if I had said yes to your questions." A small smile moved across Cheney's lips, but it was thin and mirthless. "I think we're exactly like ordinary men anywhere. Perhaps our circumstances were different for one brief period of time, that's all." The old man shrugged. He thought now he sensed rain in the air: the humidity was growing and the sky seemed heavier than before. He thought of all the years of rain that must have fallen in this meadow— seeping, seeping down through the surface, collecting in forbidden subterranean places.

Estaban's hand slid from the old man's sleeve. *It was here in this field,* Hugh Estaban thought, *when I last came face to face with my private monster. It was in Sutter's Meadow when that ugly misshapen thing had last been released.* The thought settled on him as if it were a claw digging in the soft core of his brain. He gazed at the old man but you could never read Edward Cheney's heart from his face: you could never get down to the deeper surfaces of the man. *Does he feel as I do?* Estaban wondered. *Does he feel crucified in this meadow?*

The big black birds had returned, cawing as they dropped into the trees. In the beak of one a small creature hung suspended. A mouse, a young rabbit, Cheney couldn't be certain.

Estaban said, "There's only one name left on the list, Edward."

"You think I'm not aware of that?" Cheney asked. The old man stared bleakly at Estaban.

"What are you going to do?" the accountant asked.

Cheney said nothing. His eyes searched the meadow, as if an answer lay out there in the grass—but the only things the meadow threw up were questions, deep impenetrable questions.

"Are you going to talk with George?"

"I don't know . . ."

Cheney strolled away from his companion. Estaban's presence, his questions—these things oppressed and disturbed him.

"He's your son, Edward," Estaban called out. "And I don't have to remind you that he has a son too."

Cheney came to a stop beneath a tree.

"My daughter was taken," Estaban said. "Who's going to be taken from you? Have you asked yourself that?"

The old man gasped for air. He experienced a strange eclipse in himself, a darkness in his brain. Talk to George. Tell George. *How could you ever do that?*

Then there was Danny.

A small boy in a Cub Scout uniform.

Something ached in Cheney's heart.

"Have you asked yourself that, Edward?"

Cheney walked a little farther. He was standing directly below the tree that harbored the crows. Something fell through the air just in front of him.

It was a tuft of bloodied fur to which was attached a scrap of raw meat. He walked around it, sickened. And then he was moving back out through the damp grass, returning the way he had first come.

He looked back once when he'd reached the trees on the far side, but Hugh Estaban was gone and the meadow was empty under the slate sky and all around him there was a sense of lifelessness, almost as if the whole planet had run its course and there was no time left to anyone.

Out there, many yards away from him in the center of the meadow, the wind created a sudden eddy in the grass, a darkly vacant space where the blades were twisted sideways and driven apart.

It might have been in that exact spot laid naked now by the random motion of a breeze. *It might have been in that very place*. The wind died again and the stalks of grass closed around the opening in the meadow and it was as if nothing had ever been disturbed.

Ronald Kelly said, "I hear you took a guy called Arthur Rigley into custody in connection with those missing kids. That true?"

"Where would you hear something like that, Ron?" Cheney asked.

Cheney looked for a second at the map on the wall of his office. Any one of the workers at Slattery's might have told Kelly that Arthur Rigley had been taken out of the plant—but how could anyone have known the reason for it?

"Do you deny you have a man in here you're questioning?"

"I don't deny anything. And I'm not confirming anything either."

"George, I'm going to find out anyhow. It's better if I get it straight from you." Kelly took out his notebook and held a blunt little pencil at the ready. "So what's the score on this Arthur Rigley?"

"I'd like to know the source of your information," Cheney said. A slight shadow moved at the back of his mind a moment. There was one person, perhaps only one, who might have told the reporter.

"A little bird," Kelly said. "Come on, George. You know I can't tell you anything like that. It was an anonymous call. Is Rigley responsible for the three kids?"

"*Three* kids?"

"Don't act surprised. I do my homework. Rick Dove, early this morning, vanished from his home, blah blah blah. I just talked with Fred. He confirmed his son was missing. Something of a windbag, Fred Dove. Likes to sound off. Fred's an unhappy man who doesn't like the way this investigation is being handled." Kelly flicked the pages of his notebook a second. "I quote. *Sheriff Cheney should have called in outside help. He isn't experienced in this kind of investigation. He's a fast man with parking tickets.* End of quote."

"Dove's entitled to his opinion." *A fast man with parking tickets*—Fred Dove was repeating himself. For a moment

Cheney considered this definition of himself. Were those the limits of his abilities? Parking tickets? Shuffling paperwork? Was that all he had to offer?

Kelly said, "He has opinions on everything from missing kids to the fiscal condition of Hamland to Ethiopia and back. I won't print some of his stuff, of course. But none of it's going to reflect well on you, George. Especially when it comes out that you're holding some guy and you won't give the good old *Progressive* a whiff of information. Catch my drift?"

"Drift caught," Cheney said. He propped an elbow on his desk and laid his cheek against the palm of one hand. He had the curious feeling of artillery being lined up against him. Out there the streets were filled with potential ambushers, each of them waiting to waylay the sheriff. "How did you find out about Rick Dove?"

"You ask embarrassing questions, George."

"Did it come from the same source as Arthur Rigley?"

"Could have. I don't deny anything and I'm not confirming anything either. We're even now."

Cheney stood up. What if Lily Hubbard, say, had told Kelly about the missing Dove boy? how had she gotten hold of *that* information? He was locked in a maze now and the paper-trail he'd left behind to guide him back out had been whipped away by a breeze: it was that kind of feeling which went through him. There were devious movements in the shadows—only he couldn't understand them, couldn't get them to make sense.

"So what's the scoop on Rigley?" Kelly asked.

"He's answering a few questions, that's all."

"About the kids?"

Cheney nodded. "I might point out, though, we don't suspect him of anything."

"Yeah yeah. So why bring him in?"

"Certain facts have to be confirmed—"

"Don't speak Cop-Dutch, George. I don't understand that language. Neither do my readers. They're into plain talk."

Cheney walked round his office. "I can't tell you anything else without jeopardizing the investigation—"

"Ho hum," Kelly said. "The intrepid sheriff and the

mudslinging reporter are getting nowhere fast. Look, George, I like you. I think you're a decent man. I think, too, you're an honest man who finds himself in a thankless situation and I don't want to write anything in my newspaper that's going to slap a little egg on your face. You know what I'm saying, don't you?"

"I'm listening."

"I don't want to tell my gentle readers that George Cheney isn't coming clean with them. They like to think they're getting an honest deal. What am I supposed to tell them, George? This is something that affects every goddam household in this burg. The people have a right to know, especially when they're nervous the way they are right now. Three kids. Anybody else's kid could be next. That's what they're thinking out there."

"I know what they're thinking, Ron."

"So give me something to reassure them." Kelly paused, waved his notebook as though it were a subpoena. "Is this guy Rigley guilty or is he innocent? Either answer is acceptable. Either way, I've reported the news and the burghers sleep happy."

A goddam sneaker and a baseball cap and a bracelet.

Things that had been dropped in his lap, a gift from the patron saint of policemen.

Cheney stopped by the window, pressing his face lightly against the glass. "I can't answer your question, Ron. A man is assisting us in our inquiries. That's it."

"Yeah, but why this particular guy? Did you just drag him in off the street? Just fish him out at random and tell him he was needed to answer some questions?"

"We acted on information received," Cheney said drily.

"What information?"

"I can't go into that."

"Off the record."

"With you there's no such thing, Ron."

Kelly smiled, closed his notebook. "Sheriff Cheney was remarkably reticent when it came to discussing the man he was holding in custody—"

"Christ, Ron, do you have to print the guy's name? Suppose I release him in a couple of hours, some kind of shit is still going to stick to him even if he's as innocent as a baby. You know that. You know the way people's minds work—"

Ron Kelly stuck his notebook away. "I only write the news, Sheriff. People can read into it anything they like. If it happens to be shit, I'm not responsible for it."

"Kelly—"

The reporter paused in the doorway and turned around. "Yes, George?"

"I wish you wouldn't print the guy's name."

Kelly shrugged. "It's my job. Thanks for your time anyhow." The journalist stepped out in the hallway, paused again, looked back. "You know, it's funny how there's a really thin dividing line between ordinary respectable people and a mob with blood on its brain."

"Which you'll encourage—"

"The news is the news is the news," Kelly said, then he was gone.

Alone, Cheney could feel a pressure begin to build inside him. A solid thing, forcing its way up through his body and into his brain. Pressure to find the kids. Pressure to make an arrest. How long before he buckled under it? Or had he buckled already, without knowing it because he was too far gone?

He went out into the corridor toward the interview room, where Charlie Bannion sat with Arthur Rigley. He looked through the small window. Like two characters in an existential drama whose theme was the futility of communication, Bannion sat motionless at one end of a table and Rigley, his eyes shut, at the other.

Cheney tapped on the glass. Bannion came out into the corridor, closing the door behind him.

"He doesn't remember, George," Bannion said. "Not the sneaker. Not the bracelet. Not the fucking baseball cap. It's like trying to talk to a block of wood. I feel I ought to be a ventriloquist, answering my own questions. Would you mind standing behind Rigley and operating his mouth?"

Cheney smiled in a weary way.

"Do we release him?" the young cop asked.

"Not yet," Cheney said.

"Shit, he's sitting there and he's not doing anything."

"Yeah. I know."

Both men were silent for a moment. Cheney peered through the pane of glass. Rigley had his hands flat on the table and was studying his knuckles.

"Let me run something past you, Charlie."

"I'm ready."

"Can you think of any reason in the world why Lily Hubbard would plant those objects in Rigley's apartment?"

"Plant? *Crazy old Lily?*" Bannion looked surprised. "What makes you think she'd do something like that?"

"I don't know. I'm playing a guessing-game. Assume she did, why would she?"

"Christ, I don't know."

Cheney turned away from the window. Rigley, looking up, had caught his eye a moment, reminding Cheney of a cow sentenced to death in Slattery's. Why was Lily Hubbard so goddam adamant about this poor bastard?

"If she planted them," Bannion said. *"If* she did, it's because she wants you to make a wrongful arrest."

"Okay. Why?"

"You're the sheriff," Bannion said. "You get paid more to answer the biggies."

"A wrongful arrest—what kind of sense would that make?"

Bannion plunged his hands in his pockets. "Maybe she's trying to throw you off the track . . ."

"You mean because she took the kids herself?"

"Or she knows who did," Bannion said. "Of course, if she did plant those objects, she could have done it to make you look goddam stupid, George."

"For what reason?"

"I don't know. Did you ever rub her the wrong way? Is there some ancient grudge or something? Jesus. I don't have answers to that one."

An ancient grudge, Cheney thought. What could that possibly be? His own history barely intersected that of Lily Hubbard, except where his father was concerned. The old man was the one with connections to the Hubbards, not him.

There was no grudge. There was nothing he could think of. At least not between himself and Lily.

Nor did he imagine that Lily, a frail wispy woman, was

capable of stealing healthy young kids, who would presumably be struggling against her—

And yet. And yet.

There had been no sign of a struggle in any of the cases. It was as if those kids had gone willingly with whoever took them.

If indeed anyone had.

What kind of thought was that? They hadn't vanished of their own free will, for Christ's sake.

Cheney took a deep breath. The next consideration was the possibility Lily was covering up for somebody. Who and why? Those were biggies.

And they went nowhere.

Like everything else, they led back to confusion.

"None of it makes sense," he said.

"I agree with that one, George." Bannion raised a hand, tapped the surface of the small window a second. "How would Lily Hubbard get a hold of the kids' stuff? From an accomplice?"

"I don't know."

"Then you dismiss Lily altogether and you concentrate on the guy sitting in that room," Bannion said. "If you ask me. And you did ask, didn't you?"

Cheney clapped the young cop on the shoulder. "Yeah, I asked."

"So what now? You want me to go back in there and keep old motor mouth company?"

"For a while longer, Charlie. The guy's got to have some alibis for the times when those kids vanished—"

"Not that he remembers," Bannion said. "I've asked more times than I can count. Arthur's memory is a bit like the moon, George. Mostly barren with some empty craters." Shrugging, the young cop entered the interview room. Cheney went back to his own office.

Ellis Diamond was standing at the window, looking out into the street.

She turned to him with a nervous smile.

Fred Dove looked down at the face of his wife Marge. She was lying on the sofa in the living-room, a damp cloth spread across her forehead and little slivers of water running down her cheeks. She had one hand pressed to the cloth and her mouth was open very slightly.

"I didn't see any harm in talking with that reporter," Fred Dove said. "In fact, it might even do some good. Somebody might remember seeing Rick . . ."

Marge said nothing. The damp cloth lay on her brow like a tiny shroud. She had said nothing for a long time, withdrawing into silences Fred Dove couldn't penetrate. Marge had the ability to create foxholes in her brain and she could crawl into them whenever reality became too much of an intrusion. She had been this way ever since Cheney's messenger boy, Bannion, had called to ask the color of Rick's sneakers.

Dove stared at his wife. Even when he'd mentioned the banking arrangements he'd made, the ransom money he had gathered, she hadn't responded. Catatonic, as if everything that floated in front of her eyes were meaningless, she seemed to look only into the interior of herself. Hadn't he been telling her that the boy would be fine? that the money would buy his safe release?

She had looked at him as if to say *You keep telling me this, you keep trying to convince me, but I haven't heard the voice of the kidnapper on the telephone, I haven't seen any evidence of a kidnapper . . .*

Fred Dove felt a surprising calm right now. Since he was sure he had worked it all out, since he was convinced that Rick would be home in a matter of hours, and since he knew the name of the man who had taken the boy, he felt it was simply a time for some patience because things were going to fall neatly into place at any moment. Hugh Estaban, whom Fred had always found wishy-washy and uncertain of himself, might choose to think what he liked: but Fred Dove knew otherwise.

He wandered to the window where, his hands still behind his back, he gazed out into the street. A girl went past on a bicycle. She wore tight blue jeans and an OP T-shirt emblazoned with parrots and her long yellow hair floated out behind her as she rode. Fred Dove tightened his jaw, watching the kid disappear along the street. Her buttocks

THE PIPER

were lifted a little from the seat of the bike as she pumped the
pedals for speed at the place where the road began to rise.

A girl on a bike in the street. Such casual grace. What filled
him just then was an envy of her youthfulness, the way her
tight trim body pumped that bike, the effortless flow of
muscles, the gorgeous coordination.

He wandered out into the kitchen and stared into the back
yard where Jenny was squatting in the grass. Her dolls and
animals lay in disarray nearby. Dove leaned against the jamb
of the door, studying his daughter. Her brown hair fell
untidily against her shoulders and there were green smudges
on her pale blue jeans. Fred Dove stepped out into the yard
and kneeled down beside the girl. He had never been
anything but awkward when it came to conversing with small
children, which was something they always seemed to sense
whenever he tried.

He stroked his daughter's hair clumsily. "How are you?"
he asked.

"Thinking," she answered.

"Yeah? What are you thinking, baby?"

"About Rick."

"Rick's going to come home, baby."

The little girl shook her head. "Unnnn."

"Sure he is. He'll be home before you know it."

She kept shaking her head. "Unnn-unnnn."

"What does unnn-unnn mean?"

"Means he isn't coming home. Not soon anyhow."

"What makes you think that?" Dove asked.

"Cause somebody told me."

"Is that so?"

"Yep."

"Who?" Dove asked. God: they have imaginary play-
mates, they hear voices, they don't have a strong connection
with the real world.

"Lady told me."

"A lady?"

"She was out in the alley there," and the child pointed to
the door in the back fence which led to a dirt alley that ran
behind the house. The door, halfway open, revealed a couple
of large green plastic trash cans.

"There was nobody out there," he said. "You're making it up."

"No," she said. "A lady was walking down the alley. And she called to me."

"When?"

"A little while ago."

Kids, Dove thought. They have no sense of time passing. "What did she say?"

The little girl stood up, shifting her feet round in the grass. "Something."

"What, baby?"

The girl looked at the ground. "She said he was being looked after."

Looked after, Dove thought. What was that supposed to mean? And who was this mysterious woman anyhow? Kids, he knew, could make up anything, they could fantasize from dawn to dusk, they didn't live in anything that approximated the real world. His daughter was clearly fabricating this tale. He let her wrists go, and he moved away from her.

"Well, it's nice to know Rick's being looked after, isn't it?"

"Yeah," the girl said.

Dove gazed toward the alley, the trash cans. A cluster of sparrows squabbled in midair a moment, then dispersed. Dove turned toward the house now, saying, "Why don't you stay out here and play for a while longer? Mommy's got a headache. She's pretty upset. You can understand that."

"Yeah," the girl said.

Fred Dove moved toward the back door of the house.

Then his daughter called out to him.

"Don't you want to know who's looking after him, Dad?"

"Suppose you tell me."

"Somebody called Mona."

"What?"

"Somebody called Mona."

There was a sudden dryness in Dove's mouth, a pulse beating at the back of his throat, a sense of moisture being drained out of him.

"Mona?" he said.

"'Sright."

"A woman told you this?"

THE PIPER

"Yep. So you don't need to worry, do you? Do you, Dad?"

"Are you absolutely sure it wasn't a man who told you all this, sweetheart?"

"I know the difference between a man and a woman," the child responded.

Fred Dove turned once more toward the house.

To his surprise, he saw Marge standing in the doorway, one hand to her forehead, the other hanging limply at her side. She had no color on her face. Her skin had the texture of chalk.

"Who the hell is Mona?" she asked.

Fred Dove stepped past Marge and went into the kitchen. He poured himself a shot of brandy and sat at the table, staring into the liquid.

"Who the hell is Mona?" Marge asked again.

"The kid's dreaming, Marge—"

"Is she somebody you screwed, Fred? Is that who she is? Some little girl you fucking molested?"

Fred Dove raised his face to look at his wife.

What he saw there wasn't Marge at all.

It was a person filled with violence and hatred, somebody who had nurtured the poison of resentment until it had filled every secret crevice of her being. Somebody who stared at him as if all she had on her mind was murder.

Dove sipped his drink.

Who was the woman in the alley? he wondered.

Who was the kidnapper's accomplice?

There was a wife, wasn't there? There was a wife called Hilda or Hildy or something like that.

He watched Marge go out into the back yard.

Wax.
Wax and wires.
Electrical circuits.
Switches.
Here we go round the mulberry bush . . .
The smell of burning.

Mr Zanzibar stops at the foot of the stairs.

Then he moves through the living-room and into the kitchen.

THE PIPER

The girl sits at the table.

She sits silently.

Zanzibar says, "Everything's ready. It's almost time."

The girl says nothing to him.

Zanzibar, moving toward her, pulls silks from her open mouth in one colorful flourish.

"There and there and there and there!" he says.

He wants an expression of admiration from her.

He wants applause.

"You're not impressed?" he asks.

No. She isn't impressed. Not at all.

He watches the girl a little while longer, noticing the absence in the eyes and the distended mouth and the way her earrings, small emerald globes, hang almost as low as her shoulders.

Zanzibar goes back upstairs.

Back to wax and wood and wires and all the wonderful bits and pieces of the Great Illusion.

SIXTEEN

IT WAS RAINING LIGHTLY WHEN GEORGE CHENEY REACHED THE house on Dolores Street. The gray sky that had hung all day over Hamland had blackened and cracks had appeared in the texture of the clouds. He parked his car and moved toward the Sears's house where a light burned on the porch, even though it was only late afternoon and not yet dark. Climbing the steps, he turned the collar of his jacket up.

The screen door swung open and Thomas Sears stood there. The fat man's white shirt hung outside his pants and the pants themselves appeared to have slipped from his waist, suspended someplace in mid-thigh. There was a streak of blood on his shirt pocket, and his breath, musty with stale beer, floated across the porch.

Cheney said, "I had a report of an incident at the park, Tom."

"Hell, it was one of them misunderstandings—" Sears waved the whole thing away with the motion of a hand.

"It doesn't sound like a misunderstanding," Cheney said. "What I hear is you beat up Max Crouch."

Thomas Sears, contrite, shuffled his feet. "I'd been drinking, Sheriff. I ought to quit it. Sometimes it takes me the wrong way," and the fat man laughed. "You know how it is."

"My report is that you accused Max Crouch of kidnapping your son." Cheney tucked his thumbs in his belt, spreading his legs.

"Hey, I was mistaken. Is he pressing charges?"

Cheney shook his head. He looked away from Sears the length of this leafy street. Rain pattered on leaves, millions of dull whispers, a drumming that might—over a period of time—drive you quite mad. Lily Hubbard and Arthur Rigley and the cache of objects in his apartment: people and things congregated in his brain, pressing against the backs of his eyes. Quite, quite mad, he thought.

"I don't know about charges, Tom. What I'm wondering is why you accused Crouch of having anything to do with your son."

"I was drunk, dammit, and I'm still a little drunk."

"Tom, don't give me this drunk shit. You must have had *some* reason for attacking Crouch the way you did. I don't care if you were drunk or stone-cold sober, you must have had something in mind."

"A drunk does all kinds of off-the-wall stuff, Sheriff. All I can say is I'm sorry."

Cheney leaned against the porch rail. He had never disliked this town before but he did so now, annoyed by its smug frame houses and the smell of Mexican food blowing through the drizzle: it was as if the boyhood he remembered so fondly in this place had never taken place. Someone might have implanted false sunny recollections in his brain.

"I'll pay his medical expenses, Sheriff."

Cheney shook his head at Sears. "Goddamit, Thomas. I don't give a flying fuck about his medical expenses. I don't even care a shit about the assault. I'm interested in knowing why, out of a town of some fifteen thousand people, you apparently considered Max Crouch guilty of kidnapping!"

Thomas Sears stepped back, surprised by the way the sheriff was shouting. "I swear. I don't remember."

Cheney sighed in exasperation.

"Did you also think Crouch was responsible for Vickie

Estaban? Did you happen to think that too? Did you imagine he'd also snatched young Rick Dove? While you were trying to beat him senseless, Sears, were you thinking about all three kids?"

"I was only thinking of my own kid, Sheriff."

"But why Crouch, Thomas? Why not the barman at the Crawford or some waitress at the Royal? You must have had some goddam reason for picking Max Crouch!"

"No, I didn't. And if I did at the time, I've forgotten what it was. Booze, I guess. The bottle let me down." Sears chanced a smile but Cheney, in no mood for cheerful expressions, felt an urge inside him to slam Sears back against the wall and pistol-whip the truth out of him. Sagging, letting his arms fall loosely to his side, Cheney wanted to lie down and sleep the rest of his life away. Mysteries in the rain, and no end in sight.

Goddam.

It was a fucking carousel with skeletal horses you rode on, up and down, down and up, and the loudspeaker didn't emit music, it chanted a litany of names like they were cryptic clues in a carnival game—

Estaban and Dove and Sears.

And Arthur Rigley.

And Lily Hubbard.

And somewhere else, lingering at the far edge of his consciousness, there was Zanzibar too, Zanzibar who had promised to call him with those Social Security numbers and who hadn't done so yet—

Max Crouch. Why Max Crouch of all people?

"Does Max Crouch know your son?" he asked.

"Don't think so."

Cheney stood upright. "Tom. Think hard. Did your son ever do anything that might outrage Crouch? Did he ever steal from him? Offend him in some way? Try, Tom."

"I'm sorry, Sheriff."

Cheney nodded. He looked down the porch steps to the damp lawn. Doors were closing against him. He watched rain bend tiny stalks of grass and he thought about his son coming home—when was it? tonight? tomorrow morning? Christ, time had slipped away from him—and he tried to imagine taking Danny and Anne and a tent and trekking off into the wilderness somewhere, far away from this cesspool of puzzlement.

"If you happen to remember, call me," Cheney said. He started to go down the steps. When he turned to look back at Sears, the fat man was watching him, head tipped to one side, a nerve at work in the plump jaw.

Cheney crossed the lawn to his car. Hamland was prematurely dark, as if all the wandering rainclouds of the world had chosen to congregate over this town out of some celestial spite. Cheney looked up. He didn't think he could stand another deluge of the kind he'd gone through when he'd driven out to Gowrie Canyon.

He didn't think he could stand much of anything any more.

He looked back one last time to see Thomas Sears Senior leaning forward against the porch rail, a fat man made to appear jaundiced beneath the yellow porch-light.

He knows something, Cheney thought.

But he isn't telling me.

Lily Hubbard said, "In Arthur Rigley's possession there was a sneaker belonging to Rick Dove and a bracelet that was Victoria Estaban's. In addition, Rigley had Tommy Sears's baseball cap. These objects are now in George Cheney's hands and have been for a few hours."

There was a silence at the other end of the line. Lily could hear the reporter shuffling papers.

"Did you get that?" she asked.

The reporter said, "I got it, lady. But it would be a whole lot more credible if you gave me your name."

Lily sighed, drawing her shawl up over her shoulders. She was cold: a window was open and a damp breeze floated past the drapes, causing them to shiver. "My name is of no importance. Didn't you check the earlier information I gave you? Didn't you find out that was true? Why wouldn't you believe me now?"

The reporter said, "If what you're saying is true, lady, why did George Cheney tell me he didn't suspect Rigley of anything?"

"George Cheney, as you must know, is an indecisive man. I doubt if he could do up his zipper without assistance." Lily laughed for a second. "But in the circumstances, how could he fail to arrest Rigley? Answer me that."

Again, the reporter was quiet. Then: "How come you happen to have this information, lady?"

"That's my affair."

"Sounds to me as if you don't like George Cheney much."

"I can take him or leave him. The thing I cannot abide is incompetence in law and order, Kelly. I can't stand it when things are left undone that should be done."

"I get the picture," the reporter said.

"You get only part of the picture," Lily answered. Rising, dragging the telephone across the room, she shut the window.

"There's more?"

"There may be more. But not now."

A pause. Lily was still cold. She sat down, rubbed her feet with one hand. She said, "George Cheney is a fool. George Cheney wouldn't understand evidence if it hit him in the face."

The reporter coughed into the receiver. "I'll have to check the things you've told me—"

"Check to your heart's content," Lily answered.

"You sure you won't give me your name?"

"Think of me as a person interested only in justice. Which is long overdue."

Lily Hubbard put the telephone down.

Long overdue, indeed.

She sat back in her chair, huddling deep inside her shawl. Justice, as the Judge always used to say, had no face. Justice was featureless.

She cocked her head to one side, listening to the rain at the window. She would have to go out again and although the prospect excited her, just the same she was aware of an edge of weariness around herself.

She could set that aside for now. When you have been consumed by one consideration for years, when you have thought of nothing else during all the passages of your time, when your existence isn't just a matter of breathing and eating and sleeping but something else, a burning objective you must achieve regardless, a white-hot passion that steams and seethes inside your brain, then a little tiredness is no inconvenience.

There had been a flame in her mind for a long time now: and suddenly it was brighter.

Clear skies, she thought.

Clear skies very soon, Elmer.

She picked up the photograph that George Cheney had been curious about earlier, the one depicting herself, The Judge, and the boy. She ran the edge of her shawl across the glass to clean the frame.

The Cub Scout master, a large cheerful man called Bubba Shankland, stood up front in the old yellow school bus. He stared at the tired faces of his pack of Cub Scouts and made another effort to get their spirits up. Sixteen small boys frowned at him, every boy utterly tired from hiking and climbing and doing the kinds of chores they never had to do at home. *Mom always does the dishes, Bubba! Mom always does the laundry!* Sixteen small boys, none of them very much in the mood for singing.

Bubba Shankland peered out into the rain that fell against the side of the bus.

"Twenty-nine miles to Hamland, boys," he said, grinning. "How about another chorus of *The Old Gray Mare*, lads?"

Groan. Groan. Sixteen small boys wondered what the old gray mare had been like in her youth before she had been immortalized in a song concerning her advancing years.

"After three," Bubba Shankland said. "Okay. One. Two. Three. *The old gray mare she ain't what she used to be, Ain't what she used to be, Ain't what she used to be . . .*"

At the rear of the bus, Danny Cheney and his friends Davie and Donnie Territo—the Terror Twins—began to sing *She'll Be Coming Round the Mountain When She Comes,* setting up a cacophonous counterpoint. They had come to perceive Bubba in recent days as a kind of cheerful jailer and the fact that they were interfering with his choral efforts was a small form of rebellion—like prisoners rattling tin mugs against the bars of their cells.

Bubba stopped singing. "I hear small dissenting voices back there, don't I?" And he laughed good-naturedly.

At the front of the bus, Dustin Fish, the runt of the troop who had been christened—naturally—The Minnow, wanted to know how far it was to Hamland now.

"Only twenty-nine miles," Shankland answered.

"I thought it'd be twenty-eight by this time," said The Minnow.

"Let's try again," and Bubba Shankland smiled, sticking a conductorial finger in the air. "After three . . . One. Two. Three."

> *The old gray mare she ain't what she used to be*
> *Ain't what she used to be*
> *Ain't what she used to be . . .*

The Minnow made a weird choking sound and threw up his lunch of baked beans on the floor.

At the back of the bus, Danny Cheney rubbed his eyes. He was tired, but it was a different kind of tired from what a long hike might have produced. It was like there was something dead at the center of his brain.

Kinda spacey, he thought.

Cheney parked his car on Strasburg Street and stepped out, moving toward the house where Max Crouch had a small apartment he shared with his wife. It was one of those old houses that had systematically been butchered down the years by a series of landlords. It had been turned into two apartments, then into four: and now there were six bells on the front door, each with a faded nameplate. Cheney rang the appropriate bell and waited, surveying the ruined front yard and the way broad-leaved weeds wilted beneath raindrops.

Max Crouch opened the door a little way. One arm hung against his side, strapped to his body, and there were bruises across his cheeks. He peered out at Cheney as if he'd expected the sheriff all along, but it was clearly a prospect that hadn't delighted him.

"Can I come in?" Cheney said. "You look like you've been in the wars, Max."

Crouch stepped back from the door and Cheney went into the corridor. It was long and gloomy.

"I don't have anything to say," Crouch remarked.

Cheney looked toward the stairs. A door was halfway open at the top and he could see the bloated form of Hildy Crouch standing there in large silhouette.

"Can I come up?" Cheney asked.

"Suit yourself. Won't do you much good though."

Cheney climbed, followed by Crouch. Hildy had disappeared somewhere. Inside the apartment, small and brown, wallpaper faded, a TV played. Cheney glanced at it. There was an old *Hawaii Five-O* rerun and Jack Lord was saying *I want him under surveillance twenty-four hours a day. When he sneezes I want to know it. When he blinks an eye, tell me.*

Max Crouch said, "And when he shits, I want the color of it at once."

Cheney smiled feebly, looking round the room. A door opened and Hildy Crouch, dressed in a bag-shaped shift, came into the room. It was obvious she had just gone to put on some makeup because her lipstick looked fresh and new. Rubbing her hands together nervously, she smiled at Cheney.

"We don't get many visitors, Sheriff. You want to sit down?"

Cheney shook his head.

Hildy, waddling across the floor, sank into a sofa. With a remote device, she turned the volume on the TV down so that Jack Lord whispered. *Danno, check the guy for priors.*

"I figure you're here about that animal who attacked my Max," Hildy said.

"Yeah," Cheney said.

"I told Max. I said to him. Press charges, why don't you? Put the sonofabitch behind bars, I said. Max is too good-natured. He won't lift a finger."

Cheney looked at Max Crouch. The custodian turned his bruised face aside: the useless arm was motionless against his body.

"The guy said it was a mistake, Sheriff," Crouch remarked.

"One hell of a mistake, Max."

"Happens."

Cheney moved around the room. On a small circular table

273

by the window there was a white birthday cake with unlit candles. He gazed at it a moment, wondering whether it was Max or Hildy who was celebrating a birthday. He counted the candles quickly. Twenty-seven, twenty-eight, he wasn't sure. Whatever, they represented a number of years that neither Max nor his wife would ever see again.

"Press charges, why don't you?" Hildy asked.

Max Crouch shrugged. "The guy said he made a genuine mistake. Anyhow, he was drunk."

"What puzzles me is why Sears would think you had something to do with his kid," Cheney said.

Hildy, sipping on a glass of sherry, said, "Yeah, that's the strange part. Max told me all about that. The way I see it—"

"Nobody's interested in how you see it, Hildy," Crouch snapped. "It was a mistake. A goddam mistake. I don't want the fuss of pressing charges and going to court. I don't like courts."

Cheney looked back at the birthday cake. "Thomas Sears must have had something going on in his mind, Max."

"I see where his kid's missing," Crouch answered. "Guy's not in full control of himself, that's all. Call it anxiety. Call it worry—"

"I call it violence," Hildy said.

Cheney said, "Even if he was bombed out of his mind, Max, why would he associate you with Tommy?"

"Search me."

Hildy Crouch set her glass of sherry down. "Time!" she said.

"It can wait, Hildy."

"Let's do it now."

"We've got company, Hildy—"

"The Sheriff won't mind. Will you, Sheriff?"

"Mind what?" Cheney asked.

"It's time to light the candles."

"Go right ahead," Cheney said. "Whose birthday is it?"

Neither Crouch nor his wife answered the question. Hildy Crouch struck a match and hovered over the cake, lighting the candles one by one. When she turned to look at her husband tears were running down her cheeks. Max Crouch, apparently embarrassed, moved toward the table. He held one of his wife's plump hands in his own and silently gazed at the flickering candles. The impression Cheney got was of some private ritual being played out here, and he felt curiously like a trespasser. He looked at the cake, seeing how the tiny dance of flame illuminated a name frosted on the top of the cake.

MONA
TWENTY-EIGHT TODAY

Puzzled, Cheney watched as Hildy Crouch blew the candles out. The air was filled with the smell of wax. Mona, he thought. Who was Mona?

Max Crouch looked at the sheriff. "You want a piece?"

Cheney shook his head.

Hildy Crouch took a knife and sliced it into the cake. There was a collapse of candles.

"Twenty-eight. Twenty-eight," Hildy said. Having cut the cake, she turned away from the table without eating any. She gazed at George Cheney, who felt incongruous in this room, as if he were the only non-member at the meeting of a cult.

Max Crouch said, "The sheriff doesn't remember, Hildy. This doesn't mean a damn thing to him."

"I don't follow," Cheney said.

"Mona," Hildy said. "Mona is our daughter."

"Was," Crouch said.

"Is. Is. Is."

Max Crouch sighed, shaking his head. "Whatever you want, Hildy."

Cheney moved to the center of the room. What the hell was going on here?

"If she's alive," Crouch said, "she's twenty-eight years old today."

"If she's alive?" Cheney asked.

"We haven't seen her for fifteen years."

Hildy Crouch, her face hidden inside a handkerchief, had her head bent low across the darkened cake.

"Before your time, Sheriff," Max Crouch said.

"What happened to her?"

"She went away," Crouch answered.

Hildy moaned into the folds of her handkerchief.

"Away?" Cheney asked.

"Yeah. Away. One night she went out and she never came back and that's all she wrote."

"She ran away?"

"Ran. Walked. Took a bus. Flew. How the fuck do I know?"

Cheney said nothing. Fifteen years ago. Mona Crouch would have been thirteen then. There were little echoes here, things that resonated inside his brain. Another missing kid. Back then in another sheriff's history.

"You never heard from her again?"

"Never," Crouch said. He picked up a slice of cake, looked at it with disgust, set it down.

"What did the police do?"

"They took notes, Sheriff. That's what cops do."

"Who was the sheriff at the time?"

"McClanahan."

Cheney nodded. McClanahan, if you believed local lore and rumor, had been one of those sheriffs who liked nothing better than to be seen riding in his marked car through the streets of Hamland, a sort of smalltown Mussolini, but one who approached his job with a lackadaisical quality that amounted to a kind of benign neglect.

"They found no trace of the girl?" he asked.

"Sure," Crouch said.

"Like what?"

"She was seen last in the parking-lot of the Crawford, stepping into a car. Nobody remembered the make of the car or the face of the guy driving."

"Then what?"

"Then nothing. Gone. Swallowed up." Crouch shrugged: it was a bitter little gesture.

Hildy Crouch licked frosting from her fingertips. "She'll come back. I have this feeling. Sometimes I dream. I see her walk right through that door." A sad smile went across the plump face.

"Dreams," Crouch said.

"The cops never found the car or the driver?" Cheney asked. "They discovered absolutely nothing?"

"Nothing."

Cheney looked at the broken cake. "I'm sorry."

He leaned against the sofa. A missing girl. He imagined the world of Max and Hildy Crouch, a big empty place in which, with every passing day, expectations and hopes would diminish to a point where optimism had no meaning, where only vague dreams would give you sustenance. Mona Crouch. Another aspect of Hamland's history that had passed him by, just like the news of Lily Hubbard's dead son.

He hesitated: it was time to bring everything back into the present. "I'm still left with the behavior of Thomas Sears."

"Forget it," Crouch said.

"It sticks to me, Max. It's hard to forget it."

Crouch shrugged. "All I can say is that I don't have his kid, which is what I told him at the time. What would I want with another guy's kid anyhow? And Sears isn't much of a prospect for a guy in the kidnapping business, if you ask me."

Cheney nodded. He had nothing, nothing from either Thomas Sears or Max Crouch: a snippet of information about a child who vanished years ago, and nothing else. He gazed at the sad birthday cake and wondered about Mona Crouch who, fifteen years before, had stepped inside a stranger's car and driven off to nowhere—to a place without witnesses, a place from which she had never returned.

How did you live the rest of your life wondering what had happened to your kid?

Cheney turned toward the door.

"Thanks for your time," he said.

"We got lots of time," Max Crouch answered.

Hildy blinked moistly at Cheney. "She's twenty-eight today."

As Cheney went down the flight of stairs to the front door he heard Hildy Crouch's voice singing brokenly: *Happy Birthday to Mona, Happy Birthday to Mona* . . .

After a second, Max Crouch joined in.

Fifteen miles out of Hamland Bubba Shankland made the driver stop the bus because The Minnow had to go out and pee. The small Cub Scout disappeared behind a tree while the rest of the troop pressed their faces against the windows and jeered at the sight of Dustin Fish pissing in the rain.

"Wet your pants!" said one of the Terror Twins, his face stuck through an open window. "Piss into the wind, Fish-face!"

"He can hardly find his dong," said another Scout.

Danny Cheney, half-asleep at the back of the bus, experienced an odd sensation. It was the feeling you always get when you know there's something you're supposed to do only you can't remember what the hell it is and so it *nags you*. He opened his eyes, aware that the bus had stopped.

Bubba Shankland was saying, "Behave yourself, boys. You've all seen somebody pass bodily fluids before."

Outside, The Minnow struggled with his tiny member. The windy rain caught the arc of his urine and blew it back against his bare knees. The small boy's face was red. He flashed one finger at the bus.

There was an outbreak of cheering, because Dustin Fish was moved only rarely to such vulgarities.

Danny sat up in his seat.

There was an uneasy sensation in his stomach.

Not quite sickness. Something else.

He looked at his watch.

It was six twenty-nine.

Time seemed suddenly very important to him, although he wasn't absolutely sure why. He stared at the second hand of the timepiece, watching it sweep the face.

The Minnow boarded the bus to much cheering and the dirty yellow vehicle ploughed on through the rain.

Edward Cheney called Anne. He stood by the big bay window of his sitting-room and watched wet mist blow along Montrose, creating a shroud around the oak tree.

Edward asked, "When is Danny expected home?"

"At seven. At least that's what he told me. But I wouldn't bet on it. I don't trust that big yellow bus."

Edward Cheney was quiet a moment. He had a feeling of something stuck at the back of his throat. "Where is he due to arrive?"

"The Lutheran Church."

"I wonder if you'd mind very much, Anne, if I accompanied you to meet him."

"I think that would be lovely," Anne said. "Is something wrong, Edward?"

"Wrong?"

"I don't know, you sound . . . forlorn."

"I'm fine."

"If you say so."

Cheney laughed: it sounded like a very small pebble rattling against his teeth. "I'll meet you at the Lutheran at seven."

When he had hung up, Cheney went out into the back yard. He stood at the edge of the grass and looked at the sky. He needed to see the boy, that was what it came down to. He needed to be there when Danny stepped off that bus because then nothing could happen to the child, nothing could happen if he was around to make sure.

Family.

A sense of blood ties.

Edward Cheney folded his hands in front of himself. Estaban and the others might have lost their children, but he wasn't about to lose the only small child left in his life, not if he could help it.

He shut his eyes. He was dizzy in the rain.

There was a demon, certainly, and it rose from its mildewed grave in Sutter's Meadow and it sucked children back into the ground when it foraged the blind places of Hamland.

But he wouldn't let it take young Danny.

Not down into that swampy grass where it had its lair.

He went back indoors.

He sat down on the piano stool. His hands fell over the keys, creating a discord.

The sound rolled and echoed into the farthest rooms of the house, rising upstairs and reaching as far as the vast gloomy attic where—diminished by the distance it had travelled—it had the faint timbre of glass breaking in a faraway place.

Charlie Bannion stood in the doorway of Cheney's office. "Arthur Rigley fell asleep in the interview room, George," the young cop said. "He was telling me about how he should have been an artist because he has all these natural gifts—then, wham, he was out of it. What do you want me to do?"

"Let him sleep," Cheney said. He was searching through a filing-cabinet, one of several that filled one wall of the room. They were antiques that had been painted time and again over the years and where they were scratched you could see different layers of colors—gray, dark blue, khaki, and a kind of murky sea-green. Dust rose into his nostrils from old manila folders. "Did Zanzibar call?"

"No," Bannion answered. "Not that I noticed. Your wife did, though."

"Yeah?"

"Your son's coming home tonight."

Cheney smiled. A bright spot in a dark day.

"Anne says she'll pick him up."

Cheney nodded. "I'll be glad to see the boy. If I ever find the time to get home." A noisy house, he thought. A kid clambering up the stairs. Clumping around in the kitchen. All the sounds of a vital life being lived. A small shaft of warmth went through him. Danny.

"Do something for me, Charlie. See if you can get a hold of Zanzibar. He promised he'd call. And I don't intend to let him off the hook."

Bannion went toward the phone, glancing at Cheney as he crossed the room. "What are you fishing for there?"

Cheney took out a folder and smacked it against the cabinet and pale dust filled the air. "This," and he brandished an old manila folder in the air. "The file on one Mona Crouch."

Bannion shrugged, picked up the telephone, asked for Directory Assistance. Waiting, the receiver tucked between jaw and shoulder, Bannion said, "I'm going to feel pretty damn stupid asking for the number of a man with a name like Zanzibar."

Cheney went to his desk, opening the folder.

He found a single sheet inside marked MONA CROUCH: it was flimsy, crinkled, and it had been typed on a machine with a feeble ribbon. The officer who'd made the report was called Patrick McDonald, a name that Cheney had never heard before. The report was dated July 7, 1970. Cheney spread the sheet flat on his desk and read. He was vaguely conscious of Charlie Bannion talking into a telephone, but the young cop's voice was a murmur on the edge of Cheney's awareness because it was the sheet that had gripped his attention, the pale words rising up off the paper at him.

It was all here, pretty much as Max Crouch had indicated.

The girl, Mona, was last seen getting into a car on the evening of July 6, 1970, in the parking-lot of the Crawford Steak & Chop House. The car, according to witnesses, was variously a black or dark blue sedan, perhaps with two doors, quite possibly four. None of the witnesses seemed able to agree. Nobody could describe the driver.

Cheney's head ached.

The words kept coming up at him, like letters thrown carelessly by a tide. They jumbled before his eyes, then rearranged themselves, even as the pain in his head started to get worse, dimming his vision. Charlie Bannion was putting the telephone down, saying something about how there was no listing for anybody called Zanzibar and asking what he should do now, but George Cheney barely heard him.

Cheney folded his hands over the report.

He massaged the sides of his head.

Witnesses, he thought. The people who saw Mona Crouch get into a car. The people who saw her being driven away. *Witnesses.*

He stood up, gazing out at the rainy facade of the Matter-horn Motor Lodge, which had the look of a place abandoned right then. All the windows were dark. Even the neon sign was unlit.

Witnesses.

People who saw the girl.

The pain in his head was growing.

"Knock, knock, George," Bannion said. "Are you home?"

Cheney nodded, went back to his desk, picked up the report again. Officer Patrick McDonald, who must have done at least some of his homework, had listed the witnesses who happened to be in the parking-lot of the Crawford at the time when the girl vanished inside the mysterious car and set off to a destination unknown.

Cheney, whose blood seemed cold to him now, circulating

through his body like ice-water, fingered the flimsy sheet of paper as if he expected it to turn into something else—like one of Zanzibar's tricks in which an ordinary piece of paper becomes a rose.

There was no rose.

Only this crumpled old sheet, smelling of age.

What he had in front of him, typed on a weak ribbon, punched out on paper by a cop who didn't know his way around a keyboard, were scraps of history—scraps he was suddenly afraid to reassemble because he had the feeling that the whole picture was going to be more murky than the most stagnant water.

Bannion said, "Hey, are you okay?"

Cheney nodded. "I've got to go out for a while. Keep trying to find that phone number out in Gowrie Canyon."

"But George, there's no listing—"

Cheney moved toward the doorway now and passed out into the corridor. He saw Richard P. Bacon come in through the front door, his fashionable British raincoat open, a silk scarf knotted at his throat.

"Cheney," the Mayor said. "The man I need to see."

"Not now," Cheney said.

Richard P. Bacon blocked his way. "I'm up to my ass in complaints, George—"

"I said not now," Cheney answered.

"Don't try and brush me aside, Cheney. We need to talk, you and I. We need to sit down man to man. We need to *confer.*"

Cheney side-stepped Bacon, but the Mayor reached out and gripped him by the wrist.

"I understand you're holding a man—"

"Christ."

"My information is that he's the one who took the kids—"

"Who told you that?" Cheney yanked his arm free.

"I received two calls, Cheney. One from our intrepid newspaper reporter, Ronald Kelly. The other anonymous. Both of them telling me the same thing, you understand. Both of them highly interesting." Bacon moved his body slightly and something in his coat pocket rattled. "What I need is the comforting confirmation from you that you've officially charged this madman you've got down here."

Cheney shook his head. "Nothing's official."

"I want to know why not—"

"Not now," Cheney said again, stepping toward the front doors.

"You value that badge, Sheriff?" Bacon asked.

Cheney reached the doors, shoved them open, paused. What was he supposed to say? He wasn't certain if he placed any value on his office right then.

"Do you, George?" Bacon asked.

Cheney stepped out into the street without looking back.

He heard Richard P. Bacon, Mayor of Hamland, call after him. "You going to charge this fucker or do I have to get your goddam deputy to do it!"

Cheney got into his car.

Danny heard Bubba Shankland say it was ten miles to Hamland. He gazed from the window. Familiar scenery appeared. The gray flatlands that stretched to the foothills, the rain-covered mountains in the far distance. He looked at his watch.

Six forty-one.

It nagged him still, this feeling of having something to do. He tried to shove it out of his mind. Beside him, the Terror Twins were telling sick jokes. They were of the "Mommy, Mommy" variety. *Mommy, Mommy, why am I running in circles? Shut up or I'll nail your other foot to the floor.* Danny had heard them all before. Up front, Bubba Shankland was no longer trying to get everybody singing. He simply stared out of the window from time to time, nodding his head and smiling the way he often did.

Something, Danny thought.

Something I'm supposed to do.

But what?

He shut his eyes.

He was feeling very sleepy.

SEVENTEEN

WHEN EDWARD CHENEY SAW HIS SON'S CAR DRAW UP OUTSIDE the house on Montrose Drive, his first reaction was a slight flicker of resignation. He had expected George all along and now, as he saw him come up the driveway, he realized he would have to think of him as the *sheriff,* not as his own son, not as his blood and flesh.

It was strange to make this adjustment: he was like a man who, so divided by his ambidextrous talents, could use neither hand in the end.

He moved out into the hallway. He had already put his raincoat on because he intended to meet Danny's bus at the Lutheran Church.

He opened the front door.

George looked strange to him. There was a tight lock-jawed expression on his face Edward Cheney had never seen before. It scared him a little.

The old man backed away, thinking: *He knows, George knows.*

George Cheney stepped inside and shut the door behind him. For a second, he didn't move: he scanned his father's face.

"Going out?" George Cheney asked.

"I was going with Anne to meet Danny."

The sheriff ran a hand across his jaw. He swept past his father and moved on into the sitting-room where he stood in the center of the floor, tapping one foot on the floorboards.

All the black nights of Edward Cheney's life, all the flashes of doom he'd ever experienced, seemed to congregate in his heart and he felt suddenly heavy, weighted down, sagging. Waiting for George to say something, waiting for George to speak whatever it was he'd come to say: until George said something, he would wait indefinitely, his life halted, his whole being suspended in a place where he trembled.

Edward Cheney passed one hand over the other, palm upon knuckles. This was the moment he had dreamed and dreaded.

George moved to the piano. He surveyed the keys as he said, "Tell me about Mona Crouch, Dad."

Edward Cheney felt that his head had become a steeple in which a forlorn bell was ringing. "Mona Crouch," he echoed, his voice dry. He gazed past George to the clock on the mantelpiece: six forty-three. Time filled him with fear. Time passing. There was a yellow bus approaching Hamland and his grandson was a passenger and if he wasn't there to meet that bus—

But Anne would be there.

"Tell me about her, Dad. Tell me about the night of July six, nineteen hundred and seventy."

"That's such a long time ago . . ."

"I know."

Edward Cheney drifted away from his son, turned his back, watched the minute hand on the clock move. "You were in Los Angeles then, weren't you?"

"Yes," Cheney said.

"My memory's poor, George."

George Cheney rapped the upraised lid of the grand piano with his knuckles and strings vibrated a moment. "Mona Crouch. What does that name mean to you?"

Edward stared across the room at the window. The rainstorm that had been threatening before was gone and there was all at once a watery whiteness in the sky over Hamland.

In such a sky it was easy to imagine an angel of vengeance spreading great white wings. Edward paced, turned out of the room, wandered down the long hallway and into the kitchen: the spaces of this enormous house whispered at him. George Cheney, following his father, his footsteps hard on the wood floors, was still asking the same question.

"What do you remember about a child called Mona Crouch?"

Was she a child, that big-breasted girl with the wide hips and the skin smooth as an oyster-shell?

He supposed she was. A child.

In the kitchen he fidgeted with things in the sink.

"Dad," George Cheney said. "You were there in the parking-lot of the Crawford on the night of July 6, 1970. You saw Mona Crouch get into a car. A car you couldn't describe properly when a cop called Patrick McDonald asked you."

And the sheriff thrust a sheet of paper in front of his father's face, holding it there like a weapon.

"It's here. It's in black and white, for God's sake."

Edward moved his face away from the paper.

"The girl stepped into a car. She was never seen again, Dad."

"So long ago," the old man whispered.

"Goddamit, don't tell me you don't remember. Don't play games with me. I'm sick and fucking tired of games."

Edward Cheney looked at his son. It was strange, but he couldn't see any trace of the child he had helped raise in the man before him now. Stripped, hardened, all that childish innocence gone, the man who stood beside him was a stranger to him. Somebody who had gone away and had never returned.

"Games?" the old man said. "Games, George?"

George Cheney said, "You saw Mona Crouch get into a car. Not just you, Dad. Hugh Estaban was there. Elmer Hubbard was there. Thomas Sears was there. What was that little gang doing in the parking-lot of the Crawford, watching a girl get inside a strange car? Or was it really such a strange car, Dad?"

George Cheney paused. A look of confusion crossed his face and Edward, filled with an old loving urge, wanted to hug his son and hold him. "I don't remember the car, George." Lie upon lie. He could no longer remember any truth because he had fallen out of favor with reality. Recollected events were what you wanted them to be. Nothing more, nothing less. There was an eclipse of actuality.

"I'm working round coincidences here," George Cheney said. "Estaban and Sears. Two of the men who were in the parking-lot that night have their children stolen from them. A third man, Elmer Hubbard, blows his own goddam brains out."

Edward Cheney leaned against the sink. "I don't recall," he said.

The sheriff sat down at the table, propping his face in the palms of his hands. He sighed a couple of times, then spread the paper out on the surface of the table. "Do you see what I'm trying to get at, Dad? I've got half of a picture staring me in the face. Fifteen years after a kid vanishes to God knows where, children start disappearing. The fathers of two of those kids were in that parking-lot on that night. Strange, huh? A third man present at the same time takes his own life. Why does he do that? What is it that he can't stand to think about? What is it he can't tolerate about his life that makes him pick up a goddam revolver and pull the trigger? Somebody else drives the girl off in a car. Was that person Fred Dove?"

Silence. Edward Cheney could feel the dynamo of total quiet throb through him.

"Dove," the old man said. "You're looking for neatness. You're searching for something tidy. Life isn't quite that way, George, it doesn't fall into convenient little boxes the way you want it to—"

"And you, Dad. You're there on that same night. Why?"

George Cheney pushed his chair back from the table, ran one hand through his hair. Edward glanced at the clock on the old stove. Then remembered it hadn't worked in years. It was stuck forever at two fifty-six.

"I'm not looking for neatness," George Cheney said. "I'm looking for an ending to all this. I want those kids back if there's any way in hell I can do that."

Edward Cheney picked up a stale dry cracker that was lying

287

on the counter by the stove and began to break it between his fingers. When it was nothing more than a pile of crumbs, he brushed them out of his hands on the floor.

He said, "Fred Dove was the man in the car."

There. A door was halfway open. But he wasn't going any further, he wasn't about to step into the room beyond because that was where the dead lay.

"Fred Dove and the girl?" the sheriff asked.

Edward Cheney nodded.

"What next?"

The old man looked down at the crumbs he'd made. He said nothing. The door that was halfway open hung on rusted hinges and he knew they'd squeak if he pushed any harder.

"He drove away."

"What happened to the girl?"

Edward shrugged. The faucet was dripping again. He watched tiny globules of water fall reluctantly from the tap. They seemed, in defiance of gravity, to hang suspended in midair too long.

"You and Hugh Estaban and Sears and Elmer Hubbard— all of you protected Fred Dove in some way. Is that right? When you were questioned about the missing girl, you lied about the car. Is that how it happened?"

Dear God, the old man thought.

If it were only that.

"Fred Dove went off someplace with the child," George Cheney said. "And she never came back."

"The five of us used to meet on Thursday nights. There was a plan, George. A very ordinary business venture. It came to nothing. It dissolved as these things do sometimes."

"What plan?" the sheriff asked.

"We were going to form a corporation to purchase the Crawford," the old man said. It was feeble now in his mind, and his memory felt like a wasted limb. "Estaban was the tax consultant. Thomas Sears fancied himself as a maitre d'. Strange to think of old ambitions. Elmer Hubbard and I were to provide the finances. The Judge was in charge of all the legal matters too. And Fred Dove—well, to put it bluntly, he was going to smooth the way when it came to building permits and expanding the size of the property. It was a matter of re-zoning and acquiring some additional property. It was going to be *the* place to dine in this town . . . You see, it was a simple, very ordinary business consortium, George. Just five men with different motives."

The old man paused.

"For Sears it was a step up in his career. He knew the restaurant business. Estaban perceived all kinds of tax breaks. Dove liked the notion of owning a fashionable place because all his life he's sought status. I was thinking about retirement and I wanted an interest in something. And Elmer Hubbard—well, it was simple enough for Elmer. He just wanted a decent place to eat and a regular table always available where he wouldn't have to make a reservation. The Judge's Table is what he always used to call it. I remember thinking that part was funny, George."

"The girl?" George Cheney asked. "What about the girl?"

"The girl," the old man said. He desired nothing more now than silence, the quiet of a grave, a dead place. "Fred Dove drove away with the girl."

"And when the cops questioned you, you said you didn't know who had taken the girl?"

Edward Cheney licked his dry lips. "Something like that."

"That's not exactly good enough."

"You want precision, George? Fifteen years after the event and you expect precision?"

George Cheney nodded. He was sticking to this thing, the old man saw that. He had the bone of this whole thing between his teeth and he wasn't going to let it go.

"Where did Dove take the child? And what did he do with her?"

"George, listen to me, we had all been drinking that night. Keep that in mind. As we drank, the more attractive the notion of our little consortium became. It glowed out there in the future. We drank toasts to it. We drank more than we ever should have done. Alcohol interferes with one's memory of events, and I can't bring anything back with clarity now."

George Cheney wasn't going to be moved. He asked his question again. "What did Fred Dove do with the girl?"

Edward Cheney roamed out of the kitchen, back down the hallway, into the sitting-room. The clock read five minutes to seven. The bus would be in Hamland any moment now. Danny Cheney would be home. Anne will be there, the old man thought again. Everything will be fine.

The sheriff, who had followed him back inside the sitting-room, sat on the arm of a sofa. "I'll tell you what doesn't add up for me. A young girl goes off in a car with Fred Dove and four men lie to the police. Some time later, one of the four blows out his brains. Why does he do that? Because he told a simple lie? If that was a reason for suicide, Dad, there would hardly be anyone left on the planet." George Cheney closed his eyes a moment. "Now we come to the missing kids. Fifteen years have passed. Kids, who weren't born on that night of July 6, 1970, have vanished. Their fathers were present in that parking-lot and one of them drove the car. Why? Where's the goddam connection? Don't tell me coincidence, because I'm not stupid. And don't lie to me either, because I won't accept it."

Edward Cheney listened to the way the clock ticked. It had a faint metallic echo after every tick, something he'd never noticed before.

"Did Fred Dove kill the girl? Is that what you're hiding?"

"Fred Dove didn't kill the girl, George."

"Then what the hell happened?"

A great sweeping calm entered Edward Cheney, the last sensation in the world he expected right then. He might have been afloat in a bathtub of warm water, or succumbing to the effect of a narcotic. He sat down, stretched his legs, gazed at his son.

It had been a summer evening of uncommon beauty. Sutter's Meadow had been alive with wildflowers and butter-flies and a variety of night moths. Fred Dove had taken the girl there in his car, where he had taken her many times before. She's a wild little thing, Fred said. She'll do anything you ask, Fred said. Forget she's only a kid because she behaves like a whole woman, Fred said. She's hot shit, Fred said.

Fred said.

Edward Cheney looked away from his son: streaks of colorless sunlight lay upon the window, creating a white film.

The sheriff asked, "If Fred Dove didn't kill the girl, what happened to her? Why didn't she ever come home?"

Edward shook his head. "I always tried to live a decent life, George. I always thought I had certain values. A measure of integrity. I would always place more trust in a man's hand-shake than I ever would in a written contract because the connection of flesh and good intentions were always more meaningful than any scrap of paper, George. My life was constructed around what I thought was a civilized code of honor . . ."

The old man paused. These were all lies as well: honor and integrity and trust—what right did he have to be using words like that? He had lived an underhand life, he thought, one of passably respectable surfaces: inside, where it really mattered, was something else again. Inside there was darkness. He couldn't even give himself a character reference to present to his son. *I used to cheat on your mother, George. Doesn't that make me a fine fellow? Even when she got sick, George, with the disease that finally killed her, even then, George, I would take my trips up to Denver . . .*

He stood up. It seemed to him now that his body was one complex mass of nerves. He stared at the open door and imagined the ground suddenly breaking open in Sutter's Meadow.

"The four of us followed Fred Dove when he drove away with the child in his car," Edward Cheney said. "I use the word child. Appearances deceived me then. I didn't think of Mona Crouch as a child, George. Whatever, it's no excuse because there can't be any excuses. Some things are simply inexcusable by their very nature, George. As I said, Elmer Hubbard and Estaban and Sears and myself—we followed Fred Dove's car to Sutter's Meadow."

George Cheney, listening, felt something tighten in his heart. He was trying to make pictures, but they just wouldn't come. He saw Fred Dove and a girl, a child, but it was blurry and faint. He had a sense of motion sickness, as though he himself were trapped in a car going through some long tunnel.

There was no light at the end of it.

"Sutter's Meadow," and Edward Cheney placed a hand to his face, rubbing his cheek nervously. He was cold all over.

"I'm listening," George Cheney said. *You don't want to hear the rest, do you, George? You can feel it rolling toward you with the inexorable force of thunder on an empty landscape.*

"I used to think they'd build something in Sutter's Meadow. I used to see land-surveyors there now and again, staking out the property. When I think of it now, I realize they never built on the meadow because the place is haunted. They knew it and so they took their instruments and they went away . . ."

George Cheney went closer to his father. The old man was rambling and had to be prompted. "The girl, Dad. You were telling me about the girl."

"Yes, the girl."

Edward Cheney walked to the window and stood looking out. He saw the big oak as if he'd never really perceived it before, he saw every leaf, the twist of every branch, the gnarled roots visible above the surface of the ground. The intensity of his vision was hallucinatory: wasn't this heightened sense of reality said to be experienced by men facing their own execution?

"We took turns, George."

George Cheney said nothing. There were no pictures in his head at all now.

"We took turns with that young child. Five men and a young girl. Five men, I said. What I really mean is five people who for a short period of time were less than men. Who lost something essential to themselves."

Turns, George Cheney thought.

Edward Cheney saw shapes in the branches now.

A horse. An angel. A man hanging there by a thin length of rope.

You could see anything in that oak.

"At first the child seemed to welcome it. At first she seemed ready for anything. It was one of those moments in a life when, for myself, I was standing outside the boundaries of myself. I wanted that child, George. I wanted her badly. I stood in the trees at the edge of the meadow and I watched the others as they took turns. I saw the child accommodate Thomas Sears. Then Estaban. Dove. Elmer Hubbard. And when it came to me I didn't stop to think, I didn't understand the meaning of the word consequences. I don't think I believed there would be any. When it came my turn, George, I took it."

The old man paused.

"The girl lay there in the grass. Her jeans were around her ankles. Her underwear had been drawn to her knees. She lay there with her legs apart. Somebody had torn her T-shirt. There were bruises on her thighs. I remember all this clearly, George."

George Cheney stared at his father. The word *turns* kept going through his mind like a locomotive at a distance.

"She held her arms up toward me," the old man said. "I lowered myself. All this time I was aware of the others watching. It didn't make any difference to me because I had lost any self-consciousness I might have had. I could blame drink, George. But it wouldn't do the trick. You see, this flaw in me was there already as it was in the others. As it is, I daresay, in any man. I took my turn with the girl. And after that it changed and I don't quite remember why. It changed."

"How? How did it change?"

"It was almost as if the girl had awakened from a troubled sleep, George. She dressed herself, she started to cry, she seemed suddenly appalled by what had happened. Then she accused us of molesting her. She made all kinds of threats. She was going to go to the police. She was going to expose us all. I don't recollect her exact words. You see, George, I was already beginning to feel the first flicker of guilt. It was already happening inside me. July 6, 1970—I sometimes think it was on that date I began to die . . ."

"Go on," George Cheney said. "What happened after that?"

"I remember now the girl screaming. Yes, she started to scream. I remember she began to run across the meadow. We caught her. We stopped her." Edward Cheney turned away from the window, the sight of the oak against the watery white sky. "We stopped her, George. Do you understand what I'm saying?"

George Cheney looked into the palms of his hands a second. He understood. He understood what his father was telling him. It was a horror story, it was a tale of men who had created their own nightmare and didn't know how to escape from it. It was sad and brutal and it made him feel a strange palpitation in the center of his chest.

"Fred Dove and Thomas Sears—they pinned her to the ground. And then it happened all over again, George. It began a second time. I want to tell you that I tried to prevent it. I *want* to look you straight in the face and tell you I tried to claw those men away from the girl. I didn't. I took my turn again. It wasn't the same girl as before. It was somebody else by this time. It was a creature I hated. I loathed her under me. I couldn't stand her crying. I hated her flesh . . ." Edward Cheney inclined his chin against his chest. "Of course, it's easy to say now that what I really hated then, at that moment in my life, was myself and my own brutality. But that thought didn't cross my mind back then, George. I wanted destruction . . . I was filled with disgust. I don't remember ever having a feeling quite as strong as that one."

The old man looked at his son a second, then away.

He couldn't take George's expression, which was without pity: a kind of numb accusation lay on the younger man's face.

"I can't tell you who struck that first blow and even if I could I don't think it would matter. I only remember the blood now. I remember thinking what a surprising amount of blood a human body contains . . . When she was no longer crying, when she was no longer breathing . . . we buried her in the center of Sutter's Meadow."

The old man paused again in his narrative. He ran a hand over his entire face, like someone trying to remove a mask. "I think I believe in ghosts. I think she rises out of her grave in Sutter's Meadow and takes the children of the men who killed her."

George Cheney shook his head. For a long time he wasn't sure what was expected of him: he fumbled for words, but none came. He was confined by the insane brutality of his father's history and by that of other men who had been Edward Cheney's associates. He thought of a child screaming in a summer meadow. He thought of the savagery of it all. He had a quick impression of a child's terror, of the way in which Mona Crouch's comprehension of the situation must have changed abruptly.

He was lost all at once in the madhouse.

It would begin with the girl being flirtatious. He could see that. He could also see how the flirtatious moment could lead to something else, the way the girl might just throw all caution to the winds because five men—five *adult* men— wanted her body in Sutter's Meadow and maybe she thought it was the way grown-ups were supposed to be, maybe she'd even been drinking herself before they all reached the meadow, and maybe she just didn't know any better.

Even so, how did this wretched history connect with the missing children of Hamland now? Cheney felt lost in the tangled nature of time, seeking threads that might bind the chaos of the past to the present.

"There aren't any ghosts," he said.

Edward Cheney shrugged. He was feeling an odd light-headedness. He stared once more at the oak tree. It seemed to shimmer there in the moist white light.

"And if there aren't any ghosts, who the hell has taken those children?"

The old man shook his head.

George Cheney, standing now alongside his father, gazing out at the same picture, said: "Hugh Estaban and Fred Dove and Thomas Sears—they all lose their kids. Elmer Hubbard commits suicide. And then *his* son dies . . ."

The old man turned his head to George. "Whose son dies?" he asked.

"Elmer's—"

"Where did you hear that one?"

"Lily mentioned it."

The old man smiled in a curious way. "She sent the boy away after Elmer's suicide. She wanted him brought up away from Hamland. An aunt took the child, I seem to remember. Some eccentric maiden aunt tucked away in either Idaho or one of the Dakotas, I'm not sure which. As for his being dead, I don't think you've got the right story there."

"Then why did she tell me her son had died?"

"I don't know. I can't read Lily Hubbard's mind." There was a touch of sadness in the old man's voice: a tone of resignation. He raised a hand to the window so that the oak was framed between his thumb and forefinger. He knew what

295

he was going to do. It all seemed so damned simple to him now.

George Cheney watched his father. He had a sense of layers of tragedy and deceit, subterranean passages leading down through lies and anguish and pain. Why had Lily Hubbard lied about her son, for instance? To what end, what gain? Suddenly, despite his father's awful narrative, he was back at the place where he'd started, back at the beginning when a newspaper boy had vanished in mid-route.

And just as suddenly he was filled with the cold touch of fear. The chill of realization.

It lay lodged at the back of his mind like an ice cube.

Three men have lost their children.

Elmer Hubbard, avoiding retribution, stepping away from any possible consequences, put a bullet through his skull.

And Edward Cheney—

Edward Cheney—

What was going to be taken from Edward Cheney's life?

The old man said, "What are you going to do now, George? Are you going to arrest us all? Are you going to condemn us all?"

George Cheney hardly heard these questions.

Three children had gone. Three. There was a fourth child out there now. A kid on a bus. Edward Cheney's grandson. On a yellow bus. Dressed in a Cub Scout uniform.

His own son.

And the grandson of the man who, fifteen years before, had taken part in a crime that had resonated through time, echoing down to this very moment, down through bloodlines, down into the hearts of blameless children.

Edward Cheney's grandson was next.

Anne parked her car across the street from Hamland Lutheran Church. She lit a cigarette as she observed the front of the church, which was white clapboard with a blunted steeple rising from the roof. A bird flapped around the steeple, then was gone into the albino disc of the faint sun which threw a slanted light across Hamland. A queer kind of light, Anne thought: anaemic.

She barely noticed a small red Datsun that slid past her and moved across the parking-lot of the church, crunching over gravel as it wheeled behind the clapboard building and disappeared from her view. Other cars were arriving now, lining up along the edge of the curb, each of them filled with mothers anxious for the return of their sons.

Anne crushed her cigarette out and wondered when Edward Cheney was going to arrive. She eased back in her seat. She looked at her watch.

Seven oh-seven.

The big yellow bus was late.

Ellis Diamond said, "I don't mean to trouble you, but I was wondering if you'd heard anything about the kids."

"Nothing yet," Charlie Bannion, telephone in hand, answered.

He looked at the woman standing in the doorway. She stood, rather coyly, one foot in front of the other, her hands clutching a big embroidered purse.

Bannion put the telephone down and smiled. He hadn't much felt like smiling until she'd come in the room, because Richard P. Bacon, an irate man whose demeanor had made Charlie Bannion think of a hangman, had only just left and the air was still filled with the echoes of Bacon's upraised voice.

"Oh dear." She came across the threshold of the room and tossed a curl from her brow as she moved. She had eaten alone in the dining-room of the Royal Hotel, a sparse meal of quiche lorraine and spinach salad. All the time she'd been there at the table her mind had kept coming back to the scene between Max Crouch and Thomas Sears. The encounter—as she'd told Sheriff Cheney before—nagged at her: it was an odd thing for a man, even a drunk, to accuse another of stealing a child. To be so insistent about it. So violent.

She stood in front of Charlie Bannion. "I was hoping the information I gave your sheriff might help . . ."

"About the fight?" Bannion asked.

Ellis Diamond nodded.

Bannion said, "It hasn't led him anywhere as far as I know. Of course, George sometimes forgets to tell me things."

Ellis Diamond watched Charlie Bannion pick up the telephone. "I've been trying to get your Mr Zanzibar's phone number. I don't suppose you happen to know it?" he asked.

Was there a touch of sarcasm in the way he asked his question? "I'm sorry," she answered. "It's just one more item of information I didn't get—"

"You apologize too much, Ellis."

"Well," was all she answered, uncertain of what to say. Maybe she *should* quit saying sorry all the goddam time. You couldn't go through life, after all, as if you were sorry for breathing.

"The mysterious Zanzibar," the young cop remarked. "George wants me to find the number. So I'm jumping through hoops."

"You sound disenchanted."

"Just tired. That's all. I like working for George Cheney. He's a good man once you know him. But this case has us up shit creek, pardon the French."

Ellis smiled. "Perhaps Zanzibar doesn't have a telephone," she suggested.

"George saw one in the house out there. The trouble is, it isn't listed under Zanzibar's name, and I can't get through to anybody who can give me the information I need because all the supervisors are apparently at home eating supper. Where any sane person should be about this time."

"I wish I could help," she said. "Perhaps it's still listed under the name of the owner of the property. If Zanzibar is renting the place, that is."

"Good suggestion," Bannion said. George Cheney had mentioned a family that had owned the property out there, but the name eluded him now. Besides, the house might have changed hands. George had said that the former occupants had been a long time gone. If that were the case, then the telephone wouldn't still be listed under their name, whatever it was.

"How do I go about finding the name of the owner?"

"It's a matter of public record, Charlie."

"A deed somewhere, you mean?"

Ellis said yes, a deed, City Hall: that's where *she* would check anyhow, if it were up to her. She said all this a little breathlessly, as if by coming to the young man's assistance she was in some small way cancelling out her own past sins of omission where Zanzibar was concerned.

"City Hall's shut by now," Bannion said.

"You're the cop. You should have access, if you need it."

"Damn right. Now suppose you tell me *how* I get this access if I happen to need it? Which I do."

"It shouldn't be hard," she said. Her head was spinning. She had a vision of being suddenly indispensable to Charlie Bannion. "The Town Clerk is a man called Arnie Schroeder. I happen to know him because he's on the Board of Directors of the Youth Program. He's a helpful little man. If you were to call him at home, I'm sure he'd do whatever he could."

Bannion smiled at the woman. "What would I do without you?"

"Oh, I'm sure you'd manage," Ellis said, watching Charlie Bannion start to flick the pages of the Hamland phonebook. "His number, by the way, is 332-6655."

"You're really on a roll, Ellis."

"Well, it's such an easy number to remember—"

"When you're hot, you're hot," Charlie said. He punched the numbers and after a few moments he heard the thin, reedy voice of Arnie Schroeder, the Town Clerk of Hamland, a career bureaucrat who took the phrase "public servant" to mean exactly that.

Charlie Bannion mentioned the property out in Gowrie Canyon. He said it would be very helpful to Sheriff Cheney if Arnie Schroeder could somehow supply—*as soon as humanly possible, of course, since it was after all a matter of some urgency*—the name of the present owner. Schroeder made a noise as if he were removing a chicken bone from his mouth.

Anything to assist the sheriff, he remarked. Could he have twenty minutes to get down to his office?

Bannion put the receiver down, smiled at Ellis Diamond. "What can I say?"

Ellis Diamond, who had the feeling Charlie Bannion was just being nice to her, answered, "You could have done all that without my help, Charlie."

"Might have taken longer, though."

Ellis shifted her feet around on the tiled floor, embarrassed and pleased, filled with a sense of having—to some extent anyhow—redeemed herself.

The yellow bus chugged round the corner of Brush Street. It was engulfed in its own exhaust fumes. Anne leaned forward in the seat of her car, watching the vehicle advance darkly toward the Lutheran Church. The bus came to a shuddering halt. Anne opened her car door. She saw Danny's face pressed briefly against a window and she waved, but the boy didn't see her.

She stepped out of her car.

She saw Bubba Shankland emerge first from the bus, his large good-natured face smiling. And then boys spewed forth in a confusion of sleeping-bags and backpacks and fishing-poles, a pile of arms and legs and bright little voices shattering the quiet of Brush Street.

Anne started to cross the road to the bus at the same time as several other mothers, all of them hurrying to claim their uniformed offspring. Again, Anne had a brief glimpse of Danny in the throng and again she waved—but the child's face was momentarily lost from sight in the crowd.

So many small boys. So many faces and heads. Bubba Shankland awash in a sea of Cub Scouts and looking now like some befuddled whale.

It was as if these kids were being evacuated during a fire or bomb scare—the confusion of movement, the shouts of mothers, the skirmishes of boys crowding each other to get off the bus.

Then, where faces parted, Anne saw Danny again.

He wasn't moving toward her.

He had turned and was walking up the path that led to the front doors of the church. He had turned away from her.

Puzzled, she started to move after him. Somebody she vaguely recognized clutched at her arm and wanted to detain her with questions about the missing children of Hamland but Anne smiled politely and skipped past the woman. Ahead, she saw the front doors of the church close behind Danny.

She had the odd impression of a mouth closing around her son. She went after him, pushing the heavy doors, entering the church. The air was stuffy, stale, a smell of mildewed Bibles. In the dim light she stared ahead at the plain altarpiece, a simple brass cross with a narrow stained-glass window behind it.

"Danny," and her voice echoed.

No sign of her child.

The sense of being chilled closed around her and she felt suspended in frigid air, unable to breathe.

"Danny?"

She went toward a door at the side of the altar, pushed it open, found herself going down a short flight of stairs, past a door marked OFFICE (she tried it, locked), past a second door marked SUPPLIES (also locked), and then she was hurrying along a corridor in the direction of the rear exit.

"Danny!"

Fumbling with the crossbar, she thrust the rear exit open and found herself in the parking-lot behind the church. And still she was unable to breathe.

Danny.

The parking-lot was empty.

It stretched before her, seamless gray concrete spotted here and there with slicks of oil and liquids that had dripped from cars.

Empty—

And yet she had the strangest impression that a vehicle had been there only moments before. She couldn't say why, except that the air seemed to contain a tremor, a suggestion of something having recently vacated the space it occupied.

She went back the way she had come.

She surveyed the pews, which lacked luster in the terrible light. Beneath the vaulted ceiling she felt tiny and useless.

"Danny," she kept calling.

Searching and calling. Getting no answer.

She went back out into the street where Cub Scouts were milling around and Bubba Shankland was caught in the center of a group of women.

"Mr Shankland." Anne pressed herself forward. "Mr Shankland, have you seen Danny?"

"No." Bubba Shankland shook his head, looking very flustered.

Anne turned and looked back at the church, thinking how squat and secretive it appeared suddenly, as if it were the gateway to another dimension. Which, in one sense, it was supposed to be: but it wasn't the kind of dimension that might have swallowed one small boy. Confused, she moved along the sidewalk, asking boys if they'd seen Danny.

Nobody had.

He'd been on the bus, sure, and some of them had seen him get off, but nobody knew where he was now.

Anne felt dizzy.

She'd have to go back inside the church again, she'd have to make sure, but she couldn't bring herself to move. She stood leaning against the bus, gazing at the short, silly steeple and the sight of two birds—starlings—squabbling up there as if some territory were being disputed.

Birds. A steeple.

Dizziness.

Danny

She caught her breath.

Then she was conscious of somebody grabbing her arm and she turned to see her husband standing alongside her.

"He got off the bus, George," she heard herself say. "He went inside the church. I looked for him. I looked for him."

George Cheney didn't say anything.

"Why did he go in there?" Anne asked. "It doesn't make sense."

Cheney put one arm around his wife's shoulder.

"It's like the others, isn't it?" she asked. "He's gone just like the others, hasn't he?"

Cheney stared at the inscrutable front of the Lutheran Church. He had the impression of a facade, a set, a front propped up by wooden struts and supports. With nothing behind it, no pews, no altar, no stained-glass windows.

And no small boy.

It was seven fifty-eight when Charlie Bannion received his expected phone call from Arnie Schroeder, who told him that the house in Gowrie Canyon had been purchased from somebody called Walter and Laverne Burford in January of that year. The new owner had paid the sum of $58,000 for the house and adjoining land, some 9.7 acres. Bannion listened to this recitation patiently before he felt obliged to ask the name of the owner.

When Schroeder told him, the young cop put the telephone down and looked at Ellis Diamond, who had waited with him in the office.

"Well?" she asked.

"Surprise, surprise," Bannion said.

EIGHTEEN

GEORGE CHENEY DROVE THE STREETS OF HAMLAND FOR MORE than an hour, along Center and past the Municipal Park and out to Naughton's Hill. He drove past Slattery's and Rosita's Food Factory and Hamland High, travelling narrow leafy streets where darkness fused with the trees and only an occasional streetlamp punctured the lightless air. When he reached Sutter's Meadow, that square of grassland hidden behind stands of trees, he thought of the dead girl lying out there under the earth, he thought of bones, old savagery, five men driven to kill by monstrous urges inside themselves—and a horror filled him, something he couldn't grasp because it reached out into places beyond both his understanding and experience.

The secret, humid night pressed against him.

A boy gets off a bus and disappears inside a church. Five men kill a girl fifteen years ago. What was missing from this awful equation? What had he left out?

He couldn't think.

His brain was a blunt instrument.

He'd taken Anne home and left her there and now he was driving down Montrose where his childhood lay and he was thinking about Danny and none of his thoughts made sense because they were all heading toward panic, to that place where reason and control have all the substance of sand-castles rotting in a tide.

Somebody had to be waiting for the boy at the back of the church. Somebody in a car. But why had Danny gone inside the church in the first place?

He thought of Anne, thought of her sitting in their empty house, remembered her white face and the last thing she'd said to him: *You'll find him, George. I know you'll find him. Won't you?*

Insects sang terrible songs in the dark green night.

He parked his car in the parking-lot of the Crawford and sat there a while, his eyes shut, his fingers drumming the side panel of the car.

Here, fifteen years ago, he thought.

From this spot they took the girl out to Sutter's Meadow and brutalized her. He couldn't imagine it now: he couldn't get a grip on five ordinary men, five men who were innocently planning a business venture, driving that child out between the trees and, as Edward Cheney had put it, "taking turns" at her.

Danny, he thought again.

His sense of loss was something he'd kept damped down, as if to yield to it would harm whatever slight professionalism he had left to him. But now it surged through him and his eyes blurred as he gazed at the discreet neon which read

THE CRAWFORD CHOP & STEAK HOUSE

Five men. Fifteen years ago.

And now there was revenge as heavy as the humidity that lay across the town itself. He looked up past the neon at the night sky, which was moonless, starless, an expanse of unlit dark. And he wondered where, under all this cover of blind cloud, his son could be.

Think, George Cheney.

Force your mind to work.

Think who might have taken the children. Think who might have taken Danny. Jesus Christ, his heart ached, his body felt leaden. He might have been looking through a telescope and seeing the universe speed away, stars diminishing then imploding, drawing all kinds of objects into their dead centers where they were lost forever.

Lily Hubbard.

Why was she so *adamant* about Rigley?

And why had she lied about her own son being dead?

He beat his clenched hands upon the steering-wheel, then he drove out of the Crawford, which had begun to fill him with dread, and back in the direction of the station. He studied doorways as he moved, stared at dark trees, shadowy porches, convinced he saw small shapes taking form and substance out of the shadows.

When he reached his office, he found Charlie Bannion there. Ellis Diamond was present also, sitting across the room from the young cop.

Charlie Bannion said, "Anne called."

Cheney said nothing. The room seemed stark and awful to him.

"She wanted to know if there was any news of Danny, George." Bannion looked miserable and his tone of voice was flat. "Christ, George, I'm sorry. I don't know what to say . . ."

Cheney leaned against the wall. He didn't have any energy. The rush of adrenaline that had helped him drive through the town had deserted him.

Bannion was quiet a moment: a man uncertain of himself at a funeral. He shifted around uneasily, shuffled a piece of paper in his hands.

Ellis Diamond twisted her fingers together. Cheney noticed this with a strange clarity, this tiny gesture of despair.

"I've been trying to reach you, George," Bannion said when the silence in the room had run its course. "Did you have your car radio off?"

Did he? Cheney didn't remember. He only remembered driving. The damp night. The way the town was suffocating him.

Bannion indicated the piece of paper in his hand. "I'm not sure what this means, George. But I tried to get the phone number of the house in Gowrie Canyon, which led me eventually to City Hall and the Town Clerk . . ."

Cheney wondered where this was leading, what Charlie was babbling about.

"The house out there was sold by the Burfords," Bannion said.

"And?"

"Well, it was bought by Lily Hubbard, George."

"Lily Hubbard?"

"And she apparently rented it to Zanzibar."

Cheney stared out of the window. He felt as if something had struck him, something hard and metallic rapped against the side of his skull like a tuning-fork drummed on ivory.

Zanzibar.

"Which means Zanzibar is her tenant," the young cop said.

More than her tenant, Cheney thought.

More than that!

He moved toward the door, where he paused.

"Release Rigley. Tell him to go home, Charlie."

"That's going to piss off our Mr Bacon. He suggested I charge the guy—"

"Fuck Bacon," Cheney said.

"You're the boss."

And then George Cheney was gone, leaving a faint sense of air being disturbed around him.

Charlie Bannion went after him out into the corridor, just in time to see the front doors swing shut behind the sheriff.

"George?" he called out. "Are you going to Gowrie Canyon?"

But there was no answer from George Cheney, only the sound of his car roaring down the street.

Cheney drove to Lily Hubbard's big dark house on Gunnison, drawing his car in to the curb and staring at the black windows of the place. Lifeless and empty: even the trees in the front yard seemed as inert as things sketched on paper. He went up the driveway to the front door and rang the bell, hearing it chime in the recesses of the house. He waited. The impression of emptiness inside the house grew.

He pushed the front door open and stepped inside, moving down the darkened hallway to the stairs. He climbed up to Lily's apartment. There, he knocked a couple of times on the door. No answer. He tried the handle, found it locked, then forced the lock with the blade of his penknife.

An empty sitting-room, the same room he'd been in before. He turned on a lamp.

Here, in this house, perhaps even this room, Elmer Hubbard had taken a gun to his head. Cheney imagined this. He saw the shadowy form of a small man, his hand trembling, lift the gun to his face and press the barrel against the side of his head. Maybe not—maybe Elmer had inserted it between his lips and pulled the trigger quickly, blowing himself forever into dark realms.

Had there been a note? a letter?

A suicide's confession?

Cheney sat a moment in a wingbacked chair, placing his fingertips to his lips. He hadn't come here to reconstruct Elmer Hubbard's violent death; he had come to look at a photograph again. But his mind turned on the notion of Elmer scribbling on paper just before inflicting the fatal wound on himself.

Did it describe the nature of the crime?

Did it describe the girl in Sutter's Meadow?

Cheney stood up, wandering to the table that held the framed pictures. If Elmer had not gone out of this life in total silence, if he had indeed left a paper souvenir, had he named names? Mentioned his collaborators in the deed?

The naming of names. Lily Hubbard discovers the note.

Then, then what?

From that moment on is she set on a course of utter madness, determined to bring some form of her own crazy justice to the men who had been Elmer's allies in the crime?

By taking *their* children?

Or grandchildren, as in Edward Cheney's case?

Cheney ran one tired hand over his face. He looked down at the photographs on the circular table. He picked up the one he had come to see.

A small boy jammed between Elmer and Lily.

Resemblances. Impressions.

He tilted the picture directly into the light from the lamp.

The boy was sent away to be raised elsewhere.

Raised to become *what?*

Cheney put the photograph down. There was a ringing in his ears.

If Lily had planned this whole thing, if she had spent fifteen years constructing this delicate mechanism, if this is what Lily Hubbard had done, then Cheney realized he had stepped beyond the bounds of anything he'd ever experienced before. He couldn't imagine vengeance devouring somebody for that length of time, couldn't understand the daily chore of adding yet another tiny building-block of hatred to the structure she spent all her time making. He just couldn't see it. Minute by minute, hour by hour, all of it spent planning. Seasons would change, years slip past, and still she was scheming.

Maybe she didn't notice the real world: times and seasons and events went past her without her ever being aware of them. Because she would sit here and be devoured by her own monster. Sit here, in this room, and scheme. And maybe one day she came up with a little spice to throw into the general concoction—she'd toss Arthur Rigley to Sheriff Cheney and Cheney would be pressured into making an arrest, a false arrest, which would serve two purposes for her. It would humiliate George Cheney; perhaps more importantly, it would create a little extra space for Lily to complete her mission.

A mad mission.

He felt very cold suddenly in this room.

It was coming to an end. It was all coming to an end.

And he knew where the last act was to be played out.

Feeling haunted, George Cheney left the house and moved quickly toward his car.

The last place, he thought.

The only one.

The road to Gowrie Canyon was dark and the washes were still running, though not quite with the same force as they had been on Cheney's last drive this way. Now, water simply slid whimpering through the funnels in the land. Without a moon, the surrounding hills were little more than suggestions of presences in the landscape. Despite darkness, despite the mud that made his wheels spin, Cheney drove quickly, urgently, beset by a sense of time running away from him.

When he reached the track that led down through the canyon itself, he saw lights in the distant house. They were incongruous out here, creating a soft yellowy glow. There was something almost welcoming about them and it crossed Cheney's mind that he was expected in any case, that Zanzibar and Lily Hubbard knew a time would come when George Cheney was destined to arrive.

Cheney parked his car and sat a moment staring at the house. Beside the black Packard was a small red Datsun he didn't recognize. He opened his door very softly and, fifty yards from the house, stepped out into the soft clinging soil.

He placed the palm of his hand over his gun as he went toward the porch. He caught the porch rail and hoisted himself in the air a couple of feet so that he could see through the lit downstairs windows. The rail creaked under his weight. Glimpsing an empty room for a second, he lowered himself over the hand-rail and on to the porch. He tried to move softly but the boards under his feet trembled.

He stood to the side of the window, gazing into the room.

He went past the window to the door.

He reached out, turned the handle, the door opened soundlessly and he found himself in the hallway with the stairs ahead of him. A curious smell assailed him, as if somebody had burned something in the kitchen. And yet it wasn't quite that either: it was a scent of scorched wood, perhaps—but certainty eluded him.

Now he stood on the threshold of the room containing Zanzibar's equipment. Everything was still. Everything silent. He had the sudden feeling he was all alone in this house, that whoever had been here was gone now, that he was too late to find what he had come for.

He gazed across the magical equipment.

He kept his hand on the butt of his gun as he crossed this room, passing the screens, the guillotine, the manacles, all the strange shellacked boxes and cylinders and the playing-cards. The ventriloquist's dummy hung over the screen where it had been before. It seemed to observe George Cheney as he moved toward the kitchen. Glass eyes caught light, sparkled; the stiff hinged jaw appeared to shift.

Cheney shook his head.

This house. His fears. His anxieties.

He paused in the doorway of the kitchen.

A stove, a refrigerator, clean surfaces. The hardwood floor under him shone in the overhead light.

The room was empty.

He stared back into the magic room like a man waiting for somebody—something—to come into view.

The overhead lights flickered suddenly.

Down to dimness, then back up full again.

Then dim. Like house lights in a theater fading before the show.

They stayed that way, barely as strong now as a candle, casting a weird misty light over everything, more pale brown than electric white.

Cheney stepped out of the kitchen. He had taken his gun from its holster and he was holding it out in front of himself, conscious of its dead weight in the palm of his hand. In the terrible light, all Zanzibar's equipment had regained its mysteriousness. Cheney gazed at the guillotine, expecting it to come plunging suddenly downward. Then at the dummy, waiting for it to move, to leap, to change from inert wood to flesh and blood.

Nothing happened.

Nothing moved.

The lights remained dim.

He went to the doorway, stared in the direction of the stairs which rose upward in deepening shadow where the light didn't penetrate. He wanted to call out—his son's name, anything, any kind of sound—but he made no noise.

The silences of the house came down around him like rain in a deaf man's world.

Across the hallway the door to another room faced him. It lay halfway open, the spaces beyond it bathed in the thin brown light that permeated the entire house. He walked across the floor, nudged the door open, peered into a room furnished only with a solitary chair in which somebody sat, looking away from Cheney.

Small hands dangled over the sides of the chair.

A kid.

A kid in that chair.

Cheney felt a great vulture of terror rise in his brain.

Those motionless hands—were they attached to a body that couldn't move? a lifeless body?

Danny, say, perhaps Danny, dear God no

Cheney was still. For a long time he stood staring at the tiny hands that hung down in the brown light, hesitant, scared, unwilling to take the step which would bring him face to face with the person in the chair.

He moved his dry lips soundlessly. He realized his body was smeared with perspiration, that the gun in his hand adhered to his palm, metal stuck to flesh.

He took one step forward.

With the gun extended in front of himself, he stepped closer to the chair.

The girl was Vickie Estaban. Cheney remembered the face from the photograph of the child. She sat, face forward, her expression glum, features flat, as if she'd lost a dimension of herself. The eyes were closed.

Vickie, he said. Vickie . . .

Around her waist, strapping her to the chair, was a strip of metal, a band that held her body in place.

He saw something else: leading away from a place beneath her body was an electrical cord, snaking into the shadows in a sinewy manner.

He glanced at the length of cord and even as he did so the figure in the chair moved slightly, prompted by electrical impulses running the length of the wire.

The small hands swelled.

The fingers twitched.

The body contorted and the eyes opened abruptly. Expressionless eyes looking into a far distance Cheney could not measure.

Smoke curled out of the body, the hair, rising in dark fumes from the sides of the face.

An electric chair, Cheney thought and then he was reaching out to pull the child out from the smoke and the small flutters of flame rising from the clothing, reaching out to haul the child free from the metal band that held her strapped to this monstrous chair.

He touched her. Her flesh peeled in his hand. It stuck to the tips of his fingers, hot and gummy.

Horrified, he stepped back.

The air was filled with the smell of burning wax.

The face began to dissolve and drip.

It ran, slithering over the sides of the chair. The eyes withered and puckered and slid over the sudden fissures in the cracked face. The legs melted. The body buckled from the hips, bending across the metal band. He watched the figure dissolve like some grotesque candle, the eyes moving out of their waxen sockets and the lips twisting, shrivelling, the fingers distending and dripping to the floor. And then there was nothing before Cheney but the sight of an effigy beautifully crafted, sculpted in stunning detail, that had melted down into the smoky, smoldering puddle still sliding, like hot slime, from the chair to the floor.

There was an unfathomable sickness here. He was walking on the floor of some polluted ocean and his air-supply was running out and he was dizzy from lack of oxygen.

Lily Hubbard finds her husband's dead body. The head blown away. Somewhere in her mind she wonders why, if four other men took part in the same molestation and murder, her husband was the only one to die. Cheney backed further away from the melting figure, as if what it truly represented were the twisted workings of an old woman's demented brain. The insight made him freeze, made him feel as though he were suspended in aspic.

If this was a wax mock-up of Vickie Estaban, then where in the name of God was the real child?

He closed the door of the room and stood in the hallway at the foot of the stairs. The hall, which went around the side of the stairs, led to another door. Cheney regarded the shadows there a moment before he decided he'd go upstairs. He put one hand on the bannister rail and realized his hand was covered in flesh-colored wax.

He climbed. Halfway up, he paused.

Zanzibar stood above him, looking down, smiling.

He wore a dark suit and a cloak and a pair of white gloves that struck Cheney as incongruous.

"Enjoying the show so far?" the man asked.

"I only want the kids," Cheney said. "Give me back the kids."

Zanzibar shook his head. "It's up to you to find them, Georgie. You're the clever sheriff."

Cheney made a motion with his gun. But it didn't impress Zanzibar, who looked at the weapon with the contempt of a man who has total control of his environment, someone who could—if he chose—make both gun and sheriff disappear.

"Don't you feel sleepy, George? Don't you feel a little sleepy? Don't you feel nicely relaxed? Isn't your body beginning to become just a little heavy? Aren't you lulled?"

Zanzibar had taken a crystal out of his cloak and was swinging it back and forth, a pendulum that barely gleamed in the bad light.

Cheney shook his head. "I'm a bad subject for that kind of thing. You're wasting your time."

"I always think a good hypnotic subject needs a whole lot of imagination and an open mind. Children are wonderful that way, George. They're so open. So receptive. To put it another way, they're a snap, Sheriff. Impressionable and easy. They don't have all their mental barricades in place."

Cheney moved two steps up, stopped again. He saw it now. He should have seen it before. He'd been slow. Very slow. And now he was irritated by his own lack of perception. He watched the crystal swing back and forth. "That's how you got the children," he said. "Post-hypnotic suggestion. You made them come to you."

"Oh, aren't we bright, George? Aren't we swift with the old deductions tonight? Good for you, Georgie."

Cheney, his hand on the gun, was filled with the sudden urge to blow this young man away. A killing impulse, strange to him—but a tension ran through his hand right then and he had to fight the urge aside. He thought about Danny, wondering how and when Zanzibar had managed to get to the boy while the kid was away at camp—but these considerations didn't matter a damn now. It had been done somehow.

Zanzibar said, "I wish you wouldn't point that at me. It could go off. Then I'd bleed, which would be messy."

Cheney sighed. The destructive impulse had gone and he felt now a wariness, an uneasy quality.

"Where are the kids?"

Zanzibar made a vague gesture with his hand.

"Are they still alive?" Cheney asked.

Another vague gesture, meaning nothing. Meaning nothing except *find that out for yourself, George.*

"Are they?" he asked again. *Say yes.*

Zanzibar ignored him. "There's a girl buried in Sutter's Meadow, George. And my own father shot himself through the head. I consider the world an inequitable place."

"That hasn't got anything to do with those children," Cheney said. "Christ, they weren't even born then."

"The best victims are the innocent ones," Zanzibar remarked. "When you punish the innocent, the ones who are really guilty suffer more."

Zanzibar paused. A strange smile crossed his face.

"I wish you'd lower the gun, George. If you use it on me, it would be inconvenient. Because then you'd never find the precious children, dead or alive."

Zanzibar stepped back, losing himself in the shadows. Cheney heard the sound of the cloak flapping, the whisper of footsteps, then a door closed somewhere overhead.

And then silence.

He quickly climbed the rest of the stairs. There was no sign of Zanzibar at the top. Doors stretched ahead of him on either side of the landing. *The best victims are the innocent ones.* Would he find any of these innocent ones beyond the doors that faced him now? Or more waxen illusions designed to self-destruct at the first surge of electricity? He stood very still.

Rooms beyond doors.

Rooms created by Zanzibar's imagination, which had been fueled in turn by the mind of his mother.

Cheney paused. The closed doors around him were menacing. Pick one, he told himself. Choose, Cheney.

He tried the door nearest him.

It was a bedroom with a narrow cot beneath the window,

315

nothing else. Something lay beneath a white bedsheet, a human form. Cheney stared at it, conscious now of a faint noise coming to him from an indeterminate point within the room.

From speakers, from some kind of outlet, the whispered voices of children issued. He gazed up at the walls, seeking the source of the sound, but he saw nothing save for an air-conditioning vent set high on one wall. Whispers—almost as if the missing children themselves were trapped behind that vent, imprisoned between the walls.

He tried to ignore the whispers as he moved toward the cot. But they came at him as if they were murmurs of ghosts reaching out over great distances.

And one of the voices belonged to Danny.

Daddy. Can't you find me, Daddy? Please find me . . .

Cheney remembered the cassette Hugh Estaban had received, thought about the phone call Courtney Sears had taken.

Daddy, come get me, please, come get me . . .

Cheney stood over the white sheet, the covered form on the narrow bed. What illusion lay under this?

What had Zanzibar left here for him?

Find us, Sheriff . . . Look for us . . .

Cheney reached out to touch the sheet.

Slowly he pulled it back.

It was the neck he noticed first. The band of dried blood that created a violent ring around her neck, as if she'd been garrotted by something thin and vicious and sharp like a piano wire.

Cheney stepped back, breathless.

He closed his eyes a second. Then looked again.

From the girl's open mouth flowed a string of knotted silks—a crazy sequence of oranges and pinks and yellows and reds that hung from her lips and flowed down the front of her blouse as if a rainbow of violence had emerged from her.

And this one was real, this was no illusion, this was no wax statue carved by Zanzibar . . .

Cheney wanted to take the silks out of the dead girl's mouth but then he dropped his hand, sickened. He couldn't touch this girl, this Zena, whoever she'd been. He couldn't touch her long enough to remove the indignity of her dying. Couldn't bring himself to press her eyelids shut, not even that. The sickness he felt became a hot coal in his stomach. He turned his face away from her and shuddered.

And still the whispers.

He moved to the window and forced it open and drew damp black air into his lungs. A sticky liquid filled his mouth and he was sweating as he leaned out into the darkness of the canyon.

Dear Christ.

He understood something now.

He understood that with one hand Zanzibar was showing him an illusion—with the other he was demonstrating reality. To trick Cheney, to confuse him, to make him uncertain about anything else he might encounter in this house.

You may find a wax effigy melting, George. Or you may find a girl truly dead. But you'll never know until you look and touch and feel . . . You'll never know.

This room of death was silent now.

There was no more whispering.

In a reflex action, he drew the bedsheet up over Zena's face, covered her bruised neck and the revolting silks that hung from her mouth. He stepped away from the corpse: this, all this, was a descent down the rungs of somebody else's madness. If Zanzibar could kill Zena, it meant . . .

Angry and sick, he went back out on to the landing. He gazed down the flight of stairs into the brown emptiness of the hallway, seeing nothing. And then he tried the other doors along the landing, kicking them open fiercely, looking for Zanzibar, finding nothing but empty rooms, abandoned rooms, scraps of litter, *nothing*—until he reached the very end of the landing.

It was a workshop.

And something else besides.

He wandered among electrical cords, power-tools, jars of putty, tubs containing flesh-colored wax, hammers, saws, nails. The air was filled with the smell of wood dust.

But the tools didn't interest him.

It was what lay in the middle of the floor, isolated from

everything else in the room so that he couldn't fail to notice it.

A bundle of clothing.

Kids' clothing.

T-shirts, sneakers, a hair-ribbon, blue jeans.

A Cub Scout uniform.

Cheney bent down, running the palm of one hand over this pathetic little bundle of belongings. Danny's Scout knife. His sneakers. His shirt.

Cheney turned his face to the side.

He pictured the dead girl on the narrow cot and he stood up. He went back out on the landing and then down the stairs. In the hallway, his attention was drawn toward the magic room.

He went inside the room of paraphernalia.

Zanzibar—where the hell had Zanzibar gone?

He crossed the room: all Zanzibar's paraphernalia seemed to assail him, imbued with a curious animation of its own. The figures on the lacquered Chinese screen, pale green and yellow against the deepest black, suggested delicate movement. The ventriloquist doll, eyes vacant and idiotic, looked suddenly as if it knew something Cheney could never know. A secret locked in its wooden head.

Cheney moved toward the screen.

A faint noise, a metallic whine, made him swing abruptly round.

The guillotine—

Swift, dreadful, sliding down with a deathly whisper, the great angled blade fell in its shaft even as Cheney realized a small figure lay in the direct line of the blade—and Cheney stuck his hand out uselessly as if he might still the blade in its descent but it whistled past him and struck the neck of the child who lay trapped at the bottom of the shaft and the head, rolling away from the torso, tumbled across the floor to stop at Cheney's feet.

Real, unreal—*for a moment Cheney didn't know. Didn't want to know.* He felt he was standing in a place where nightmares blended faultlessly with reality, where you couldn't tell one from another.

318

He looked down at the face of Tommy Sears. It stared up at him with bleak sorrow, the sadness of a life abruptly ended.

And then he bent.

The head had been made from clay, soft clay that stuck to Cheney's hand as he touched it. The whole body, decapitated, pierced by the blade, nothing more than a clay figure carefully sculpted. Streaks of the pink substance adhered to the blade and had splattered here and there about the room.

Tommy Sears.

As if it were a score in some dreadful game, Cheney realized that of the three apparent corpses, only one had been real. He stepped away from the sculpted head of the boy and stood motionless in the middle of the room. Then he looked behind the lacquered screen. Saw nothing.

He stepped into the kitchen.

Quiet, empty.

The only sound now was that of his own hard breathing.

He let the gun in his hand fall to his side: his arm was weary. He walked across the kitchen. Pantry doors, closets, cupboards—all these ordinary surfaces seemed potentially terrifying to him, as if behind them might lurk a monstrosity he wouldn't be able to absorb, an assault he could never withstand. He was conscious of his own edges, those unlit margins of himself that were treacherous and slippery and led down, inexorably, into a private madness all his own.

Cheney left the kitchen.

He surveyed the magic room again, ignoring the crumbled clay shape crushed by the guillotine blade. Somebody must have placed the clay figure there when he'd been upstairs because he hadn't noticed it on his first tour of this crazy room. Were there secret passageways in this house? concealed stairways enabling Zanzibar to move freely and surreptitiously?

Cheney moved out into the hallway. There, he gazed at the door behind the stairs.

Go there.

You know you have to, Cheney.

Go there to what is presumably the basement of this house.

Go, see what waits down there in darkness.

* * *

The smell that came up to hit him in the face was sulfuric, the stench of things that had rotted down here in the damp darkness, releasing their gasses into the air where they hung unchanging, trapped in spaces where nothing moved and no windows allowed fresh breezes to pass through. He stood on the first step. What lay below him was a chasm, an unlit expanse of space.

He lowered himself slowly, quietly, testing each step beneath him before allowing his full weight to descend. Under the palm of his hand, the rough wood of the handrail was slightly damp, unpleasant to feel. When he judged himself to be halfway down, he stopped. The smell was suffocating and seemed to assail him through the pores of his flesh as well as his nostrils, almost as if it were laying a fine skein of decay across the surfaces of his skin.

The steps crumbled under him. Darkness engulfed him. He had a sense of flimsy things hanging just above his head— webs, the filaments of spiders that had decayed in the center of their own strands. And he had an instinct that if this room were to be flooded suddenly with light he would see all manner of insects scamper for shadows.

He reached the bottom of the stairway.

He might as well have been blind. The brown light that filtered from the basement door at the top of the steps was feeble, falling no further than a small area inside the door.

He moved carefully.

The light that struck his eyes was blinding, a sudden burst of white that might have emerged from a firework. He shaded his eyes and felt vulnerable, afraid, conscious of the stab of light piercing him. He was a target, a dead target, if whoever held the flashlight wanted to shoot him.

Cheney looked down at the floor of the basement, away from the flash. He saw the edges of things, impressions that came at him out of the dark where the flashlight barely penetrated. There were reel-to-reel tape-recorders, tangles of electric wire, cords that stretched off into the gloom.

But there was something else, something he couldn't quite delineate properly. It lay, shadowy, just beyond the range of the flashlight. And he couldn't take his eyes away from it.

From beyond the circle of light he heard the soft laughter of a woman and he knew that Lily Hubbard stood there with the flashlight in her hand. He blinked, looked away from the core of light, his attention drawn to the shape on the far side of the room.

Danny, was it Danny?

"Are you entertained, George Cheney?" she asked. "Are you enjoying yourself?"

Cheney moved slightly. He didn't speak. The shape in the gloom was small and seemed to be hanging from a rope attached to the ceiling but he wasn't sure of that.

"He was always a smart boy," the woman said. "He always had talents in every direction, you know. This whole show here—he put it on specially for you, George. You should feel honored."

The urge to fire his gun was intense. The urge to *feel* the bullet puncture that dreadful light and the insane woman who held it was overpowering. The rancid air of the basement seemed stronger now. He felt faint, choked.

"We're not over yet, George," the woman said. "The show has a way to go."

"Lily," he said drily. "Lily, there's a dead girl in a room upstairs—"

"And a dead girl who was buried in Sutter's Meadow, George. Do I need to remind you of that? Do I need to say anything about that event?"

Cheney peered across the basement. The shape hanging there appeared to move as if stirred by a vague draft. What was it? What the hell was it?

"It wasn't very fair that Elmer died," the woman said. "It wasn't fair that he was taken away from me like that. That none of the others who had led Elmer on into the only questionable act of his life were still alive and breathing—"

Led Elmer on? Cheney wondered.

Lily Hubbard's interpretation of reality, her assessment of history, afforded Cheney still another insight into the woman's madness: she could take past events and alter them to fit whatever suited her. What was it like inside her mind?

He knew the answer to that question.

This house and everything in it—*this was it, this was the inside of Lily Hubbard's mind.*

"The Judge would never have done anything like that to the poor girl in Sutter's Meadow, George. I am very sure he was forced by the others to participate in the shame. However, he was a sensitive man, and he couldn't cope with his guilt. Some people can't cope, George. They can't do it."

Forced by the others, Cheney thought.

"I'm sure," Cheney said. "I'm sure you're right, Lily. I'm sure he was dragged down to that meadow and made to participate in the murder of the child—"

"Exactly," she said. "That's exactly how it happened, George." She was quiet a second. "But The Judge told me how to plan all this, George. Nights he would speak to me. Nights he would tell me which step to take. I would lie in the darkness and listen to his voice. Get them, he'd say. Make them suffer. Make them experience the pain of it all. Estaban. Dove. Sears. Cheney. Make them go through anguish. The worst kind of anguish. Take Edward Cheney's grandson, he said. Get him through his grandson. As for his own son—as for you, George—you were to be given the bone of Arthur Rigley to gnaw on for a time. You were to arrest him, Elmer said, and when that simple-minded man provided alibis, you were going to be vilified by a community that couldn't trust an incompetent sheriff. For you, George, you were supposed to lose both son and office. The Judge often provided nice touches like that one."

Nice touches, Cheney thought.

He watched the flashlight move. Lily Hubbard's shape could barely be seen beyond it: a stark silhouette, nothing more. She was backing away from him now and the light was dwindling.

"The children, Lily," Cheney said. "Give me back the kids."

"I think it's a little too late for that. If you could have given me back The Judge, we might have made a bargain. Good-bye, George."

The light went out. The blackness was complete. Cheney, stumbling in the direction where he thought Lily had gone, collided with something. It was soft and papery and it rubbed against his face. He reached up blindly to touch it: it felt like a small child suspended in mid-air.

Hanging there.

Cheney opened his mouth, moaned, his hands clutching the body that dangled against his face.

Then, as if it were the interval of a play, a time for the curtain to come down, there were lights in the basement. Soft overhead lights suddenly shining through the dark.

And the tape recorder was running.

Sheriff, help us, come find us . . .

Daddy . . . Daddy, please . . .

Cheney stared at the body hanging by a rope from an overhead beam.

It was Rick Dove.

And it wasn't.

Cheney tore the effigy down from the ceiling and crushed it against his chest, feeling it tear and splinter as he held it. Then he let it drop from his hands to the floor, where it lay broken—papier-mâché, fibrous, painted eyes and mouth, hair created from synthetic material, a rope knotted round the broken neck. A boy made out of paper and water and hung from a rope as if he'd been found guilty of an awful crime and condemned to death . . .

Wax and clay and papier-mâché: the substances of madness. And in each instance what had gone into the creation of these figures was a talent of an extraordinary kind.

He moved toward the tape recorder and brought his fist down hard upon the slow-turning reels and the whispered voices became hauntingly distorted, like sounds from beyond the grave. He tore the plastic reels out of the machine and threw them across the floor of the basement and then, breathing heavily, his anger barely assuaged, his fear running through him like a fever, he turned his face in the direction Lily Hubbard must have taken.

There was a narrow crawlspace. He peered inside it.

It was a passageway of rough earth at the end of which he could see only darkness. But there was air, fresh air he drew into his lungs gladly. Lily had gone along the crawlspace and presumably through an opening that led outside.

Out into the dark canyon.

The space was too narrow for Cheney to attempt.

He turned, crossed the basement, sprinted up the shaky

323

stairs and moved quickly along the hall to the front door, disturbing air all around him, air that was still heavy with the aroma of burning wax.

He hauled the front door open, stepped out on to the porch.

Which was when he saw the bones.

They had been assembled in a sitting position in the center of the porch, propped up in a fragile way in a chair. Cheney gazed at the skeleton, aware of how the slightest tremor of wind might blow this delicate structure apart. He reached out to grip the handrail, his movements cautious.

The sockets seemed to regard him with a mild bewilderment. The face, set in that ludicrous grin of death, hung a little to one side and the fingers of bone dangled in the bleached-white lap. From the top of the skull, like the tendrils of some ghastly plant, hung a few lank strands of rotted hair.

Cheney stepped away.

He knew.

He knew this was the skeleton of Mona Crouch, that somebody—Zanzibar, his mother, perhaps both of them—had gone down to Sutter's Meadow and dug up this dead girl and transported her here to this place where they had lovingly reassembled her as part of their whole gruesome performance, bone by bone they had put this dead child back together and even as he stared at the thing he could see flecks of soft black earth adhere to the cage of ribs and tiny globules of dirt set deep in the hollows where the eyes had once been—

He went down the steps of the porch and the reverberations of his movements made the edifice of Mona Crouch collapse, bone slipping away from bone, ribcage falling apart, skull sliding from shoulders to strike the wood slats of the porch—and it was like the sound of some awful ivory bell.

Cheney looked out across the canyon.

There was all at once a withered moon bleakly surveying matters from a cloud break, but then it was gone, sucked back into darkness, and Cheney felt an intolerable solitude.

He looked toward his car.

Both the Packard and the small red Datsun had gone and the landscape was empty.

He moved quickly to his car.

He rammed the key in the ignition, glancing for some reason into the dark rectangle of the rearview mirror.

Something sat in the back seat, framed by the mirror.

Cheney swung around.

Danny Cheney's face was tilted back, his mouth wide, his lifeless eyes staring at nothing.

Half of his head had gone, blown away by a pistol fired from pointblank range. There were powder burns on his cheeks. Dried blood adhered to the shattered skull.

For a second George Cheney stepped outside of time, felt himself drift away into a place of such timeless silence no clocks ever ticked, where there was nothing but a dark void of grief where you were doomed to linger forever, going over and over the same mental image time and again until eternity. A place of no escape, of endless repetition. A hollow where your heart was meant to be. He thought: *This thing I am looking at now will stay with me forever. This horror will never go away.*

And then he reached back into the space behind him, his hand encountering the gun that lay in Danny Cheney's slack grip.

It was a toy, a dark plastic toy pistol placed between fingers of fiberglass. He gazed a second at the shattered face of the boy and it was more than he could stand: this illusion was the last and the best and it pushed him beyond his own limits. He struck out at the thing, flailing away with both hands and then with the butt of his gun until he'd smashed this fiberglass obscenity, until there was nothing left of this travesty of a suicide but tiny shapeless pieces littering the back seat of the car.

When he stopped he felt weak and empty and drained.

Someone might have gone inside his brain with a scalpel and said, *This is how it's done, Cheney. This is how we put you in a place beyond all sensation. This is the final comfort of all. You'll never feel anything again as long as you live . . .*

He caught his breath, staring out through the windshield at the black spread of the canyon. Then, shaking with the effort of his rage, he turned the key in the ignition.

As the car rolled forward it swayed and bounced, groaning.

Cheney braked and stepped out: the tires had been slashed.

He stared in dismay at the cuts in the rubber and how the car sloped now at a weird angle. He reached across the passenger seat for the radio microphone, knowing even as he did so that the thing had been disabled: the wire had been cut as certainly as the tires and the microphone came away uselessly in his hand.

Fighting panic, he stared out across the canyon.

And it crossed his mind, with a cold jolt, that Zanzibar's Packard had formerly been a hearse.

That all hearses went only one place in the end.

Nowhere else.

He went back inside the house. He found the telephone among the illusionist's paraphernalia and he snatched it up quickly, punching buttons before he realized there was no dial tone, only a recorded voice flowing into his ear.

It was the voice of Zanzibar.

If you are listening to this message, Sheriff Cheney, you have approximately thirty seconds to live . . .

Cheney dropped the receiver.

Thirty seconds to live . . .

He moved away from the useless telephone, noticing the cord from the receiver did not lead to the usual phone-jack, but to a small black plastic box fixed low on the wall.

A small black plastic box, ominous in its very functional appearance.

30 seconds—

He knew there was something in this house counting down toward destruction, that by lifting the telephone receiver he had activated an explosive device.

He sprinted across the floor, raced down the hallway, tumbled down the steps of the porch and past the bones lying scattered there and by the time he'd made it to the far side of his car the old house had exploded in a swift violent flurry of light and smoke.

First the downstairs windows blew out and scattered the dark with glass and then the porch roof was sizzling with fire which spread to the upper floors, and after that the whole building was burning, filling the sky with yellow flames whose heat Cheney could feel from forty yards away. He watched the night sky change color above him, saw an enormous plume of black smoke drift up and churn in the air like a great storm cloud, showers of red ash, tiny sparking missiles, floating scraps of flaming paper tossing in the updraft like small fiery bats and birds.

His face red in the reflected glow of the fiery house, he turned away and stared the length of the canyon. What crossed his mind now was the notion that the missing children might have been in that house, they might have been incinerated by the blast, but he had gone from room to room, he had wandered through the house and hadn't seen them—

Zanzibar's hearse.

That's what he kept coming back to.

He moved further away from the pyre of the house, which hissed and crackled as the flames coursed through timbers and struts and beams.

George Cheney considered the only course of action he had left to him. It had been a long time since he'd run and he knew he was in no shape to sustain any prolonged effort, but what alternatives did he have? He could run as far as the highway and then stop some passing vehicle, but he wasn't sure he could even make it that far without passing out. What else was there?

He drew air into his lungs, turned once to stare at the bonfire of the old Burford house—which rose into the night like some doomed comet—and then he ran.

Conscious of time slipping away from him—

Aware of his own physical inadequacies—

Ignorant of the fate of those kids—

George Cheney ran.

Mud. Breathlessness. Physical pain. His head became liquid. His mouth dry. Pinpoints of light danced in front of his eyes.

Keep going.

How many miles to the blacktop?

He didn't know.

Didn't know how far he'd come.

Across wet washes, scrambling up slopes, his breathing impossible, he kept going.

He was one mass of motion but whatever fuel propelled the machine—fear, anxiety—was dying away inside him.

And then there was his sense of direction. The darkness of the canyon obscured landmarks, interfered with his radar, he had no way of knowing if he was moving in the right direction.

Even if he reached the blacktop, would any vehicle come along to help him?

It was a lonely road.

And that lonely road was his only chance.

Breathing wildly, his heart like some palsied muscle in his chest, he ran.

Just goddam running.

Just the old machine hammering across the kind of wet soil that worked against motion because it sucked at your feet and ankles and tossed pellets of mud into your eyes.

He stumbled through a wash where he lost his balance a moment and sat down in chilly water, which shocked him as it spread through his pants and shirt.

He got up again but now it was even harder to keep going.

He couldn't breathe. He had to stop.

Bending at the hips, he let his arms dangle to the ground. There was the jolting pain of a stitch in his side and he moaned.

But he had to keep moving.

He made it up a slope, sucked air into lungs that were failing him, reached the summit, had to pause again.

Far back down the canyon the burning house sent fire up into the sky.

How far away was it?

You couldn't judge distances out here.

Two miles. Three.

Was that all he had covered?

Running. He couldn't feel himself. He had no sense of his own being. He was a numb machine traversing a terrain.

Down a slope, over a narrow wash, up a bank. Then he

wasn't even really running, he was half-stumbling, staggering, moving as if lead ran through his veins.

On. Keep going. Move. Don't stop.

Slipping and slithering, his feet yielding to the treachery of mud, he pitched forward into darkness and when he forced himself to stand up he knew: *I can't keep it up, can't keep moving . . .*

He urged himself forward but there was nothing left to urge and no mission control to send out the messages of urgency either. Everybody in the control room had gone off-duty. Suppertime in the commissary of the brain.

Hopeless, Cheney.

You can't go another step.

He hauled himself up a bank of mud and as he was about to sink face down from sheer exhaustion the headlights of a car struck his face and a door slammed and he heard, from a place very far away, the sound of Charlie Bannion's voice.

"I don't normally stop for hitch-hikers," Bannion said, helping George Cheney to stand upright. "I want you to know that this is an exception. Don't tell the sheriff or I'll lose my goddam job."

Cheney slumped in the passenger seat.

For a long time he couldn't speak.

Then, when he did, all he said was, "Sutter's Meadow."

It seemed to Cheney an endless ride back to Hamland. Miles translated into hours, whole long passages of time he couldn't measure. And yet he knew Charlie Bannion had the gas-pedal floored and was taking the bends in the blacktop in a dangerous fashion, making the tires squeal each time he swung the wheel in his hands.

Then, on the edge of Hamland, George Cheney told him to slow down. The stand of trees that hid Sutter's Meadow from view was motionless and dark. Cheney groaned as he stepped out of the car. Something in his legs had given way: or maybe it was just that the muscles had locked in a frozen position. Whatever, pain coursed through him with every slight movement.

He stood staring in the direction of the trees.

Charlie Bannion stood alongside him. Sutter's Meadow was a place the young cop never visited, for reasons he didn't understand fully: there was a creepy feel to the meadow, something he sensed. He would never have brought a girl out here. His hand went to the butt of his gun nervously.

George Cheney was stepping toward the trees. He wondered if this was the wrong place: maybe he'd guessed badly, maybe Zanzibar hadn't come here to Sutter's Meadow with the kids, but somehow—given the twisted nature of the whole scheme, the insane logic of it all—it made sense: it was an act of closing the circle. A wheel turning the whole way round. The condemned child Mona Crouch had been brought here: why not the others fifteen years later?

He stood among the trees, Bannion silent at his side.

The meadow before them was dark and quiet: it lay like a black carcinoma attached to the side of Hamland.

Cheney took out his gun, the butt of which was slick with mud, greasy in his hand.

He moved closer to the meadow's edge. Bannion followed him quietly.

Out there in the center of the grassy land something was barely visible. Cheney didn't know what: it was more an impression than a perception.

Something sat there.

And then a faint sound drifted across the stalks of grass toward him. He realized that all the normal movements of his body had become stilled.

Pulses.

Heartbeat.

Circulation of blood.

"Zanzibar's car," Charlie Bannion whispered.

"You sure?"

There was a sudden brief light and the soft click of a car door. Then darkness and silence again.

"I'm sure," Bannion said.

Cheney squinted across the meadow. Then he moved forward a little way. He wasn't sure he could truly make out the Packard but something *did* sit there in the middle of the field. Blades of long grass rose up against his knees.

Another sound floated out to him.

A puzzling sound like that of a thing being dragged across soft grass.

He narrowed his eyes, as if by so doing his night-vision would improve, but there was nothing out there in Sutter's Meadow save the ghostly dark and the whisper of something dragging through the damp green-black stalks.

"What is it?" Bannion whispered.

Cheney said nothing. Speech needed an effort he didn't have it in him to give any more. Now, out of nowhere, a faint breeze stirred the meadow and shook the thick trees gently, and for a moment there was clear clean air passing through layers of humidity. Cheney found some energy in the draft, a sense of being revived.

He kept moving forward, Bannion a couple of feet behind.

There, dark as the shaft of an abandoned mine, stood the black Packard, half-submerged in the dense grass. A light went on inside the vehicle briefly as the door was opened. Then it was dark again.

But Cheney had seen two figures carry something between them.

For a second, he'd seen something being lifted from the Packard and lowered to the ground. Something rectangular. Something that wasn't very heavy because the two figures lifted it with ease.

And now he knew.

Sutter's Meadow was to be the burial place for the kids.

He fired his pistol without really thinking, a reflex action, and he heard the thud of a bullet against a metal surface, followed by the soft rattle of glass breaking. And then he was running in the direction of the Packard, aware of Bannion trotting through the grass beside him. The sound of the gunshot, trapped by the trees, echoed around the meadow.

When he reached the big black car he stopped. The passenger door hung open and the tailgate was raised. The interior light was burning feebly, casting a strange glow over the contents of the car.

Cheney looked toward the back of the hearse. Charlie Bannion stood by the open tailgate, gazing at Cheney across the boxes stacked in the back.

Three boxes.

Three rectangular pine boxes with lids.

Coffins. Beautifully carved, immaculately finished.

For a moment neither man moved. Bannion looked paralyzed suddenly, his mouth slightly open.

Cheney was the first to act.

He scrambled over the seat toward the back of the car.

He slid the lid of the nearest coffin aside.

Tommy Sears lay there, hands crossed on his bare chest, legs straight, eyes shut.

In the other boxes they found Vickie Estaban and Rick Dove. All the time Charlie Bannion kept making an odd choking sound as if what confronted him here in the darkness of Sutter's Meadow was beyond anything he might comprehend now or in the future.

Cheney lowered his hands toward Tommy Sears's pale face, cupping the boy's cheeks in his palms. He raised the face upward, not knowing if the child he held against him was dead or alive.

Charlie Bannion said, "The girl's alive, George. She's breathing."

And so was Tommy Sears. Cheney saw that now: he could feel the faintest whisper of warm breath escape the kid's lips.

"This one's okay too," Bannion said, indicating Rick Dove. "They're sleeping . . ."

Sleeping, Cheney thought. It was more than sleep.

Danny, where was Danny?

Cheney stepped out of the car.

Danny . . .

He stumbled through the dark, whispering his son's name over and over again. He had to be around here somewhere. He had to be.

Danny . . .

Then Cheney was falling suddenly. Falling through blackness. The earth opened up abruptly and swallowed him and as he regained his balance he understood he had stepped into a hole at the center of the meadow.

A dark opening, five or six feet below Sutter's Meadow.

The grave.

There was a wooden surface beneath his feet.

He knew what it was.

He pressed his back against the wall of the grave and quickly kicked the lid of the coffin aside. He raised Danny up out of the box and held him tightly in his arms.

In his sleep, Danny Cheney made a soft moaning sound.

Cheney felt the balm of a relief so total that his legs buckled. He kissed the boy's face, ran a hand over the scalp, wept.

Then he slung the boy across his shoulder and scrambled up from the grave even as the damp earth started to crumble softly around him. When he reached the top he looked across the darkness of the field. Overhead, a blackeyed moon threw aside its cover of cloud and illuminated the field, turning it to stark silver.

Cheney stared down into the hole. And realized two things.

The first was that this same grave must have held Mona Crouch for fifteen long restless years. Widened now, deepened, it had been intended as a burial place for four kids.

It was the second insight that laid ice across the surface of his flesh.

The kids would have been . . . *buried alive.*

Cheney stared across the meadow now. He saw nothing move out there in the grass or the trees—as if Zanzibar had contrived to pull off one final illusion, that of making both himself and his mother vanish to places the moonlight couldn't touch.

They had disappeared so completely they might never have existed in the first place. Cheney turned to look at Charlie Bannion and said, "Find them . . . if you can."

"Is Danny . . . ?" Bannion asked.

"He's going to be fine," Cheney answered.

The young cop turned and moved swiftly across the meadow, vanishing between trees where he was no longer visible.

Bannion went down through the grove of trees, disturbing a night owl that screeched overhead, distressing a skunk which slunk into thickets, leaving the air malodorous behind it. He moved down a slope of grass to the place where the trees yielded to a narrow road, which created a moonlit ribbon in front of his eyes. He saw, parked some distance away, a small red car.

When he reached it he opened the driver's door and looked inside. In the pale yellow glow of the interior light he saw a dark shape hunched in the passenger seat and he put his hand out. He had the impression of a person sitting there, but what his hand encountered was soft and yielding.

It was the illusionist's black cloak, spilling coins and cards and silks from all its secret pockets as Charlie Bannion lifted it in the air. It seemed to the young cop that if he shook the thing really hard, Zanzibar himself would fall out.

He let the cloak drop on the road.

He looked this way and that, seeing nothing. Once, he heard the strange cackle of a night bird he couldn't identify, but even that faded and the silence came back.

Gone, Charlie Bannion thought.

Swallowed by the night. Conjured away. He had the strange anticlimactic sensation he always experienced whenever a show came to an end and the stage was empty, the sets struck, the auditorium nothing but a great hollow space, the footlights turned off. At the heart of this feeling there was something else: a small core of expectancy—because all this inactivity, all this emptiness, was just waiting to be filled up again.

With fresh illusions.

A meadow. A moon. Trees coated with silver.

George Cheney closed his eyes.

Buried alive, he thought.

It was a phrase that would keep coming back, inexorable as any tide, through his dreams.

And sometimes he would wonder if Mona Crouch, when she had been raped and buried in a shallow grave, had been dead at the time of her burial.

Or if consciousness had perhaps come back to her slowly and she'd felt the weight of earth against her flesh, filling her eyes, the spaces beneath her fingernails, if she'd opened her mouth to scream and soil had stuffed her throat with silence.

THE PIPER

George Cheney clutched his son, stroking the boy's hair with a touch so light no instrument could have measured it.

Two events occurred in Hamland shortly after dawn. Amanda Thurston, waking early from a troubled sleep, looked out of the bedroom window of her parents' house on Montrose Drive and saw—refracted, like a stick placed in pale green water—the sight of a white-haired man hanging from the big oak tree that stood at the edge of the curb.

He seemed to twist very slowly as he hung there, his body disturbed by passages of air. When her brain had cleared of sleep, when she realized she recognized the man, she went to wake her parents.

And Randy Claybourne, delivering copies of *The Progressive* which had the out-of-date headline

NUMBER OF MISSING KIDS GROWS TO THREE: SUSPECT IN CUSTODY

found the body of a mutilated cat stuffed into a drainage ditch not far from Gunnison Avenue.

Somebody had cut its head off.

Epilogue

---❖❖❖❖❖❖❖❖❖❖❖❖❖❖❖---

ON CERTAIN FALL NIGHTS GEORGE CHENEY THOUGHT HE COULD *hear* the weather changing. Winter was out there in the soft darkness, audible in the whisper of a tree or the massed, dying hysteria of insect noises.

A barbed season was coming.

Sometimes, when he would drive through the streets of the town—which seemed smaller to him than ever before, sunken like the face of an old man who has removed his false teeth—he understood there were other changes unrelated to the shift of a season. They were inside himself.

He had lost his own sense of place. He was constantly uneasy in a town that had once been as familiar to him as the sight of his own reflection in a mirror. When he drove streets that had become alien to him, he found himself looking beyond the porch lights and store-signs into areas of darkness, as if what he expected to see most of all was Zanzibar's face gazing back at him from the shadows.

It was this darkness that haunted him, this nervous sense of anticipation that nightly stalked his dreams. Every shadow he encountered contained a suggestion of Zanzibar and still another terrifying illusion. Some nights, when he'd force himself out of sleep, he'd hold Anne close to his body before he'd get up and go along the landing to Danny's room—where he'd stand on the threshold for a long time, just watching the boy as he slept. It was the vigilance of a man dogged by conditionals. *What if I hadn't reached Sutter's Meadow in time? What if I had been blown apart in the explosion of that house in Gowrie Canyon?*

Watching his son, Cheney would go over these questions again and again in his mind. He was being damaged by possibilities that hadn't happened, a chain of events that had never taken place. But still he had to work hard at the idea that his son was safe, asleep in his own bed. Often, he'd sit on the edge of the mattress and stare at the boy until his eyes ached.

The barbed season he knew was coming existed already in his own heart: he was living on the edge of an old nightmare and he was tense, exhausted, filled with dread.

Sometimes, as he walked through the dark, he'd hear Anne calling to him from their bedroom, her voice soft and filled with concern.

"You don't have to relive it," she told him once. "It's over, George."

"I know it's over," Cheney answered. "I have to keep reminding myself."

"Let it go, George. Just let it go."

"Have you managed that?"

Anne didn't answer his question. She lay beside him in silence, her fingers clutching his hand. Cheney gazed at the cloudy moon pressing lightly against the window and thought of it spreading its feeble glow across Sutter's Meadow or spilling through the foliage of the oak tree on Montrose Drive.

He closed his eyes, picturing Edward Cheney hanging from an upper limb, the frail body turning slowly in the fragmented dawn. He felt grief, but it seemed—like many of his responses these days—to be one step away from himself, almost as though he were spying inside another man's skull. Still, he couldn't bring himself to drive along Montrose or see that oak tree or step inside the big gloomy house. When he thought of Montrose Drive he thought of blood and death and an old man's rambling confession and the justice Edward Cheney had assigned himself.

One fall afternoon, long after the last of the reporters had gone back to the city desks that had sent them scurrying across the country to Hamland, long after they had picked the story clean and gleaned from its bones the most sensational elements, long after Zanzibar and Lily Hubbard had been scrutinized in print by popular psychologists and their particular psychoses simplified for mass understanding, George Cheney had a meeting with the County Attorney, a stoop-shouldered man called Sam Bowles who occupied an office at City Hall.

Bowles said, "It's a hard case to make, George. When you've got something this old, it's damned hard."

Cheney, seated by the window, said nothing. He was looking out into the street below. He saw Charlie Bannion and Ellis Diamond get inside a car, the young cop solicitously ushering the woman through the passenger door, his hand on her elbow. Cheney understood, from hints Charlie Bannion had dropped, that they were seeing each other on a regular basis. Romance from the ashes of things, a mythical bird.

"Sears and Dove and Estaban have indicated, through their lawyers of course, that they would plead not guilty to the murder of Mona Crouch," Bowles said. He tapped the surface of his desk with a skinny hand. "Strange how they all rushed out and got themselves lawyers, George. Folks in a panic do that kind of thing."

Cheney looked at the County Attorney. Panic, he thought. Was that the last sensation which rushed through Edward Cheney's mind as he took his drop into oblivion? when he felt the noose tighten round his neck? Or was there at the very last a sense of calm flooding through the old man?

"Basically, all we've really got is this," Bowles said, taking a sheet of yellowed paper and spreading it on his

338

desk. "We found this in the basement of the Hubbard house. Locked in a desk. Apparently, it's Elmer Hubbard's suicide note."

Cheney gazed at the paper. He had no urge to read it. But he reached for it anyhow, holding it delicately in his fingers. It had the texture of a dried moth. His eyes scanned the page quickly. The handwriting was uneven and spidery and there were stains of smeared ink spread across the paper. Basically, it was the same story his father had told him. *Five men, a young girl, a meadow on a summer night* . . .

"As you can see, George, it names names. It's a confession," Bowles said. "How much mileage we could get out of it in a court of law is debatable . . . Any defense attorney worth a spit would question the state of Elmer Hubbard's mind when he wrote that letter, and the veracity of what he says there."

A confession, Cheney thought.

He didn't need to hear confessions: they were locked away in another time, a dead time that had withered all around him.

"The postscript is interesting," Bowles said. "On the back of the sheet."

Cheney turned the paper over.

He read.

. . . this is what keeps coming right back to me, Lily . . . the fact I saw or I think I saw and it doesn't matter which . . . that poor girl's hand move even as we were shovelling dirt on to her face . . . and at the very last just before we had her covered with soil one of her eyes opened and looked straight at me . . . I can't get that out of my head, Lily . . . Forgive me if you can find a way . . .

Cheney tossed the note back on the County Attorney's desk. The hairs on the backs of his hands stirred and something very cold moved through him.

Bowles stood up. "We could make a case on this confession, I suppose. I just have this gut feeling it's not very strong." The County Attorney paused and leaned across his desk to pick up the suicide letter. "Your father . . ." Bowles paused, as if he had no desire to pursue anything so delicate as Edward Cheney's death.

"My father left no note," Cheney said.

Bowles nodded. "If he had, it might have helped. It might have substantiated the essence of Elmer Hubbard's letter."

"No note, no confession." Cheney rose from his chair. No note, no confession. Would Edward Cheney have wanted this denial? What are you protecting here, George? Your father's memory? Or is it something inside yourself—some totally overwhelming desire to close a goddam door and get on with your own life if you can?

Bowles said, "I guess we'll just see where this leads," and he shrugged. "Like I say, it isn't much to go on, George. Not after all this time has passed. Things grow cold."

Cheney walked to the door.

Bowles said, "Everybody and his brother keeps seeing Zanzibar and Lily Hubbard. According to the FBI office in Denver, the pair was sighted yesterday in Galveston, Texas, Culver City, California, and Aberdeen, Maryland. It's funny how even after the guy's gone he keeps creating all these illusions of himself."

Cheney smiled thinly.

Galveston.

Culver City.

The moon.

Cheney stepped out of the office. He went down into the street, which was empty. Charlie Bannion and Ellis Diamond were already gone.

Later, in the twilight, George Cheney took his wife and son up to the crest of Naughton's Hill and together they looked down across the town of Hamland. Here and there, the dying day receded in small pockets of shadow between the houses. Cheney put his arm around Danny's shoulder and drew the boy close to him. It was always this way lately: he would grab his son and hug him every chance he could get and he'd see, in Danny's perplexed eyes, a strangeness, a sadness, as if the small boy didn't understand the changes and the needs in the man who was his father.

Cheney wondered how long it was going to be like this, if he was going to feel this overpowering urge to be close to the boy for the rest of his life, to watch over him always, protect him from demons he couldn't name himself.

Danny Cheney wandered to the edge of the hill. Anne, sighing, put an arm through her husband's and pressed her face close to his shoulder. Cheney realized he should have had a sense of family right then, a sense of some unity, but instead he felt only a vague threat rising up from the streets of the town.

How far had Zanzibar gone into the boy's mind? How deep had his control gone? Was it something that would forever leave a scar? Cheney couldn't know the answers: Danny hadn't talked about the experience, because he'd locked it in a far place inside himself. One day, though, it would have to come out, it would have to be rejected from the kid's system like a poison—and then what form would it take?

Cheney, tired of questions, weary of what had been inflicted on his life, moved closer to the boy.

Danny asked, "Do you think he'll ever come back?"

"Zanzibar?" George Cheney hesitated before replying: a simple and terrifying thought crossed his mind. *Zanzibar could be down there somewhere even now, lingering in shadow, hiding, waiting until he'd been all but forgotten. Behind a tree. In a dark alley. The basement of an abandoned house. Anywhere.*

"No, I don't think he'll ever come back, Danny," Cheney said, and his voice was dry.

"Good view," the kid said after a pause.

Used to be, Cheney thought.

He looked down at the dark square of the municipal park, the humpbacked outline of Slattery's Meat Packing Plant, the chimney of Rosita's factory; he looked down at spires and rooftops and pinpricks of light that glowed from porches and shops and there, in the distance, the stand of trees surrounding Sutter's Meadow seemed to reach up toward him, as if they were calling him down to another kind of darkness—that of loss.

George Cheney turned away from the view. He understood something then: he was seeing Hamland from Naughton's Hill for the very last time. He was seeing it as night fell, layer upon inexorable layer, as if the oncoming dark were coat after coat of black paint applied by a steady hand.

Anne Cheney touched the back of her husband's wrist and said, "I'm ready any time you are, George."

The following morning, Saturday the twenty-seventh of September, George Cheney packed his family into the car and headed out of Hamland in a westerly direction, lured by a coastline he had conjured out of his imagination, drawn by the notion of cleansing sea winds and brisk tides and the deafening music of an ocean crashing upon rocks.

Westerly, with no particular destination in mind.

On Center Avenue, at a stoplight, Max and Hildy Crouch crossed the street. Max was dressed in a new plaid jacket and slacks and Hildy wore bright bermuda shorts and electric-blue sneakers. The pair smiled at Cheney, waving a little shyly, then they were gone arm in arm around a corner.

Cheney smiled back at them. Something had come out of all this for Max and Hildy Crouch, he thought. A sense of certainty, a door that opened into the future instead of the past: at least now they didn't have to live suspended in a twilight world of unspoken hopes and pathetic birthday celebrations. It was the only instance where Zanzibar had worked to destroy an illusion rather than foster it.

Cheney drove on.

Danny, bouncing in the back seat of the car, asked, "Are we going away for good?"

"Ask your father," Anne answered.

George Cheney glanced at the boy but said nothing. He

watched Center Avenue recede in his rearview mirror, saw the small storefronts and the bleached-out canopies dwindle, and then there was nothing left of Hamland but a freeway ramp and a ring of dark trees around a meadow and two big black birds flapping above the dying cottonwoods.

CAMPBELL BLACK

The Wanting

COME ON IN
THE FAMILY'S DYING TO MEET YOU . . .

It was the perfect summer home for Max and Louise and their twelve-year-old son. The California pine forest was peaceful, silent, isolated, and the old couple who lived nearby just loved to entertain young Denny. It was perfect . . .

Until Louise made a horrifying discovery: something was happening to her son. Something dark and evil, draining his innocence, twisting his mind, his body and soul. A nightmare too frightening to believe.

But Louise believed it. And only she could bring it to its terrifying conclusion . . .